MW00975217

NOT SO LONG AGO NOT SO FAR AWAY

Sally-
Jo. my blogging
buddy & a true
inspiration. Even
though the names & labels
we place on our spirituality
are different, I think
we are more alike
than not. :)
Jinske

NOT SO LONG AGO NOT SO FAR AWAY

TRISHA SLAY

Deeds Publishing | Atlanta

Published by Deeds Publishing, Marietta, GA
www.deedspublishing.com

Library of Congress Cataloging-in-Publications Data is available on request.

ISBN 978-1-937565-58-9

Books are available in quantity for promotional or premium use. For information write
Deeds Publishing
PO Box 682212
Marietta, GA 30068
info@deedspublishing.com.

First edition 2013
10 9 8 7 6 5 4 3 2 1

The following quotes are from the *Star Wars* movies:
"This could all be happening right now." | 25, "Feel the Force flowing through you." | 90 , "Stay on target. Stay on target." | 90 , "...some damn fool idealistic crusade." | 102, "...a galaxy far, far away?" | 143, "Your eyes will deceive you. Don't trust them." | 184 , "I'm here to rescue you." | 191, "That reminds me. I have something for you...your father's lightsaber." | 204, "They're not going to get me without a fight." | 206, "How could I be so stupid?" | 218, "...wretched hive of scum and villainy." | 233, "And may the Force be with you." | 238, "You have to do what you feel is right, of course." | 255, "He was killed by a young Jedi named Darth Vader—" | 262, "A direct hit and only a direct hit will start a chain reaction." | 266, "We have no time for our sorrows, Commander." | 284, "Hokey religion is no match for a good blaster at your side." | 303, "The Force is strong with this one" | 306, "A little short for a Stormtrooper?" | 306, "I don't like you either." | 306, "...the Force will be with you...always." | 308,

The following characters/items are from the *Star Wars* movies:
Force, Darth Vader, C-3PO, R2-D2, Stormtrooper(s), Jedi, Princess Leia, Death Star, Chewbacca & Chewie, Empire & Imperial, Tarkin, lightsaber(s), Tatooine, Mos Eisley, Han Solo, Obi-Wan Kenobi & Ben Kenobi, Jawa & Jawa Juice, Wookiee & Wookiee Cookies,

Excerpt from *Hotel California* | 55, written by Don Felder, Don Henley, and Glenn Frey, © 1976

Excerpt from *The Candy Man* | 150, written by Leslie Bericusse and Anthony Newley, © 1971

Cover | Matt King and Mark Babcock

Illustrations | 10, 120, 222, 298 by J. B. Jones | gonzoearth@yahoo.com

For my mother,
who is nothing like
Erika's Mother Monster.
She never left half-moon
marks on my body or my spirit.
And in memory of my
grandmother.
She was a little bit like Anita
and too much like me.

"Your eyes can deceive you; don't trust them. Stretch out with your feelings."

Obi-Wan Kenobi

Star Wars Episode IV, A New Hope

JUNE 1977

"We had to wait almost half way through the month of June before we could glimpse that rebel blockade runner fleeing the Imperial cruiser somewhere above Tatooine.... In Ohio, fourteen godforsaken days went by before we could go to a movie theater and see the first *Star Wars* movie."

Tom Hanks

33rd AFI Life Achievement Award: A Tribute to George Lucas (2005)

Friday June 3, 1977

Dear Cassie,

Maybe it's stupid to write this letter. I can't possibly mail it without an address, but sleep is a million miles away and I'm sick of rolling around in sweaty sheets trying to make my brain stop screaming. So I pulled my daisy bedspread out on the porch roof to look for cooler air and shooting stars. Suddenly, it seemed like a good idea to write down everything that's happened since you left.

It's been four awful days since I last saw you. I miss you so much! Where are you now? Does the sky look different there? Are you wondering what is going on back here?

Don't worry, I haven't told your father anything that will help him or the sheriff track you down. I just wish they didn't know I saw you that night. It was such a stupid mistake!

Walt called my house when he got home from the fire station and found your room empty.

The Mother Monster hollered upstairs asking if you came over last night and I said, "Yeah."

That one little word has changed everything.

Anita yelled, "Cassie, your dad's on the phone. Pick it up!"

I yelled back, "She's not here now."

Next thing I knew, Walt was hammering on the back door and then he was standing in my bedroom hammering me with questions. Mother Monster stormed in and dragged me out of bed in my ratty old nightshirt. Walt kept yelling at both of us non-stop. Anita yelled back. I know I should have tried to say something to trick Walt, to get him looking in a totally wrong direction, but all I could think to do was grab the sheet off my bed and hug it around my body.

Anita managed to make Walt back off with promises of helping him find you. When he left, I was almost grateful to her…until the evil witch pinched the flabby place below my bottom and said, "This ain't baby fat, young lady. Cover it up!"

By 4:00 that afternoon, Sheriff McCombs himself was standing in our kitchen asking the first round of official questions. Anita kept muttering snide comments about how the sheriff wouldn't move that quickly for most teenagers, but he jumps right in to chase down the fire chief's daughter.

That gave me goose bumps because it reminded me of the time you went camping with Jeff even though Walt said you couldn't go. I never told you I was standing in our kitchen watching from the window when he yanked you out of his car and dragged you into the house while you screamed and screamed. Anita may be the Mother Monster sometimes, but Walt is just plain scary mean. And he keeps getting meaner every day you're gone.

Even though I miss you, I hope you are really far away from Walt by now.

Your friend forever,

Erika

| one |

It's a terrible thing to live under a question mark. The lies and the truth keep getting tangled and twisted in my mind. That's why I can't stop examining every minute, every second, every breath of that last night, looking for some shadow or flaw that might reach out to drag Cassie back to this prison she fought so hard to escape.

On the night Cassie finally broke free from this hell hole, I sat up until the wee hours of the morning waiting for her to come home from Jimmy's party—partly because she'd promised to stop by and tell me all about it, partly because I was afraid Walt was going to come home in the middle of his shift and discover she'd snuck out again. I guess I thought staring at the light from her bedroom window would somehow get her back there safe and sound.

I was nursing a bottle of warm Tab Cola to stay awake, every sip like battery acid on my tongue. I remember the swish and swoop of cars on the old state road as my Mickey Mouse alarm clock ticked and clicked its way beyond midnight. I think I heard the strains of the *Star Spangled Banner* before the Mother Monster switched off our TV.

After an eternity of waiting and watching and listening, Cassie finally popped through my bedroom window a few minutes after 1:30 am with an oversized straw bag in one hand and a bottle of pink champagne in the other. That bottle was cold and wet against my spine when she threw her arms around me and spun us in a circle, but I didn't mind. I was buzzing with relief to see her safe and so happy.

When she pointed outside and slipped back out my window, I followed without hesitation. Without question. Just like every other time she appeared.

After leaving my bedroom, we walked across the south porch roof and climbed down the old hollow pear tree that grew too close to the house, its branches all tangled up with the splintering wood trim. Once we were both on the ground, she pressed a finger to my lips and walked in exaggerated tip-toe steps past the row of dark bay windows on that side of the house. Those windows belong to the studio rooms where my Mother Monster teaches ballet, tap and jazz to all the pretty little princesses in town, so there was no real danger of being seen or heard by anyone in the middle of the night. Cassie knew that. She was just being silly for my benefit and I had to bite down hard on my lower lip to fight back the giggles.

When we reached the unlit alley that ran between our back yards, Cassie twirled a few steps away with both arms stretched wide to the glittering stars and declared, "Once I escape Nowhere, Ohio, I'll figure out how to breathe the sky."

There was a nearly full moon hanging over the trees and not a single cloud to hide the stars. Despite the heavenly lighting, my eyes were slow to adjust to the night and my footsteps were awkward, shuffling. Cassie continued to dance ahead until we left the streets and alleyways of our neighborhood, crossed the state road to the Catholic cemetery and found our way to the grassy hill beyond the graves. As soon as I caught up, she wrapped her arms around my shoulders and planted a loud kiss on my forehead.

"It's time, Erika. I'm leaving tonight!"

"Tonight? Why?" It was a struggle not to panic.

But her eyes were sparkling as she said, "Let's celebrate!"

Cassie took a few hopping steps and then she was running up the shallow slope. I followed, working hard to ignore the terrible weight in my feet and my heart. When we reached the top to hug the lone poplar tree, she just kept giggling like a maniac while I tried to hide how puffy my breath sounded. Soon we were rolling down the hill and racing back up to roll again.

When she was finally tired of rolling and running and rolling again, we both flopped down on the hillside near the poplar tree. She produced two Dixie cups from the depths of her straw bag and opened the pink bubbly. We sipped and giggled and talked about all the things we would do in Hollywood. The places we would visit. The movie stars we would date.

"What will you do when you first get there?" I asked, still a little breathless.

When Cassie rolled onto her stomach, it seemed like she was searching every inch of my face for something. It was so intense. What was she looking for? Bravery? Trust?

I'm glad it was so dark, because I'm sure my face was flaming red by the time she laughed and said, "The very first thing I'll do is buy a gorgeous postcard with a palm tree on it and I'll mail it off to you."

"With nothing written on it except my name and address, right?"

Our secret signal.

"Right. No one will know who it came from, but you'll know I've made it." Her finger lightly tickled my shoulder. "Second thing I'm going to do is get one of those maps that show where all the movie stars live. Then I'll go pick out the mansion I'm going to buy when I'm a movie star."

"But how will you get there? Where will you stay until you're famous?" I wanted to know more. I was hungry for details the way she was always so hungry for freedom.

"I'll stay wherever I want and no one will be able to tell me what to do or when to do it."

"But, you know what I mean Cassie," I insisted. "How will you live?"

"Don't you worry about that, Worry Bird. I've got everything worked out."

"But, if I don't know where to find you...." My voice wobbled at the terrible thought.

"You'll always know where to find me," she promised. Eyes locked on the horizon, her voice was pure calm certainty. "We're a team. Soon you'll come join me. You'll write the movies I'll star in. We'll be millionaires and we'll spend every weekend next to a pool drinking expensive champagne from real crystal glasses. We'll own the world."

That's the part I keep replaying over and over in my mind. Whenever it feels like too much work just to breathe, I remember that promise and it makes breathing just a little bit easier.

Around 3:00 AM, we scrambled back the way we came. I left her humming and waltzing around my back yard while I scuttled up to my bedroom to retrieve our secret stash of money. My whole body was shaking so hard it took ten deep breaths to calm my nerves before maneuvering back down the pear tree. When I handed over the shoebox of money, we linked pinkies and pressed our foreheads together.

"Don't you dare cry," she whispered, "Stay strong. Promise you'll never, ever let them guess you know a thing."

"I promise," I whispered back.

And I am trying to keep my promise. I am. It's just so damn hard to keep the lies and the half-truths straight when the questions never seem to stop.

Monday June 6, 1977

Dear Cassie,

The police were at school again today. I had to talk to the same officer, Deputy Wayne Todd. Remember him? He was the cop who caught us hitchhiking back from the Millersport Corn Festival. You said he looked a little like Burt Reynolds. I thought he was just hairy.

Now that hairy deputy has become my interrogator, pushing me with question after question. His eyes are always glued on me. Sometimes it feels like I'm nothing more than a smudged fingerprint he's examining under a microscope. I am getting so sick of that hairy man!

He keeps showing up at my classes with Principal Nelson. Then they both walk me into Nazi Nelson's office to answer the same stupid questions over and over. Do they ever get me out of Algebra or Gym? Of course not. They pull me out of the only classes I don't hate—Art and English. Some of your other friends have been called to the office too, but I'm the one they torment the most.

Everyone has noticed.

Now they're oinking at me!

It started today when I left Nazi Nelson's office after third period. My feet were walking toward Biology class while I tried to shake off another round of the deputy's endless, brain-draining questions. First, there were these gross, grunting pig noises that seemed to follow me down the hall. Then a piggish squeal echoed right behind me. Just before I stepped into Mr. Ray's classroom, some guy yelled out that "Soowee!" pig call and the hallway exploded with laughter.

All during the review for my Biology final, I tried to tell myself the noises and the laughter had nothing to do with me. But then Tammy "Big Red" Costas stopped me on the way to lunch. After looking me up and down carefully, she said, "Do you mind moving downwind? I hate the smell of bacon." Everyone milling around us cracked up like that was hilarious.

During lunch, three different voices belted out "Soowee!" before the lunchroom monitor promised the next offender a whole hour of detention. People I barely know would stage whisper things like, "Squeal like a pig, Erika!" or "You're gonna get chopped, Suey" as they walked past my lunch table.

It was Dana Spivik who finally took pity on me.

Yes, that's right. Nose-picking, spit-spraying, brace-faced Dana Spivik—the freshman who carries her French horn to every class and had her head stuck down the girl's room toilet at least three times this year—SHE looked at ME with a face full of pity as I stumbled out of the lunchroom.

"You really don't know what it's all about, do you?" she asked.

All I could do was shake my head.

"Pigs...that's what the Dopeheads call cops."

Deputy Wayne Todd! This nightmare is all his fault!

Dana says everyone thinks I squealed to the hairy deputy about a party at Slim Jim's that got busted Saturday night. The cops found drugs. Lots of crazy stuff. Some kids got hauled off to jail and might not be allowed to take final exams, which means they'll flunk this term. All because of one wild party. And since Deputy Wayne Todd led the charge into Jimmy's garage and he's always interrogating me at school, now people are saying I told him about the party and the drugs. They're saying the whole mess is my fault.

Like I had any idea there was another party at Jimmy's! Nobody invited me. I know you used to love his parties, but I'm not even sure where Slim Jim lives. Whatever led Deputy Todd to Jimmy's door, it had nothing to do with me. But how can I spread the word it wasn't my fault without looking even more guilty? I bet you'd know what to do...if only you were here.

Oh, Cassie! There's only three days left of this school year, but I don't know how I'm going to survive without you. I know I shouldn't wish it; I know you'd hate me if it happened and I was the cause, but sometimes I wish you'd come home. I wish you'd drive up and jump out of the car glaring bullets at this whole town. At least you'd be back here again.

I wish everything could be like it was before you decided to leave.... even though I know that's impossible. I know you had to get away from Walt and I'm trying to be happy that you escaped. I am.

It's just that tomorrow and all the ugly tomorrows after it are coming at me too fast right now.

Your friend forever,

Erika

| two |

Somehow, I manage to survive Tuesday by scuttling around the edges and corners of school, clinging to the shadows like a teenaged cockroach. The pig noises are always there. At times the grunting and squealing threaten to suffocate me, but I keep my eyes down and my feet moving. Instead of going anywhere near the lunchroom, I stand next to the baseball practice field eating a peanut butter sandwich. Deputy Todd doesn't show up all day. I'm not sure if I'm relieved or disappointed by his absence. There are questions I need to ask that horrible hairy man.

Wednesday starts the special two-day schedule for finals. Juniors and seniors with a grade point average of B or higher don't need to stick around school when they aren't taking an exam. That, plus the fact that some students and some classes are exempt from the whole thing, leaves the campus much less crowded than usual. There's not a single oink before morning announcements, not a single squeal.

I dare to think the storm has passed. Big mistake.

The two bottles of Tab I sucked down before school hit me during my second exam. I barely manage to scribble out the final translation "en Français" before dropping my blue booklet on Madame Renard's desk and rushing out of the room. In my hurry to reach the girls bathroom, I forget to scuttle and hide. As I approach the doorway, someone shoves me hard between my shoulder blades, slamming me into the doorframe.

"Hey, lookey who came to the *girls* bathroom!" a female voice calls out from behind me.

A dark, scowling creature wearing bright blue eye shadow emerges from a cloud of cigarette smoke in the doorway. She squints at me for a few seconds before grabbing a handful of my hair. "Oh no, I am not sharing toilets with this dirty little freak."

She yanks my hair and plants her foot on my hip, kick-shoving me toward the opposite doorway. Next thing I know, I'm on my hands and knees in the boys bathroom…within full view of the urinals! There's only one guy in there, and he's just washing his hands, but I can't make myself look up. I try to scoot back out, but the evil she-troll stomps her foot on my butt.

"What the hell, Tracy?" The guy's voice booms out. "That's wacked!"

"Walk on by, Toad. This little freshmeat is nothing more than a sicko leg licker."

A what?

"Leave her alone, Tracy. Go crawl back to your hole."

Everything stops. Tears of shame are scalding my eyes and my bladder is threatening to burst all over the filthy bathroom floor, but my body is locked in that miserable position waiting for the next blow.

It never comes. The pressure from Tracy's foot disappears and the guy she called Toad helps me to my feet.

"Don't let Tracy get to you. She's messed up…and not in the good way, you know?"

I still can't make myself look at him. My lips refuse to move. So, instead of thanking him, I break away and stumble toward the exit. Once outside, I realize I'm not going to make it through the next five minutes, let alone the rest of the day, without peeing. There's other student bathrooms, but now I'm terrified to go anywhere near them.

"There's a toilet in the janitor's closet in the next building."

When I turn around, Dana is pressed into a corner, hugging her French horn with one arm and shoveling Buckeye potato chips into her mouth with the other. I am practically dancing around with the need to pee.

"Kenny the janitor leaves the door open for kids who don't feel safe in the student bathrooms." She stops to push in another fat wad of potato chips, chews and swallows while I wiggle in pain.

"Through the door, to the right, down three steps, then right again. The door says 'private' and the handle won't turn, but if you pull hard enough, it will open…unless someone's already claimed the space. Then you're out of luck."

I mumble some gratitude in her direction and waddle away as fast as my aching bladder will allow.

Wednesday June 8, 1977

Dear Cassie,

You will not believe this! There is a tiny psychedelic trip of a bathroom hidden under the stairs to the Freshman lockers. I'm sitting here right now surrounded by a kaleidoscope of florescent colors. It is absolutely wild! I can't believe this place was under my feet all year.

When I first opened the door, it looked like nothing more than a sad little supply closet with a toilet in one corner. Truth is, I didn't pay much attention at first because I had to pee so bad it was hard to breathe. But once I answered the call of nature, I started looking around and realized this is no ordinary janitor's closet.

To start with, the back of the door is painted to look like you're standing at a window that looks out over the Milky Way. A flock of exotic birds made from folded notebook paper hangs from the ceiling. A step ladder climbing one wall is filled with magazines. Some of the covers, like *People*, *Mad* and *Time*, are familiar. But who reads magazines with names like *Starlog* and *Famous Monsters*?

Time had a feature about "The Best Movie of the Year," but I can't tell you anything about it. When I opened the pages, the words swam into a soupy mess. It has not been a good day and that headline made me realize I won't be going to see any movies anytime soon. Without you, there's no way I'm going to hitchhike to the Cineplex or sneak into the Valley Drive-In. Safe in this weird little space and with no exam this period, I let myself sit on the toilet and cry it all out until the tears refused to flow. Then I forced myself to stand up and splash cold water on my face.

Above the sink, I found an aluminum bucket filled with hundreds of well-used florescent crayons. That really puzzled me…until I noticed a lamp with a black light bulb on the floor.

When I turned on the lamp and switched off the overhead light, the puke-green walls disappeared; replaced by a mural of words, symbols and drawings in every one of Crayola's eight florescent shades. The effect is impossible to describe, but there is one part I have to tell you about. Someone sketched a drawing of you in there. I don't know who the artist could be or how that person managed to capture your personality in crayons, but you look amazing. You're wearing a slinky dress, a pageant sash and the most incredible set of rainbow wings that seem to embrace the whole room.

Underneath your magical portrait, someone wrote, *This could all be happening right now.*

I'm not sure what that means but it sounds beautiful, doesn't it?

Love,

Erika

| three |

The Mother Monster and I are staring at each other over boiled chicken and Brussels sprouts. She's decided we're on a diet again. I'm counting the seconds until she gets up and leaves me to clean the kitchen. Maybe I'll be able to scavenge up some real food.

She frowns down at my fork as it circles around the disgusting things on my plate. To divert her attention, I say the first thing that pops into my head.

"What's a leg licker?"

Anita's fork clatters to the floor. "Where did you hear that?"

"Some girl at school called another girl a leg licker. I just wondered…."

"That's a filthy way of calling someone a lesbian. Don't let me ever hear you say it again."

It's a good thing I have not eaten because, hearing that, I would have puked it all back up right there on our dinner table. Why would Tracy Troll call me that?

The screen door slams open and Chief Walter Abbott barges into our kitchen. He doesn't bother to knock or ask permission or even look at me. He just points two fingers at Anita and tells her he'll be driving me to school tomorrow to clean out Cassie's locker.

"Erika knows the combination. I don't want that negro janitor cutting open the lock or going through my little girl's personal items."

Anita shrugs and says, "Whatever you say, Chief," without noticing that I'm begging her with my eyes to say no.

"Be ready by oh-six hundred," he barks at the wall behind me before slamming his way back out of our kitchen.

My fate is sealed. Walt and I will be digging through Cassie's locker tomorrow morning, probably with Principal Nelson standing by to take custody of school property...which is not going to improve this torture that has become my life. Not one bit.

***

Walt is pounding on our door before the sun has a chance to make an appearance. Even with sleep crusty eyes and a skull full of mush, I know who is wham, wham, whamming on our kitchen door. No one pounds on a door quite like Chief Walter Abbott.

"Said I'd be here. Why aren't you dressed?"

No "good morning." No "thanks for doing this."

"They want to search her locker," he practically spits the words in my face. "It's not just about getting her stuff. That idiot Nelson is tryin' to tell me there's some missing money my little girl might have stole."

What to say? I was up half the night trying to figure out how to deal with this man. He knows I saw Cassie right before she left, so now he won't leave me alone. Unless....

There has to be some way to play this so that he thinks I've given him a clue to follow. Not a real clue. Something false that will send him out thundering fury in the wrong direction. If I plant a fake lead that points everyone in the wrong direction, maybe they'll all leave me alone, but I can't seem to figure out how to fool anyone, especially not this early in the morning.

"Don't worry, Chief. They won't find anything."

Chief starts rubbing his buzz cut and glaring pure poison at me. "And just how do you know what they will and won't find? Did you steal the money?"

"What? No!"

He keeps eying me like some messed up version of the Mad Hatter without a hat. It's impossible to breathe, let alone think of something clever to say, with Walt looming over me staring.

Suddenly, he's back to barking orders. "Get dressed. Move, move, MOVE!"

So I turn and run for my room like a scared puppy.

On the way to school, Chief hammers me with a non-stop verbal assault. Some of what comes out of his mouth is phrased as if he's asking questions, but, really, he isn't interested in anything I might have to say.

"You know what's going to happen, don't you? I'm going to find my baby girl and I'm going to bring her home. She comes up wild sometimes. My Cassie is too much like her mother that way, but she always comes home. Remember last March? She had some wild idea she was going to Nashville to sing on the street until she got famous. Remember that? Then she calls me from the truck stop up off Interstate 70 begging me to come rescue her. Didn't make it more than thirty miles from home. What's happened this time? That's what I want to know. What's different? This escapade has dragged on way too long. Someone else has to be involved. You know who's messing with my family business? Better tell me now if you have any idea who might be involved. When I find my little girl, and I will find her, I'm going to figure out who had a hand in this and I'm going to gut them like a fish. You hear me?"

His diatribe goes on and on and on. If there was any chance to tell him something, anything to get him away from me and looking for Cassie in all the wrong places, I let it slip away.

When we get to school, Principal Nelson, Deputy Wayne Todd and Kenny the janitor are lined up next to Cassie's locker. Kenny has these huge metal clippers that look way too big to cut off one tiny little combination lock.

"Put those cutters away!" Chief snaps. "No use ruining a perfectly good lock she can use next year."

Nazi Nelson launches into this long speech about how all students are required to report their lock combinations to the office, but the combination Miss Abbott reported doesn't work and this constitutes a serious violation of the school's code of conduct....blah, blah, blah. Other kids wander in early for the first exam of the day and every single one of them stops to watch this little scene. I hear a few piggish grunts and squeals in the crowd. My guts are dissolving.

Finally, I just walk up to her locker and open the stupid thing.

The heavy *chunk* of the lock opening sets off a terrible chain reaction. Deputy Todd grabs my arm and yanks me away just as Chief's hand slams into the locker door right where my head used to be.

"I'll be the one going through my daughter's things."

Deputy Todd slams his hand right next to Chief's and says, "That is NOT the plan, sir. Please stand by."

Nelson tries to act tough by saying, "This is school property and there is money missing from our student council funds. I think the school needs to conduct this search."

Kenny rolls his eyes at me, but keeps quiet. I wonder if he knows I've been peeing in his toilet and reading his *Time* magazine.

The three big men continue to yell and argue. I keep my eyes glued to the hallway linoleum and imagine myself sitting with Cassie next to a turquoise pool under a palm tree. The first bell shakes me out of my lovely daydream. Out of the corner of my eye I watch the feet of the other students start to drift away. I want to get moving too, but I don't want to open my mouth and bring anyone's attention my way. The flecks in the linoleum start to dance and quiver at the edges of my vision.

I'm not sure which one of the men ends up opening the locker. I have no idea how they manage to dump most of Cassie's books and stuff onto the floor. What I do know is that some Polaroid pictures fall out of the pile and slide right into my line of vision. I get a really good look and immediately realize these are some pictures Cassie never intended her father to see—pictures of her posing in skimpy underwear with pouty, glossed up lips.

Chief takes one look and he just about loses his mind.

He gets down on all fours, scrambling around on the floor and covering them up with his hands. He's howling–really howling, like a wounded animal–and babbling at everyone, "Don't look. Don't you dare look. Shut your eyes."

The other three men stand there with their jaws hanging open, even when Chief's crazy scrambling almost knocks me down. Suddenly he looks up, latches onto my ankle and starts bellowing, "Who took these? Who took these filthy pictures? Answer me! Answer ME!"

I can't make my lips move.

Principal Nelson grabs my arm and pulls me away from Chief. "Better go to your classroom Miss...uh, Miss..."

Deputy Wayne latches onto Walt's shoulder and yanks him back, breaking his painful grip on my leg. "Get lost, Erika."

My lips may have failed me, but my feet move just fine. I hustle out of there and over to my own locker in the freshman section as fast as possible.

Head deep in my own locker, I listen to two sophomore girls from the yearbook staff gossiping about Cassie. From what they are saying, it's obvious some of the fundraiser money for the senior class graduation picnic is missing and someone told Nelson that Cassie took it.

Cassie? That makes absolutely no sense. She isn't even on student council and she would never volunteer to help with the senior picnic. Only pep rally idiots and snot-nosed cheerleaders do that sort of thing. But who's going to listen to me?

Thursday June 9, 1977

Dear Cassie,

Last day of school. Do you remember this day last year? Bicentennial summer stretched in front of us like a birthday gift waiting to be opened. Everything was brighter, bolder and better back then. I wish I could flip a switch or jump down a hole and go back.

You were still dating Charlie and you made him pick me up from my last day of junior high school in style, in his dad's candy apple red street rod with the rumble seat open. We sat back there in the rumble seat drinking rum mixed with real Cokes instead of that horrible Tab my mother makes us drink. You were wearing a white peasant blouse that my mother gave to you instead of me because you "had the body for it."

Halfway through my rum and Coke, I told you Anita said that. Then I showed you the moon-shaped marks where Anita digs her nails into the fatty place above my hip. You stood up in that seat—right there at the traffic light at Main and Oak—and you pulled that shirt off. Within a block of downtown! You stood there wearing only your bra, handed me that shirt and said you would never wear it again because Anita was a bitch.

Up until then I would have said you really liked Anita. After all, she was your dance teacher before you were my friend. But I saw the green fire in your eyes and I took the shirt because you insisted. The guy behind us started honking so Charlie flipped him the bird and revved the engine.

The guy in the other car yelled, "You gonna take off any more clothes, Baby?"

"I'll take off whatever I damn well please," you yelled back and flipped the bird just like Charlie. Then you said, "Take off your shirt, Erika."

And I did it. Even though my skin puffed out around the elastic of my Playtex bra, Charlie whistled and hooted like I was every bit as great as you. We laughed and everything felt so good, I even flipped the bird at the car behind us before Charlie sped off.

Then we were driving so fast my skin almost felt light for about sixty seconds. When I closed my eyes, I could picture myself with long, flowing hair like Ali McGraw's in *Love Story* and a tiny, thin little body.

When we stopped at the park, you grabbed my old Pittsburg Steelers shirt faster than I could think to move. You tied the front in a knot that exposed your flat stomach and made that ugly old shirt look adorable. I was forced to put on a flounced white half shirt even though my mother was absolutely right and I absolutely do not have the body to wear it.

"There we go!" You were so happy, and you looked so proud of me. So I smiled. And I walked with you and Charlie to the clearing in the woods where a bunch of high school people were drinking beer and smoking those weird-smelling cigarettes. My flabby sides were flapping out at everyone so I kept my arms wrapped around myself and my chin down.

I know you didn't mean to embarrass me, but I felt like a fat and jiggling freak at my very first high school party. I never told you. Thank goodness you never noticed the way I squirmed and kept my arms crossed over my midsection.

Someone did notice. I don't know her name. She gave me a big scarf that was wrapped around her jeans gypsy-style. She said I looked cold when she draped it around my back and arms, but her eyes said she knew I was feeling exposed. They were nice eyes, golden chocolate brown, and I never did figure out who she was.

That was the night you fell in love with Jeff. You told me Charlie was too small town. You said Jeff had poetry, but he also had a football player's body. You probably didn't remember me telling you about my secret crush on Jeff. Not that it mattered. It wasn't like he was ever going to look at me twice anyway. I was just Cassie's pudgy tagalong friend.

I remember thinking, yeah, Jeff has poetry and Cassie has magic. A poet needs a pretty muse, not a chubby brown moron mooning over him.

But then you fell out of love with Jeff almost as quickly as you fell out of love with Charlie. Now you've moved on again....but I can't seem to ever move on and I'm still wondering why you had to leave without me.

I'm sorry. That's not fair.

I remember how Walt went after you with his belt that night because we got home so late. I'll never forget his voice yelling, "You stink like sin!" Or the sickening crack his belt made every time it bit into your skin. Or the angry welt marks all over your body the next day. I can still see you curled up like a sick kitten on the foot of my bed, sobbing and sobbing until you threw up in my trash can. Most of all, I remember the terrible green fury in your eyes when you sat up and said, "Erika, get your camera."

Whenever I start feeling sorry for myself, I have those pictures to remind me…I know why you had to get out of here, Cassie. I do. I just don't know if I'm strong enough to survive this aching emptiness you left behind.

Love always,
Erika

| four |

I WAKE UP TO THE TERRIBLE SOUND OF MY MOTHER SCREAMING obscenities. Crashing noises vibrate through the floor and walls. For a full five minutes, I'm pinned to the sheets unable to move or even swallow the sour taste pooling in my mouth.

KATHUNK! It sounds like she's tearing down a wall with her bare hands. I squeeze my eyes shut getting ready to sneak out my window and run over to Cassie's house to hide...until I remember she isn't there anymore. Memory slams into me like a freight train. No Cassie. Nowhere to hide.

Before I can even get my breath back, I hear a familiar voice whisper, "Erika, are you sleeping?"

My eyes snap open and there's Suzie standing in my bedroom. This is bizarre! Suzie Ellis has been our dance receptionist for a whole year, and a dance student for ten years before that, but Anita has never, ever let herself turn into full Mother Monster mode in front of our sweet Suzie Q.

"Hey, Honey Girl," Suzie whispers when our eyes met. Her voice is wobbling like crazy. "I've come to say goodbye."

BOOM! The noise downstairs makes us both look down at the floor.

"Goodbye?" My voice barely croaks. This can't be happening!

I watch Suzie's tiny feet cross over to my bed. She sits and wraps her little bird arm around my shoulders to give me a quick squeeze.

"Sorry, Sweetie," Suzie's voice is barely more than a breath.

"What's going on?" I ask, trying to keep my morning breath away from her minty freshness.

"We're getting married," she sings, with a lopsided smile.

What to say? We all know Suzie is getting married. She's been pawing through bridal books and flashing around that microscopic diamond chip ring since her boyfriend Hank gave it to her at Christmas. So what?

Anita storms into my room with both hands clenched in fists at her hips. "Stop cuddling up to my daughter, you traitor."

"Oh, Anita! Stop being so mean," Suzie says, but she drops her arm away quickly. "I told you I was sorry, but we have to go now." She's whining like a baby ballerina from the toddler class. I have never heard our practical, efficient, ever-cheerful Suzie-Q whine. Something ugly stirs at the pit of my stomach.

"Then get out." Anita snaps her fingers at me in rapid fire. "Erika Shaina Williams. Out of bed. Move!"

Reflexes kick in and I start to stand, but Suzie stops me in a surprising sideways bear hug.

"Suzie, get your crap and get your idiot boyfriend out of my house," Anita's voice is pure poison. Another loud bang from downstairs makes us all look down. Suzie's arms drops away from me again. She starts twisting her engagement ring round and round her finger. The thing in my stomach is doing summersaults.

"You're really leaving now?" I ask. "This minute?"

Suzie locks her eyes on the window and babbles out a long line of gibberish something like this, "Hank took a job out west and I'm going with him and we have to go today, right now, so we have to get married out there and that's just how it has to be because I'm not getting left behind here no matter what anyone thinks, I'm not losing him."

Anita snorts. "Recital is in five days. My star student is missing. The sheriff has been talking to all my girls and their mothers. The phone is ringing off the hook because of this mess. My own daughter is being questioned like a common criminal. And now I have to deal with this garbage from you? You can't wait six damn days to ruin the rest of your life?"

Smothering silence locks all three of us in place. Down below, in the main dance studio, there's another *KATHUNK* that just about causes me pass out.

Hank's voice booms up the stairs.

"All right, that's the last of yer damn boxes Anita. Stop throwing yer hissy fit and pay Susie her salary for this week. We gotta get going."

Quick as lightening, Mother grabs Suzie by the arm and pulls her downstairs like she's a misbehaved child. I follow, watching in horror as my mother bodily flings our poor little Suzie at her ugly boyfriend, Hank.

Anita points to Suzie. "You want me to give you money? You show up five days before recital and you tell me you are quitting without any notice. Do you really think I'm going to pay you anything?" Her voice is squeezed so tight her head might pop off.

"Either pay Suzie what you owe her, or I will light these stupid boxes on fire," Hank's voice is even more vicious than Anita's, sending bile right up my throat.

Anita doesn't even flicker an eyelash his way. Instead, she steps closer to Suzie and says, "This is who you're marrying? What a pathetic little idiot you are, Suzie."

"Anita, you don't understand..." Twist, twist, twisting at her ring.

"I mean it, Anita. Pay up." Hank pulls out one of those silver Zippo lighters and starts flicking it open and closed with quick jerks of his wrist. Bile is burning my nose hairs.

"Mom..." I whisper, begging her to back off. But will she? Of course not.

"Let me tell you what I understand," she grinds the words out in the same squeezed-tight voice. "Number one, I helped Suzie-Q here plan her wedding on my phone, used my credit card to reserve the hall and bought all that extra film for the movie camera so we could film this wedding. Now you're going to elope?"

"Anita..." Suzie's twisting is about to rip her own finger in two.

"Number two, I let you take vacation days you didn't have so you could trot off to Virginia Beach with this loser while my own daughter worked your job during her spring break. I looked the other way every time you talked Erika into covering your desk for three hours. And why did you need all those three hour breaks, Suzie? So you could sneak off with this ape and come back with your skirt on backward. Did you think I didn't notice? Everybody noticed."

Suzie's head is sinking lower and lower. Her eyes never look up. Anita's tirade is now directed at the part in Suzie's hair.

"The way I do the math, Suzie, you owe US money!"

"Number three..." At this point, Anita swings her glare toward Hank and cocks one thumb toward the supply closet. "You light that flame, Hank, and you will never see the landscape outside this state. I have a loaded shotgun behind that door. I'll put a load of shot through you before you get to the car if you so much as drop that lighter by accident. I swear to God! Now get out. Both of you."

Hank looks ready to fight. "Look here...."

"Out! Now!"

"I swear I'll...."

"OUT!"

Finally, Suzie hooks Hank's arm and pulls him toward the reception area. There's some more cussing and yelling on both sides. On the way out the front door, Hank picks up the hideous brass ballerina from the reception desk and throws it through the skinny window next to the door.

Anita screams, "You bastard!"

Then it's all over. The sound of Hank's souped-up Camaro squealing away is the most gorgeous sound I've ever heard. Anita swirls down, from standing to sitting cross-legged on the bare wood floor and presses both fists to her forehead. When she speaks, her voice is drained of all energy.

"What a mess."

I open my mouth to say something, but she keeps talking. "Most of what Suzie did, you're going to have to do. No moping around the shadows this year. There are programs to be picked up, the place cues need taped on stage and the theater...you'll have to deal with Nick about all that." Her head suddenly pops up. "What about the camera?"

"The camera?" I ask.

"I spent all that money on a new Super 8 camera with sound so Suzie could film this recital with the music. You'll have to figure out the camera before Wednesday night. Do you hear me?"

"You mean I get to use the movie camera?" This is the first good news I'd heard since Cassie disappeared. My hands have been itching to hold that camera since the day Anita bought it. The promise of filming a movie, even if it is only her stupid dance recital, makes me a little dizzy until her next words bring me back to earth.

"If you screw this up, I will rip your face off."

"I'll go get the camera now. I'll practice today."

"No. First you get down to the Pit Stop and get more Tab. We're out. I need Tab and I need it now."

After I scramble to get out of my nightgown and into a t-shirt and cut-offs, I practically run for the store with Anita's voice behind me yelling, "Get the cold stuff from the back of the cooler. Don't bring home warm bottles."

Friday June 10, 1977

Dear Cassie,

I walked to Pit Stop with enough money in my pocket for Anita's Tab plus 37 cents to spend on candy.

I know. I'm going to get my weight down this summer. I will. Starting Thursday after the recital is over, I'm going to start jogging. I'm going on a strict diet. But today is the first day of vacation. Everything has been so horrible. And 37 cents doesn't buy that much candy. It was just going to be a little treat for tonight's TV shows.

Walking across the tiny parking lot next to Pit Stop, I was busy fingering the money in my pocket thinking about which candy I would choose. Suddenly, I was eye to eye with you.

There's a new poster in the front window of Pit Stop. It's taped to a piece of white cardboard with the word *Missing* written in thick black marker across the top. Whoever made the poster made the *M* too big so the *n* and *g* are all squished together at the right. That plus the ten or twelve pieces of electrical tape slapped all around your picture makes it look so sloppy that I didn't even realize what it was at first.

Missing since Memorial Day. Last seen in the vicinity of Pine Street and Main.

In other words, near my house.

Must have been your dad who put it up, right? I mean, who else would write *in the vicinity of*? Oh, and then there's the picture.

I know what you're thinking. Which picture did he put up? Well, it's not the gorgeous picture from the Miss Junior Independence pageant that we all loved. And it's not the one that ran in the newspaper when you played Glenda in the *Wizard of Oz* last fall. It's not any of your modeling pictures for Cooper's Department Store. Sorry to tell you this, but it's that last school picture. The one you hated. The one with your hair absolutely straight and held back in gold barrettes like a school librarian.

Sorry, but you were the one who said you looked like a librarian. You also said you made yourself look like that just to keep your dad happy. So I guess this means you were right and he likes that picture as much as you thought he would. That is, if he really is the one who made the poster. But who else would make it?

After staring at it for too long, I walked into the store and stood in front of the magazines, but everything felt weird. I couldn't read a single word. It seemed like the store was too bright and too loud and too open. So I just left. Not without Anita's Tab and my candy, of course. I still managed to buy the coldest bottles and exactly 37 cents worth of sugary stuff. But instead of saving it for tonight's TV shows, I ate the candy walking home. Right out of the little brown bag. Piece after piece. It was all gone by the time I got back home.

I don't remember tasting any of it.

Love,

Erika

| five |

IT TURNS OUT THREE OF THE BOXES HANK WAS FLINGING around are full of blank film cassettes for the Super 8 camera. In the closet behind Suzie's desk I discover two more boxes of film stacked under the camera case. There must be enough Kodachrome around here to capture ten recitals and ten weddings.

When I ask Anita why we bought so much, she waves her hand at me like a magician trying to make something disappear. "Erika, I told you to deal with the camera."

So that's that. If she doesn't care about all this wasted money, then I'm certainly not going to worry about it. And this means I have plenty of film cassettes to practice my camera technique.

All day Saturday, I'm like Steven Spielberg on a ten-speed, searching for the perfect shot. There's just one problem. Without Cassie, I can think of no one and nothing in this town worth filming. Plus, I don't dare go anywhere near the places other high school kids hang out. Even pedaling past the YMCA parking lot causes me to duck low and stare at the pavement whizzing under my front tire, praying no one will recognize me. Feeling defeated, I'm just about ready to go home and film the repair guy replacing our busted window when I notice a banner fluttering over the football field gate.

Senior Graduation Commencement
Sunday, June 12th – 2:00 PM
Valedictorian: Jeffery Johannson

Jeff! Now there is someone who can light up any camera like a rock star. Do I dare? It's risky, but a plan starts forming as I peddle home.

At precisely two o'clock Sunday afternoon, I leave home to walk the eight blocks down to the football field with the camera case snuggled in my arms like a precious baby. I've timed it so that I'll get into filming position just late enough to avoid everyone going into the graduation ceremony, but still in time to capture Jeff's speech.

Nearing the field, I veer off the sidewalk and carefully inch down the cement slope under the Church Street overpass to the grassy path along Raccoon Creek and follow the water to the point where it passes right by the chain link fence behind the western goal post. Cassie and I used to sneak down here during football games to drink that strawberry wine she always seemed to have hidden in her purse.

As I get close to our spot, I realize it isn't empty. There's a group of older students drinking liquor from a square bottle. The first person I recognize is Jeff's cousin, Sonny. Damn!

It is so ridiculous that Jeff and Sonny are related. Not just related, their fathers are identical twins. It seems impossible. Everything that is light and golden and beautiful in Jeff is dimmed and tarnished and plain in Sonny. And their personalities could not be more opposite. I've spotted Sonny first because he's standing on the largest rock, arms crossed over his chest, glaring down at someone as he yells, "You need to shut up before I shut you up."

That is enough to send me running back the way I came, but then I hear Slim Jim say, "Oh come off it, Sonny! Don't even act like Cousin Jeff didn't know what our little Cassie was up to."

What Cassie was up to? I creep forward to listen, hugging the camera tight to my body, but they aren't saying anything else worth risking my neck to hear. Just a lot of:

"Shut up."

"No, you shut up."

"Think you can make me?"

"Why don't you both shut up."

That last line comes from Big Red. I can't see her, but I recognize the voice. That gets me moving away, but it's too late.

A voice behind me on the path says, "Hey, Erika, what are you doing here?"

I spin around and find myself nearly nose-to-chest with Vince, one of the AV geeks from school. The group behind me gets really quiet, until a couple of people start up with the pig noises and Big Red says, "Hello, little piggy. Wee, wee, wee. Run all the way home."

I want to run, but a hand hooks my arm and spins me around hard enough to hurt. I don't exactly recognize the guy holding my arm, but he looks kind of familiar. I'm just about certain I've seen him somewhere, but I can't think where. Not at school. He looks older than everyone else, older than high school. He isn't very tall, but he's a thick block of solid muscle with a bush of blond fuzzy hair, a darker blond mustache and dead brown eyes.

"Hello, Erika," he says. "Where have you been?"

Does he know me? Because it sounds like he knows me.

Another girl—one of those scary-looking senior girls who always hang out at the smoking pit—stands up and points at me.

"Erika? As in the Erika who got us kicked out of graduation ceremony? Is that her?"

"That's her," Big Red's voice again. "Erika Williams. She was Cassie's little girlie. Now she's the sheriff's best buddy."

Another girl's voice says, "Hey, I got suspended and stuck in summer school because of you!"

All I can do is drop my eyes so I don't have to look at anyone. That's when I remember the camera cradled in my arms. Not good. Not good at all. If anything happens to that camera, my mother will kill me and chop me into little pieces.

The blocky guy reaches out a finger to touch the edge of the camera case peeking out from behind my crossed arms. "What have we here?"

I hear Sonny jump down off his perch and see his legs walking closer to me. Suddenly, he yanks me away from the other guy and gives me a nasty little shake.

"What are you doing here? You weren't invited. Go home." He forcibly turns me back toward the path and gives my arm a rough shove. "Get going before I plant my foot in your butt."

A chorus of laughter erupts as I run away, but I don't care. I'm thrilled to be free with the camera in one piece.

The graduation music starts echoing over the loudspeakers as I climb back up to Church Street. Despite what just happened, my feet refuse to walk toward home. Instead, I turn and walk to the east end of the stadium. No one is anywhere near the visitor's entrance, so I duck under the gate and hide under the metal bleachers closest to the podium.

When Jeff stands up, my hands are shaking too hard to keep anything in the frame. So I just rest the camera under my chin and listen with my whole body.

Sunday June 12, 1977

Dear Cassie,

If you were here with me, you'd have giggled and snorted through Jeff's graduation speech, saying things like, "Why did I date him, again? He's such a nerd sometimes."

As if that word could ever really attach itself to Jeff Johannson—class president, wide receiver for the state championship Cardinals, valedictorian. He is absolute perfection. Golden haired, golden skinned and, as it turns out, golden tongued.

It really was a great speech, Cassie. People laughed at the places they were supposed to laugh and they cheered at the places he meant for them to cheer. Except for me....I just cried. From the beginning to the end and then I cried harder when he walked off stage.

What if that's the last time I hear Jeff's voice?

Truth is, I've been in love with Jeff Johannson since the first day of second grade. That was the year I had to start wearing those horrible leg braces and all the kids were so mean. At recess, someone tripped me on the playground and I couldn't stop myself from falling. Humiliating! But then Jeff stood over me with the kickball tucked under his arm. He'd stopped the fifth grade kickball game to help a second grade girl in leg braces.

When he gave me a hand up, he whispered, "Don't worry. It'll stop now."

And it did stop. For the rest of that year, no one dared bully or tease me. I've always wondered how he made that happen.

I wish he would work that magic for me now.

Your friend,

Erika

| six |

I'm outside the Bixby theater with my arms loaded—Suzie's overstuffed three-ring binder, the Super 8, electrical tape in every possible color and a bunch of Anita's junk are piled up to my chin. A nasty pair of her ballet shoes are balanced on top, right under my nose. Does the Mother Monster help me at all? No. She speeds off as soon as I'm out of the car, leaving me to struggle up to the side entrance alone.

With my arms full, I have to kick at the door a couple of times instead of knocking. A hollow gonging sound echoes on the other side. I wait. And wait. Then I kick again. Five times and harder. Then I wait and sweat and wait some more. Aggravated, arms about to give out, I turn to rest my backside against the door and mule-kick backwards as hard as I can. On my third kick, the door swings inward without warning and I stumble backward into a wall of muscle.

I mumble, "I'm sorry" a few times before turning around to get a good look. Sonny Johannson scowls at me. Twice in two days. My bad luck is unbelievable.

A low muffled voice behind Sonny says, "The pounding. Stop the pounding...."

Jeff is leaning against the open doorway of the men's bathroom with a white towel tied around the top half of his head. Even though I can't see his whole face, my heart recognizes him instantly. My pulse flutters in my ears, making me dizzy.

"The pounding is over, Party Animal," Sonny says. "Get back in the bathroom and hug the toilet."

Jeff peels one edge of the towel up to uncover his right eye. "Erika?" His voice is just above a whisper. "Shhh. Okay?" I nod and he gives me a lopsided smile, then suddenly frowns.

"Cuz, if you puke on the lobby rug I'm going to kick you in the head," Sonny yells, hurrying toward him. Over his shoulder, he says, "Nick's in the theater messing with the stage lights. He wants to talk to you." He shoves Jeff into the bathroom just as Jeff starts making ugly gurgling noises.

"What's wrong?" I ask.

Sonny gives me a hard look. "Graduation parties until dawn. You tell Nick about this and I'll…" The door swings shut between us.

Since when does Sonny work here? Guess it's been a long time since I've watched a movie at the Bixby.

When I walk into the theater, I don't see Nick anywhere. "Nick? Are you here?" My voice echoes despite all the velvet draped on the theater walls.

No answer. So I walk up to the stage, dump my armload into one of the front row seats and look around.

Oh, the Bixby! There is something so magical here. I'm not talking about all the old fashioned fanciness. The magic is not in the big crystal chandeliers. It's not in the miles and miles of rose velvet draperies. It has little to do with the gilded plaster or the mahogany seats or the painted murals of twilight skies. Standing there, it feels like I've fallen into a whole other world; a safe place where anything is possible. I close my eyes and inhale a few breaths just to savor it.

Above my head there's a clattering noise. Nick is crawling along a narrow metal catwalk with a tool of some kind clenched in one fist. His coveralls look like they haven't been washed in months. His bald head is already dripping sweat. He looks so much older than the last time I saw him…a year ago? Still, the sight of him makes me smile. Makes me remember how he used to dress up like Frankenstein every Halloween and hand out popcorn balls in front of the theater. The way he used to sneak a box of candy to me when Anita would come to discuss recital business in his office.

The year I was stuck in a wheelchair after my ankle surgeries, Nick carried me up to the balcony to watch *Snow White* because I told him those were my favorite seats.

I cup both hands around my mouth and yell, "Nick! I'm here!"

The sudden noise must surprise him. For just a few seconds, it looks like he might lose his balance up there and my heart lurches with him.

Once he's back in control, he looks down and yells, "Well hello! Is that my gypsy girl?" in his usual cheerful voice.

Gypsy girl. Nick calls me that because I was always a gypsy for Halloween. Every single year. No matter how much I cried for another costume, Anita always made me be a gypsy. Probably because we could make up that costume using the scarves and jewelry that was already in her closet without buying anything special for me.

"Yes, it's me. Be careful!"

"Oh pooh," Nick laughs, waving the wrench-like thing in his hand toward me. "I've been crawling over every inch of this theater since before your mother was born. Don't you worry. I never fall."

I watch him crawl back and climb down the skinny access ladder very, very slowly. He's moving so much more slowly than he used to. My chest hurts just watching.

When he's finally down on the stage, he claps his hands together and says, "How's my girl?"

What can I say? Nick lives in his own world here at the Bixby. Even though this theater is right next to the main fire station where Chief Abbott looks out over the downtown square, I don't know if he's heard anything about Cassie leaving town. But he definitely knows Suzie.

"Suzie eloped with her boyfriend on Friday and Anita is in a complete tizzy."

"Oh goody," Nick says, pulling out a red handkerchief to rub his forehead. "As if her normal temper isn't awful enough." I laugh and he tilts his head sideways. "I'm afraid it's going to get much worse too. You might want to hide when she gets here."

"I can't," I tell him, "I'm taking over most of Suzie's work. In fact, I've got to talk to you about some stuff." I pick up Suzie's binder and look for the page with notes from Anita.

"About the lights, Little Gypsy—" Nick says.

"Yeah, the lights," I break in, "and some other stuff." I stop talking when Nick holds up his hand.

"I'm telling YOU something," he says. "There's problems with some of the lights. There's some shorts in the wires, some rust I can't explain…"

Nick rattles on and on with a list of technical catastrophes. Everything—from the lights to the air conditioner to the backstage toilets—is on the fritz. I scribble furiously as he lists all of the problems. When he's done, I definitely want to hide.

I look up at him with my saddest eyes, "She's going to get really, really mean."

Nick gives me his widest ear-to-ear grin. "That's one way to say it. Bette Davis would say, 'Fasten your seatbelts it's going to be a bumpy ride.'"

Monday June 13, 1977

Dear Cassie,

Today was the first day of rehearsals for Wednesday's dance recital and it is now official. My mother is the devil in tap shoes.

So far she has made six different girls cry. One baby ballerina peed all over her leotard and tights because my Mother Monster kept the group on stage too long. Do five-year-olds really need to "learn their marks" on stage just to hop and shuffle-ball-change for two minutes? Anita even got one mother crying because she informed the woman that her child was an overstuffed oaf. The munchkin in question did not cry. I heard her tell her mom that she would be very happy to quit dance classes forever so Mommy wouldn't be upset by Miss Anita ever again. I gave the kid a thumbs up behind Anita's back.

Worst of all is how Anita is treating poor Nick Papanos. If I were him, I'd kick her out of this theater and tell her to shove her recital money where the sun don't shine. But he just keeps nodding and putting up with her abuse. In fact, I think I hear her now. Better go figure out what she's screeching about.

Love,

Erika

Wednesday June 15, 1977

Dear Cassie,

Another year, another recital, another reason to dig a hole in my back yard and jump in.

I'll spare you a full description of the recital. Lost ribbons, ripped tutus, missed cues....it's the same chaos covered in sequins every year. We've seen it all before.

Oh, except for the part when Big Red tried to kill me.

There is something seriously wrong with that girl. She should be locked up like *One Flew Over the Cuckoo's Nest.*

I was supposed to film the recital, but I had this idea about using one film cassette to record some backstage images. You know the stuff I mean...ballerinas tying up their shoe ribbons, little girls getting powdered and painted by their mothers, baby starlets twirling in their costumes. I thought it would be something artistic and cute Anita would appreciate. Stupid me.

Everything went fine with the younger dancers getting ready in that huge room under the stage. Then I climbed the stairs to film a few shots of Anita and the high school dancers up in the real dressing rooms. The first thing I saw when I pushed open the door to Dressing Room Three was Tammy pressed close to a huge mirror smearing on cherry red lipstick while her mother fluffed and fussed with her big red hair. She was wearing a circus ringmaster's coat with shiny black hot pants and fishnet stockings.

Wasn't that supposed to be your costume?

As soon as I saw her, my stomach dropped. I would have closed the door and snuck away, but Mrs. Costas saw me and said something like, "Oh look, here's Anita's daughter with a camera."

Well, Tammy spun around like she'd been pinched. Her face went very white, while all the splotchy freckles on her chest turned an angry purplish color. She looked at me and then her eyes locked on the Super

8. From the expression on her face, you would have thought I was holding a fist full of greasy gopher guts.

Out of nowhere and for no good reason, she started screaming at me in Technicolor. I'm not even sure what all came out of her mouth, but I know it was absolutely foul and too disgusting to write on paper. It was insane! You want to know what's even crazier? The whole time Tammy was throwing this tantrum, her mother just stood there fluffing her hair. Do you believe that?

When the beast finally ran out of obscenities, she kept stomping her feet and screeching, "Get out!" about a hundred times. I should have run. I have no idea why I didn't. Tammy suddenly lunged at me and shoved me with both hands. The stairs were right behind me. I could have died!

Never, ever in a million years would I have expected to be happy to find Deputy Wayne Todd lurking around Anita's recital, but he saved my life. He was coming up the stairs behind me, no doubt trying to figure out what all the screaming was about, when Tammy pushed me. He caught me from behind and held me up until I could get my feet back under my body. My legs were pure jelly, so he had to help me sit down on the steps. Thank goodness I managed to keep my grip on the Super 8!

I was hugging the camera to my chest, trying really hard not to cry, when Anita walked up. Would you believe she started asking me what I had done to upset Tammy!?!? And then she walked right past me to apologize to Tammy's mom for MY behavior!

Deputy Todd leaned down and whispered, "Wow. I guess the customer is always right, but your mother can be a hard one, huh?"

I didn't want to talk to the deputy and I didn't want to cry. So I just got up and left. Of course, I couldn't leave the theater. I still had to film the whole stupid recital.

In the final number, when my mother was in the middle of the chorus line doing high kicks with her teen princesses, I pretended the camera lens was a super-powered rifle and I was an assassin.

Missing you like crazy,
Erika

| SEVEN |

THE EMPTINESS IS THREATENING TO SUFFOCATE ME.

My chores are finished before noon. The only thing on TV is the stupid news. Q-FM is playing awful "Hometown Rock" that makes my teeth ache and every other radio station on the dial is filled with garbled static or commercial jabber. Every song in my record collection seems to echo with Cassie's laughter. I can see her spinning in circles to "Rhiannon," or singing "Hotel California" into my hairbrush, or demonstrating how to "(Shake, Shake, Shake) Shake Your Booty."

My skin feels like it wants to crawl right off my body and run out the front door so I switch off everything and sneak downstairs to raid the kitchen, but there's nothing to eat in this house, not even one single bottle of cold Tab in the fridge. At least that gives me an excuse to walk over to Pit Stop with three dollars I found in Anita's jeans—one of the few perks of being her laundry slave.

There's an unpleasant surprise waiting for me when I get back home. Deputy Wayne Todd is sitting on our wooden picnic table, glass of ice water in his left hand, chatting away with the Mother Monster. He looks comfortable, like he's planning on hanging out for a while.

Damn! Why can't he just forget I exist?

For her part, Anita is lounging in her favorite lawn chair all slicked up with baby oil and wearing her itty bitty white bikini. Hair tucked into a white turban, she's stretched out on one side like a Coppertone model. Something about the scene makes me wonder if she knew we were going to get a visit from a six-foot-something law man today.

"There's my dumpling," she says, all saccharine sweet.

Dumpling? Translation: There's the lumpy fat thing that lives here.

To emphasize her point, she looks at the bag of Buckeye potato chips in my hand and spikes one pencil-thin eyebrow at me. I hold up a case of sweating Tab bottles with my other hand.

"Went to get some pop. We were totally out."

Translation: You drank all the Tab. Fry in baby oil and die.

I wait, not looking at the Deputy, even though the clink of ice in his glass makes my eyes itch to peek over in that direction. Silence.

"Wayne was just telling me all the latest news."

They are both staring at me, but Cassie's coaching kicks in. *Never offer anything. Always let them talk first.*

Finally, the deputy breaks the stand-off. "Only news is there's no news." He waves his glass and shrugs casually, but his eyes are searching my face. "You have any news, Erika?"

I wave my bag of chips and shrug back at him, imitating his exact gesture.

Oily skin slithers restlessly against the plastic lawn chair. "Erika."

Translation: I'll slice you into shreds if you don't behave.

I lock my eyes on the tip of Deputy Todd's nose. "No, sir, no news."

"All right. Relax." He wiggles his glass toward Anita. "No need to get intense. This isn't an official visit.

"Then I can go now, right?"

Anita nods once, but the Deputy holds up a hand like he's directing traffic.

"Hold on there just a minute. I come in peace. No more Cassie questions, I promise." He flashes the peace sign. "You and I seem to have gotten off to a bad start. Let's try again."

I stare at his nose and keep my lips pressed together.

"You heard about this new movie; I think it's called *Space Wars*?"

Huh?

He doesn't bother to wait for a response, just keeps babbling on like we're good buddies. "*Time Magazine* called it 'The Movie of the Year.' Friend of mine with LAPD says every teenager in the city has been lined up to see this movie over and over for weeks. Says it's the damndest thing he's ever seen...and that's from a guy who patrolled West Hollywood for over ten years."

All I hear is LAPD. As in the Los Angeles Police Department. As in the people to call if you want to track down a runaway...in Hollywood. Does he know something? Or is he fishing?

Words are still flowing out of his lips, but I can't follow any of it. When he finally shuts up, Anita makes nicey noises before poking one of her talons into my hip.

"Right, Erika?"

I nod, even though I have no idea what I'm agreeing to. Deputy Todd flashes all of his teeth at me and says, "Great. I'll pick you two up at five on Saturday."

Oh, no! Did I just agree to go see some weirdo space movie with the Mother Monster and the hairy interrogator who is ruining my life?

Cassie's voice seems to echo around me as I stumble back to the house.

We are all just prisoners here, of our own device.

Saturday June 18, 1977

Dear Cassie,

STAR WARS!!! Have you seen it?

Everything is different now. Everything.

All of these crazy feelings and ideas are pinballing through my body and I can't seem to focus on anything. I want to close my eyes and breathe myself into that other galaxy far, far away. I want to walk with droids, fire a blaster, fly over metal moons and drink bubbling cocktails in a space bar full of aliens. I think I can already feel the Force flowing through me.

Here's the thing…I need to see that movie again.

There's no way Anita will take me. She hated *Star Wars*. Big surprise. As if we needed more proof that the Mother Monster is a cold, evil, hollow creature without a soul.

Never mind. I don't want to waste any energy on her right now. I just want to think about that movie and how to get back into that theater.

If you haven't seen *Star Wars* yet, you have to go see it. Now. Immediately!

It's better than a thousand new episodes of *Charlie's Angels*. More fantastic than sipping pink champagne after midnight. It's even more exciting than a plane ticket to Hollywood.

This movie will BLOW your mind!

May the Force be with you,
Erika

| EIGHT |

When the final credits roll, I feel turned inside out and scrubbed clean. The blank half of my birth certificate, years of stumbling around on crooked legs, every single question mark looming over my head—it all disappears. Surrounded by an energy field of all living things, I'm eternal. Weightless. Free.

The transformation lasts all of thirty seconds.

As soon as we step out of the theater, Deputy Todd starts laughing. "What the hell was that? Two hours of my life wasted watching a rolling vacuum cleaner, a queer robot and a giant monkey dog."

"Good Lord!" Anita adds, "Have they run out of pretty girls in Hollywood? What kind of space princess was that? All brown and round with a nasty mouth."

The two of them start snickering like Muttley, the evil cartoon dog.

Why does my chest hurt like this? I want to smash my box of Lemonheads in both of their smug faces. Glaring down at my own hands gripping the half-eaten box of candy, I'm hoping to see something new glowing under my skin.

"So what do you think of all that spaced-out weirdness, kid?" It's Wayne's voice. I can't look up.

It's painful to make my lips form words.

"Kind of crazy, I guess. The music was cool."

"That music was the whole movie," Deputy says, eying me carefully.

I keep staring down at my candy. There's a few seconds of quiet where I can almost feel him trying to find the best way to say something.

"I need to use the bathroom before we leave," I blurt out, desperate to escape.

Inside the last stall, I press my back against the door and close my eyes. For just a few stolen seconds I can imagine the world of space and laser fights sweeping back over me. Then a little girl in the next stall starts breathing through her hands to sound like Darth Vader. Another little girl giggles and the spell is broken.

The ride home is torture. Deputy Todd drives a pickup truck so I'm stuck sitting between the two of them while they make fun of *Star Wars* all the way home.

***

Two days have gone by. Nothing seems real to me. My head is in the stars. Time plays tricks. Some hours dissolve into seconds, but then seconds stretch into eternities.

The Mother Monster is blathering on and on about her recital ticket sales and wallpaper. I guess the profits from this year's recital are enough to make some improvements at the studio, which almost certainly means I'm expected to perform slave labor. I should be listening, but I can't focus. Instead, I let my eyes wander over the wallpaper samples she's spread across the kitchen table. They're shiny metallic paper in soft shades of baby blue, mint green and powder pink with a raised fuzzy pattern that looks like powdered sugar. I let my fingers run over the pink one, feeling the stubble texture of the pattern.

Anita looks at the sample I'm touching and says something like, "That would be perfect for the ballet room."

Private sleeping quarters on a luxury spaceship with bubble windows and a panorama of stars. The powdery patterns shift and change to reveal the swirling invisible patterns of the galaxy….

Anita's voice has switched to barking orders so I try to focus my brain. Chores. No TV. No moping on the couch. Blah, blah, blah. She's shaking her car keys at me as she leaves. The door slamming between us is sweet relief

Once she's out of the house, I finally let myself breathe.

The chores fly by in a blur. The vacuum cleaner is my own little droid. The handle of our ancient lawn mower is the steering mechanism for a supersonic space cruiser. Even the feather duster becomes an exotic alien pet that carries secret messages between spies. I name it Fizzwicky.

Anita isn't back by twilight. I find myself staring at a blank screen on the TV, unable to turn it on. There's something so earthbound about TV. I don't want to be earthbound. So I take a glass of lemonade outside to watch the sky change colors. The light in Cassie's room is on. Everything freezes. My feet start walking toward her house. I'm not thinking, just walking. When my bare feet step onto the asphalt alley, still warm from the day's sun, I stop. Walt is standing in the back yard under the crabapple tree. He doesn't seem to notice me at first. He's standing there staring down at his own feet with a cigarette dangling from his left hand, right hand over his eyes, rocking side to side.

The sound of breathing—deep and heavy and hollow like Darth Vader's—seems to surround me, turning my skin to ice. I tip-toe a few baby steps backward, hoping he won't notice me. Then I turn slowly, holding my breath, and start to retreat.

"Just doesn't make sense, does it?"

His question hangs in the air as the sound of breathing gets louder, more intense. This is crazy. Where is that sound coming from?

"You'd say something if you knew, wouldn't you, Erika?"

Swallowing over the bitter taste of metal, I open my mouth, but nothing comes out.

"Look at me, girl."

Against my wishes, my feet obey. When I turn around he's standing on the other side of the alley and I nearly jump out of my skin to see that he's gotten so close to me when I never heard him move.

"You'd tell me or the sheriff if you knew anything at all that would help us find my little girl, wouldn't you? You wouldn't let me suffer like this?"

I manage to choke out "No sir…I mean, yes sir. I mean…I don't want you to suffer."

Anita chooses that particular moment to bust open our back door and yell "Erika, where the hell are you?"

I've never been so glad to hear that witch's voice in all my 15 years! I run back to our house without looking back and find her glaring out at the gloom behind me.

"What were you doing?" she asks. Before I can form an answer, she hooks her claws into my shoulder and pulls me into the kitchen

Her lips say, "I brought home some chicken and cole slaw for dinner." But her eyes are glued to the apple tree in Cassie's back yard.

Monday June 20, 1977

Dear Cassie,

I'm back up on the porch roof. The light in your bedroom is on, but I haven't seen any movement. Maybe Walt figures you'll come back if he lights up your room. Weird, huh?

Weirder than that, he's been standing in your back yard for hours, chain smoking and staring at the same patch of dirt under your apple tree. It's going to be a long, horrible summer if I can't hang out in my own backyard without seeing your dad. Just thinking about it makes my stomach itch.

I really, really want to go see *Star Wars* again but I know Anita won't go near it. Right now she's on the phone gushing with her friend Penny about some guy she met at the fuzzy wallpaper store. Will she drop me off at the Cineplex while she looks at more wallpaper?

After what happened last time, thumbing a ride freaks me out. But if Anita won't take me, I might risk it. There's a set of steak knives in the kitchen cabinet that we never use. I can slip one in my purse.

As for getting in to see the show, well, I'd better start searching for money. I'm not even sure how much it costs to get in. None of this was ever a problem when you were here.

Okay, you're not here. I need to start figuring this stuff out on my own… unless I want to be trapped here all summer, always hiding from Anita, from Walt, from Deputy Wayne Todd. No! I've got to figure this out.

May the Force be with you,

Erika

| NINE |

EVEN THOUGH IT'S EARLY AFTERNOON, BROAD DAYLIGHT, AND I have our sharpest kitchen knife in my purse, I'm too terrified to stick out my thumb. I walk at least two miles down the state road to get away from our neighborhood. My guts are twisting and squirming. At least twenty cars zoom right past me before I finally get up the courage to point my thumb westward, toward the city. Some guy in a rusted bucket of a car throws a can of Mountain Dew at me as he speeds past. That is almost the end. Like the littlest piggy, I'm ready to run wee, wee, wee all the way back home.

Suddenly, there's a pickup truck stopped next to me. A woman's voice says, "Are you okay, Honey? You need a ride?"

The voice sounds sweet and kind of familiar. I inch closer, just close enough to make out a stiff beehive hairdo and rhinestone-crusted glasses. I know this person. She's the one and only waitress I've ever seen working at the Landmark Diner. Last time we were there, the Mother Monster slapped her hand when she tried to put extra whipped cream on my cocoa. Dora? No, it's Doreen.

"Hey! Aren't you Anita Williams' little girl? Your mother know you're out here?"

I step back quickly, lips opening and closing while I try to come up with some excuse, but not one single sensible word comes out.

"Don't fret." She leans over and opens the passenger door. "I was young once, too. You trying to get to the mall?"

"How did you know?"

"Never met a girl hitching on this road wasn't going to the mall. I'll give you a ride if you agree to meet me at five o'clock on the dot to come on back home. I can't be leaving you in the city."

Doreen drops me off in front of Sears and watches me walk inside. After her taillights disappear, I walk across the parking lot and dodge six lanes of ferocious traffic to get to the Cineplex Four. The familiar glass front of the theater is suddenly terrifying. Maybe I should have gone to a different movie theater. There's got to be at least twenty theaters in the city. This is not my tiny nowhere town with only one single movie theater with only one movie playing.

It used to be so easy to sneak into this place when I was with Cassie. Half the time, I could see the usher knew what we were doing. He'd look into Cassie's dazzling green eyes and wink, like they had a secret understanding. I never could figure out exactly how she managed it, but she sure got us in to see movies. Staring into a wall of smoky glass windows with no money in my pocket, I feel utterly and completely alone.

Slowly, I circle around the building to survey the side exits, one for each theater. All I need to know is which of the four possible doors leads to the theater showing *Star Wars.* Simple enough on the surface, but I don't know any way to find my movie behind these identical, anonymous, metal rectangles. I'm about to give up and go back to Sears when I hear the *Star Wars* music.

That music wraps around my middle, hooks into my belly and pulls me right out of my miserable life. There is nothing else like it.

I twirl around and watch three girls wearing Peter Frampton shirts walk away from the first exit. As the door clicks shut, the music dies. I've found my target.

More people pour out along with that amazing music. The trick is to look like I just walked out and need to go back in for something I forgot. I pass another group as I walk toward the magical opening, a man and three boys. Two of the boys are pretending to sword fight while the third whines, "I want to play, too." I walk on past the theater door as it opens again and two more people came out. Two girls who look like cheerleaders emerge. One looks right at me with this smirk that says she knows exactly what I'm doing. So I duck my head and keep walking. I'm about ready to forget this whole thing and go home.

Hurrying back toward the parking lot, I find myself in a stream of six or seven senior citizens walking the same way.

"Well, that was really something wasn't it?" A woman with a white poof of perfectly curled hair asks a bald and blue-veined old man in a stained cardigan.

"Something weird if you ask me," he snaps back.

"Oh come on, you old grouch," the little woman chirps back, "I thought it was very creative. Very modern and..."

"Childish. No class in the movies these days."

I don't want to listen to another painful bashing of my movie, so I slow down to let them get ahead, pretending to look in my purse.

"Forget something?"

I look back and see a familiar face looking down at me. The ground jolts under my feet. I can't believe I'm this stupid. It's the usher who used to wink at Cassie...and it's also the mean guy who grabbed me on Graduation Day. I thought he looked familiar, but I guess I didn't recognize him without the red jacket and brass buttons. Who is this guy?

Before I can make my mouth say anything, he points into the theater. "If you left something in there, better move fast. We've got another crowd waiting to get in for the next showing."

He doesn't seem to recognize me.

Keeping my head down, I keep digging frantically until I nick my pinkie on the kitchen knife. "I'll just take a quick look," I whisper as politely as possible while rushing past him.

"Take your time," he answers with a shrug of one shoulder, still showing no sign of recognition. He lifts a bag of trash, "I'm dumping this then I've got to get into Cinema Three to start cleaning."

The door closes and he's gone. Did he give me permission to stay in the theater? The cut on my finger throbs in time with my heart, which is beating wildly in my throat. I hurry to the far back corner of the theater and go through the motions of poking around for something. To my left, a group of three walks in, laughing loudly. I track them out of the corner of my eye, peeking out from under my bangs. They aren't even looking toward me. More people come in. I hear young voices; a girlish squeal. No one is paying any attention to me. I perch on the edge of the chair, suck on my injured finger and pretend to poke around in my purse with my other hand. Before long, I'm one of about a hundred people in the theater.

So easy…and yet I still feel all short-circuited and tense.

Why did he let me in? Anita always says, "There's no such thing as something for nothing. It's always something for something."

When the house lights finally dim, I settle back and swallow my discomfort. After the preview for a stupid car movie starring Burt Reynolds I make the move from the back corner of the theater to the middle of the last row. Finally, the movie rolls and the camera drops me back into space. Just like the first time, reality dissolves away.

He waits until the droids are trudging through the desert sands before he sits down beside me. My stomach drops. Busted.

"Hello, Cassie's friend. Enjoying the movie?" The words are spoken right next to my left ear; his breath burns my skin.

I swallow, my mouth suddenly stale and sour, and nod once. His finger brushes away the tiny hairs in front of my ear and I flinch.

"Shhhhhh, relax," he whispers.

I'm trapped. Up on the screen, C-3PO reunites with R2-D2. My skin is crawling.

"Cassie said you were cool. Said she trusted you completely. Like a sister."

He takes my chin in his hand and pulls it to look at him. "We need to talk, Little Sister."

My brain is screaming, but my lips are zipped tight.

"You need to make it right. Hear me?"

There's slight pressure on my chin. I let him move my head up and down in a puppet's nod. Then he leans in close to my ear until his nose is touching the upper fold. "Wait out by the dumpster after the movie." He leans back, stares into my eyes for what seemed like a very long time.

"Dumpster. Got it." I whisper back, wondering how private and hidden it is back there.

"Good girl," he answers and walks away from my row. The exit door doesn't open or close. There's no tell-tale flash of light from the lobby. Is he still in the theater? Neck burning, I fasten my eyes on the screen and blink back tears. I feel raw, stripped naked.

There's no way I'm going back to that dumpster. No way. When the movie ends and a new stream of people leave by the outside door, I press right through them and run, not stopping until I'm back at Sears with a hot stitch of pain in my side.

First, I find a van to hide behind. Then I start thinking he might sneak up on me, so I crouch down and look for feet coming my way. A hundred million years creep by before Doreen finally pulls up in front of Sears in her battered yellow pickup. I practically yank the door off its hinges to duck inside. It's all I can do not to yell, "Drive away, drive away!" While I struggle to control my panic, she's looking at me sort of weird.

I need an excuse for the way I'm acting. "Um, I think I saw someone from school who used to tease me."

She smiles this sad smile, puts the car into gear and we're out of there. All the way home she talks non-stop about how mean the kids were when she was in school and how they're all fat failures now. She doesn't ask me a single question. I really should pick some flowers and take them to the Landmark Diner for Doreen. Under all that goofy hair, the woman is an angel.

***

Lazy Bones,

It's going to be another scorcher. Apparently, you plan to sleep the coolest part of the day away. I went shopping with Penny to escape the heat. When you finally drag yourself out of bed, I need you to take this check over to the Bixby. Tell Nick I am only paying him half the agreed amount due to maintenance issues.

When was the last time you did the laundry?

Mom

PS – Better not find you loafing on the couch watching TV when I get home.

| TEN |

My day starts with an evil note from Anita next to the coffee pot.

The house isn't just hot, it's boiling. The water out of the kitchen tap is like soup and the air makes me sweat just to breathe it. Every window in our house is wide open as if we heard some rumor there might be a breeze on the way, but there's no breeze. Blistering sunlight pours into every room. Why? Because Anita can't stand a gloomy house.

So she drives off to go shopping and leaves her daughter to roast in a solar torture chamber. On top of that, she expects me to drag myself back to the Bixby to do her dirty work with Nick. Then she wants me to do the laundry and, after all that, I'm not allowed to sit on the couch and watch TV?

Hatred for that woman sizzles in my throat.

There's no way I'm touching the laundry. No way! It doesn't matter what fury she unleashes when she gets home. If I'm even still alive by then. I stomp from window to window, pulling the shades and trying to block out some of the blasted heat. It's no use. The heat is inescapable.

They're probably going downtown to the Lazarus Department Store. Anita says it reminds her of shopping at Macy's in New York. There are multiple movie theaters along their route where, I'm sure, *Star Wars* is playing in at least one. Did it occur to her to wake me up and offer to let me go with her? Did she even think for one second about letting her daughter watch a movie in air conditioned comfort while she spent ridiculous amounts of money on clothes?

No. I have the most selfish mother in the history of the galaxy.

I walk back to the kitchen and stare at her note, pick it up to...I don't know, wad it up maybe. Underneath, there's a five dollar bill and her payment check made out to Nick Papanos. The Bixby isn't the Cineplex Four, but it is air conditioned. And there's ice cream at the Dairy Dream across the downtown square.

My anger doesn't evaporate, but it cools down a notch or two.

When I pull my bike out of the shed, Walt is sitting on his back porch smoking another cigarette, staring at the curl of smoke climbing away from his clenched fist. His legs are draped over the cinder block steps. When does that man go to work these days? Every time I look toward Cassie's house, he's there. Waiting. Every time I see him, the sound of Darth Vader's breathing seems to echo in my brain and I forget to breathe until a pain in my chest reminds me.

But once I'm on my bike moving away from Chief and my overheated house, I feel free. Pumping the pedals, my brain lets go of every dark thought.

Hellish heat bubbles up from the asphalt. How hot can it get before a bike tire will melt? How hot would it be on a desert planet with two suns? It would have to be ridiculous crazy hot there. How come none of the characters in *Star Wars* seemed to be sweating? After less than five minutes on my bike, I'm already dripping.

When I get to the Bixby, I'm sticky and gross. With our one single angry sun hammering heat into my body, I'm looking forward to the cool, darkened world of the theater. I'm not happy to see Nick standing outside. He's directly in front of the theater with a long pole in one hand, staring up at the letters on the marquee—*Nasty Habits*. It's a comedy about nuns in garter belts or something like that. Some nutball religious people complained to the newspaper about the movie poster before the film even opened.

I prop my bike against a parking meter. My eyes scan for the "offensive and degrading" poster to see what all the fuss is about, but only the sun's reflection glares back at me from the glass. Nick is busy mopping his face and bald head with a blue handkerchief when I walk up.

"Is that the Gypsy Girl?"

"Hi, Nick."

"Well, you're getting so grown up I barely recognize you these days!"

The man saw me last week during the rehearsals and the recital, but I don't say that. I'm feeling extra guilty. First he had to endure all of Anita's insults. Now I have to short pay him for the recital. Except for Anita's dance recitals, we never come to the Bixby any more. Instead, we drive forty minutes or more to one of the big multiplex theaters in the city—Nick's competition. Everyone knows the big theaters are putting him out of business. Everyone, it seems, except Nick. Today, baking in the intense sunlight, I can see the front of the place is looking older and more faded than usual. The marquee letters are from three different mismatched colors. I feel dirty, like a wad of discarded gum on the sidewalk.

Nick stuffs his hankie back into his pocket. "Hot day for a bike ride."

One of the front doors pops open and Jeff walks toward us. Jeff! He sure is looking better than the last time I saw him; all six foot two of him. He's wearing dark blue jeans with a plain black t-shirt that hugs his shoulders and...oh, wow! He's holding up a *Star Wars* poster. I'm stunned. Completely speechless.

"Nick, I'm moving this to the feature display window," he says, then looks at me. This slow, incredibly sweet smile creeps over his face. It's a real smile that lights up those heavenly blue eyes. All he says is, "Hey Erika," but it feels like he's really happy to see me!

I say, "Hey" back, but no one seems to notice.

Nick slaps the air in front of him in a gesture that says he doesn't really care about the poster and turns back to the box of letters open at his feet. Jeff looks down and his perfect face folds into a frown. There's a large S and W plus two smaller r's laid out on the sidewalk. I keep my head lowered, but peek up at Jeff through my lashes. He's frowning harder, his eyes locked on Nick as the old guy pulls out the same limp handkerchief and rubs at the back of his neck again.

"You should go inside and cool down," Jeff says, "I can change the marquee."

"I'm fine. I've been changing this sign for over forty years and in plenty of summers hotter than this one." Despite the words, Nick's voice is heavy with exhaustion. "I changed this sign in a blizzard this year."

"All the more reason you deserve a rest." Jeff's perfect china blue eyes flicker toward me and lock on mine. In a split second, there's an electric communication between us.

"Nick? My mom asked me to come talk to you. Um…." Jeff's eyes are so distracting!

"Anita?" Nick heaves a gigantic sigh that wheezes in his chest and sounds wet. "I suppose she's still upset."

"Right. She asked me to come here and talk to you about something."

"Well…" Nick draws out the word and leans both hands on the metal pole, "You know I think your mother should probably come here herself."

"If I have to tell her that, she's going to be so mad at me! Please, could we go inside to talk? Do you mind? It's really flaming hot out here."

Jeff turns and walks away. I feel his walking away like a pain, my body leans toward him. When he stops in front of one of the poster display windows, I catch his reflection in the glass. He looks back at me in the reflection and winks. The jolt flip-flops my heart.

Nick coughs into one hand, breaking the spell. I could stand out here forever and watch Jeff work on the poster, but I know he wants me to get Nick out of the sun. So I make a big deal out of fanning my face with my hand and say, "Please? Could we go inside?"

"That woman," Nick grumbles, looking around for a place to prop up the pole.

Jeff is there instantly, reaching out his hand. "I'll get started taking down the letters."

He doesn't look at me again, but I can feel the warmth of him there; just a few inches away. My brain is still floating around on that secret wink. I picture my hand reaching out to touch his arm. Running my fingers up to his shoulder. Burying my face in that black t-shirt.

"Well, let's get on with it," Nick says, pushing the pole at Jeff. He limps away from us toward the front door. I lift my eyes up to Jeff's face, but he's looking after Nick with another frown. I want him to look at me and say something. Anything.

"You were brilliant, Erika." Or, "You're the best, Erika." Even "Thanks, Erika" would be fine.

Instead, he bends over to rummage in the box of letters.

Nick jerks open one of the main doors and yells, "Well, come on then, Gypsy Girl."

Once inside, I peek back at Jeff, still crouched down in front of the letters. I watch him pick out a letter and then I walk straight into a wall of solid muscle. The wall grunts and turns around. It's Sonny. Again. Why am I always running into Sonny when I would give anything for some contact with Jeff?

"What are YOU doing here?" he asks, pushing one finger into my shoulder to emphasize the word "you" even more.

That really bugs me. It's like a swarm of Stormtroopers could bust into the Bixby Theater firing lasers in every direction and that might be okay with Sonny. But me, I'm a real problem.

I look over at Nick standing in front of the candy counter, rubbing at his neck with that nasty sweat-soaked hankie. No help there.

"Who do you think you are?" I whisper spit back at him.

"I work here and this is—"

"Wait, wait, wait!" Nick's agitated voice cuts off whatever Sonny was going to say. "What is this?"

I give Sonny my nastiest, "that's what you get" look, but he isn't paying any attention. His eyes are fastened on Nick.

"What's wrong, Nick?" Sonny asks.

Nick waves his hankie at the candy counter. "This! What is this? Why doesn't this look right?"

Sonny closes his eyes and takes a slow breath, then walks over to Nick.

"We talked about this. Remember?" He sounds like he's talking to a five-year-old child throwing a tantrum, not his boss.

"No, I do not!" Nick's voice is crackling with anger.

"We've gotten rid of the suckers. That's all," Sonny says. "We added more Lemonheads and JuJu Bees in their place. They sell better."

"There's always been suckers," Nick snaps.

"No." Sonny crosses his arms in front of his chest. "There's been the same bags of suckers for seven years."

"What are you saying?"

"Those bags of suckers have been sitting in the candy case since 1970. They were seven years old Nick."

"What? That's not right."

"Yeah, it is." Sonny tilts his head to one side. "They were always there, but no one bought them. I've never seen a single customer buy them, so I checked the old invoices. Had to go back seven years, Nick! You bought a case of suckers once. Back in March of 1970. By my count, you've sold three bags."

Nick seems so confused and lost. Why is Sonny being so mean about candy?

"Only three bags?"

"Yeah. In seven years. It's time to let the suckers go, Nick."

Nick's bald head swivels around, finds me.

"Gypsy girl?" he asks. The hairs on the back of my neck stand up. He looks so confused.

"Yes, sir?"

"You like suckers?"

Sonny glares at me.

"I like one sucker at a time," I say and feel Sonny's glare grow hotter, "but a whole bag is a bit too much."

There's a warmth at my left elbow. I know what it means even before Jeff's voice says, "We talked about this, Nick. We'll sell some candy that makes more money in the case and toss the old suckers to kids at the Fourth of July Parade. Don't you remember?"

"Why does everybody keep doing that?" Nick asks, very agitated. "You all keep saying…" his voice lifts to a weird falsetto, "Remember? Remember this? Remember that? Don't you remember?"

The room is silent except for the muffled pops from the popcorn machine. Then a smoky voice drifts down to us from the shadows above.

"Stop being so ornery."

Nick raises his face upward. "Did I say the candy could change?"

"Yes," the voice answers. I can't tell if it's male or female. Or where exactly it's coming from. "You agreed to let them change the candy yesterday."

Nick shakes his head like he's trying to clear it. "Well, I'll be damned."

When he looks at me, something is sharper in his eyes than before. "Where's Anita again?"

"Shopping," I tell him. "She sent me to talk to you."

"Well then, let's talk," he says in a bright, cheerful voice and turns toward the curving staircase that leads up to the balcony seats and offices.

Jeff nudges my arm gently and whispers in my ear, "Go on. It's okay."

I love the feeling of his breath near my ear. I wait a split second, hoping he'll say something else. Instead, he walks away. Sonny is looking at me hard, so I move quickly to follow Nick upstairs.

Nick is standing in the middle of his office holding up a movie poster in one hand and scratching one eyebrow with the other. He lifts the poster higher for me to see. It's the *Nasty Habits* poster. There's a picture of a nun with her skirt, I guess they call it a habit, hiked up and one sexy leg with a garter belt showing. The religious nuts got crazy over that?

"The movies these days." He shakes his head again before fixing me with a sad, watery look. He points two gnarled fingers at me, then he sweeps them toward the wall behind his cluttered desk. My eyes follow his fingers to the framed posters that have been on his office walls as long as I've known him. One is for *Gone With The Wind*. The other is for *Ben Hur*. I've never seen either movie.

"We've shown all the great masterpieces here," Nick's voice seems to come from far away. "Such big, gorgeous pictures. Stories that would sweep a person right out of this life and into something magical. But these days?" He makes a disgusted noise and drapes the *Nasty Habits* poster over the stacks of papers and empty Styrofoam cups on his desk. "These days the pictures seem to be getting dumber and smaller. We don't even have to roll back the curtains all the way to show this stuff. They don't make pictures big enough to fill the screen any more."

He moves slowly to the other side of the desk and lowers himself carefully into the chair. "Characters cussing instead of talking. Colors so dull, it's a waste of Technicolor. Doesn't surprise me people don't come to the movies so much these days. What's to see?"

Nick sits back and studies another framed movie poster on the wall to his left, behind the open office door—*Cleopatra*.

I think about the line at the Cineplex Four and the crowds of people in Hollywood waiting to see *Star Wars*. "You'll have to roll back the curtains all the way for this next movie, Nick."

"What? This kid's space movie?"

"It's a big movie. Like those older movies," I tell him. Nick looks doubtful.

"Really, Nick. There was a story in the paper on Sunday from some big movie critic in Washington. He said this movie is pulling lots of people to the theater. Not just once. Some people are watching it over and over. It's making lots more money than they thought it would."

Nick smiles at me, but the sadness is still in his eyes. "That would be nice, but it won't be enough. One big picture won't be enough."

"Enough?"

Nick looks down and picks at a loose thread on the arm of his office chair. "Business hasn't been so good lately. I'm thinking about selling the theater." He keeps his eyes down.

"You're going to sell the Bixby?" The sadness of it tears my breath away. Nick and the Bixby have always been here. Always. Even though we don't come here so much any more, I've never thought about it not being here.

Images ricochet through my mind: the mismatched letters on the marquee, the bulbs that always seem to be burnt out, the problems with the stage lights, the cracked tiles in the bathrooms, the rusting spots and the moldy smells. Most terrifying, the way Nick seems to be forgetting things and limping more than he used to. It's all so sad. I have to blink like crazy to stop the stinging in my eyes from turning into waterworks.

Nick plows on with words that seem to flow right past me. His eyes never leave the arm of his chair. I only catch bits and pieces of what he says. In my pocket, Anita's short check burns like an accusation.

"…guy coming from the city to look over the place…back rooms need cleaned out…been letting Anita keep some stuff there…got to get it moved…."

I force myself to blurt out, "Anita sent me with a check for the recital but she didn't pay the full amount."

Nick stops talking and focuses his eyes on me with a half smile. "Oh, I know. She told me ten times she wasn't going to pay the full amount."

"I'm so sorry." How I wish I had something better to say!

"Don't be sorry, Gypsy, none of this is your fault. That's for sure."

There's a knock on the office door frame behind me and I turn to see Jeff standing there. "Sorry to bother you, Nick, but Mrs. P left."

Nick pops out of his chair like he's been hit with electricity. "Left? What do you mean she left? We just got here and the old woman can't drive! Where would she go?"

Jeff shoves both hands into his pockets and looks at Nick with a puzzled face. "Today is the twenty-third of the month. Cemetery Day."

Nick plops back down into his chair and slaps one hand over his eyes with a groan. "That woman! My brother has been in the ground for over twenty years. Twenty years and still the old fool is in mourning. Always in black dresses! Walking over to St. Francis Cemetery every single month to stand there over the gravestone and mumble in Greek."

"Mrs. P is the lady who works the ticket booth," Jeff explains to me in a low voice when Nick pauses to take a breath. I nod and don't tell him I already know this.

"My dear sister-in-law is also supposed to be the bookkeeper and there's a stack of bills that need attention today. Not next week. Today! There's a whole list of work that needs done today. We're opening a new picture tomorrow. There's no way we can get it all done if I am stuck up here struggling with paperwork that's all in her crazy shorthand scribbles!" Nick's voice is getting louder and louder.

"We can get it done, Nick."

"No, no we can't!" Nick thunders. "There's not enough bodies even with Theodosia here." He slams his palm down on the desk and a cascade of papers fall to the floor in front of me. Nick doesn't seem to notice or care so I kneel down in front of the desk to pick up the papers. Most of it seems to be flyers that are months old. I look up to ask if I can throw the stuff away and notice that Nick's face is turning an alarming shade of red.

"I can't afford to hire more people! I sure can't afford to pay people who don't work, even if they are family."

"I can help," I say.

My name is Erika Williams. I'm here to rescue you.

"See, Boss." Jeff points at me. "Erika can help us out some."

"I said, I can't afford to hire more people." Nick's voice is losing the anger. Now he sounds tired.

"You don't have to pay me." I stand up. This is too perfect. I'm so excited I have to stop myself from jumping up and down.

"One day of free work is nice, but it's not going to help much, Gypsy Girl."

"Wait, please listen. Please?" A bitter metallic taste is burning my mouth. I have to swallow hard to keep talking. "I can do lots of work, not just today. I can mop and scrub and anything you tell me to do. I'll come every day. You don't have to pay me anything. If you let me watch the movie for free, that's enough."

Nick holds up a hand to stop the flow of my babble. "Well…I don't know."

Jeff puts his hand right in the middle of my back. "What's not to know? Why not give it a try?"

It's almost too much for me. Jeff is touching my back and my head is swimming. What if I pass out on Nick's desk, face down on the naughty nun, right in front of Jeff?

Nick heaves a big sigh and drops back into his chair. "I've seen the way Anita works you for those recitals of hers. You work hard. You're a good girl. It seems wrong to let you work for free. What will your mother say?"

"She won't care. I swear. She'll be happy to get me out of the house." I can see Nick wavering. When he pulls out the sweaty handkerchief another thought hits me. "Nick, our house is so hot. It's hot enough to give someone heat stroke. We don't have air conditioning, but there's air conditioning here. That's another reason I want to be here. And…and…."

"Okay, okay," Nick lifts both his hands up in surrender. "You win. Who am I to stop such an eager girl from working for free. You're welcome to help us out a little bit today." Then he points his two fingers at me again. "But I want to be sure about your mother. She's got a temper, that one. Have her write a note like they do for school trips. You know; a permission note. Bring it tomorrow, okay?"

I think my lips are saying okay and thanking him. I'm not sure. My skull is buzzing and whirling like crazy. I'm so happy!

"And don't forget to tell Anita about moving her stuff," Nick says, reaching for the phone on his desk.

Jeff taps my shoulder and tilts his head toward the door before walking away. I follow him in a daze, mesmerized by the golden hairs on the back of his neck. He's the best part of this whole thing. Jeff! I'm actually going to be working with Jeff. I'm going to see Jeff every day.

And I'll be able to watch *Star Wars* for free. Every day.

Jeff stops halfway down the stairs and turns to look up at me with that dynamite smile full of perfect teeth. "Nick's right. You are a good girl, Erika. Now let me introduce you to the glamorous world of the janitor's closet."

It isn't glamorous. I quickly discover Sonny is sort of like the assistant manager to Nick. So I'm stuck taking orders from Sonny. He tells me to clean all of the glass surfaces in the place. There are a million glass surfaces in a theater. I never realized how many there are until I'm stuck cleaning them, but there is an upside. Jeff is there and cleaning glass is an excellent way to watch someone without looking like you're watching them.

Wednesdays are "dark" at the Bixby. That means they don't have any movie showings all day and all we have to do is clean, clean, clean. After the glass, it's tiles. Then it's wood. When I finally run out of wood surfaces to clean and polish, Sonny tells me to head home. He doesn't say thanks or tell me I did a good job or anything, but Jeff looks at me and asks, "We'll see you tomorrow, right?"

Like he really, really wants to be sure he'll see me tomorrow.

Once I'm outside, the court house clock chimes six times. Pure panic surges through me. I haven't touched the laundry yet! Even though it's still a million degrees outside, I pedal home like there's a legion of Stormtroopers behind me.

The Force is with me.

The Mother Monster doesn't get home until nine-thirty. By the time she waltzes through the front door, I'm in the basement folding the final bit of laundry. I've already swept Fizzwicky over most of the open spots, run the vacuum droid quickly around the furniture and stuffed a bunch of junk under my bed. The bathroom isn't exactly scrubbed, but I've wiped it down.

Anita isn't alone. I can hear her friend Penny's chirpy laughter and both of them walking around. At one point, I distinctly hear Anita say, "Good. She's not here." Then she says, "I tell you, ever since our pretty Cassie flew the coop, I have not been able to turn around without tripping over this lump that is supposed to be my daughter."

I hold my breath waiting for her to say more, but there's only the sound of the ice cubes on glass. Cocktail time.

"Do you think that guy will call you?" Penny's voice already sounds boozy.

Well, I'm not going to sit down in the basement listening to them get plastered while discussing my mother's love life. So I sneak out the cellar door and walk to the front porch like I just got back from somewhere.

"Mom?" I yell out as I walk in the front door.

"What is it, Sweet Potato?"

She only calls me something cute when there's an audience. I cross my fingers and plow right into the kitchen.

Mother Monster flashes a smug smile in my general direction before taking a huge gulp of what looks like her usual cocktail—rum with a splash of Tab.

"I sort of got a job today."

That has a bigger effect than I ever would have imagined. Anita's eyes bulge and her mouth makes an exaggerated O. Penny lets loose her infamous squeal. Both of their glasses thump down on the kitchen table.

"It doesn't pay exactly and I'm not really officially working there."

"Well, what are you sort of doing?" Penny asks.

"Cleaning and stuff for Mr. Papanos."

"What?" Anita asks.

Before I can answer, Penny dives right in with, "Nick? Over at the Bixby?"

"Yeah. I'm going to clean up popcorn and taking out the trash and stuff. It's not like he has much money to give me, but it will keep me out of the house some days."

"Well, hot diggidy dog!" my mother is trying to sound cheerful and humorous, but her sarcasm can peel paint. "Did you hear that,

Penny? My daughter's actually going to get out from in front of the TV and out of the house this summer. Will wonders never cease?"

Even Penny cringes at her tone. Mom stands up and gives me a brief hard hug while I stand still and straight.

"Good for you. And the house looks decent, too," she says and sweeps back to her chair.

I nod and turn to go, thinking I've escaped, but she can't let me go without one last poke. "Don't let me find out he's paying you in movie junk food. You need to get your eating under control. If you start porking out more, I'm going to make you stop working there and send you to one of those fat camps. You hear me?"

"Yes, ma'am," I force myself to say through clenched teeth.

I don't bother to ask her for Nick's note. I've been writing my own notes for school since seventh grade.

Wednesday June 22, 1977

Dear Cassie,

You will never believe what I pulled off today. I can barely believe it myself.

This summer, I'm going to work for Nick at the Bixby! Can you believe it? Because I can barely believe it.

Technically, I guess I'm not exactly working for him because he's not paying me any money. But I don't care about money. What I'm getting is a hundred, million times more valuable than money. I'm going to help clean and do some chores. He's going to let me see *Star Wars* as many times as I want. I'll get to see *Star Wars* every single day until the next movie premiere.

But wait, it gets even better. Jeff still works at the Bixby. So this means I'm going to be seeing Jeff and talking to Jeff every single day all summer long.

Oh my stars! I think I might die of happiness before this summer is over.

Love & Hyperdrive Happiness,
Erika

| ELEVEN |

When I get to the theater, Sonny is standing in front of the concession area with his back to me. No one else is in sight so I take a deep breath and walk over to him. He's doing some kind of math calculations in a thick black binder that's spread out on the glass counter and he's deep, deep into it.

"Sonny?"

He jumps like I shot off a canon at his back, knocking the binder off the counter.

"Where did you come from?" he snaps at me. It takes all of my willpower not to turn and run.

I point back toward the rear door. He looks that way and squints. When he squints, I can really see that y-shaped scar next to his left eye. There's a rumor that Sonny beat a varsity linebacker to a bloody pulp last November. Is that how he got the scar? Or was it from that fight at the pool hall? Cassie told me he was hauled off to jail that time. It's hard to remember all the Sonny Johannson fights I've heard about in the past year. Why would Nick hire this guy?

Suddenly, he slaps down the pencil on the glass. It seems like he's going to say something mean, but then he sort of stops and rakes a hand through his hair.

"You're early," he says in the same tone of voice people use when someone screws up.

So I say, "Sorry." But I'm really thinking, *Is that a crime?*

Sonny assigns me to clean up the cement part of the floor in the theater, the part that slopes down under the seats. First with a broom and dustpan, then with a mop. It's really hard work. I have to walk down every row and try to work all around and under the seats. It has to be the worst job in the place. Sonny turns up the house lights as high as they can go—which isn't very high because at least half of the bulbs are burned out—so I can sort of see what I'm doing. It's hard to believe how gross the floor is! The cement is all chipped and pitted and there's this blackish sticky sludge in the pits. Black funk is caked around the cracks where the seats are bolted to the floor. No matter how many times I jam a mop under some of those seats, the mop comes back dirtier and dirtier, but the floor never looks any cleaner.

I'm bending over and sitting and standing and squatting down and bending over again. Over and over. My whole body is aching within fifteen minutes. There are a total of one thousand six hundred seats in the Bixby. I think about quitting every two seconds, but, if I quit, Sonny wins.

While sweeping the next to last row, my broom pulls out this dirty, sort of deflated balloon-looking thing. It's kind of white see-through, like hospital gloves, and long with a wide opening. The floor grime is mixed with slime on the outside. I'm leaning down to pick it up when a memory from three summers ago bursts into my brain. Me curled up in a comma suffering through my first ever bout of cramps. Anita standing over me saying it's time for another discussion about the birds and the bees. The little square packet she waved in my face saying, "It's a woman's best weapon against pregnancy. Open it."

Oh, disgusting! This is a used rubber! Somebody must have had sex in the next to last row at the Bixby then tossed the dirty rubber under the seat.

I push the awful thing into the dustpan and try to throw it away with all the blackened popcorn and hairy jawbreakers, but it sticks on a loose metal edge. Even when I shake the dustpan, it stays snagged. I didn't want to touch it. Good grief! I try to use the broom, but then I knock the dustpan off its long handle and into the trash barrel. Looking down into that mostly empty trash barrel thinking about reaching down to get the dustpan is too gross. It's all coated inside with black grime.

There's no way I can ask for help because.....well, there's no way.

So I sneak back to the janitor's closet to look for something, anything, to use. I find some sort of long tongs and rescue my dustpan out of the trash. I can't stop looking over my shoulder, praying no one will ask me what I'm doing. Once the dustbin is on the floor, I have to use the tongs to pluck the rubber out and finally throw the nasty thing away. Then I dunk the pan and the tongs in the mop water and end up having to mop three times in that area. When I'm finally satisfied there's no evidence, I dig both hands into the small of my back and stare down the remaining seats of the last two rows. Suddenly, I'm worried about what else is lurking under these seats. Leaving the tongs propped next to my mop bucket, I grab one of the flashlights from back stage and search under the remaining seats.

In the very last row, about half way toward the center of the theater, there's this brown paper bag pushed under a seat. Poking it with the light, it seems to have a solid block of some sort inside. Using the tongs, I manage to pull it out from under the seat and tear open a little corner. A stack of magazines peeks out. They seem innocent enough...until I pick up the bag and get a better look inside. I'm looking at pornography magazines. Not like Playboy. Really gross, raunchy stuff. So raunchy it burns my eyeballs.

Right then, a strange voice says, "What is thing you find?"

I jump, fumbling to keep hold of the bag. The little hole I created tears wider and those horrible magazines spill out all over the place. A shadow separates from the wall and comes toward me. It's Nick's sister-in-law, Mrs. P, in one of her black dresses with a black scarf tied over her hair. She's looking down at all these pictures of....well, every angle possible of fully naked people doing all these sex acts. I mean, Cassie showed me a Hustler one time, but I have never seen this stuff.

Mrs. P leans over with her hands on her knees to get a really good look, then starts clicking her tongue. My world stops. I'm mortified, frozen to the spot. Mrs. P puts her thumb and forefinger to her lips and issues a series of ear-splitting whistles until somebody suddenly appears to my right.

Vince. The AV Department goon. The goofball who nearly got me beaten up on Graduation Day. Here he is, at the worst possible moment, standing next to me in a red usher's jacket that's at least two sizes too small, scratching at his zits. This is how I find out he now works at the Bixby, too.

"Oh hey, Erika!"

I keep my lips pressed together.

"Is something wrong?" Vince asks, his eyes moving to Mrs. P. From where he's standing, he can't see the display of pornography on the theater floor.

"Pick up," Mrs. P snaps her fingers toward the floor then hooks my elbow and pulls me away from the mess. "Good girls go now."

I'm dying! Every inch of my skin is on fire. Tears start burning my eyes. If I could make my feet move faster, I'd run all the way home. Instead, my feet only shuffle as Mrs. P guides me toward the doors to the lobby.

Somehow I keep my feet moving, past the mop bucket and the trash can. Into the lobby. Nick is vacuuming away with this ancient Hoover that looks like it's kicking back out as much dirt as it's taking up.

"Hey, Gypsy Girl!" Nick waves at me all nice and normal. I feel like what I've just seen is branded on my forehead.

Mrs. P pulls me toward the concession stand where she finally lets go of my arm. She pushes a Styrofoam cup filled with ice and Sprite under my nose and pats my shoulder. The Hoover switches off.

"Anything wrong?" Nick asks.

I look at Mrs. P with pure terror in my eyes, silently begging her not to tell Nick what happened. She waves her hand around and unleashes a stream of Greek.

"Of course she can have a cold drink," Nick says. "I'm no slave driver." Then he switches back on the vacuum cleaner.

She pats my shoulder one more time for good measure and shuffles away from me toward the ticket booth. Whew!

Somehow, I manage to stay all day and keep working. Vince tries to crack jokes about what happened, but I ignore him until he finally gives up. Does that guy think we are friends or something?

Thursday June 23, 1977

Dear Cassie,

The Bixby has lost a little bit of its magic for me.

When Sonny pushed a broom and dustpan at me, he warned me to watch out for rats in the theater. He said to come get him if I saw any rodent activity at all. I thought the jerk was trying to scare me. Now I realize rats are not the worst thing lurking under the seats in the Bixby

I can't tell you what happened today, what I found, because it is far, far, FAR too humiliating. I cannot even think about it without feeling sick, let alone write it all out.

Never mind that.

The premier of *Star Wars,* at least the premier for this hick town, was at six o'clock. I got to sit in the balcony all by myself with a bag of popcorn, Lemonheads and a large Coke.

That made the day's hard work and humiliation worth every minute, but I'll tell you one thing. I'm going to be extremely careful when I clean under the seats from now on.

Love,

Erika

Saturday June 25, 1977

Dear Cassie,

Like I promised Nick, tickets are selling like crazy. There was a line out front before the first showing at twelve-thirty. Nick kept shaking his head and saying stuff like, "Look at that. When was the last time we had a line for the Saturday matinee?"

We had to open the balcony for the four-thirty and eight o'clock show times. That's a big deal. Nick only opens the balcony for a movie showing when more than two-thirds of the General Admission tickets are sold. I guess they haven't had to open the balcony since the Shriner's charity show was here in April, so we weren't really ready. Jeff, Sonny, Vince, and I had to run around with brooms and mops to be sure it wasn't too gross up there. The whole time, I was nervous about what we might find, but it was just a few wrappers and lots of dust.

While we were up there in the balcony, I got to see the projectionist. Did you know the Bixby projectionist is now a female? A shaft of daylight caught my eye and there was this tiny woman standing outside the projection booth. She was wearing a big green army coat even though the air conditioning barely cools the balcony below eighty degrees. She popped open the outside door and lit up a cigarette. She didn't just smoke; she sucked in so hard her cheeks turned into two dark craters. When she exhaled, she leaned toward the outside and blew out a big huff of smoke. The whole time, she kept jiggling around like she had to go to the bathroom. When she saw me looking up at her, she sort of saluted me with two fingers to her eyebrow.

What happened to that wrinkled black man who used to show the movies?

We were so busy I didn't have time to ask anyone. Nick had to help Jeff at the concession stand. After a while, I had to get back there and fill orders, too. Because I'm only fifteen and not really an official employee, I didn't touch the money, but I noticed something. Half the time, they didn't even ring in the amounts. They hit the "cash open" button, stuffed money under the drawer and counted out change. It's kind of amazing that they knew how much people owed or how much change to give, but I never heard anyone complain.

Mrs. P was selling so many tickets I guess she got nervous about all the money in the booth. I saw her stuffing wads of cash down the front of her dress. Once the movie started and the lobby was all clear, she would come waddling in with both hands pressed over her boobs and disappear upstairs in Nick's office. The thought of her up there shaking all that money out of her bra is still making me giggle.

Even with all the customers, I still got to watch the movie three whole times.

If you count the time I snuck in to the Cineplex Four, I've now seen *Star Wars* seven times. Know what? I can't wait to watch it again and again. It leaves me feeling all filled up, like I'm full of Force energy. Which is probably a good thing since it's almost midnight and we still need to clean this place. From up here in the balcony, I can see all popcorn bags, cups, candy wrappers and junk all over the place. Can't people use a trash can anymore?

May the Force be with us,
Erika

| TWELVE |

THANK GOODNESS I'M CURLED UP IN A CORNER SEAT IN THE balcony writing to Cassie when Sonny bursts into the lower theater on a rampage. He's growling at Vince, asking where I am. I immediately switch off my theater flashlight and scoot down in my seat.

Jeff's voice asks, "Jesus, old woman, what's stuck in your craw?"

Sonny ignores him and keeps drilling Vince with questions: Where's Erika? Did she go home? When did she leave?

"I don't know. Was it supposed to be my job to babysit?" Vince mumbles.

Babysit. The baby. Me. Ouch.

Then Sonny yells, "Uh, curfew? Does anyone here remember there's eleven o'clock curfew in this town? Cause I'm betting Deputy Todd hasn't forgotten and he's poking around out front."

Silence. Then Jeff says, "Doesn't that guy ever take a break?

Vince chimes in with, "I think she's gone. I haven't seen her since…."

"Erika?" Sonny's voice calls out with a hard bite to it. "Hey, Erika, are you still here?"

Suddenly it seems like I'm doing something wrong by sitting up here listening without speaking up earlier. So I duck down even lower and stay quiet.

I forgot all about the city's curfew. Anita never cares where I am at any hour, especially on a Saturday night. I know there are parents out there that care about that stuff, but our town's curfew has never been an issue at my house. I honestly don't have any idea what kind of trouble you get in if you break the curfew. Do they take you to jail?

Knowing Deputy Todd is poking around out front, I decide to try something crazy. When Sonny disappears backstage, still calling my name, I sneak up toward the projection booth and ease open the outside door where I saw the projectionist smoking earlier. She's banging around in the projection booth, so I slip outside on the lower roof that's over the lobby. I'm standing about fifty feet behind the darkened marquee sign. Everything is pretty dark up here. It's easy to sneak up behind the sign and peek out onto the street.

At first, I can't find Wayne. Then Jeff walks out the lobby exit door and walks toward a big shadow.

"Hey Wayne, good thing you're here. We might need an escort over to the bank."

"Why is that?" Wayne asks in a casual voice, like he hangs out downtown in front of the movie theater all the time.

"Blockbuster day here at the Bixby. I don't think we've sold that many movie tickets in one day since....maybe since I've worked here."

"Even better than *Jaws*?"

"Yeah, I'm not sure Mrs. P can make it over to the bank night deposit with all the cash she's got stuffed in her girdle."

I have to pinch my nose hard not to laugh out loud.

"Thought she shoves it in her bra."

"Ran out of room. Can you believe it?"

"That's a lot of cash, son."

The door behind me cracks open. Luckily, I'm already well hidden in the shadows so I crouch down into a ball and stay still. A flame flares up then is replaced by a red glowing cherry and a huff of smoke. The projectionist. I stay still and watch for any sign she sees me, but there's only the glow of her cigarette tip.

"Hey, Wizard, have you seen Erika?" Sonny's voice comes from somewhere behind her.

"Dark-haired thing with eyes all over her face?" Her voice is husky and deep; the same smoky voice that stopped that stupid candy argument.

Sonny laughs. "Yeah, that's the girl."

"Haven't seen her since she was up here cleaning for the eight o'clock. Why?"

"Oh, the deputy dog is sniffing around. I want to be sure she gets home without any hassles."

"You sure you want to take on Wayne Todd again?"

Again?

The door clicks closed. Jeff is still standing out on the street shooting the breeze with Wayne. So I hurry back toward the door to climb the metal ladder up to the higher roof. I'm planning to hide out for a while, but the door clicks back open when I'm on the tenth rung, halfway between the two levels.

"There's a fire escape down the back side," Alex's smoky voice says. "Perfectly safe. We use it all the time." Another big puff of smoke pours out; then the glowing red butt sizzles into a Sprite bottle by the door

I don't risk saying thanks. Instead, I climb the rest of the way as quietly as possible.

The roof up there isn't empty. There's a metal table and some lawn chairs set up in a loose circle. Part of me wants to sit and catch my breath, but the larger part wants to get gone. I have no idea why it's such a big deal if I'm caught out after curfew. Maybe Nick or the Bixby can get into some kind of legal trouble.

So I head straight for the far wall and the fire escape. Actually, at the top, it's more like metal rungs bolted into brick. Scary! There are some bigger metal rings that form a cage tunnel around the rungs so it isn't like I'll be hanging out in bare space three stories above asphalt. Still, it's a long way down. Taking deep breaths, I count to ten. The fear is only getting worse. I can't do this. There's no way!

Feel the Force flowing through you.

I close my eyes, take more deep breaths and imagine I'm a Jedi student. This is a test I must pass or I'll be sent back to my home planet in shame.

Slowly, hands locked on the outside ring, I boost myself up and swing one leg over the wall. Eyes focused on my white knuckles, my foot finds a metal rung. It takes ten more breaths to get my other foot out there. Now I'm clinging to the side of the building chanting, "Stay on target, stay on target." Inch by excruciating inch I lower my right foot until I find the next rung. Then the left.

And on it goes, each successful step slows my racing heart a wee bit until I'm standing on the metal platform outside the window to dressing room three. Looking up, a wave of energy surges through me. It is nearly impossible to believe what I just did. From there, the two flights of metal stairs down to the parking lot are super easy. When my feet touch the ground, I don't even stop to breathe. I duck behind Jeff's van, sneak out of the parking lot, and zigzag through all sorts of private property on my way home.

If anyone asks, I'm going to say I left halfway through the last showing. I'm hoping Alex won't tell anyone what really happened.

Sunday June 26, 1977

Dear Cassie,

Vince must be one of the dumbest people on Earth.

Today, Sonny assigned him to work with me cleaning the main seats before the first matinee. I was so annoyed! I've cleaned those seats on my own for the past three days. Why did Sonny need to pair me with Vince? With his sticky lips, thick pop bottle glasses, purple zitty forehead and his gurgling way of breathing…I swear, that guy breathes louder than Darth Vader!

So I was already in a funk when we walked into the main theater. Then he turned up the house lights all the way and…whoa! What a nightmare. It was ten times worse than it looked last night. A hundred times worse. Do people buy stuff at the concession counter so they can throw it all around the theater before they walk out?

My face must have shown how shocked I was by all the garbage because Vince looked at me and said, "Welcome to Sunday mornings at the Bixby. Watch out for rats."

Uh, what?!?!

"Actually, this isn't too bad," Vince called back over his shoulder. He was walking toward the front of the theater, dragging the giant trash can. "Wait till the holiday drunks come in next weekend. It's going to be four days of this and worse."

"Holiday drunks?"

"Yeah, you know how it is." Vince was already grabbing the larger pieces of trash and tossing them in the bin, but I felt unable to move. He kept talking as he was working, "There's always lots of beer at the carnival. Then there's no telling what other party supplies people get into, if you know what I mean. Last year it seemed like the most messed up drunks and wasted zombies all stumbled in here for the late show… uh, hello? Earth to Erika. Are you still here?"

I had forgotten that next weekend is the Independence Festival. My head was spinning. I was lost in memories from last year's festival and this terrible sadness over the fact that you won't be here this year. And I was also thinking about how everyone from school will be downtown next weekend and the sound of pig noises will be all around.

"Of course you being here at the Bixby might scare away some of the more hearty partiers," Vince said, and gave me this big ugly smile. "Hey, yeah! Maybe there's a bright side to this whole mess with you spying for Deputy Dog."

"I am NOT!" I shouted at his ugly face.

Vince shrugged. "I'm just saying what everyone's saying."

Really? And if everyone was saying Vince is a slimy pile of zit puss, would he repeat that too?

I should have said something. You would have put him in his place so fast, he'd have gotten whiplash. But I didn't have much time to respond.

Suddenly, Vince jumped back from what he was doing and started screaming like a little girl. Then he was whacking at the floor with the dust pan handle over and over. Some of his whacks made a terrible squishing noise. That's when I remembered about the possibility of rats. I hurried toward the lobby doors, but Sonny rushed in before I could get there. Jeff was right on his heels. Neither of them stopped or even looked at me. They both ran down the aisle to Vince.

Sonny grabbed the handle while Vince was in mid-whack. "Hold up! I think you got him. Calm down."

Jeff made a terrible face, looked up at me and said, "Ben is not our friend no more."

Sonny pushed Jeff away. "Cuz, get Erika started on cleaning the Ladies room."

Jeff walked back toward me. "What he's really saying is the two of us need look no more."

The rest of the day, Jeff was either whistling Michael Jackson's theme song for *Ben* or he was singing a slightly different version of the lyrics that made me giggle. Vince told him to "shut up" a few times, which only made me giggle more. Then I'd think about what happened, the terrible squishing sounds, and my stomach would feel queasy.

Seriously, Cassie! All of that hysteria over a rat? My sixth grade class had a pet rat and we used to take turns feeding him. Mr. Whiskers was so sweet! The thought of somebody beating him to death makes me nauseous.

Your friend,

Erika

| THIRTEEN |

On Monday morning, Sonny tells me to clean the big windows in the ticket booth out front. Instead of Windex and paper towels, he hands me a huge jug of white vinegar and a stack of newspapers. I think maybe the jerk is messing with my mind, but there isn't any hint of a joke on his face. So, instead of cleaning, I end up standing out front chewing on the skin around my thumbnail. The temperature is already somewhere around a million degrees so I'm sweating like crazy.

When Deputy Wayne Todd's reflection appears in the glass, I almost jump out of my skin.

"Hey, Erika." He sits down on the bench in front of the pharmacy next door. He's sweating ten times worse than me, but he leans back and stretches out his legs like he's as comfortable as can be.

Maybe if I was more like Cassie, or Princess Leia, I would tell him to keep walking. Being me, a dumb cow, I stand there and gnaw harder on my thumb.

Wayne looks up at the marquee. "I see Nick is showing our movie,"

Our movie. Like Deputy Wayne Todd and I have anything that is ours.

The door on the left side of the theater opens. Sonny walks out with a bucket, but stops when he sees the deputy sitting there. With Sonny on my left and Wayne on my right, I feel like I'm standing in the Death Star trash compactor between two walls closing in. That feeling only got worse when Wayne stands up and swaggers a couple steps closer. Sonny puts down his bucket and moves closer, too.

"Johansson," Wayne says in this low growl.

"Deputy Wayne," Sonny draws out the "ay" into this exaggerated twang. Wayne's forehead twitches.

Time hangs heavily with the two of them eyeballing each other. Then one of the front theater doors bangs open and Nick comes out.

"Deputy? Something wrong?" Nick asks. Wayne looks over and half smiles, breaking the tension. I could kiss Nick's sweaty bald head.

"Mr. Papanos," Wayne's greeting seems half-hearted, like he's humoring an old man. "How are you doing today, sir? Hot enough for you?"

A gentle tug on the inside of my elbow causes me to look down and see a finger hooked there. I look up, confused, into Sonny's dark blue-gray eyes.

"Get inside," he growls through clenched teeth.

There isn't any reason to argue, so I go inside, sit in a seat and stare at the stage curtains. That gets boring quickly, so I get up and start poking around the seats half-heartedly with the broom and dustpan.

"Can I ask you something?"

The voice, suddenly coming down from what I thought was an empty theater almost gives me a heart attack. Spinning around, I bash my elbow on the hard edge of the seatback in front of me. The impact brings tears to my eyes.

"Whoa there!" Alex the projectionist is leaning casually over the railing with a smile on her face. "Didn't mean to scare you."

I shake my head, not trusting myself to speak without bawling like a baby. Alex is tilting her head a little bit to one side and looking at me carefully.

"You're Anita Williams' little girl, aren't you?" Before I can answer, she slaps the banister and points at me. "Yes you are! Multiple ankle surgeries three, no, maybe four years ago."

I'm sure my mouth is hanging open. "How did you know?"

"The way your mother laid into every nurse who crossed her path every chance she got? After that ordeal, who could forget you?"

"Oh, wow. Sorry."

"Hey, no, forget I said anything. As much as we cursed your mother, we all fell in love with you. No whining or crying from Anita's little girl. Most of those kids were sniveling all night long, but not you. Almost bit your way through your bottom lip trying to be a tough soldier the first time your doctor looked under the dressings." Her smile is pure sunshine, waiting. "Don't remember me, do you?"

I shake my head.

"Some of the kids called me Nurse Dread."

That's a thunderbolt from the past! I remember a nurse with a tight cap of short mouse brown hair, sharp ice blue eyes and three pinkish worms of burn scar wiggling up from above her right eye. The person above me has longish brown hair falling in her face, smiling sky blue eyes and....

"Looking for the scar?"

"Sorry," I say, quickly averting my eyes.

She waves it off. Lifting the hair away from the right side of her face, she says, "It's faded but still there."

In the twilight of the theater, the old scar is barely visible.

"Good thing about working in the theater," she says, dropping her hair back down. "You can avoid looking at yourself in the full light of day for weeks at a stretch."

I'm searching for something to say. "So...you don't work at the hospital any more?"

She makes a terrible face. I've said something wrong, so I quickly add, "Sorry."

"Don't be," she says. "I hated it there. It was like a sick joke putting me on the pediatric ward. I hate kids. Most of them anyway. I kept showing up until they told me to stop...like a trained monkey or something."

There's a bitterness in her voice that hints at more than she's saying.

"Sorry," I say yet again.

"Erika…it is Erika, isn't it? Listen to me. You have got to stop apologizing so much. It drives people bonkers."

Right. As if that's easy. I nod though, like I'm taking her advice to heart. "Did you want to ask me something?"

"Yeah, just wondering what was up with the Spiderman escape routine Saturday night?"

Pow! I totally forgot about that. What to say? Lucky for me, Sonny slams his way into the theater and marches down the aisle toward me repeating, "Stupid, stupid, stupid" and shaking his head. Above, Alex grips the rail with both hands and leans way out.

"Take it easy, Sonny. What's going on?"

"Stupid!" he yells up at her then stands in front of me with both hands tucked under his arms. Is everything over? Is he sending me home?

"Who is?" Alex asks calmly.

At the exact same moment, Sonny and I say, "I am." Then we stare at each other.

"I am," Sonny repeats quietly, with extra heavy emphasis on the I. "What the hell was I thinking, putting you out front like bait on a hook?"

I'm too astonished to say a word, but Alex breathes out a long "Oooooh."

"No more working outside, you hear me, Erika?" I think I'm staring at him like he's sprouted three extra heads. "Somebody else tells you to do some outside work, especially if it's out front, come get me, okay?"

"Uh…okay."

Sonny nods and marches back out of the theater.

"What's going on? Did the sheriff or Chief Abbott give you some trouble out front?"

Alex's question sends an electric jolt from my belly to my toes. I have to force myself to look up into her eyes.

"Deputy Todd, actually."

"Wayne? Damn it!" She rubs both hands over her face then rakes her fingers through her hair. "Has Deputy Wayne Todd taken a special interest in you?"

I nod, fascinated by the intensity of her reaction.

She looks up at the ceiling. "Double damn it! What is that dumbass up to this time?"

"This time?"

"I think we need to have a special meeting."

"Meeting?"

"Question is…when?" she continues, tapping her fingers in a fast one-two-three-four repetition on the rail. Then she nods her head like she's come to some decision and looks down at me again. "What are you doing tomorrow night after the last showing, Erika?"

"Nothing." Does she think I have hot plans for a Tuesday night?

"Good. Make yourself scarce until Popples leaves. You can hang out in the balcony or up on the roof."

"Popples?"

She smiles. "Uncle Nick." I guess I must still look confused because she adds, "The owner of this mighty fine theater you're cleaning." Then she stands up straight, checks her wristwatch and announces, "Time to smoke!" before disappearing from my view.

***

Just before the final showing on Tuesday, I knock on the projection room door. Alex appears and pushes a tightly rolled sleeping bag at me with her free hand.

"The boys usually stay and camp out. That way I don't have to worry about them driving. I'll have Sonny walk you home or you can sleep out under the stars with us. It's kind of a rooftop slumber party. If you want to stay, call Anita on the office phone. Tell her it's chaperoned; no funny business." The door slams shut in my face

If I want to stay? Is she kidding?

Our home phone rings eight times with no answer. I wait fifteen minutes and try again with the same result. Anita is probably over at Penny's or the two of them are getting boozy at the Sheridan bar. She probably won't even notice if I don't come home tonight. I'm not going to call around town looking for my mother and I'm definitely not going to miss this rooftop slumber party with Jeff. No way.

I watch most of the movie from the last row of the balcony, then slip out to climb up to the upper rooftop. Unfortunately, Vince is already sitting up there picking at his zits and drawing something in a thick, oversized pad of paper. When he sees me, he slams the pad shut and glares. The silence stretches. This is not a good way to start.

"Does it matter where I sit?" I ask, more to break the tension than anything. He shrugs and stuffs his sketchpad into a book bag under his chair. Hugging my borrowed sleeping roll, I sit in the chair furthest from him. The silence continues to press in on us.

I'm so relieved when I hear Jeff and Sonny's bickering down below, I jump up and rush over to the ladder.

Jeff's head pokes up, sort of like Chewie's head popping up out of the smuggling compartment. Instead of growling, he flashes that megawatt movie star smile and says, "A little help here?"

He starts handing things to me: a beat up transistor radio wrapped with electrical tape, four six-packs of Pabst Blue Ribbon, a grocery sack full of junk food, and bundles of beach towels and blankets. Then he climbs all the way up and vaults over the top of the ladder. Sonny appears right after Jeff and shoves him out of the way.

Sonny takes one look at me and frowns. "Does your mother know you're here?"

"Would you mellow out?" Jeff says, cracking open a can of PBR. "I seem to remember bringing you up here when you were fifteen."

"It's fine," I say, but no one is listening.

"Do you really want to get on Anita Williams' bad side?" Sonny asks Jeff. "Cause that woman could peel paint just by looking at it. You want her thinking we're corrupting her little baby girl here?"

"Really, Sonny, she doesn't care that I'm here."

Sonny gives me another sour look, cracks open his own beer and drops into a chair.

When Alex arrives, we're all sitting in a loose square sipping from cans of PBR. Well, I'm sipping. Jeff and Sonny are taking enthusiastic gulps and arguing about "corrupting minors." Vince is chugging the stuff down like drinking beer is his job and he wants a promotion. Alex taps his shoulder as she walks past.

"Take it easy there, Vincent, or you'll be practicing your Technicolor yawn before midnight."

"What's a Technicolor yawn?" I ask.

Alex smiles at me. "Just a funny way of saying vomit." Then she looks around and asks, "What's with the tense energy tonight?"

"I'm not in love with the idea of corrupting Anita Williams' fifteen-year-old daughter." Sonny grumbles.

"Whoa. Relax. Who's corrupting anyone?" Alex cocks her head to the side and looks me over with such intensity I have to look down. "We're here to help."

Everyone is absolutely quiet. Even Vince stops slurping and wheezing.

"So...tell me, my little one," Alex says in the same low, soothing voice, "what is this mess you've gotten yourself into?"

Dead silence presses in. The air feels so thick; it's difficult to force my lungs to breathe in and out.

"I'm not sure what you mean."

"Really?" She leans forward and, with two fingers, gently tips my chin up until we are eye to eye. "Why are you working so hard to hide from the world, Erika? Why is Deputy Todd lurking around you? And why does Vince think Chief Abbott assaulted you on school property, right under Principal Nelson's nose? That can't be true, can it?"

I shrug while Vince sputters, "It is! It is true!"

Alex never looks away from my face. The intensity of her scrutiny is making me squirm. "I'm only asking these questions because we want to help you, Erika."

"Can you teleport me off this rock?" My voice is barely more than a whisper.

The ghost of a smile flits across Alex's face then quickly disappears. She gently pats my cheek a couple times before sitting back. "Let's hope that's not necessary." She looks off toward the fire station for several long, excruciating seconds, absently gnawing on the skin around her pinky nail and muttering something under her breath, but I can't make out a single word.

"Erika?" Jeff says, then takes a huge swig of beer. "I don't want to freak you out or anything, but there's something we should tell you."

I nod, unable to trust my voice.

He carefully stretches out one leg, then the other and leans back to stare up at the sky. "Deputy Todd, Chief Abbott, Sheriff McCombs…you have got to be super careful how you deal with those old boys. Especially the sheriff. You understand?"

"Yeah, I guess so. I mean…maybe?"

Sonny snorts loudly. "You don't have a clue, do you?

I let out the breath I've been holding. "I don't know what clue I'm supposed to have!" I look around at everyone. They're all looking back at me, waiting for something more. "What do you want me to say? What?"

"Erika." Alex's voice breaks in. "Has your mother ever told you anything about the sheriff or…anything about local politics?

My brain starts clicking through some of the things I've heard Anita say about Sheriff McCombs. Most of it is too filthy to repeat, but I remember something I heard her say just recently. "She says his soft voice and quiet manners fool most people, but he's really the worst kind of trouble—a bible thumping bigot with a badge. She says he makes Archie Bunker look like Mother Teresa."

Alex scrubs both hands over her face, laughing in a way that sounds more sad than happy. "Yeah, that's about right on." She crosses her arms and looks around at the guys. "Any one of us could tell you some horror stories about what it means to be on the Sheriff's bad side."

Sonny snorts again, much more loudly.

"Some of us," she says, directing a fierce glare at Sonny, "Could tell you more than others about the Sheriff's bad side…and the dangers of going off on some damn fool idealistic crusade."

Her words startle me. Does she know that line is from the movie?

"Like my father did," Sonny says without skipping a beat. I have no idea what they are talking about, but my view of Sonny shifts in that moment. He lifts his beer can toward Alex with a wicked grin. "And I have no regrets."

"Of course you don't." Alex starts rummaging through the pockets of her Army jacket. "Never mind. I'm not in the mood for your 'might for right' crapola tonight. We're getting off track here." She pulls out a crumpled pack of Kool cigarettes and a Bic lighter. After lighting up, she squints at me through a cloud of smoke. "Let's get back to you, little one. Seems like you've already figured out the best strategy for this situation—lay low and always keep one eye on the exit." She winks at me, but her words sting.

"Being a coward is a strategy?"

"Erika, you know I got this beauty mark when I was an Army nurse in Vietnam, right?" She rubs her ring finger over the scar above her right eye while the cigarette makes a halo of smoke around her head.

I nod, even though I had no idea.

"Being in a filthy war like that, it gives you a very different view of what people like to call courage." She shudders and takes a deep drag of her smoke. "Listen, I don't know what all is going on with this Cassie Abbott mess and, frankly, I don't want to know, but there is something not quite right about the way the sheriff and his deputy have been acting since Chief Abbott's daughter disappeared. If Deputy Todd has been circling around you, that worries me. I'm telling you, best thing to do is fly beneath the radar and hope the storm passes over soon. In the meantime, we'll keep our ears on and watch your back. Right, boys?"

Jeff is the only one who nods. Sonny mutters, "Aren't you supposed to fly over a storm?" while, at the same time, Vince bursts out with, "What have you been telling the Deputy Dog?

"Vince." Alex's tone is a warning, but Vince either doesn't notice or doesn't care.

"Everyone says you're a snitch helping the sheriff with this big stupid crack down on the stoners and the party crowd."

"That is pure nonsense," Jeff says before I can respond. "Anyone who knows Erika knows that is the dumbest rumor they've ever heard." The most incredible wave of relief and gratitude surges through me.

"Okay, fine. Then what has the deputy been asking and what have you been saying?" I notice Vince has twisted his empty beer can into the shape of an hourglass and keeps twisting and twisting it in his hands.

Alex reaches over and wrenches the beer can out of his grasp. "I called this little meeting together to offer this poor kid some support, not to cross-examine her."

"But how can we help her if we don't know what she knows?"

Everyone looks at me. No one says a word.

Finally, Jeff breaks the silence. "Vince does have a point." He tosses his empty beer can into an open grocery sack, scoots his chair up close to mine and puts a hand on my arm. My entire universe collapses into the few inches of my skin touching Jeff's skin and his pure blue eyes searching my face. Breathing is nearly impossible.

"Besides, I have got to admit, I am curious as hell how she pulled it off this time. You do know more than you are saying, right?"

I want to tell him anything he wants to know, but the heavy weight of the promises I made to Cassie presses in. It takes every ounce of my willpower to keep absolutely still and silent.

"I don't think there's much of a mystery about where she went," he continues. "She was always talking about Hollywood when we dated. Always getting you to take her picture. I know you were helping her put together one of those actress portfolios."

"Yeah," Vince adds, sloshing a fresh beer around. "She had pictures of Hollywood in her folder. I used to see them in Study Hall."

I'm careful not to look at anyone or make any sudden movements. "I don't know where she was going, how she was getting there or where she would be right now."

Jeff holds up both hands, palms facing outward. "Okay, answer me this. Did she definitely tell you she was leaving that night? Was she all packed up and ready to go? Did you say your final good-bye that night knowing she would be gone the next day?"

There doesn't seem to be any danger in answering that set of questions, so I nod. The three guys start shifting around looking at each other and saying things like, "Far out" and "There you go." Alex doesn't react at all.

Jeff scoots his chair even closer to mine. "You know what Chief Walt Abbott has been saying, right? He thinks Cassie didn't run away on her own. He keeps spouting nonsense about his little girl being kidnapped. Or murdered."

Kidnapped? Murdered? This is the first time I've heard anyone use those words in connection to Cassie. My whole body turns to Jell-o and I can barely sit up in my chair.

"Listen, honey," Alex leans forward and puts her hands on my shoulders. "We don't think that's what really happened. Don't freak out. Cassie was a wild child, but not stupid. This crazy kidnapping theory, I think Walt is losing his marbles. Do you know if anyone had threatened her? Was she in any trouble?"

I shake my head.

"She'll turn up eventually," Sonny says. "Nobody murdered her or locked her in a basement. I promise you. She's probably holed up with some poor sucker paying her way to California or Mexico or Timbuktu. That girl was a cat who always landed on her feet."

"You never did like her," Jeff says with a shake of his head.

"And you should have listened to me," Sonny shoots back. "You had a great girl and you tossed her aside to go out with the beauty queen. Cassie spent a few months making your life miserable then she tossed you aside when she got bored. Was I right or was I right?"

"It wasn't her fault she was so messed up, Son."

"Um, cool it," Alex says. "We are talking about someone's friend."

Sonny looks at me. "She wasn't exactly a good friend for you, was she? That's why we've got Deputy Dog sniffing after you." He stretches out his legs and leans back the same way Jeff did earlier. "You want my advice? Listen to Alex. Stay out of Wayne's sight. Lay low. We'll do our best to run interference.

I'm confused, but mostly amazed that Sonny is saying he's going to help me.

"All right," Alex says, lighting another cigarette. "We've talked about this Cassie Abbott business enough. Turn on the radio or something."

Jeff stands up, grabs the radio and twists the knob through static, static, and more static until he finally gives up and switches the radio off. He looks over at Sonny and asks, "So what's your favorite movie?"

"What the...why would you ask me that?"

"Because there's no good music and we've got to lighten up this party. So say something. What's your favorite movie?"

"I don't know. *Clockwork Orange*, I guess."

"Why that one?" Vince asks.

"I have no idea." Sonny shrugs. "Probably means I'm thoroughly screwed up."

We all laugh and I feel another surge of pure love for Jeff, silently thanking him for changing the subject.

"What about you?" Sonny asks Alex.

"*One Flew Over the Cuckoo's Nest.* Nurse Ratchet is my hero which means I'm definitely screwed up."

For no good reason, that makes us laugh harder.

"Van Gogh?" Sonny is pointing to Vince, but Vince is too busy gulping beer and staring down. "Hello? Earth to Vince? Favorite movie?" For some reason the weirdo keeps his eyes down and shakes his head.

I'm starting to feel a little disturbed and uncomfortable, but Jeff smiles and says, "The artist is in one of his moods. What about you, Erika?"

"This one," I answer quickly, "Because it makes me forget everything I've screwed up."

That sounds more clever in my head, but everyone laughs anyway. Even Vince smiles at me.

After that, we talk about a whole lot of things and nothing. Jeff and Sonny get up and perform an impersonation of the "Wild and Crazy Guys" from *Saturday Night Live*. I don't think I've ever laughed so hard.

A beer or two turns into six or seven for Alex, Sonny and Jeff. Vince sucks down five then falls asleep in his chair. I only drink one before Sonny hands me a large Coke and a box of Lemonheads from downstairs. That makes me feel sort of prickly, like he's telling me not to drink, but I love Coke about a million times better than I like PBR and Lemonheads are my favorite candy, so why get resentful?

Tuesday June 28, 1977

Dear Cassie,

You will not believe where I am right now. Not in a million, trillion years

Up on the top roof of the Bixby, stretched out on an old sleeping bag. The Milky Way is sparkling up above....and Jeff is sleeping just inches away.

Yes, that's right. Jeff. As in JEFF!!!!

Okay, everyone else is here, too. Sonny, Vince, even Alex. And Jeff's body is actually more like five feet away instead of inches, but our feet are pretty close. He probably doesn't even realize that my bare foot is so close to his that I could stretch out my leg and brush the sole of his right foot.

But I can practically feel his heartbeat in my toes.

Of course, I won't stretch out to touch Jeff because Alex would notice.

Alex is the new Bixby projectionist I saw the other night. She's also one of the nurses who took care of me in the hospital, the one with the terrible scar I told you about. We called her Nurse Dread. That makes me feel pretty crappy now, because she is wonderful and so cool. I really think you'd like her. And you would not believe the stories she's been telling me about fighting with Anita when I was in the hospital!

Right now she's sitting up in a lawn chair watching over us and smoking cigarettes. That woman is the most energetic smoker I've ever seen. In and out, in and out, with great big whooshing breaths. One cigarette right after the other.

Maybe it has something to do with her time in Vietnam. That's where she got the scar. She was an Army nurse, like Hot Lips on *M*A*S*H* except Vietnam was a whole lot more bloody, filthy and rotten than Korea. (Her words not mine.)

The reason she's sitting up watching the group and the sky instead of stretched out sleeping is she doesn't sleep when it's dark any more.

Crazy, huh? She works at the Bixby most days, so when does she sleep? Anyway this slumber party is all her doing. Seems like they do this pretty often. I hope she invites me back because this has been the most incredible night! I finally created a happy memory that's all my own without you to take center stage.

Don't take that the wrong way. I still love you all the way to another galaxy and back and I hope that you are safe and that we'll see each other again soon. I guess some people are saying you might have been kidnapped…or worse. I guess that explains why Deputy Wayne Todd keeps asking me about hitchhiking and why your dad is acting so crazy. But I think I would know if something awful like that happened to you.

It would be a terrible disruption in the Force.

My eyelids are feeling sticky. It's time to get some sleep before the sun comes up.

Love and safe wishes,

Erika

PS – Alex is kind of dozing in her chair. I wonder…if I stretch out my foot just a little and scooch my body down like I'm getting comfortable… could I touch Jeff's foot? Do I dare?

Wednesday June 29, 1977

Dear Cassie,

Last night, I gambled with my freedom and I won. So why do I feel this miserable?

I was betting Anita wouldn't care if I spent the night at the Bixby. I wondered if she'd even notice I was gone. But part of me was more than a little afraid. I mean, I've never stayed out until after sunrise without telling her I was going to be sleeping at someone's house.

When I got home this morning, there was Anita going through her morning ballet barre routine. First position. Plie. Second position. Plie. Then she looked over one bony shoulder, lifted her eyebrows like she was slightly surprised to see me in her house and said, "You're up early."

Third position. Plie. Point and flex and point and flex the toe.

I was thinking, this is it. She's going to cream me. This is the day I went too far. I should have left a note or tried to call again or something.

"Since you're up early, please take the trash out to the alley before the garbage truck gets here."

Arm up. Then down. Plie.

That was it. I waited for more, but she looked at me and said, "The trash, Erika? Hustle it if you please."

Can you believe that woman? She didn't even notice that I didn't come home last night!

I know, I know. I'm being a complete idiot. Getting mad because she didn't get mad at me. Weird. It's not like I want to get in trouble. But still...all those times your dad was checking up on you. Reading your private stuff. Nailing your bedroom window shut so you couldn't climb outside on the TV antennae. I know it was a total pain. But, as annoying as he was, at least you never wondered if he cared if you were dead or alive.

My mother. My one and only parent. The only family I know. She doesn't care one tiny little bit about me. You were the only person who ever really cared about me, but now you're gone.

Oh good grief! I'm starting to tear up. No! Last night was wonderful and I'm not going to let the Mother Monster ruin my mood. I can't become some weepy pathetic thing. Luke didn't sit around crying over his dead family. He went out and found a new life; a better life. You didn't sit around crying every time your dad used the belt. You figured out how to escape. And that's what I need to do, too.

Erika

PS – Anita has decreed that I will be taking Super 8 movies of all the dance routines at the gazebo during this year's Independence Festival. She gave me some cash in case we needed more film. I didn't remind her of all the boxes we already have in the closet. It's her own stupid fault if she doesn't bother to open the door and look. I pocketed her cash and shut myself in the basement with a notebook and a week's worth of laundry.

| FOURTEEN |

I WAKE UP BRIGHT AND EARLY TO THE SOUND OF ANITA'S CAR tearing out of our driveway and zooming away. It's such a huge relief to walk around the house in my nightshirt without her scowling at me. That woman sucks all the fresh air out of the house when she's here. This is the first time I've been able to breathe, really breathe, since Tuesday. Even better, I'm free to pour a huge bowl of Boo Berry cereal and mix chocolate syrup in my milk glass without hiding my food from her evil eye.

Big Bad Bob on the KJCM morning show is babbling on about which downtown streets are closed for the Independence Festival. It's always the same sections of the same streets so why do they have to announce them fifty thousand times every year? Then he starts listing all of the events. It's always the same events on the same days. Blah, blah, blah...then, wham!

Suddenly he's talking about Cassie Abbott. He's saying stuff about "our missing Miss Junior Independence 1976" and how the pageant will be "under a black cloud of mystery and grief" this year. Then he urges anyone who knows anything about the whereabouts of Cassie Abbott to call an anonymous hotline.

My cereal turns to mushy blue sawdust and the chocolate milk tastes sour on my tongue. I flush most of my breakfast down the toilet, grab the Super 8 and lots of film cassettes, and then leave the house early.

Just as Big Bad Bob warned, the streets around the downtown square are blocked off with lots of wooden sawhorses and orange cones. What Bob hadn't warned me about was the total chaos going on all around the square and spilling over the sidewalks, including the one right in front of the Bixby. Everywhere I look there are sweaty, grease-stained strangers.

I've lived in this town and gone to the Independence Festival every single year of my life, but I've never seen the exposed guts of the carnival being pieced together. It's totally surreal. A giant plastic clown face emerges from one of the trucks and wobbles past me on two sets of blue jean legs. Something about the black gaping hole between the clown's creepy grinning lips makes my skin crawl. To shake it off, I move away to watch five or six guys piecing together the metallic skeleton of a Ferris wheel. Beyond the wheel crew, two guys are pitching a small red and white striped awning over one corner of the courthouse lawn where four very bored, very stinky ponies stare back at me. Beyond the ponies, a ridiculously tall man with a bushy black mustache is setting up a game that involves dolls shaped like umpires and piles of baseballs. Finally, I remember the Super 8 and slip in a film cassette so I can try to capture some of this crazy stuff.

I get a cool shot of a shriveled gnome-looking guy standing on a step ladder to spin pink cotton candy onto a white paper cone. After that, I catch an even better scene with a big hairy ape of a man, smoldering cigarette butt dangling from one lip, weaving thick black power cables into some intricate pattern that looks like a monster spider web. I even manage to get the clown head—now minus the human legs—being hoisted into the air behind the ticket booth.

I'm so absorbed in my little behind-the-scenes carnival film that I back up to the Bixby without realizing anyone is standing out front. Camera still stuck to my face, I back right into someone who is all bones and elbows. Two hands grab my shoulders to keep me from falling on my butt. Off balance, I look down through the lens to see a set of freckled, skinny legs poking out of a pair of cut-off blue jeans. The legs end with a very familiar pair of dirty green basketball shoes.

Slim Jim.

For a split second, I seriously consider running away.

Then Slim Jim leans around sideways to look right into the lens of my camera and says, "Hey, Erika. How's it hangin?"

I'm so shocked, I yank the camera away from my face like I've been burned. There's Slim Jim's face smiling at me while Sonny stands beside us with a fierce scowl on his face. I start apologizing to Slim Jim, which is pretty stupid, because I'm also telling him I didn't tell any cops, or anyone else for that matter, about his party. So why do I keep saying "sorry?"

"Aw forget it, kid."

But I can't let it drop. I beg like a desperate maniac for him to believe me or at least tell me that he believes me.

"Poor baby," Jimmy says and clucks his tongue a few times. "You don't get it."

"Get what?" I ask, dreading the answer.

"What was really happening there. With Tammy and the oinking and everything. You have no idea what was really happening, do you?"

I shake my head.

"You ever watch *Mutual of Omaha's Wild Kingdom*?" he asks, his voice changing to a pretty exact impersonation of the one on the show.

I stare at him.

Slim Jim starts laughing and pokes at Sonny's arm with his elbow. Sonny isn't laughing, though. Apparently he doesn't get the joke either. In fact, he looks even more annoyed than usual.

"Jimmy, what the hell is so funny?" Sonny asks.

"*Wild Kingdom,* man. *Wild Kingdom* is a riot!" That sends Slim Jim off into another fit of giggles.

I'm starting to feel a whole lot less confused and a whole lot more suspicious. Sonny rolls his eyes at me. I think he's suspicious of the same thing.

"Wait, listen man." Slim Jim is pressing both hands to his sides and fighting to take a deep breath. "See, there's these goofy British dudes with cameras and stuff. All sitting around watching animals fight and hunt and hump on each other—" A high pitched girly giggle escapes, before Slim Jim sucks in more air and gets himself under control.

Sonny crosses his arms over his chest in that way he always does when he is not happy. "Jimmy? Are you high?"

"Wait, wait," Jimmy says, rubbing at one eye, "Wait! Listen, man. Then you got Ma and Pa America sitting in their safe living room watching the animals fighting and hunting and humping while this snooty British voice tells them all about the animals and why they fight and hunt and—"

"Where is this going?" Sonny practically shouts at him.

"High School!" Jimmy looks at us both with this proud look on his face like he just pulled a rabbit out of a hat.

"You're totally baked, aren't you?" Sonny's voice is no longer loud or angry. He sounds exhausted. I'm feeling more and more sick to my stomach.

"High school is like *Wild Kingdom*, man. We're the animals. It's like this thing with Tammy and Erika, man. It's like when the old gorilla gets killed and the other gorillas have to fight to see who's in charge, you know? Cassie was like the leader of the gorillas. And then Cassie was gone and Tammy had to make her move. So she got rid of you, Erika. I mean, no one really thought you, like, went to the police and sent 'em over to my place to bust up a party. That would involve, like, you talking to strangers, you know?"

"No one really thought I did it?" I ask.

"Nah. No way."

"But everyone oinked at me and stuff."

"What do you mean they oinked at you?" Sonny asks through clenched teeth.

"Aw, they were vicious, man. That Tammy is not one to mess with," Slim Jim answers for me while my brain fumbles for words.

"But I didn't ever mess with her," I protest.

"You were, you know, a casualty of war. You were Cassie's little buddy. Her co-pilot. Her lieutenant. When Cassie went, you had to go. If anyone would have stuck up for you or tried to say anything, Tammy would have wiped the floor with them. No one was going to fight the red gorilla to help out a freshman."

Tears are threatening to gush, so I nod and duck my head to hurry inside.

Behind me, Jimmy keeps going. "Look, don't be upset, Erika. Tammy....she's not worth it. With Cassie gone, you can hang out with your own friends."

My own friends? Did he think I was keeping a spare group of friends in my pocket? Saving them for a rainy day?

I'm in a black fog for most of the day. I keep my head down while I sweep, mop, scrub and haul trash. At some point, I tell Sonny's feet that I have to film Anita's dance stuff during the festival so I won't be available all the time this weekend.

"Sure, Erika. Listen—"

I don't listen; I just keep moving. I do not need Sonny's pity.

Sometime during the four-thirty show, the numb wall around my heart starts to buckle. My eyes are burning, my throat is itching and every breath feels like torture. I manage to stumble into the black sub-stage shadows and find a safe hiding place before the tears pour out. In the largest storage room, the one next to the spiral stairs up to Stage Left, I curl my body into a nest of old ropes and let myself sob, sob, sob until my eyes refuse to produce another drop. Finally empty, I sit in the dark and listen to the distant sound of my movie, wishing there was some way to blow myself into millions of bits like a tiny version of the Death Star. The salty tears drying on my face make my cheeks feel tight and itchy. I really need to wash my face, so I emerge from my closet... and nearly jump out of my skin.

Nick is standing right there, less than three feet from the closet door, scratching his ear with one hand and holding a mop with the other. Faint yellowish light is spilling into the hallway from the open doorway of the janitor's closet across from the supply room, but it's still pretty dim in that cement tunnel under the stage. Maybe I should sneak away, but there's something about the way Nick is standing there all alone in the subterranean twilight.

When the door to my storage room closes with a sharp click, Nick turns to me and whispers, "I think maybe our old theater is crying."

My own skin is still itching with dried tears, but I inch closer to Nick and look down where he's looking. He pulls a battered flashlight out of one of his many pockets and directs the beam toward the corner behind the spiral stairs. Sure enough, there's a puddle of water in that corner and the cinderblock walls are streaked with drips of water.

We stand there in silence for a while with the faint sound of dripping water barely tickling my ears whenever the booms and explosions of the movie soundtrack stop.

Nick finally shakes his head and whispers, "Poor old girl. It's not rain. There's no water pipes here. It must be tears."

"I'll clean it up," I whisper back, pulling the mop out of his loose grip.

That's when Nick looks at me, really looks at me. Grabbing my shirt sleeve he whispers, "Let's keep this our little secret, Gypsy Girl. No need to get the others down here poking around. There's no rain and no pipes. It's just a few tears."

Nick's eyes look kind of unfocused and a little too upset.

"Okay, Nick, it's our secret," I promise.

When he nods and shuffles away, I'm more than a little relieved. If Nick wants to keep this puddle a secret, fine. There isn't much water. I'll keep checking that corner and mopping up as needed. If it doesn't get any worse, then there can't be any harm.

When I'm done mopping, I pat the wall and press one cheek against the cool gray cement blocks. "Every girl needs a safe place to cry," I tell the theater before pushing the bucket back into the closet.

Thursday June 30, 1977

Dear Cassie,

According to Slim Jim, Tammy "Big Red" Costas is responsible for all the hate and all the lies and all the oinking that made my life a living hell after you left town.

Once he told me, I could feel the anger and hatred for that Big Red bitch bubbling through my veins all day. When I got home, it only got worse. I couldn't sit still! I went down to the basement to do laundry, but all I could do was pace around like a caged tiger. When I tried to stop, my chest hurt so bad I swear I was close to having a heart attack. So I went back to pacing and thinking about being a casualty of Tammy's war.

Let's oink at Erika to prove to Tammy we're her friends. Was it really like that?

Anita yelled down to tell me she was going out for a drink and please don't forget to have the camera ready for the dance numbers tomorrow night. Dance numbers. Including a performance by one evil, Big Red bitch.

After watching Anita's taillights disappear down the street, I took the camera out the back door and started walking the alleys. Most of the windows I passed were dark, but when I got near Tammy's house, I could see her bedroom window was lit up. I stood under her neighbor's willow tree, pressed my overheated face against the bark and glared hatred at her window.

I could see flickering shadows in her room, but not much else. For a second I didn't know why the light was so weird, until I remembered the spoiled brat has a TV in her bedroom. So I crept up closer until I was practically sitting in her bushes and I could finally see her. She was sitting cross-legged on the end of her bed with her body bent forward, brushing her hair from the nape of her neck to the ends.

I watched her toss her Big Red mane back. She must have been watching herself in the dresser mirror, because she opened her lips, twisted her shoulders and tilted her chin like she was posing for her next close up in *Seventeen* magazine. The anger that had been building all day boiled up like acid in my mouth.

God, Cassie, I cannot tell you how much I hated her at that moment! If I could have had telekinetic powers like the movie *Carrie*, I would have put Big Red's face right through her own mirror. Then I would have stuffed her fancy silver hairbrush down her throat. Instead, I lifted the camera and started filming.

Inside, totally unaware I was filming her and dreaming of killing her, Tammy tossed her brush on the floor, twisted all that coppery hair on top of her head and fake smiled at her mirror. She wiggled her shoulders and smiled a different way. She tipped her chin down and frowned.

Tammy Costas is the love of her own life. That girl can't get enough of herself!

She stood up and posed in her nightshirt with her hand on one hip. Then—I'm not making this up—she used both her hands to cup her boobs and tried to look all sexy into the mirror. She tossed her hair around, wet her lips, sat on the bed and leaned to one side with her hand on her top hip. She was still at it, posing and pouting, for like ten minutes after the film cassette ran out.

When I walked away, I was bored with Tammy and bored with hating her. I still have no idea why I filmed her. I'm sure I broke some kind of pervert law, so I hid the cassette in the deepest, darkest place I could find. Maybe I should have destroyed it. Thing is, if that evil beast comes after me again, a film like that might be of some use to me.

Erika

JULY 1977

"The first bad penny dropped in San Francisco when a sweet-faced boy of twelve told me proudly that he had seen *Star Wars* over a hundred times. His elegant mother nodded with approval. Looking into the boy's eyes I thought I detected little star-shells of madness beginning to form and I guessed that one day they would explode."

-Alec Guinness
A Positively Final Appearance (2001)

| FIFTEEN |

ANITA DIDN'T EVEN BOTHER TO COME HOME LAST NIGHT. GUESS I can't complain, but it's not exactly easy to get a good night's sleep all alone in an empty house. I'm up with the sun, restless with itchy energy. So I escape the house by eight o'clock, leaving behind a note on the kitchen counter that says, *Working at The Bixby. Have dance schedule, camera and plenty of film. See you at the gazebo.*

I'd rather shoot myself in the head. The idea of standing there all exposed on the courthouse lawn, filming Anita's dance princesses, including Tammy. Agony! But I don't dare defy the Mother Monster. Sonny was right. That woman can peel paint just by looking at it. And that's nothing next to what she can do to me.

If I could choose a superhero power right now, I would pick invisibility.

When I get to the Bixby, the carnival is gearing up. The completed Ferris wheel starts moving as I round the corner, but the red vinyl seats are empty. Meanwhile, the egg-shaped Tilt-A-Whirl cars, also empty, are whirling at full speed. The hairy ape guy from yesterday, still with a cigarette on his lip, is squirting paint out of plastic bottles to create a fresh masterpiece at the Spin Art booth while two other workers watch. The horrible stench from the ponies is now mingled with the smell of frying grease at the Lion's Club French fry booth.

I decide to use one more cassette of film to catch the carnival waking up. Filming soothes me a bit. The gnome-like man at the cotton candy booth flashes me a peace sign.

Vince is standing in front of the Bixby's ticket booth rubbing the windows with wadded up newspapers when I finish the film. He takes one look at the Super 8 and lights up like a fist full of sparklers.

"Hey, what are you going to do with that?"

"What do you think I'm going to do with it?"

Vince is so excited he can hardly contain his spit. "Are you going to try to get some of the movie on a tape?"

A thought of me standing up in the theater holding out the microphone is so ridiculous it makes me crack up.

"I knew it!" Vince drops his paper and walks kind of sideways until he's in front of me. "Hey, is that a new Super 8 with sound microphone? Can I see it?"

He's a little too close so I step back, but he follows me.

"Um, I have to use it to film my Mom's dance stuff," I tell him, stepping back again. He moves forward again, looming over me.

"We work with cameras all the time in AV club. I know what I'm doing. Can I see yours?'

"It's...well, maybe later."

I take another step back.

"Hey, Vince? These windows look like they're clean to you?" Sonny is standing by the ticket booth with his arms crossed.

"You promise later?" Vince says, back-pedaling toward Sonny.

"Maybe later," I correct him, relieved to have my space back.

Sonny sends me inside to clean the seats. It's become my usual morning chore.

Once the festival is in full swing, even with all the rides, games and greasy junk food available right outside our front doors, more people are lining up to see *Star Wars* than ever before. Jeff barely has the chance to close the cash drawer at the concession stand because he's so busy.

I almost forget Anita's Friday evening dance group so I have to run for it, jumping over people's blankets and picnic baskets on the courthouse lawn. When I get there, I fully expect Anita to peel off my hide. Instead, she looks over at me and smiles. "Oh, good. There you are."

Uh oh. I know what this means. Not coming home. Not getting all over my case when I almost miss my cue. Anita must have a new boyfriend.

Oh please, let it not be Deputy Wayne Todd. Anyone but him.

Saturday July 2, 1977

Dear Cassie,

Get this. I actually stopped a crime today. Me and the Super 8.

The heat was pure torture outside and we were crazy busy in the theater. I think some of the crowd came to the theater to get a little air conditioning relief, but most of them were there for the movie. There were lots of hick farm kids who think the Bixby is the finest sort of special treat. They were looking at the poster with fish eyes, pointing and asking their parents, "What's that? What's that?"

It might have been cute if there weren't so many of them all packed in the lobby waiting for their Cokes and sucking up all the cool air from those of us who were running around like lunatics trying to work.

Today, I was very careful to keep track of the time. I almost missed my cue last night, but the Mother Monster didn't notice. You know I can't count on that kind of reprieve twice in a row. So I gave myself lots of extra time to go up to the projection room to get the camera before heading over to the dance stage area. Alex has been safeguarding the Super 8. I told her it was because of the crowds, but, really, Vince has been drooling over it and I don't trust him.

On my way back down the balcony steps, I spotted this trampy looking girl in a tiny spaghetti strap tank top and cut off short shorts at the concession stand. You could see straight through her little tank top. I'm not kidding, Cassie. You could see all of her business and I can tell you she was not wearing a bra.

The woman behind her had this pinched, I-smell-something-bad look on her face, but her big beefy husband was filling his eyeballs with all the skin he could see. The scene was too perfect to pass up. I put the Super 8 to my eye and started filming. As soon as I did that, I realized that Super Tramp was flirting with Jeff and he was flirting right back. Which made my stomach hurt. Jeff was eating her up with a spoon and not moving the line like he should. I saw Nick shoot him a stern look. Then the girl kind of giggled and stumbled to the side, causing some guy with a Coke to splash it all over the counter, his own sleeve and her nearly transparent tank top.

I've probably seen lots of girls do that sort of giggle stumble thing, but through the Super 8 it looked so fake. She was full of apologies and flirting with the guy whose sleeve was dripping Coke. Jeff was handing over stacks of napkins. Nick was shaking his head and refilling the spilled portion of the guy's drink.

Nobody noticed her skinny little right arm snaking up into the open cash drawer except me. I got a good shot of her stuffing a fist full of bills into her big macramé purse, the whole time petting on the guy's wet arm with her left hand. Then I did something crazier than all the crazy stuff I've ever done.

I charged down the rest of the stairs and grabbed that girl's thieving right arm as she dipped into the till a second time and screamed, "Hey, what are you doing?" as loud as I could.

She was quick to recover. I'll give her that. She yanked at my grip on her arm and quickly said, "Hey, I think this kid just tried to steal some money." Even though her hand was holding the cash.

"I caught you on tape," I told her, waving my camera in the air.

This whole time Jeff was standing there with his jaw open. I swear he was still staring at her jiggly chest, all confused. Nick was a pro. He was around that counter faster than I ever thought he could move and grabbed the girl by the back of her teeny, tiny tank top.

"You open your purse or I'm calling the cops!" he said.

Well, there was a little of her trying to act like Nick was hurting her and looking for help from all the big strong men around. Some of them were still looking at her chest, which was even more exposed with Nick yanking on the back of her top, but none of them were getting involved. So she reached into her ratty bag, pulled out a wad of money, and threw it on the ground. Nick let go of her clothes, but kept his hand clamped on her arm as he walked her toward the door. I crouched down to scoop up the money, while everyone else watched Nick.

"Don't you ever come back to my theater!" he yelled, pushing her out the door.

Then Mrs. P popped out of her ticket booth shaking two furious fingers at the girl and yelled, "And cover down your boobies!"

In case you're wondering, I still managed to make it to the dance stage with plenty of fresh film cassettes and a huge smile on my face. I did a pretty good job of getting the dance acts on film. I even got some good candid shots of Anita looking serene and proud between numbers. The only rough patch was near the end of the last number when Big Red was bouncing through butterfly steps and I heard someone in the crowd yell, "Cover down your boobies." The cinematography gets a little shaky there.

Erika – Super 8 Superhero

PS – In honor of my "heroism in the face of enemy breasts" (Jeff's words, not mine), there's going to be two Bixby Special Meetings in a row, tomorrow night and then during the fireworks on July Fourth. (Nick doesn't believe in scheduling movie show times to conflict with the big fireworks display.)

| SIXTEEN |

TONIGHT WILL BE A PLANNED EXPERIMENT WITH THE SUPER 8. I'm trying to capture a little bit of what it feels like to sit up on the roof with the stars above us, all of Ohio around us and the festival lights below us.

When I first start fooling with the camera, I notice Jeff is sort of hamming it up, making bigger gestures and playing to the camera. Vince can't stop staring at the camera and drooling. Sonny is being Sonny, still pretty mad at Jeff for almost letting the cash drawer disappear and making sure he mentions it as often as possible. Alex is tolerating the camera, but she's acting a little like a turtle, tucking her neck into her Army jacket shell.

I don't actually have any film in the camera at first.

We sit in our chairs and I throw out stupid questions. Jeff is quick with the easy answers. Every time he pops a wise crack, he sort of resettles his shoulders like he's really enjoying this. Instead of framing him alone in my shot, I include Sonny watching Jeff and rolling his eyes. Then Sonny stands up and disappears from the frame, but pops right back in from the side.

"How long does one of those tapes last?" he asks. From the way he says it and his lopsided grin, I can tell he knows I have not been filming anything. A giggle slips out before I can even try to be cool about it.

"Oh, I'm just practicing framing shots right now," I say.

Alex sucks down the last half-inch of a Kool cigarette and lifts her unscarred eyebrow at me. "You haven't been filming Mr. Personality's act this whole time."

I put down the camera and shrug. "It's Anita's camera and film. I need to make sure I don't use up too much of it." The lie rolls out easily. I reach under my chair to get a cassette. "I'm going to put in one now, though. Just in case."

"What?" Jeff acts put out. "I've wasted all my best material?"

"What's your bad material?" I'm kind of being sassy, but I do not expect the reaction that question unleashes. Alex drops her head back and laughs straight from her gut.

"Burn!" Sonny yells, dropping back into his own lawn chair with a fresh can of Pabst Blue Ribbon.

Vince actually peels his eyes away from my camera to say, "She just burned you."

For his part, Jeff puts his left hand over his heart and leans back. "Ouch, ouch, and ouch!"

Everyone is getting more relaxed and real. Good. I frame Jeff with Sonny behind, press the button and say, "What's the dumbest thing you ever did?"

Jeff looks at me with his John Wayne crossed with Robert Redford look. "Erika, you do know the rules up here, right? You ask a question, you get to answer it too. Squid pro quote."

"I think you mean Quid pro quo, genius," Sonny says into his beer.

"Squids or quids. Whatever." Jeff waves a dismissive hand over his shoulder in Sonny's general direction without bothering to look back. "Are you willing to answer that question, Erika? You have to be willing to answer any question you ask."

"I'll go first, if you want me to," I offer, but I keep the camera rolling.

Jeff sweeps his hand in an arc and shakes his head. "Oh, no! Not necessary." He settles back, takes a long drink of his beer and looks into my lens.

"The stupidest thing I ever did was cheat on my girlfriend," Jeff announces in a deadly serious voice. His words hit me like a punch in the ribs. It's a very good thing that I have the camera in front of my face. Jeff's electric blue eyes stay focused on the lens while my heart hammers uncomfortably in my chest and my throat goes bone dry.

"See, Erika," Jeff continues, "last year I was dating the sweetest girl in the whole world. She was the love of my life and I blew it. There was a keg party in the woods to celebrate senior graduation. Somehow I ended up thinking it was a good idea to strip down naked and go for a midnight swim with one Miss Cassandra Abbott. Some splashing, some horse play and pretty soon my sloppy drunken mouth is all over Cassie's and there were plenty of witnesses. Know what? As soon as I broke my sweet, wonderful girlfriend's heart and started dating Miss Beauty Queen, Cassie was already flirting with the next guy. I hung on and pretended we were a couple for a few months so I could feel a little less like the idiot I really was…am."

When Jeff stops talking and takes another drink, the silence is horrible.

Alex's voice snaps, "I hope you are not trying to tell us that was Cassie's fault and you were some kind of victim."

"Oh, no." Jeff draws out the word really long and low, "I said it was the dumbest thing I ever did."

"Did you hate her, though?" Vince's voice sounds pretty angry. "Did you hate her for making you—"

Alex snorts loudly, cutting Vince off. "I will NOT listen to anyone tell me a teenage girl, even a wild and selfish one, made a guy cheat on his girlfriend. Unless Jeff left out the part where he was hogtied or handcuffed with a gun to his head?" She pauses and Jeff shakes his head. "Right. Cheating is cheating. Who you cheat with or how easy a girl makes it to cheat is not important. It doesn't matter if you cheat with the town slut or the most wonderful angel on the face of the earth. Cheating is cheating."

Obviously, this is a personal issue for Alex. I think all of us, especially Jeff, are feeling pretty uncomfortable.

Sonny is still staring hard through the camera lens.

"I agree with you," he says, eyes boring into my brain. "But it does make you wonder, doesn't it?"

"Wonder about what?" Alex snaps back.

"Makes you wonder how many people Cassie ticked off in this town," Sonny says slowly without taking his eyes off me. "I mean, you play that sort of game on the wrong sort of person and even a smart little schemer could get herself hurt."

Alex snorts again, but she doesn't say anything.

"Erika?" Sonny asks. I know what he's asking, but I keep my mouth shut.

"Erika," he tries again. "If anyone in this town knows whose hearts Cassie messed around with, I think it would be you. Maybe Deputy Wayne Todd is thinking the same thing. What do you know?"

Without lowering the camera, I try to swallow the bitter taste in my throat. "I didn't—" I have to stop and swallow again. "I didn't even know Jeff had a girlfriend when he and Cassie...you know. I mean, who was she?"

"She went to Eastlake High," Jeff says. "Her name was Julie Everhardt and she was—"

"Don't get off the subject," Sonny snaps.

"Oh for pity sakes, Son," Jeff snaps back. "Erika just said she doesn't know! Relax. This isn't Let's Interrogate Erika Night."

They bicker a little more back and forth, but I'm not listening. My ears are ringing and my heart is hurting. The love of Jeff's life is a girl named Julie from Westlake High. Jeff cheated on the love of his life. With Cassie.

"What do you think, Erika?" Alex asks. Suddenly, I realize everyone is staring at me. "I just asked you if you thought it was possible that you know more than you think you do." Alex's voice is low and gentle again.

"I don't think so," I tell her. When the silence stretches on too long and Alex keeps looking at me, obviously waiting for more, I try to explain. "Cassie liked her secrets. She was always telling me she had lots of secrets. She said I was too young to know them all. When we were together, we talked about the future and stuff. We made up stories and we laughed. I never thought anyone wanted to hurt Cassie. Well, except maybe Big Red."

"Big Red?" Alex looks lost.

"That was our nickname for Tammy Costas because of her big mess of red hair. She's vicious, really hateful and mean, but...."

"Tammy would claw someone's eyes out for no good reason with a big smile on her face, but she's too stupid to make another girl disappear," Sonny says, shaking his head.

"So you were too young for Cassie's secrets," Alex says, looking away. "Oh, dear."

Sonny leans forward. "You know what that makes me wonder, Erika? That makes me wonder why you and Cassie were such buddies."

"What do you mean?" I ask the question, even though I don't really want the answer. "I know I was younger than her, but—"

"No, no, no." Sonny shakes his finger back and forth, cutting me off. "I wasn't asking why she hung out with you. I'm wondering what you saw in her. Why did you think she was so great?"

"She was my friend."

"Tell me why you wanted Cassie to be your friend. Be specific. None of this *she was great* or *she was cool.* Tell me she made you soup when you were sick. Tell me she told you jokes that made you laugh until your belly ached. Tell me she stood up to a bully who was threatening to give you a swirlie in the school toilet. Just give me one real, concrete reason why you loved Cassie Abbott so frigging much."

He's caught me off guard. My stupid tongue turns into a lump of stone. Of course I have lots of reasons why I love Cassie; as many as there are stars in the sky. But I don't say a word.

"See," Sonny says, tilting his head with a sad look. "You can't do it, can you?"

Right then the soft whirring noise from the camera announces the film cassette is over.

Sunday July 3, 1977

Dear Cassie,

There are so many reasons why I love you it's hard to know where to begin.

When you first came to town, I was broken—trapped in a wheelchair with both of my legs locked up in metal and plaster. On your first day of dance class, you found me watching TV all alone, clipping pictures out of *Seventeen* magazine. You switched off the TV and told me we were going to be best friends. You chose me. The broken one. You could have chosen any girl in this whole town as your best friend, but you chose me.

Whenever my mother acted more like a monster than a mother, you would always stick up for me. You would look her right in the eye and tell her to back off.

That one night I went so crazy I thought was going to float away into the sky, you held me here on Earth.

Sometimes you broke the rules and kept secrets, but you also opened up the world for me. You taught me how to sneak out of the house, how to put on makeup, how to hitch a ride, how to whistle through a blade of grass and how to walk into a party full of strangers.

And yes, sometimes you did make me laugh until my belly ached.

You were better than a best friend and more wonderful than any sister I could have dreamed up.

Missing you like crazy,

Erika

| SEVENTEEN |

SONNY IS WORKING IN HIS BLACK BINDER BEHIND THE CONCESSION counter when I march up to his right elbow, arms crossed over my chest.

"Something on your mind?" he asks without looking up.

"I have lots of reasons for loving Cassie Abbott, Sonny. Lots of reasons."

"Okay, then. Good for you."

"No, it's not okay. You tossed that question right in my face in front of everybody. I don't know what to do with stuff like that. I'm not like you and Jeff. I can't say clever things when someone throws stuff in my face."

That gets his attention. "Hey now, I wasn't throwing anything in your face. I just....you act like Cassie Abbott was this gift from Heaven above. You're so busy thinking that, I think you forget to take a good look how things really were. Erika, you don't need a friend like Cassie Abbott."

"You don't know anything about me."

"All right," Sonny drops his pencil and rubs a hand over his face. He looks like he hasn't slept in days. The scar next to his eye seems to be getting deeper. "I said I was sorry. What else do you want me to say?"

"I don't want you to say anything. I want you to listen."

"What's up, children?" Jeff pops out of the theater door and leans on the concession counter, looking at the two of us. "Why the serious faces?"

Behind him, Vince walks out of the men's bathroom backwards, struggling with the trash and the rolling mop bucket. I feel a little twinge of guilt, knowing I should be cleaning something instead of arguing with Sonny. On the other hand, I work faster than either of them and I clean more on most days than the two of them combined.

"Erika is just letting me know she doesn't appreciate the way I talked to her last night," Sonny says in a flat voice. Vince spins around with wild eyes like we're going to start taking swings at each other any second.

"Well good for you, girl," Jeff says. "Stick up for yourself."

Even though I hate an audience, I'm determined to get this out.

"I have very real reasons for loving my friend, Cassie."

I rub my right hand over my jeans pocket, feel the outline of the letter I wrote last night, then close my eyes and recite the list from memory. My voice gets a bit wobbly and whispery at times, but I get through it all.

There's a long silence after I stop talking. Then a long, low whistle from Jeff.

"Floating away?" Sonny asks, shaking his head. "For Chrissake, Erika, what kind of crap were you two doing?"

My temples are pounding with frustration. He's missed the whole point!

"You don't get it," I yell before marching past Jeff and Vince into the theater.

The good thing about all this anger is it helps me sweep and mop and scrub and haul and polish like a whirlwind for hours. The bad thing is I can't imagine anyone wants me up on the roof tonight.

We're all supposed to watch the fireworks—Nick actually expects us to be up there so he's provided Coke in bottles, buckets of Lee's Fried Chicken, cole slaw and a watermelon. When the four-thirty showing ends and Nick locks the front doors with a parting salute, I decide to go home, so I put my stuff away quietly and slip out the back door.

Alex is waiting for me by my bike. "Where do you think you're slinking off to?"

I try to act like I'm not sneaking away, but she cuts me off with a slash of her cigarette.

"One little squabble and you go running? I might ask what kind of crappy friends you're used to if I wasn't afraid of getting you all fired up again."

I try to apologize, but she cuts me off with another cigarette slash. "I say good for you sticking up for yourself and for your friend." Alex pinches her Kool between two fingers and uses it as a pointer aimed at me. "Good! For! You!"

"Now," she continues in a big cloud of exhaled smoke, "you march your butt back up there and look Sonny in the eye. Call a truce and we will all have a wonderful Fourth of July party. He can be a royal pain sometimes, but Sonny's heart is in the right place."

I stand there, not really wanting to leave, but feeling like that first step is nearly impossible. Stay or go? Stay or go?

Jeff's head pops out the beck door. "Hellooooo, ladies. Were you planning on joining us or is this one of those private girl talk things? Cause we could use some help carrying stuff up."

"Erika cleaned twice as much as you all weekend. She saved the concession money while your eyeballs were glued to the thief's boobs. Then she was rewarded with nothing but aggravation from Sonny during her own thank you party. Now she has to carry the party stuff up? You want her to stick a broom up her butt and sweep the floors on her way out, too?"

That gets me giggling!

"Okey dokey! See ya soon!" Jeff's head disappears.

"You ready?" Alex asks.

Still laughing, I nod and walk back into the theater.

Sonny is perched halfway up the ladder handing food and drinks up to Vince. When he sees me, he jumps down to let Alex climb up and lifts both hands up like I have a gun. "You aren't armed are you?"

"I come in peace," I say as Alex disappears above. "Truce on the roof?"

"Just on the roof? Or can we declare a truce overall?"

"I don't know. Probably. If you can manage not to act like a jerk."

"Fair enough.

Everything is back to normal…for ten or fifteen seconds.

When I climb up on the roof, there are more people up there than I expect to see. Jeff is sitting in his usual lawn chair looking at some kind of newspaper while a girl leans over the back of his chair pointing at things on the paper. She has one of those thick curtains of golden brown hair they always write about in romance novels. It's falling forward to hide most of her face, but what little bit of her profile I can see looks as perfect as the hair. Jeff keeps looking up at her with his ultra-bright toothpaste smile. They're in their own little two-person bubble.

There's a second girl sitting in the chair I usually sit in. This girl is turned around facing Alex, so her back is toward me. All I can see is a thick tangle of black, curly hair and her bony shoulders. It's obvious she's talking to Alex with her whole body, both arms weaving and jerking in wild gestures. Her long, tanned legs are draped across a second chair. As I inch closer, I notice a mess of woven hemp and shell bracelets climbing up both her wrists.

I have no idea what to do with myself. This mysterious black-haired girl is in my chair.

Alex stands over by the back ladder smoking a cigarette, blowing her smoke away from the girl in my chair and nodding a lot.

Vince, with his chair pushed back over by Alex, is the only one acting normal. Which, for him, means saying nothing and glaring down at his beer between gulps.

Sonny comes up behind me and whispers. "Don't worry, they won't bite."

As if I was worried about that! I'm wearing the same dusty black pants, sweat-soaked black t-shirt and black tennis shoes I wear to work every day. My skin is nearly as white as winter because I work in a movie theater all day and spend my free time lurking around in the basement. Now here are these two Coppertone girls with glowing skin and long hair looking like summer just breezed in.

All three guys have taken off their red theater jackets to reveal t-shirts. Of course, Jeff looks like a golden god. Even Sonny looks pretty good in his ratty old KISS concert t-shirt, the sleeves rolled up to show off sculpted arms. Where has Sonny been hiding all that muscle? He didn't bother to put his arms on display for the other two roof parties.

Jeff looks up as Sonny pushes his usual chair toward me.

"Hey, Erika!" Jeff waves at me like he hasn't seen me for years instead of a few minutes ago at the back door. He makes a sweeping gesture toward the girl and says, "This is Julie Everhardt," with all sorts of emphasis on the name.

There's a good possibility I'm going to throw up.

A slim hand with thin bangle bracelets jangling pulls back the golden brown hair and looks up at me. I know instantly that I've met her somewhere, but I can't remember where. She smiles.

"I think we may have met before?" Her voice is like clover honey. That voice is how I finally place her.

"The last day of school party last year," I blurt out, surprised. "You let me use your scarf."

"Oh yeah." Her voice sounds like she's really and truly so happy to see me again. "You were there with the Thief of Hearts."

"Oh jeez, Jules, don't go there," Sonny laughs, dropping himself onto a bright orange beach towel spread out on the ground.

"No, let's just drop that subject," Jeff agrees, but he isn't laughing like Sonny.

Julie winks at me. "Don't worry. No use crabbing over old history." I smile back because, well, she's sort of contagious. And she still has those nice amber eyes that warm you from the inside… no matter how much it hurts like a spike through your head when the boy of your dreams is drooling on her.

"I don't remember if we told each other our names last time. So it's Erika?" I nod. "I'm Julie, one of the long line of girls in Jeff's shady past."

The girl in my chair swivels around and drapes one arm over the back to get a good look at me. Her eyes are nearly as black as her hair.

"This is my cousin, Meredith." Julie sweeps her hand in the other girl's general direction. Meredith punches a fist in the air before she turns and focuses all her attention back on Alex.

Julie grabs a beer and walks over to me. At one point, her back is toward the whole group and she rolls her eyes. She opens the can and leans in to hand me the beer.

"Don't let her fool you. She's harmless."

In a louder voice, she says, "We saw Jeff at the festival and couldn't pass up his invitation to come back up here and watch the fireworks. I used to work here, too, you know."

"Oh, that's great," is what I say to Julie. What I want to say is, *Please pack up your perfect self, all your history with Jeff, and your harmless cousin and go away. Forever.*

But it isn't just Julie and Jeff making everything feel weird. Vince is quieter than usual in his gulping and glaring mode. Maybe he hates girls more than rats. Then there's Alex, who spends most of her time blowing smoke away from the group and nodding at whatever Meredith says. I hear enough to know that cousin Meredith is still all fired up about the Vietnam War. At one point, Meredith might actually be crying about it. Alex keeps her face all bland and empty, but it's obvious she doesn't want to talk about the war. Every now and then, not often, Meredith stops talking long enough to take a drink and Alex tries to ask Julie questions about college. This is how I figure out Julie is a year older than Jeff and she just finished her freshman year at Bowling Green.

By the time the fireworks start, I'm ready to jump off the roof. I stand between Jeff and Sonny to watch, but both of them are turned away talking to the pretty girls.

After the fireworks end, Jeff makes a big production of pulling a joint out of a crumpled grocery bag. I recognize what it is and immediately feel a harsh tug of fear in my stomach. When they pass around the wacky weed, I'm not invited to try it. Not that I would have done it! I would never risk smoking pot ever again after that floating off the planet thing. But still, they should ask.

I end up sitting apart from everyone else, trying not to smell that awful marijuana smell.

After her second toke, I watch Meredith sort of discover that Sonny is sitting there and that he has nice arms. She scoots out of my chair and onto his towel, putting one hand on his bicep. She starts speaking in a syrupy sweet cooing voice. I'm less than a foot away from them and my skin is crawling. To make matters worse, Jeff keeps teasing and fussing with Julie, making excuses to touch her in quick little ways. Vince fixes me in the same stare he normally saves for his can of PBR and starts asking me things about the Super 8.

When Meredith says she needs the bathroom, I jump up and offer to show her the way. On the way down the balcony stairs, she grabs my arm and asks, "Does Sonny have a girlfriend?"

"Yeah, I think he does," I lie.

I show her the bathroom door and tell her I'm leaving to walk home now. She looks scared, like she needs an escort back upstairs.

"Don't worry, the ghosts won't bother you if you don't bother them."

"Ghosts?!?!" Her black eyes look wild.

"You haven't heard of our ghosts?" I ask, enjoying her fear a little too much. "Don't worry, but stay away from any darkened mirrors. Ghosts can suck you into a mirror."

I leave her standing there looking around. Her knees are pressed together like she can barely hold it to get into the bathroom. Where, of course, she's going to find three huge mirrors. Okay, that was mean of me, but I'm in an ugly mood.

I walk out the back door and right past my bike. It will be easier to dodge any sheriff's cruisers on foot.

From the parking lot, I look up and wave to Alex. She sort of salutes me with her smoke so I know I have the all clear to go home.

***

Sonny is extremely irritating on Tuesday. As soon as I walk into the theater, he starts picking on me. He's acting like I committed a crime by walking home last night, keeps saying it wasn't cool of me to wander off without a word to him. Even after Alex tells Sonny to relax because I said goodbye to her, he's still throwing out nasty comments about "Erika's disappearing act."

Finally, I say, "Sorry, but I was bored with watching you and Meredith's episode of *Love American Style*. I wanted to change the channel before she started unbuttoning your pants."

Even though Jeff and Vince laugh, I still don't feel much better. Why do I keep letting a bully like Sonny get under my skin? This is a guy who was suspended for fighting at school last year. They say he put a guy in the hospital. How dare he judge me!

As I'm finishing with the seats in the theater, Sonny walks by and says something about being surprised that I'm the type of person who would play mean pranks when someone could get hurt.

"I guess you and Cassie really were two peas in a pod," he practically snarls at me, then stomps off.

That's when Vince decides it's time to tell me the rest of the story. Turns out Meredith ran from the ladies' bathroom to the roof almost in tears blubbering about hearing a ghost crying. She was so panicked she tripped and banged up both her knees on the balcony stairs.

My stomach feels sour and strange the rest of the day. The mention of crying reminds me to check the corner below Stage Left. Sure enough, there's a small puddle. I mop it up before anyone else notices and then wipe down the cement wall for good measure.

I pat the damp cement blocks and whisper, "I don't like her either."

Tuesday July 5, 1977

Dear Cassie,

My skin feels like it's trying to contain a million fire ants squirming to break free.

Family, Police Story, Switch! ... I can't seem to focus on any of the stupid shows on TV. Every magazine in the house is filled with boring crap. The radio is meaningless babble.

Every time I walk into a room, there's the Mother Monster. She's everywhere! Talking on the phone with the cord stretched across the hallway. Messing with her hair in the bathroom. Taping up wallpaper samples in the kitchen. Right now she's playing those scratchy old records she uses for the kids dance routines, humming and snapping her fingers while her feet tap out new dance steps.

Ugh! She isn't actually doing anything evil, but I don't want to see her. I don't want to hear her. I don't want to breathe the same air she's breathing.

I have nothing to do and nowhere to go, but I can't stay here trapped inside for one more minute.

Erika

| EIGHTEEN |

As soon as I climb out on my porch roof with the sky stretched out to infinity, everything else melts away. Down the pear tree. Through the alleyway. Across the state road. Into the cemetery. With each step I feel lighter and lighter. No one is looking at me. No one can hear me. No one is going to ask me any questions.

I actually dance a few steps, but stop. Even all alone I feel stupid dancing. I try running to the poplar tree and rolling, but that feels flat and empty without Cassie. So I press my back against the bark and stare up. I'm searching deep inside for something that can pry loose all the sticky black feelings.

I find *Star Wars*. That music is in my bones now. I close my eyes and imagine the march in the final scene; try to imagine feeling what it would be to be a princess standing in front of her soldiers feeling full of grace and poise with a velvet voice. It's no use. I'm no Leia. What would I be if I lived in a galaxy far, far away? They've already got a princess.

Actually, I'm more like Luke. I've never met my father either. What if I inherited special abilities from my father? Like psychic vision or a way to communicate with animals so that they come and do whatever I say. What if I could shift and change form to look like anything...well, maybe not a pane of glass or a drop of rain. There would have to be rules, like whatever I change into has to have the same weight as my real body.

But not this body! In the other galaxy I would be gorgeous—tons of thick, wavy hair tumbling down my back, eyes like stained glass that glow when I'm looking for psychic messages, and pretty little curves like Leia. I'll wear a dress of rainbow cloth that shape shifts with me. It changes into a ball gown or a bikini or an ultra lightweight sort of armor to protect me in a fight. My name would be something exotic, like Roxara. Or Zenna.

I'm standing in that throne room watching the heroes receive medals, knowing I have secrets to share, no, a secret message from my resistance group. They need to follow me to the planet where I live. It's full of waterfalls and blue tiger-like creatures that speak in secret messages to my kind, and we will help them defeat the Empire forever.

As I walk around dreaming up my world, I see a sky filled with purple moons, jewel-colored birds turn black when evil comes near, shimmering snakes that twine in my hair, making strange new braid patterns every day. I even say some words as I walk between the old tombstones, brushing my fingers over the rough granite and making up the story of my psychic ancestors.

"Hello, Cassie's friend Erika."

The dream shatters. I scream like someone dumped a bucket of ice down my back.

"I've been waiting for you. Didn't Cassie tell you I'm not a big fan of waiting?"

The creepy guy from the theater is sitting on a family memorial with his back against one of the angel's wings smoking a cigarette. I have no idea how long he's been sitting there. He has this gross smile on his face like he knows everything about me. I open my mouth, but nothing comes out.

Wild thoughts ping pong around my skull. *What did he hear? What is he doing here? Trapped! Need to run. Will he chase?*

"Who were you talking to just now?" His voice is slow and casual, like we have all the time in the world to sit here and chat.

"No one."

The shock is threatening to force me to my knees. How did he get to my neighborhood? So close to my house!

"No one? You expect me to believe you were chattering away like that to no one? Nice try." He climbs off the stone, moving in super slow motion. Looks around. He must see I'm all alone and exposed.

Run! ...and hope he doesn't chase.

They always chase in the movies. The girl always trips and falls and dies. With my bad ankles and knees, there's a good chance I'd never make it out of the cemetery. He gives me another ugly smile.

"Ollie, ollie, oxen free!" he calls out over the silent headstones. "Does Erika have any friends here?"

Silence answers his question.

The smile gets even uglier. "Seriously, who were you talking to?"

I look around at the tombstones. Does he think I have an army of midget friends who like to hang out in a graveyard?

"Was it one of those boys from the Bixby? You here hiding out and making out with some dude right on top of the dead?" And then he laughs this hard ripping laugh that feels like a slap. That laugh finally pushes me to act.

So I run. And not like one of those crying, tripping girls in the movies. I run like I'm trying out for the track team. Eyes forward, arms and legs pumping.

Behind me, I think I hear him say, "Now why would you do that?"

I don't stop running until I'm home hugging my own pear tree, choking on my own breath, stomach churning, throat stinging, feet burning, knees and ankles throbbing. I'm looking all around at the same shadows that have been around this house since my first memories, wondering if he's lurking inside any of them.

Fear that tastes like molten ash is eating me up from the inside, but I try to keep still. Part of me wants to crawl inside to hide, but part of me wants to know if he followed me. What if I've led him right to my house and now what? Anita leaves me here alone every time she goes off to meet her latest guy. I'll probably be home alone again very soon. Or what if he catches me some night when I'm walking home from the Bixby?

I force myself, inch by inch, to creep back toward the alley. I take a different way. Instead of walking straight to the alley, I cut through the neighbor's vegetable garden and sneak along a massive wood pile. Finally, I'm able to peek around the Hogue's garage toward the cemetery. There he is. He's leaning against a beige VW Bug parked under the maple tree at the east gate. He's still smoking; looking back and forth between the cemetery and the alley that leads toward my back yard. Is he going to wait there forever?

A light snaps on in the Hogue's kitchen and I watched Mrs. H in hair rollers open the fridge and pull out a pop bottle. I hold my breath hoping she isn't going to open the back door to release her crazy little dog. When the light snaps off, I take a deep gulp of air and look back. Creepy guy is getting into the VW. I count all the way to three hundred and eighty-six potatoes before he finally starts the engine and drives away.

***

Wednesday is pure misery.

All I want to do is dig down deep into my bed and hide inside the safety of bright daylight. Two problems with that:

One—It's insane breath of hell hot in my bedroom.

Two—Anita is not going to stand for me "lazing around all day."

She's in my room at eleven o'clock clapping her hands and telling me she's giving my mattress to Goodwill if I'm not out of bed in ten minutes.

Really? I've been working every day except Wednesdays at the Bixby. I love it, but it's hard work. It's not like I'm sitting around stuffing chips and soda pop in my mouth like I used to. And I've still kept up with the laundry and my other chores. Now I try to spend one half of one day in bed and suddenly I'm the laziest girl in the world?

When I stumble downstairs, Anita hands me a list of deep cleaning chores that makes me struggle not to cry. Then I notice prices next to each chore.

"What's this?" I ask, pointing to the column of figures.

"That's what I'm going to pay you if that item is done today," she says, then arches one pencil-thin eyebrow at me, "After today, the dollar values go down dramatically."

It's a long and terrible list, but the total dollar value is higher than any amount of money the woman has ever handed to me in my life...even for my birthday.

So my Wednesday is spent taking down curtains, soaking curtains, scrubbing the cabinets, cleaning all the windows, washing the bedding, stringing up the laundry lines, moving the furniture around, vacuuming every inch of carpet, polishing every inch of wood floor and hanging every piece of linen in the house outside to dry.

There is simply no room to imagine myself as a psychic, shape-changing, magical rainbow beauty when I'm dripping sweat from every inch of my body, smelling my own BO and up to my elbows in wet heaps of laundry.

There is, however, loads of time to worry about why a creepy guy was waiting for me in the cemetery last night.

***

One second I'm dumping the Thursday morning trash into the Bixby's dumpster, the next second Creepy Guy is standing between me and the back door. Before I have time to freak out, the theater door swings open and here comes Jeff, followed by Sonny.

"What's happenin' Candy Man?" Jeff asks, full of fun and no harm. "I thought that was your slugbug out front."

Sonny stays near the door looking confused.

"What's up, man? How's your mellow?" Creepy Guy, aka Candy Man, says to Jeff without taking his eyes off me.

"You know how it is. Summertime and the loving is easy," Jeff sort of ambles over toward me and stops between me and the guy. "What's happenin'?"

"Plenty of Alaska-grown power green this year," Candy Man says. "Drop in for a toke."

Uh what? It's like they're speaking a foreign language. Sonny looks every bit as lost as I feel.

"Right on, man. What brings you down to this neck of the woods? Right next to Smokey and all." Jeff nods his head toward the sheriff's office. We can't actually see the building from the back theater entrance, but I know what Smokey means.

"Just lookin' to hook up with my new little friend here." Candy Man's hands are in his back pockets. He jerks one elbow toward me.

"Erika?" Jeff laughs like that's the funniest joke he's ever heard. "Erika's not in the market man. She's a good girl. Good as gold. Aren't you, Erika?"

Okay, I'm not a total idiot. Candy Man. The name is starting to ring a bell. He's the guy who brings the "candy" to the party. Only it's not really candy, more like pot and pills and acid and stuff.

"Right," Sonny's voice breaks in when I wait too long to answer. "Erika's good as gold."

Well, that gets a reaction out of Candy Man! At the sound of Sonny's voice, he twists around and gets this look on his face like he's swallowing mud. It's one hundred percent obvious that he isn't thrilled to find Sonny Johansson is standing five feet behind his back.

"She owes me money," he tells Sonny in a voice that sounds kind of scared and defensive. That's weird! Sonny is only seventeen and this guy looks at least twenty.

"Stop smoking what you're dealing," Sonny tells him with a mean smile. "Erika does not owe you any money."

"Yes, she does, man. She has my money."

"What money?" Sonny snaps. "Erika, you have any money for Rodney?"

"She's supposed to pay me some money from Cassie."

"No! She didn't....I don't.....What are you talking about?" I barely manage to stutter out the words.

"She's lying," Candy Man aka Rodney tells Sonny, his voice is getting more and more nervous.

"Erika doesn't lie," Sonny says the words flat and hard. "But Cassie, now there you have a first-class, hard core, addicted-to-lying machine."

Some more words are said. It's all angry buzzing in my head. At one point, Jeff touches my chin and lifts it up.

"Do you know anything at all about six hundred dollars of Candy Man's money?"

I shake my head, but it feels like a little head movement isn't enough of an answer for such a big question. "No, but I gave her money, too. I gave her some of my mom's petty cash money. She told me she would pay me back when she got settled."

I feel so sad and alone and stupid. The tears are threatening to pour, but I can't let that happen. If I start up with the crying again, I might never stop.

The rest of the day I clean and clean and clean again. I clean things that aren't dirty. Everyone leaves me alone.

Friday July 8, 1977

Dear Cassie,

I've tried to stop writing to you, but it's no use. Even though I'm really, really, REALLY mad at you. There's just no one else I can talk to. So here I go with another letter for my secret box.

The last two days have been hell. All because your friend, the Candy Man, seems to think I have some money that you owe him. Yeah, that's right, Candy Man is looking for you.

You know exactly who I mean, don't you? Isn't he the guy who gave you the double wacky weed that almost killed me? Wasn't he the one who gave you all those little scraps of paper to fold into gum wrapper chains before the Molly Hatchet concert? You know how I know? The whole time I helped you fold those chains, you kept singing one stupid verse over and over.

Candy Man can, cause he mixes it with love and makes the world taste good.

Jeff swears he and Sonny have talked to that creepy freak and he won't ever bother me again. Still, I can't seem to stop looking over my shoulder or searching the shadows in my back yard.

Honestly, Cassie, why was that guy following me? What secrets did you share with him? What on Earth have you gotten me into?

Erika

| NINETEEN |

VINCE'S BEST FRIEND CHESTER WATCHED *STAR WARS* FOR THE first time on Thursday and now he won't leave the Bixby. He walks around pushing his glasses back up his nose and getting into these incredibly stupid conversations with Vince. They go something like this:

CHESTER: "How come there's all that metal in the trash compactor?"
VINCE: "What do you mean?"
CHESTER: "Like that big long metal pole. Was that Tarkin guy like, hey Darthness, you need this pole? Cause, if not, I'm just going to throw it away."
(Cue sound of two idiots laughing their heads off.)

Today, it was this:
CHESTER: "Are Stormtroopers guys in armor or robots?"
VINCE: "Droids. There aren't any robots."
CHESTER: "Droids or robots. What's the difference?"
VINCE: "There's a world of difference, man."
CHESTER: "Okay, so are the Stormtroopers droids?"
VINCE: "Maybe they're like super droids programmed to kill."

The two of them are bugging the crap out of me. I want to smack both of them in the head with my dirty, sopping wet mop.

I want to scream, "Shut up, shut up, shut up!" about a million times, but I keep mopping my area and focus hard on the floor.

"So what's your opinion?" Jeff's voice startles me so badly the mop handle smacks me on the side of my head. He's leaning over with both hands gripping the chair backs on either side of the row.

"My opinion?"

"Yeah. What's your opinion on the big debate?" He straightens up and crosses his arms over his chest. "What is the issue up for discussion today, boys? Where do Stormtroopers pee?"

"Ah…that w-w-was the…ah…one, one of the…ah…the things we talked about yesterday," Chester tells the chandelier. "Now we are…ah…thinking…ah…they are maybe ro-robots and so….ah…. so, they don't pee."

"Droids," Vince says. He looks sort of embarrassed for Chester. I know I am, but I'm more annoyed. Why is Chester here? Why won't he just go away?

Jeff smiles his trademark smile at me.

"So the question on the floor is, *Are Stormtroopers droids*? Erika, what do you think?"

Is he making fun of me? Or is he making fun of them? Or is he just goofing off?

Three pairs of eyes focus on me. I can feel the place where Anita used to pinch up the fat on my waist burning. This would be the perfect moment to say something cute and flirty….or deadly sarcastic. Cassie or Leia would know what to say. I'll bet gorgeous Julie would know. Me, I scrub harder with my mop and feel my energy dripping away and pooling in the dirty mop water.

Jeff won't drop it. That smile is getting ornerier and ornerier. "Just now, when your eyes were burning holes in the floor and your lips were moving a mile a minute. What were you saying to the mop?"

I want to die. I want to spin around and run away like I ran from Candy Man. But there's no way to run without feeling like a complete and total goofball.

Sonny bursts into the theater just then and glares at the whole room. "Is there any reason Erika is the only person doing any work? Chester, why are you still here?"

Sonny has been in a foul mood all day. We've all been avoiding him like the plague. Strangely enough, Chester doesn't seem to be intimidated by Sonny. Yet he's petrified of Jeff. That guy isn't right in the head.

"Hey, Sonny!" Chester calls out in a cheerful voice, "I was thinking—"

"Chester, we're trying to get some work done here." Sonny's voice softens. "This is a business, bud. You can hang out with Vince on your own time, okay?"

"Well, maybe I can help. Do some stuff and hang out. Like Erika."

Oh no, no, no. It's not possible.

"See, Erika works, Chester," Sonny's voice cuts through my thoughts. "She doesn't just hang out. As far as I can see, she works twice as hard as Vince and Jeff and they take home a paycheck. Plus she's known Nick for years."

"I can work, too. I can clean stuff."

My mop rattles and swishes triple fast as I focus all of my energy on Sonny.

Say no, Sonny. We don't need Chester here. Say no.

"I'll see what Nick thinks," Sonny says, ignoring my psychic messages, "but right now you need to take off." Apparently Sonny isn't weak-minded. I change my focus to Chester.

Go away. Give up and go far, far away. This isn't the theater you're looking for.

"Can I come back tomorrow?" Chester asks.

"I'm not making you any promises," Sonny says.

Chester smiles like Sonny said just the opposite. "Thanks, Sonny!" He squeaks and hurries out the side door.

"Well, that's that," Jeff mumbles so low only I can hear him. "We'll never be able to get rid of that doofus now."

"Work!" Sonny roars at Vince, who's standing there grinning like an idiot.

Sonny looks over at Jeff and me. "What?" he yells, then storms out.

Just to escape Vince's gloating, I leave my mop to go check the spot under Stage Left. It was dry this morning, but now there's a large puddle.

The Bixby hates Chester, too.

| TWENTY |

Deputy Wayne Todd walks into the theater Sunday morning with the cop stuff on his belt jingling and jangling, eyes hidden behind cop sunglasses. His mouth is a tight little cop line.

"Erika Williams." His cop voice is about three times louder than it needs to be. "Where have you been?"

I'm standing behind the concession counter. There's nowhere to hide. Sonny is behind me working away in his black notebook with his back to the lobby, but I hear his pencil stop moving and sense him tensing up.

"Um, I've been here mostly." My teeth, lips and tongue are sticking together in weird ways. "Why?"

Sonny turns around. Jeff emerges from the men's restroom and stands waiting with his arms crossed. Vince disappears through the upstairs balcony doors, then reappears with Alex and Nick close behind. Even Mrs. P comes out of Nick's office and makes the sign of the cross.

"Were you here mostly? Or all night?" Wayne asks.

My brain is spinning. Is it a curfew violation? Can Nick get into trouble?

"It's a simple question, Erika."

"What's the problem here, Wayne? Is Erika in some trouble?" Alex sounds both annoyed and bored.

Wayne ignores her. Turning himself sideways he holds out his right hand toward the front doors like he's directing me away from the scene of an accident. "You need to come with me."

"Now wait just a second here," Nick jumps in, hobbling down the stairs. The sight is a painful kick in my chest. Nick's knees have been hurting lately. Now he's making an extra trip downstairs because of me.

"It's okay, Nick," I say, trying to stop him from coming down. I toss down my cleaning rag, moving toward Wayne, but Sonny's hand shoots out and snags my elbow. "I'm sure it's no big deal," I try to reassure everyone.

"It is a big deal!" Nick practically shouts. "It's a very big deal. Explain yourself, Deputy, if you please." When he finally makes it to the bottom step, he plants his feet apart, hands on hips. "She's a good girl. She works hard to help us out. You can't show up here in my theater and point at Erika and tell her to walk out there without so much as an explanation. No, sir!"

Mrs. P, who rarely speaks English, pipes up with "Yes, she's good girl!"

My eyes are burning.

"For pity's sake, what is it, Wayne?" There's something about the way Alex says his name that makes it sound like a joke. "Erika was with me last night. We've got a show starting in an hour and fifteen minutes. What do you want?"

"Well, since everyone's so invested—" he pulls a notepad out of his shirt pocket that looks too tiny in his big beefy hairy fingers. "Let's start with the fact that someone broke into Erika's house last night."

His sunglasses are aimed at my face. I feel nothing. His words just deflect on my surface.

"Your mother surprised whoever it was when she got home."

Everybody is watching me. What are they waiting for me to say?

"Don't worry about your mother, she's fine," Wayne adds. "Whoever it was just ran away."

Did she bother to ask about me?

"Now," Wayne waves a pen at the room, "do any of you have any idea who would break into the Williams' residence.....or why?" No one responds. "Erika?"

"How would I know?" As soon as the words are out of my mouth, I know they sound wrong. "I mean, I wasn't home so how would I know anything? What did they take?"

"See, that's what is so odd, Erika, I'm not sure." He walks up to the concession stand and leans one of his hairy arms on my perfectly clean counter. "They broke in through your bedroom window and left the same way. Doesn't look like they went anywhere else in the house, but whoever broke in was hell-bent on finding something in your room. They left no drawer or box unturned."

That's when the nightmare hits home. Pure panic smacks me in the face. Someone has touched all of my things? They didn't touch the TV or the stereo or Anita's jewelry or the spare grocery money we keep in the cookie jar, but they went through MY things? What embarrassing items have been touched and looked at and pulled out for the world to see?

A hand presses into my back between my shoulder blades. Sonny.

Wayne is still talking. I don't hear a word he's saying until I hear Cassie's name.

"What did you say?" I ask, trying to shake off the fog cloud around my head.

"I said, it looks like the same person tore apart Cassie Abbott's room looking for something. Does that help you have any idea who it was or what they were looking for?"

I immediately think of Candy Man, but can't force myself to say anything. After what I spilled about the money, I don't want Wayne Todd tracking down Candy Man for a chat.

"Enough games, Erika," Deputy Wayne Todd practically yells the words at my face. "What were you and Cassie up to before she left? Why would someone break into your rooms?"

Faintly, somewhere in the back of my brain, I hear deep, heavy, hollow breathing.

I'll die before I'll tell you anything.

My chin snaps up. "I have no idea. I don't own anything worth stealing. Do I need to take a look?"

"Yes, you need to come look, but first, were you really with Alex all last night?"

"Why?"

"Erika—"

"Wayne." I mimic the cop voice back at him. "Am I a suspect in robbing my own house?"

It works! I can see it by the look on Wayne's face. He thinks I should just tell him whatever he wants to know because he's a cop and I'm a fifteen-year-old girl. I can practically smell his frustration.

"Watch your tone with me," is all he says.

***

When I see my room, my little victory with Wayne disappears. What a mess! All my notebooks are open on the floor. Dresser drawers have been dumped out. The junk from the top shelf of my closet is thrown around the room. Posters are ripped off the walls. My old ceramic piggy bank is smashed; the coins scattered.

It all seems so violent and pointless. Does anyone really think I'm hiding a secret safe behind my *Charlie's Angels* poster or any real money in Daisy Pig?

Anita is zipping around through the rest of the house in her bare feet with a cup of coffee in one hand. She keeps calling out the things that were not stolen.

"Bank book and checkbook are right here where I left them."

Slap, slap, slap.

"Here's my pearls."

Jingle, jingle.

"And here's my diamond studs."

Slap, slap, slap.

"My shot gun is still in the closet."

Finally, she stops in the doorway to my room and says, "Unless Erika's started hiding gold bars in her room, looks like this is just a damned vicious prank, Wayne."

Deputy Todd stands by my window, looking over toward Cassie's house.

"Wayne?"

"The sheriff wants me to bring Erika over to the Abbott house." He looks at me. "I'm getting really tired of asking this, Erika. What is it you're not telling me?"

***

When Wayne marches me over to Cassie's house, the first thing I see is Chief Walter Abbott sitting on the porch swing wearing nothing but his pajama bottoms and a sweaty undershirt. The man looks so wrecked; he seems like a complete stranger. His hair is growing out in wild directions. I don't think he's seen the inside of a barber shop since his daughter disappeared. The hollows under his eyes are practically purple and there's something about the creases in his face and the back of his neck. It looks like his misery is pouring out with his sweat and making every line deeper. When he looks toward me with those pea-green eyes it feels like he's looking straight through me. He smells kind of bad too.

Sheriff McCombs is waiting by the door—uniform perfectly pressed, white hair combed in a razor sharp part, spine straight as a flag pole.

"Look, here's Miss Williams," he announces all loud and hearty like Walt can't see me for himself. "Come to help us out?"

Walt starts shifting around. "I don't know."

"Nothing to know, nothing to know," Sheriff reaches past him, hustling me up the porch steps and into the house before Walt can say anything else. Deputy Todd starts to follow, but the Sheriff holds up his hand and says, "I'm going to ask you to keep Walter company for a few minutes, Deputy."

The kitchen door slams shut and it's just the two of us. All the doors and windows are closed. Not only is the house smoldering hot, there's a funky smell, kind of like the school dumpsters. Without really thinking about it, I tuck my nose inside my t-shirt. The sheriff's eyes twitch over toward the kitchen sink. I look over. Just about every single dish in the house is piled up in the sink. Two greasy skillets are sitting out on the stove. The kitchen trash is so full some papers have fallen out on the floor. I look back at the sheriff. He's busy looking me up and down.

"Erika Williams." He gives me a thin-lipped smile that looks more like a grimace. "Your name has been coming up quite a lot lately. I wasn't taking much notice, but now I think we need to have a serious talk."

The deep, heavy, hollow breathing starts up again, much louder and closer this time.

I'll die before I'll tell you anything.

My chin juts back up and my t-shirt falls back into place.

"You're a clever girl, aren't you, Erika?"

I have no idea what to say to that, so I wait.

"Now I hope you don't think you can just stand there and stay silent," he says, then crosses his arms over his chest. "You're pretty clever, aren't you?"

"I don't know what you want me to say, sir. I don't feel particularly clever."

"Oh, come off it." There's a harsh edge in his voice that makes my stomach flip even though he's trying to smile like we're in on a joke together. "I saw your eighth grade science project last year. I was one of the science fair judges, remember?" He leans in close, too close. "Two of my fellow judges fought hard to name you the winner, but I thought Billy's project was more appropriate. Yours was a little too artsy-fartsy for a science fair, but winning second place for the whole entire county wasn't too shabby, was it?"

A surge of resentment burns through me. I worked for two months on that project—The History, Technology and Chemistry of Photography. I'd created examples of images from every type of camera I could get my hands on, from a homemade pinhole camera to the Polaroid SX70 Land Camera we used at the dance studio. I'd even talked my teacher, Mr. Baer, into helping me create a real Daguerrotype. We spent a full Saturday in the high school chemistry lab messing with silver halide particles and noxious iodine crystals, but the result was amazing. Everyone, even Billy himself, told me I should have won first place.

"No, sir," I say through clenched teeth.

"You know what I remember most about your project? I remember those instant Polaroid pictures you took. You remember those?"

"Yes, sir." They were three pictures of Cassie posing in different lighting.

"There was a small flaw, sort of a yellowish blob, on the right hand side of all three pictures. You drew a circle and an arrow for each one pointing over to an index card where you explained the problem with the camera that caused the flaw. I thought that was mighty clever."

"Thank you, sir."

"You do remember that flaw, right?"

"Yes, sir."

Where is he going with this?

The sheriff straightens up until he is looming over me. "I'm going to ask you to look at something, a few things, with me. Before we do, I need you to solemnly swear that nothing you see or tell me will leave this house. This is all between you and me. I hear about any of this from other people and I will lock you in a cell, girl. Are we clear?"

I nod, but he continues to stand there, waiting.

"Yes sir, I understand."

He glares down at me until I'm really squirming.

Finally, he says, "Okay, then. Here we go," and walks out of the kitchen, motioning me to follow.

When we get to Cassie's room, the door is closed. The sheriff puts his hand on the knob, but then turns to look down the hall at her dad's bedroom. That door is wide open. I can see the edge of his single bed and the plain wooden dresser.

"Damndest thing," Sheriff says, but he's not really talking to me. "Man takes the spare bedroom in his own house and his daughter's living like a queen in the master."

Then he opens Cassie's door and I get a good look at her room. Her costumes! All of her beautiful dance costumes have been cut up; slashed into jagged strips and pieces. The pale blue cloud of ballet dress from last year's recital, the white and electric pink Genie costume from her jazz solo, the old fashioned telegram outfit with the gold buttons that she tapped in for the pageant—all cut up. Those mutilated costumes, even more than my smashed piggy, seem so ugly and pointless.

The sheriff stands in the doorway with his arm blocking me from entering. After a minute, maybe two, he says, "Pretty harsh, huh?"

I nod.

"Stay here for a second." He walks over to Cassie's dressing table and picks something up. I'm too busy gawking at the glittering mass destruction all around the room to pay much attention, until the Sheriff shoves something under my nose. When I look down, it gives me a terrible jolt. It's the scrapbook I gave Cassie last

Christmas. After all those hours I spent creating it, she left it behind.

Sheriff McCombs unties the ribbon that keeps the pages closed.

"Dear Cassie," he reads in a pseudo-girlish voice, "Something to help you remember me when you are ridiculously famous. Love forever, Erika."

Then he looks up at me and flips over the first page, showing me what I created with my own two hands. Pictures of Cassie during last year's Independence Festival smile back at me. The silver foil stars I cut by hand look lopsided. Then he flips another page. Pictures of Cassie from last year's dance recital. Flip. A picture of Cassie in her white dress at the homecoming festival with her arms around Jeff. I've had enough.

"I've seen all of the pages, sir."

His eyebrows shoot up. "You have? Are you sure?"

I look at him sideways. "I made the book."

"Oh yeah. Right." He looks at it again, uses his thumbnail to flip one more page, before looking up at me. "Did you make this part, too?"

I'm about to say yes, of course, I made all of it, until I see what he's showing me. There's a big square hole cut in the center of the book. All of those pages. All of those hours of work. Just so Cassie could cut a square out of the center. Why?

Sheriff McCombs is searching my face. "Did you have a falling out with Cassie?"

"No, sir."

"Cassie was your mom's star dancer, right? She got all the pretty costumes and private dance lessons. How come we never see you up on stage?"

"My legs—"

"Cassie sure had a lot of boyfriends, too, didn't she? Do you have a boyfriend?"

"What?"

"You do like boys, don't you?

I'm not sure if I want to cry or throw up.

He pulls a Polaroid photo out of the hole in the scrapbook; holds it up with the top edge pinched between two fingers like he's holding a dead mouse. The room swims in and out of focus.

I know exactly what he's holding, even before he turns the photo side toward me, but the image still makes me so nauseous I have to close my eyes.

The snapshot shows a girl facing away from the camera wearing only her panties. The exposed skin from her shoulders to a few inches above her knees is crisscrossed with angry red welts. Some of the worst welts end in short, bloody gashes surrounded by purple bruises.

It's a picture I took of Cassie after one of Walt's worst beatings. There are nine more snapshots, all equally vile, hidden beneath a floorboard under my bed.

"Erika?"

I open my eyes and force myself to focus. The sheriff is tapping one finger over a small yellowish blob on the right side of the picture. Damn it!

"Do you take many pictures of naked girls?"

"What? No!"

"Why would you take this picture, Erika? Do you like to look at pictures of other girls without their clothes on?"

I clamp my lips shut and shake my head. This is insane! This man, who is supposed to be a sheriff protecting and serving innocent people, he is looking right at clear evidence of terrible violence and he is not saying one word about the injuries. Instead, he's asking me these disgusting questions. I force myself to look into his face. This is the face of real evil. Equal parts terror and disgust are making me dizzy.

The sheriff takes a good look at the picture, then tucks it into his shirt pocket. That photo will never see the light of day again. I'm certain of it.

Next, he pulls a folded sheet of notebook paper from the ruined scrapbook, shakes it open and holds it up. It's a glamorous cartoon drawing of Cassie in an evening gown standing next to an old fashioned movie camera. Her body is only half as big as her head but her boobs are enormous.

"You're pretty artistic. Did you draw this?"

I shake my head.

"You know who did?"

I close my eyes and shake my head harder. Sheriff McCombs blows out a big breath. I think he doubts I'm telling the truth and I have no way to convince him.

"One last thing." He closes the scrapbook and tosses it on the bed. "What money was Cassie planning to use when she ran away?"

I swallow three or five times, trying to come up with something to say.

"You know, if I find out someone gave this little girl running money, there's going to be hell to pay, especially if that someone was an adult."

My throat is a clenched fist.

"Did your mother ever give Cassie any money?"

I shake my head, back teeth grinding, and try to keep my eyes on his face. We stand there, locked in a staring contest that seems to stretch out for an eternity. He looks away first.

"Can I go?" I whisper.

He makes me stand there waiting a few more heartbeats before pointing at me and saying, "Remember, not a word about any of this to anyone."

"Not a word," I repeat. Who am I going to tell?

"You can go on home now, but we'll be talking again, little girl."

***

I walk back home with every inch of my skin burning after that ugly interview with the sheriff only to find Anita in my room shoving most of my clothes into one of her old suitcases.

"What are you doing?"

Without looking up, she says, "I called Richard. He's going to have a friend change all the locks in the house. He wants me to have some security firm come out and look at wiring an alarm system. He's invited me up to his cabin on Lake Erie until the house is more secure."

"Who is Richard?"

"You'll meet him soon enough."

"I don't want to go with you and some guy to Lake Erie."

Anita snorts. "Don't worry, Darling, I have absolutely no intention of taking my teenaged daughter on a romantic getaway. Penny said you could go with her to a family reunion in Cincinnati. There'll be lots of kids your own age there. Maybe you can make some friends."

"No."

Her head snaps up. "Excuse me?"

I'm on dangerous ground, but I can't let this happen. "I said, no. I'm not going to Penny's family reunion."

Her eyes narrow to slits and her nostrils flare. She's in full Mother Monster mode now, but that is nothing compared to what I just went through with the sheriff.

"This isn't a request, young lady. You can't stay in this house after—" Her arm flaps around wildly to indicate the destruction of my room.

"I have friends here. I can stay with them. You've been leaving me alone to chase men since I turned twelve. Why is this any different?"

The silence that stretches between us vibrates.

"You ungrateful little bitch." Each word is spit at me while her eyes drill holes in my face. "You have no idea what I've given up for you."

"I didn't ask to be born."

"I didn't ask for you to be born either. Back then, we didn't have a choice."

And there it is. That's the closest she's ever come to admitting the truth to me.

"Then it shouldn't bother you one way or another where I sleep."

She throws the suitcase across the room and marches out. The sound of her bedroom door slamming vibrates the floorboards. I want out. Out, out, out! I don't want to look at my mother or my room ever again, so I grab some basic necessities from the wreckage and stuff everything into my school book bag, retrieve the cigar box from under the floorboard then walk straight out of the house without stopping.

One of the sheriff's junior deputies is leaning against a cruiser in front of our house. He waves to me as I walk away. I just keep walking.

My bike is locked up at the Bixby, so the only way to get back is on foot. Every step bumps a bruised feeling. I get as far as the Garfield Elementary playground before I start sobbing. Every sob tears up my throat, forcing me to hold on to the monkey bars for support until the tears stop. I stumble over to the wobbly old merry-go-round and sit down. Three different sets of church bells ring noon. I can hear horns honking friendly greetings and goodbyes over on Main Street. A group of three little girls in fluffy church dresses trot like ponies past the schoolyard. Their girly giggles echo though the hollow empty places in my soul.

I don't belong here. I don't belong anywhere.

The only place for me to go is the Bixby.

***

No one notices when I arrive back at the Bixby because the lobby is packed with customers. Loud voices fill the air. Bits and pieces of dialogue from the movie are mixed in with the normal jabber. I recognize many of the faces; they've come back to see the movie for a second or even a third time. Two boys, one scrawny with stringy blond hair the other pudgy with a bowl of black hair and glasses, are carrying homemade lightsabers; a couple of wrapping paper rolls painted red and blue.

Jeff and Sonny are both behind the concession counter ringing up people as fast as possible, closing the drawer after each sale. No one is going to get a hand in the cash drawer today.

Suddenly, Vince is right in front of me. "Are you here to work, because we're in trouble."

He pushes me into the theater before I have a chance to open my mouth and pushes a wooden broom through both handles of the double doors to prevent any of the patrons from following us.

For the second time in less than an hour, I yell, "What are you doing?"

Vince launches into a stream of speech I can barely follow. "I forgot we didn't mop under the seats last night and I missed a giant Coke that spilled and now I'm mopping as fast as I can and

Jeff didn't clean the bathrooms last night so he didn't tell Sonny the towels in the bathroom were all used up and we don't have any more because the supply guy didn't give us enough and Nick had to go get more supplies like paper towels from the grocery store and Alex is trying to fix the air conditioner cause it just gave up and can you help me clean in here or are you too upset because if you're upset then they will KILL me for asking you to work."

I never suspected Vince was capable of stringing together that many words.

"I'm too upset NOT to work. Where's the Coke spill?"

He points back toward the right section of seats.

I come up with a plan. Vince nods and hurries off like he isn't a year older than me with seniority. Some people need to be told what to do.

We knock through all the spot mopping really fast. By some tremendous, unbelievable piece of luck, we do not find a single rat. Maybe they had their fill of sugar last night and are now sleeping it off.

While the crowd files in to watch the show, I hustle into the downstairs ladies bathroom to check out the situation. Good grief! It looks like a brown paper bomb went off in there. And it smells worse than it looks.

I'm cursing Jeff pretty hard in my head when he walks in, sees me cleaning and blesses me with his mega-watt smile.

"Rock on, Erika!" He wraps both hands around my upper arms, plants a big loud kiss on my forehead then swoops out of the Ladies and into the Gents. It happens so fast, the truth barely registers until he's gone. Jeff kissed me! Me. It was just a friendly kiss, not really romantic, but that friendly little kiss is making my whole body tingle. And yet, I'm still so peeved with him. I mean, seriously, when is the last time he cleaned the Ladies restroom the way it's supposed to be cleaned?

By the time Nick arrives with paper towels, toilet paper and other supplies, everything is back under control. Everything, that is, except the air conditioning. It's sputtering and spitting out semi-cool air. From what I understand, that's a huge improvement over the extra-hot smelly air it was coughing up earlier.

The 4:30 showing is even busier than the matinee.

When I finally muster the courage to go up to the projection booth, Nick is leaning in the doorway talking as Alex resets the reels. Neither of them notices me lurking in the shadows.

"This is a nice surprise, huh? This plus last weekend will help get the bills caught up....long as the air conditioner holds out."

"I'm not sure how much longer it will hold out," Alex answers. "I've been trying to tell you, but you just won't listen." The terrible mix of anger and exhaustion in her voice makes me slink away.

How bad are the bills? As I sweep and polish, I think about the rusted wires that caused all the problems for Anita's recital. Add to that all the burned out lights, the "weeping" puddle, the peeling paint and the sputtering air conditioner. Lost in my inventory of problems with the Bixby, I'm startled when Alex suddenly appears at my left elbow. Her hands sandwich my left hand. Something metal and chunky is pressing into my palm. My fingers curl around it automatically.

When I look up into her eyes, all I can think is, *Help me, Alex. You're my only hope.*

"Would you do me a quick favor, Erika? Would you hang these on one of the hooks in the supply closet next time you're down below?"

I nod, lick my lips, and try to force my mouth to ask for her help.

"What is it, Erika?"

It's impossible to look directly into the heavy weariness in her eyes. I look down to find I'm holding a plain metal ring with five keys. "What is it?" I repeat, more to myself than to her.

"Nick's key ring." She looks around, before leaning in to whisper, "He keeps losing his damn keys. I found that set under the air conditioning unit. It's no use mentioning it; he'll just get ornery and blame someone else." She straightens and pats my cheek. "How are you holding up?"

"I'm fine," I lie, "but I hope Wayne won't cause any trouble about my being here last night?"

"Oh, please. I can handle Wayne. Still...we should probably avoid the roof for a few days."

That is exactly what I did not want to hear. A kick in the ribs might have felt better.

When the movie starts, I slip backstage intending to drop off Nick's key ring and mop up the puddle of tears that has, yet again, reappeared. Inside the supply closet door, I stop. There are at least twenty keys on the hooks, most look exactly like three of the keys in Nick's set.

A sudden idea electrifies me.

I drop my mop, grab a handful of loose, random keys and hurry through the cement brick passage that runs under the stage. The second key I try opens the main dressing room. It's like a little apartment. Dusty, stale and cluttered with some of the strangest junk, but it has its own bathroom, sink, closet, couch, coffee table, desk and lamps. Where the walls aren't covered in mirror, they are covered with black and white photos. The best part is that it's all underground. There are absolutely no windows for anyone to peek in…or to sneak in.

My next stop is the side entrance. Luckily, no one is around. This time it takes six tries before I find the key that operates the deadbolt. As I stand there flipping the deadbolt back and forth, tears of relief flood down my face.

During the final showing, I bike back to my house. Every window is dark and Anita's car is gone. There's a note on the kitchen counter that says, *If you get hungry, you know where to look.*

Inside the cookie jar, I find two twenty dollar bills. While pocketing the cash, I notice stacks of Chef Boyardee pasta and Dinty Moore beef stew in the pantry. There has to be at least twenty cans of my most favorite foods on the shelf. None of it was there the last time I looked. Either my mother is going to be gone for longer than I thought or she was feeling particularly guilty before she left.

Either way is fine with me.

In addition to some cans of food, I stuff toiletries, kitchen utensils, blank film cassettes and the Super 8 camera in my backpack before pedaling back to the Bixby with my heart pounding out a strange rhythm that isn't quite happiness and isn't quite fear.

Sunday July 10, 1977

Dear Cassie,

Guess what? I'm living in the Bixby.

Do you have any idea how long Anita has been trying to get Nick to open the star dressing room for her recitals? As long as I can remember. He always puts her off with all sorts of excuses. Now I hold the keys. As I write this letter, I am sitting in front of the giant dressing room mirror. It is after midnight. I'm alone in the Bixby with a whole night in front of me to explore. And yet, I can't seem to make myself move.

I have something to tell you.

Someone broke into both of our houses and destroyed our bedrooms. My room was torn apart. Your dance costumes were shredded. Whoever it was, they must have hated you very much. Maybe they hate me, too.

But that's not the worst part.

Sheriff McCombs was on the scene. At first he was acting friendly, but then he started asking questions that implied I had a reason to hate you. Everything took a really bizarre turn! I can't bring myself to write down what all happened, but I will tell you that he found one of the Polaroid pictures I took of your injuries last summer. There is not a doubt in my mind he's already destroyed that picture, but I still have the other nine. As I write this, those pictures are weighing heavily on my heart and mind.

Once upon a time, you made me promise to find a way to use these pictures against your father if you ever ended up dead or missing. I remember how scared I was, but I swore a blood oath thinking our sheriff was a real police officer, sworn to protect and serve the innocent. What happened today made me realize he is a dirty, twisted, evil man and there is no way I would ever give him these pictures.

But you are not really missing, are you? You made a plan and you escaped this place. That's what I keep telling myself, but today marks six weeks since we said goodbye and I have not received your postcard.

What if it never comes? How long should I wait? What am I going to do?

Some of the things I've learned about you since you left have been painful to swallow, but one look at these pictures reminds me that nothing I've experienced is as painful as what happened to you.

Erika

PS - I still have this crazy wacked out Super 8 film cassette of Tammy Costas preening and posing in front of her bedroom mirror. After what happened today, after some of the filthy things the sheriff asked me, I should smash the cassette to pieces, cut up the film and bury the bits all over town. Why did I shoot this film? And why can't I make myself destroy it?

| TWENTY-ONE |

On Monday and Tuesday, the final showing ends a few minutes after ten-thirty. I make sure to say goodnight to both Sonny and Alex before riding my bike away from the theater as though I'm going home. Instead, I pedal over to Garfield Elementary and hide inside the low brick wall that separates the kindergarten play area from the rest of the playground. After waiting in the darkness fighting sleep for over an hour, I head back to the theater, hide my bike behind the dumpster and let myself in through the side stage entrance.

Inside the theater walls, I'm finally able to relax and breathe out all of the aching thoughts and fears that have been pressing in on me every minute of every day since Cassie left town. As Anita always reminds me, electricity isn't free and I certainly don't want anyone to report any strange lights at the Bixby, so I rely on the reddish glow from the exit signs and the few, faint security lights that are still working until I'm forced to use my theater flashlight to navigate the spiral stairs that lead down to my safe haven below the stage.

Among all the stacks and boxes of junk down there, I find some treasures—an enormous hat piled high with feathers and bows, a black velvet cape lined in faded red satin, a recorder flute carved out of dark wood, white majorette boots that fit over my tennis shoes, and three electric lanterns that are made to flicker with a greenish glow. These bits and pieces of past theatrical productions take on new meaning in a galaxy far, far away. I spend hours teaching myself a series of notes on the recorder, imagining this device as a mystical tool to summon Force energy. It's entirely stupid, but I can't seem to stop myself from dreaming up these elaborate fantasies until my eyelids are too heavy to keep open and I have to curl up on the couch to sleep.

My old Mickey Mouse wind-up alarm clock wakes me at five o'clock in the morning when it's still dark enough to sneak out undetected. Back home, I circle the block waiting for sunrise to make sure all the doors and windows are still secure before going inside the house to check room by room for any new signs of invasion. When I'm fully satisfied the house is empty, I lock the back door and lean a kitchen chair against the knob before taking a shower. There's plenty of time to finish some chores before heading back to the theater.

With no movie times or cleaning work scheduled on Wednesday, I'm a shadow of a person with nowhere to go and too much time to get there. After cleaning up the disaster in my bedroom, I tackle the laundry, the dishes and even the lawn despite the fact that there is no Mother Monster telling me to do these things. I'm terrified to stand still for fear I might disappear into the emptiness.

By sunset, I'm stretched out on a beach towel up on the Bixby roof watching the twilight dissolve with the last rays of light. Peach, lemon and bubble gum pink clouds streak the sky. The first glimpse of a star causes me to close my eyes to make a wish... only I can't seem to think of a single wish.

Angry words erupt from the parking lot behind the theater. I roll onto my stomach. What should I do? Is someone coming into the theater?

"Calm down, damn it. I told you, I need a little more time." Deputy Wayne Todd's voice is easy to recognize.

The voice that answers him is also male, but I can't distinguish most of the words. All I can catch is, "...sick of it!"

Keeping my whole body very low, I crawl closer to the sound of the argument until I am pressed against the wall closest to the parking lot.

"It won't be much longer, I promise." Deputy Todd isn't yelling, but I can still hear him more distinctly than the other man. Curiosity is burning a hole in my chest. Slowly and carefully, holding my breath, I raise my head until I'm able to peek over the wall. One of Chief Abbott's men from the fire station next door, I think his name is Brian, is leaning against the tall wooden fence around the Bixby's dumpster. His arms are crossed over his chest and he is shaking his head, obviously upset. Wayne puts a hand on his upper arm, but the guy yanks his arm up and away, clenching his fist. For a second, I'm absolutely certain he's going to punch the deputy, but he just starts shaking his head again.

"Forget it," he says and turns to walk away.

"Bry! Come on, let's—"

"I said, forget it!" Brian yells over his shoulder and stomps toward the fire station.

After he disappears, the deputy slams his hand into the fence where the other man had been standing, then presses his forehead into the wood. From my vantage point, I can see my ten-speed is on the other side of that fence, wobbling like it may fall over. An involuntary squeak escapes my throat and the deputy raises his head. I drop back down behind the wall and focus on taking shallow, quiet breaths until I hear a car door slam and the deputy drive away.

***

On Thursday morning, Chester and Vince become embroiled in another stupid *Star Wars* conversation that makes my teeth ache.

CHESTER: "What about the whole hidden plans in the robot thing?"
VINCE: "How many times do I have to tell you? R2-D2 is a droid!"
CHESTER: "Okay, but the Empire guys have a perfect chance to blow up the escape pod and they just say, *Oh never mind there's no life forms*?"
VINCE: "So what?"
CHESTER: "First there's these two droids shuffling around dodging lasers that should totally hit them. Then they totter off with the secret plans and no one shoots at them or checks them out at all?
VINCE: "Yeah. How about the fact that C-3PO shuffles in itty bitty baby steps and R2-D2 is on these teeny tiny roller skate

wheels? Stormtroopers can't catch up with them in the middle of a dessert?"

CHESTER: "The Imperial guys can blow up a planet. Why don't they just blow up Tatooine?"

Sonny cusses and backs out from under the soda fountain rubbing his head.

"Listen up you two!" he snaps. "I've had enough. I'll tell you why the bad guys don't blow up everything."

Both of them stop and stare, mouths hanging open.

"Why? Because it's a movie! You two are supposed to watch it and enjoy it. Or you can hate it. But you are not supposed to dissect it into tiny little bits and question every part until there is nothing left to enjoy!"

Bizarre. Sonny is putting words to every feeling that has been rattling around inside me since Chester started hanging around with all of his stupid endless questions.

Chester, who doesn't seem to have enough sense to be nervous around Sonny but can barely spit out a sentence around Jeff, shrugs. "I know it's a movie, Sonny. We're just talking about other ways it could happen. Why are you yelling?"

"Never mind, Chester," Sonny starts furiously attacking some glob of goo on the counter with an oily rag. "Stop jabbering and start working."

"Even if they blow up everything, the plans could still be floating in space and they'd have to float out there to get them, like in rocket space suits," Vince says while half-heartedly running the Bissell around the lobby.

Sonny rolls his eyes at me in the mirror behind the concession stand.

"Yeah," Chester chimes in, not even bothering to look busy, "Like in *Moonraker*!"

"You're killing me." Sonny finally drops his rag. "*Moonraker* is comic book crap, like *Batman* or *Buck Rogers* or—"

"*Lost in Space*," I add.

"I love *Lost In Space*!" Chester's face is pure joy.

"Of course you do," I mumble and go back to sweeping the stairs.

Sonny sighs and rubs at his head. "You two are acting like the goofballs in English class who ask why Romeo and Juliet don't run away. Or why the old man doesn't throw his pole into the sea and row home. Every great story in the history of the world could be turned into another jumble of meaningless crap. You two are missing the point."

Silence.

"Well?" Vince asks.

"What IS the point?" Chester adds.

"The point is to watch and enjoy," Jeff's voice is suddenly heavy and tired. "You're supposed to feel…I don't know…better. More hopeful about all the crappy things in your life. That's the point."

Vince shrugs and stares down at the Bissell. Chester looks at me. I walk into the ladies bathroom to start cleaning.

A few minutes later, Sonny is filling the bathroom doorway with his arms crossed over his chest. "I was a little mean to them, wasn't I?"

I keep the mop moving.

"Come on, Erika. You can dish it out. I was an asshole, wasn't I?"

I stare down at the brick red tiles trying to find a way to say thank you.

"They get on my nerves, too," I tell the floor.

"Yeah, but you never tear into them. Even when Vince is making puppy love eyes at you, you never even say, *Boo*."

My head snaps up. "Are you making fun of me?"

"What? No!" He looks at me closely. Sonny's eyes aren't electric blue like Jeff's. They are gray and blue with dark places. They are like the ocean instead of a chlorinated pool. Something at the pit of my stomach tingles, turning liquid. It makes absolutely no sense, but I am feeling something almost romantic about Sonny. Mean, scar-faced, sarcastic, hard-headed Sonny. How is that possible?

"You really haven't noticed have you?" When I look back up, his ocean eyes are swimming with mischief. I have to fight to remember what we were talking about before my stomach melted and dripped down to my toes.

"What are you saying?"

"I'm saying that Vince has a huge, monster crush on you. And you have no idea, do you? Well, I'll be."

He walks out, leaving me confused and rubbery.

Now what do I do? I like Sonny. Sonny is…well, I can't like Sonny! But I think I do.

Vince likes me. Vince is gross.

What a nightmare!

Friday July 15, 1977

Dear Cassie,

If I were going to shoot a film of Vince, to catch what is my gut reaction to Vince every day, it would be dirty fingernails picking at purple zits. It would be a mouth speaking with too much spit. The sound of wet gurgling sucking noises every two seconds when he clears his throat. It would be the curve of a spine slumped over in a constant question mark. It would be eyes jiggling back and forth while the mouth is talking.

Right now I hate Vince. And I hate myself for hating him, because it's cruel. Sonny told me Vince has a huge, monster crush on me. Why? Why me?

Does Vince think we are....you know...the same? Oh, I'm feeling so mean. It's hard to write this out. Thing is, does Vince think we could be together like a real couple? I mean, doesn't Vince know how BAD he looks.

Or is he really the kind of guy I'm supposed to be aiming for? I can't stand it. I can't. I'd rather be alone forever or marry a little old man like Nick.

In case you're wondering, I'm also mad at Sonny. This is all his fault. I was just feeling pretty good, like a part of a group again. Now I'm feeling like I want to run far, far away from the Bixby because I don't want to deal with Vince at all.

Wish I could kill Sonny. Or at least hit him really hard and wipe away that smug look he gets on his face every time Vince tries to talk to me.

Obviously, I had a fit of temporary insanity back in the bathroom when I started feeling tingly over him. There is no way I like Sonny. He is contrary and bossy and full of himself. He thinks it is funny and cute that Vince likes me. It is neither funny nor cute.

I try to tell Sonny this with my eyes, but he just keeps looking smug and smirky. I hate him.

If I was going to shoot a film of Sonny it would be a voice saying, "Why aren't you working?" It would be a smug face. It would be knuckles rubbing hard at a freckled neck. It would be two hands scrubbing at dark copper hair until it sticks out in all directions. It would be a smile that only pops up on one side, twisting that scar, then disappearing in the next heartbeat. It would be a spine crouched down low, hooking up extra fans for Mrs. P in the ticket booth. It would be a hand pressed to my back when Wayne was looming.

Oh, who am I kidding?

I like Sonny. Stupid, stupid Sonny. I can't seem to feel anything for Jeff anymore. I've tried, because it's so much easier to like Jeff. He's soft and sweet and golden, like honey. Or maybe Jeff is more like cotton candy. You remember that you liked it once until the time you ate so much of it you puked pink and then it never tastes nearly as good again.

I wonder if you ever had this problem. Did you ever like someone you didn't want to like but you couldn't help it?

No, that's stupid. That doesn't sound like you.

Erika

| TWENTY-TWO |

It's an hour before the Sunday matinee and I'm cleaning the popcorn machine. One of the front lobby doors crashes open and Anita swoops into the theater; white scarf fluttering on her head, white wrap dress swishing around her legs and white sandals click, click, clicking straight toward me. Her best friend Penny is right on her heels. They both march up to the concession counter and stand in identical poses—hands on hips, toes tapping. It takes every ounce of self control I can muster not to duck behind the counter and cower like Scooby-Doo.

Instead, moving in triple slow motion, I back out of the popcorn machine and wipe my hands on a spare rag. I take a deep breath, hoping to inhale some serious Force energy.

"Hello, Mother."

"Hello, Daughter."

Silence. We eye each other while Penny looks back and forth between us.

"Penny tells me the sheriff stopped by her house yesterday to ask some very odd questions about you and about me."

"What do you want me to say about that, Mother?" Even though my heart is doing a wild tap dance on my rib cage, my voice is ice-cold. We sound like two arch enemies having tea.

"Where have you been? What have you been doing?" She looks ready to peel my skin off, so I take a moment to think and breathe before I say anything.

"I've been staying with a friend, Mother. Like I told you before you left town." Another deep breath settles into my core. "I promise you I have not done or said one single thing to upset the sheriff"

There's another long silence. Anita is starting to relax a bit. The danger is passing, but she won't give in entirely.

"I need you home by 10:30 tonight. We need to start cleaning up the mess in your room," she says, and turns to walk out. Penny is still standing there, looking bewildered.

"I'll be home by 10:30," I say with a sinking heart, "but I've already cleaned up the mess in my room."

"Then we'll have plenty of time to chat," Anita promises in a sickening sweet voice, then she swoops back out of the theater with a parting wave over her shoulder. Penny follows her, walking much more slowly this time.

When I arrive home, Anita is on the kitchen phone cooing sweet nothings to someone. It could only be the mysterious Richard. She waves her hand at me then points toward the kitchen table.

Annoyed, I walk over expecting to find dinner dishes to clean up. What I see instead stops me in my tracks—a flat, black, shiny square with the words *Star Wars* outlined in white. I step closer, and touch it tentatively. *Original soundtrack composed and conducted by John Williams.*

Half of me wants this album so much, wants to snatch it up and scurry away to the record player like a good and grateful little girl, happy with any crumb of affection. The other half of me wants to snatch it up and throw it at Anita's face. Unable to find my balance between the two sides, I stand still with both hands clenched in fists.

Behind me, Anita hangs up the phone with a soft click and walks over to the table. She pulls out a chair and sits, folding her hands.

"Sit down, Erika."

I take the chair furthest from her and fold my hands on the table in the same way she has hers folded. The left side of her mouth quirks up.

"It's a peace offering," she says, tilting her chin toward the record album. "I'm not proud of what I said or what I did before

I left. On the other hand, I was at my wit's end with everything, and your attitude was impossible."

"My attitude?"

"Erika, let's keep this civil. I'm not in the mood to fight with you. When I stopped at Penny's on the way home and she told me the sheriff had been over to her house looking for you and asking questions about you, I was sick. But then we walked into that theater and there you were, looking better and more confident than I've ever seen you look. The house looks great, too, including your room. And I have your word, your solemn promise that you have not done anything to draw Sheriff McCombs attention to yourself while I was gone, right?"

"Right."

"Then let's have a truce. As long as you keep up your chores and keep out of the Sheriff's way, we can move forward without any punishments or arguments, agreed?"

She holds out her hand to shake on it.

"Why did you buy me this album?"

"I told you, it's a peace offering."

"But why THIS album?"

She drops her hand, closes her eyes and sighs. "I thought you liked this movie. Isn't that why you're working away your summer at the Bixby? The night we saw it, you and Wayne were talking about the music."

"Yes, that's right."

"Do you want to return this and pick out a different one?"

"No, I want to keep this one." I hold out my hand. "Okay, Mother. It's a truce."

***

On the third Tuesday of the month, Nick has a special one-thirty matinee on the schedule marked *ARC—half-price.*

"What does this mean?" I ask, tapping the calendar.

"Association for Retarded Citizens," Vince answers with a scowl and shuffles away.

"What's wrong with him?" I ask Chester, mainly because he's the only other person within earshot.

"Vince hates ARC showings," Chester says. "They creep him out."

"Why?"

"You've never been around an ARC group, have you?"

I shake my head.

"Oh, wow." Chester comes over to me with a ghoulish gleam in his eye. "This one guy has a huge deformed head—it's worse than the *Elephant Man*—and be breathes louder than Darth Vader. Some of them wear diapers and drool so bad they have to wear bibs. And then there's this one girl—"

"Okay, Chester. I think I've got the picture."

When I try to walk away, he grabs my arm. "No, listen. Sonny gets really mean if anyone doesn't treat them all nice, even the ones with a load of poop in their diapers. He will rip you a new butthole and send you home if you stare or look at them even slightly weird. Erika, if you are not used to retards, you should probably take off when the bus arrives. That's what Vince and I are going to do."

"Got it," I say peeling his fingers off my arm.

As I'm pedaling my bike to the theater on Tuesday morning, I'm thinking about the Cantina at Mos Eisley, full of all shapes and sizes of aliens. I am going to be a female Han Solo, totally cool and above it all. That is my plan.

The second I walk through the back door, I hear, "Hey, Erika!"

It's Heidi from the Dairy Dream. I know she has Down's Syndrome, but she's been working at the Dairy Dream for the past two years. She doesn't fit at all with the image Chester gave me of the ARC group.

"Hi, Heidi!" I say, genuinely happy to see her. I haven't been to the Dairy Dream for months.

She marches right over to me with a huge smile on her face. Two yellow plastic barrettes are holding back her thin hair, making her sleepy eyes look even more exotic. "You remember me?"

"Of course, I do."

"Where's your friend? She orders medium strawberry cones with rainbow sprinkles."

"Cassie," I say, while Heidi nods energetically. "She…um, she sort of moved away."

"Oh," Heidi says in a whispery voice, taking two steps back and looking down at her sparkling white tennis shoes. "Are you sad?"

"I was pretty sad for awhile, but I'm doing better now."

Heidi smiles pure sunshine smile at me. "I have an idea. Do you want to come see the movie with us? It has robots and spaceships and magical light swords. My brother told me."

"I work here. I need to clean and stuff. But I promise you it is a super fantastic movie!"

She giggles and says, "I'll bet Mr. Nick will let you watch it with me."

I look up and see Nick smiling at us. He holds out both hands as if to say it's my choice. "Miss Erika is very important here. Very important. But if she wants to sit with you for a while—"

"Oh yes, please!" Heidi starts bouncing up and down so that one of her plastic barrettes gets a little crooked. "Some of these guys are weird and loud and sometimes Bobby cries. You could sit with me like we're just two friends at the movies."

I keep the smile plastered on my face even though her words make my heart ache. "That sounds like fun. If you really don't mind, Nick?"

"Go. Go! Take some lemon candy."

Out of the corner of my eye, I can see Sonny looking at me like I just sprouted two heads, but he doesn't look angry exactly. I have no time to dwell on it because Heidi is bouncing up and down so hard her knees sort of buckle. She almost falls, but I manage to catch her under both elbows in a sort of scooping motion. She grabs my arm with two hands and drags me into the theater to find the best seats away from the rest of the group.

What happens next is my wildest *Star Wars* experience so far. Bobby, a black man who has to be at least fifty with a full head of gray hair, starts crying as soon as the first lasers fire. A woman of about thirty walks around the theater clapping and yelling "Yeah!" every two minutes. When Darth Vader walks onto the rebel cruiser, some teenager with really pocked up skin and no eyebrows yells, "That's one bad dude!" at everyone. The whole thing is sort of surreal, but also kind of fun.

When Princess Leia marches in, Heidi looks at me and says, "She is bee-you-tee-ful! She looks like you."

My chest fills with happy little bubbles. "Heidi, that is the nicest thing anyone has ever said to me."

Even in the darkened theater, I can tell she's turning pink.

When the movie is over and everybody is done clapping and cheering and yelling "Yeah!" I walk Heidi back to the lobby and tell her I had fun but I need to get back to work.

"Don't worry. My Sonny won't be mean to you."

My Sonny? I open my mouth to ask her what she means, but she keeps on talking. "In three weeks and one day it's my birthday party. Do you want to come?"

I'm still kind of confused, my mouth opening and closing like a fish. She looks over my shoulder and says, "Sonny? I'm inviting Erika to my birthday party. She's my friend and she's nice and she's pretty like the movie princess. Isn't she?"

Finally, I get it.

Heidi is Sonny's sister! Which means she's also Jeff's cousin. I can't believe I never knew that. Sometimes I feel like a stranger in my own hometown. Once I connect the dots, I realize Heidi's thin hair is a similar copper to Sonny's and her eyes are a similar ocean blue. I guess her differences sort of blinded me to the similarities.

Your eyes will deceive you. Don't trust them.

Sonny is saying, "Erika might be busy, Heidi."

"Sure, I'll come," I jump in, not daring to turn around.

"We're going to have cupcakes and all sorts of food!"

"Sounds like fun," I tell her and she gives me a surprise hug.

As the group is waiting to get on the bus, I hear Heidi tell three different people that I'm her friend and don't I look like the movie princess. I keep my head down, afraid to turn around and look at Sonny.

"Yep, you're purty like a movie princess and sweet like sugar candy," I hear him say, but it sounds like he's making fun of me. When I finally peek over my left shoulder, he's halfway up the stairs to the balcony level.

Thursday July 21, 1977

Dear Cassie,

Finally! Another night alone with my theater. I was beginning to think I was going to die a slow, smothering death with Anita back home, hemming me in. Tonight, I found a note on the kitchen counter telling me she was staying at Richard's and wouldn't be back until sometime tomorrow.

I grabbed a few supplies and got myself back to the Bixby as fast as possible.

Here, I can imagine I am a beautiful, blue-skinned actress in an intergalactic opera. Here, I can stretch out on the roof, fill my eyes with the stars and feel what it might be like to travel through space. Here, I can invent new planets and new aliens. I can imagine I'm the sort of girl Sonny could love and the sort of sorceress who could cure Heidi's disability without ruining her sweet personality.

Alone in the Bixby, I can believe in magic, miracles, ghosts and Jedi. Anything is possible.

I could die here and never be sorry.

Erika

| TWENTY-THREE |

I'M STRUGGLING TO TIE UP AN OVERSTUFFED TRASH BAG FROM the concession area, when a plaid shirt and blue jeans leans against the counter right next to my head.

"Talk to you for a minute?"

Working hard to hide my irritation, I twist sideways without really looking up. "May I help you, sir?"

"Yeah, you can help me by stepping outside."

That gets my attention. Straightening up, I take a better look at my visitor, then blink a few times before it finally registers. This is the Wayne Todd who took us to see *Star Wars*—no tinted cop glasses, no jangling cop belt, no attitude. He looks younger, awkward, transformed.

"Yep, it's me," Wayne says like we're sharing a joke. He points to the back exit with one finger and picks up my unwieldy trash bag with the other hand. "Come talk to me for a sec, okay?"

The lobby is packed with the Saturday afternoon rush. Sonny and Nick are busy ringing up concessions. Jeff, Vince and Chester are nowhere in sight. I'm not entirely sure why, but I follow Wayne out the back door. He tosses the bag to the back of the dumpster then hooks both thumbs through his belt loops and looks at me.

"So..."

Being someone who doesn't know what to say or how to say it most of the time, I recognize the signs.

"So..." I echo back.

He takes a deep breath before plunging in. "Sheriff McCombs pulled me into his office for a private talk yesterday. It wasn't a pleasant conversation."

I wait. There's more coming, but he's having trouble pushing the words past his lips.

"This morning, I turned in my badge."

"Wait...what?"

There is absolutely no reason for me to feel dizzy right now. There's no reason for my heart to be throbbing in my toes. There's certainly no reason for the tears burning behind my eyes. This is good news, isn't it? No more Deputy Wayne Todd on the job.

"I quit. I'm done. I give up." He punctuates the last word by slamming his fist into the dumpster so hard that *my* knuckles hurt.

"Why are you telling me this?"

"Good question." He paces back and forth a few times before stopping. "You're a good kid, Erika. I never meant to mess with your head or put you in a bad spot."

"Well, you did both."

"Yeah, I'm sorry." He hooks his thumbs back into his belt loops and rocks back on his heels.

I press my lips together, unwilling to accept such an easy apology.

"Thing is, I was trying...I don't know. I thought if I could get you to trust me, I could keep my eye on you and make sure you didn't end up like her."

"What do you mean? End up like who?"

"Listen, Erika," he looks around like someone might be listening, then leans toward me and lowers his voice, "I never said this. You didn't hear it from me."

Despite my better instincts, I find myself leaning closer, waiting for some precious nugget of knowledge to drop from his hairy lips.

"Watch out for Chief Abbott. Do you hear me? Stay as far away from that nasty son of a bitch as you can get. And do NOT trust the sheriff. He's not looking to solve any mystery or find Abbott's little girl. He's looking for someone to blame. Watch yourself."

The tingling anticipation I was feeling turns into a bitter, burning frustration. All I can do is glare at him and shake my head. Is this supposed to be a news bulletin?

"No, listen! You need to hear me. As far as the sheriff knows, you were the last person to see Cassie the night she disappeared. That is not a good thing for you. But I have a little...unofficial information." He looks around and leans in again, but I step back and cross my arms. "Erika, someone else saw Cassie later that night, after she left your house. She was hitchhiking about a mile up the state road."

"No, that's not right." The words slip out before I can stop them. I bite down on my lips while my thoughts pinball out of control. *She promised. She promised me she had a foolproof escape plan this time. No more hitchhiking. No more truck stops. No more calls to Walt begging to come home. She promised.*

"The person who saw her is one hundred percent reliable; he just refuses to go on record with Sheriff McCombs. Cassie was out there hitchhiking again. We both know it wasn't the first time. Damn it." The last two words are spoken in a sad, heavy voice full of regret.

"The person could be wrong. It was late and very dark and—"

"He's not wrong. Believe me, I wish...never mind. Wish in one hand, spit in the other and see which one fills up first."

We stare at each other, each of us struggling with our own misery.

"Erika, do you know how many times I found Cassie out on that road with her thumb out? First time, I took her straight home. Had a little chat with her daddy. Just doing my duty, keeping a wild child safe, right? Wrong!" He looks over toward the fire station with a look so full of hatred, it takes my breath away. "Found her on my front porch bright and early the next morning. Told me she wanted to thank me for all I did for her, then she stood up and pulled off her shirt. At first, I just tried to cover her with my jacket, but then I saw...you know what I saw, don't you?"

I nod, unable to say a word. He knew. He knew what was happening and he didn't do anything to stop it.

"After that, I'd pick her up whenever I found her out running wild, but I never took her home or mentioned any of it to her daddy. Never again. I'd let her ride around with me for a while, then I'd drop her off near one of her friend's houses, watch her walk in." He smiles at me, but I can't make my lips smile back. "I watched her climb into your bedroom window a few times. I really thought between me and your mother, we could keep her safe. I wanted to save that girl. Crazy and damaged as she was, I really did care about her."

"You and Cassie...was she your girlfriend?"

"What? No!"

I must look as doubtful as I feel because Wayne straightens up, places his hand over his heart and says, "I swear to you, Erika. Nothing like that. Cassie Abbott was...well, she wasn't quite a child, but that's not my style. I swear."

"She was everyone's style."

"Not mine!"

He sounds so real, I do believe him. He's telling the truth... but the tingles of energy skittering over my skin tell me he's not telling the *whole* truth.

"What about Sheriff McCombs? Was Cassie his style?"

It is impossible to say which one of us is more surprised by my question.

"Now what in God's name would make a fifteen-year-old kid ask a question like that?"

I shrug and point back toward the theater door. "I'm going in now."

When I try to turn away, Wayne grabs both my arms. Big mistake. Something terrible inside me lashes out, kicking and scratching and screaming like a wild thing. Wayne quickly steps back with both hands lifted, apologizing. I turn and rush back inside, diving into the theater's darkness hoping to escape everything Wayne just told me.

***

Sonny is waiting for me outside the supply closet with his arms crossed and his back against the old bricks. I walk past him to dump floor cleaner into the mop bucket.

"You know, you don't have to get clean water every hour," he says.

"I like clean water."

"We need to watch how much cleaner we use. The janitor supply truck isn't coming until we pay the last three bills."

I stand there, chewing on that piece of information. "I can bring in some Mr. Clean from home."

"What did Wayne want?" Sonny asks, like that has been the topic of conversation all along.

"You know, just Wayne stuff." I dunk the mop up and down in the soapy water, churning up unnecessary soap bubbles.

"He tell you he quit?"

"Yeah."

"He tell you why?"

The water in my bucket is sloshing around wildly, but neither of us looks down.

"No."

"He tell you he hauled in ten of Cassie's friends last night, including Rodney, and locked 'em in a cell until morning?"

Panic climbs up in my throat.

"I didn't tell Wayne or the sheriff anything," I say.

"No one said you did."

"Right!" I push the mop down hard with both hands, slopping the water on the concrete floor. "Everyone will say I did!"

Sonny shushes me. "No, they won't."

I'm too busy panicking to listen. "Candy Man will come after me like before."

"No, he won't." The dead flat certainty in his voice cuts through my panic like a steel knife. I look up into Sonny's ocean blue-gray eyes, almost black in the sub-stage lighting. Those eyes transform my panic attack to dim-witted mooning in two seconds.

"He won't come after me?" I ask.

"No, he won't." Sonny pushes off the wall and gives me a hard look. "Listen to me. Rodney is a dumbass piece of work and, yeah, I think he did break into your house. Stupid, stupid thing to do. I don't know why he did it. But I do know this, Rodney will not hurt you. Do you hear me, Erika?"

"I don't know Rodney."

"You know me. I'm telling you how it really is." At this point, he settles both his hands on my shoulders. Our foreheads are practically touching. "You don't have to like me. Just trust me a little bit."

I'm Sonny Johannson. I'm here to rescue you.

"Okay."

"Erika, every instinct I have is telling me something freakish is going on with this whole Cassie thing. Stay low, stay safe."

With that, he bumps a very gentle knuckle against my forehead and walks away.

Sunday July 24, 1977

Dear Cassie,

Last night I dreamed a nightmare kaleidoscope of things. One minute, I would be in a dazzling magical sort of place, but then everything would crack and tumble and jumble before falling back together all wrong.

I remember standing in a room full of mirrors, but the reflections from every direction showed you smiling and waving in your red, white and blue dress from the pageant…except for one tiny, cracked mirror that showed no reflection at all. That broken mirror seemed to call to me, so I moved closer and suddenly Darth Vader was looming over me, the sound of his breathing shaking the glass.

Then the mirrors shifted and I was standing among hundreds of glittering balls like they have at the skating rink. Around me, people in fancy disco dresses were roller skating in couples. I tried to film them with the Super 8, but through the camera lens, I could see big brass keys sticking out of everyone's backs. When I lowered the camera, I realized they all had black holes in their faces instead of eyes. And all around, the sound of that terrible breathing.

I ran away and ended up lost in a maze of metal tunnels sort of like the ones on the Death Star. The tunnels were echoing with the sound of breathing and it was getting closer and closer.

Then the floor tilted and I was sliding down, down, down…until I was sitting in the middle of the Garfield Elementary playground. There were little girls in fluffy dresses and shiny tap shoes all around me and the sky was filled with hundreds of hot air balloons. When I looked through the Super 8, I realized there were giant hairy spiders in the baskets all spinning one giant web that was covering the sky and I had to get those little girls inside, but they wouldn't stop giggling and tap, tap, tapping.

There were more places—a circus big top with clowns on old-fashioned bicycles (all with flat tires), a fountain full of swans (all with crooked metal necks) and a party room filled with baby ballerinas (all on strings with smeared faces). And everywhere I went, the breathing would follow.

The nightmare seemed to go on forever. I woke up feeling like I had run a thousand miles without any clothes on. Every cell in my body is exhausted. How am I going to make it through today?

Still, there's one good thing about that dream that's giving me a little bubble of hope to hold onto. You looked so safe and happy waving back at me from those mirrors. It has to be a sign. It has to be.

Yesterday, Deputy Wayne Todd quit his job. Then, for some reason I cannot figure out, he walked straight over to the Bixby to talk to me. He told me some things I never wanted to hear. That man has me so freaked out, I can't think straight. I don't want to write down what he said. I can't even begin to describe the sickening feeling pressing in on me. What I can do is hold on to that happy image of you and pour every ounce of my living energy into hoping that Wayne has it all wrong.

Erika

| TWENTY-FOUR |

It's Sunday night and there's another party on the roof, but I'm wishing everyone would just go home.

Chester and Vince keep asking each other stupid *Star Wars* questions. Jeff and Sonny keep bickering about everything and nothing. Alex is stationed away from the group smoking up a cloud and staying silent. My head is still swimming with the things Wayne told me.

Things go from bad to worse when Julie and Meredith show up wearing short shorts, halter tops, and a haze of Love's Baby Soft. Meredith's massive bush of black hair is swept back in a big leather and wood barrette so I finally get a good look at her face. She's much prettier than I thought. That Muppet hair and non-stop mouth are deceptive. She's a tiny bird-boned girl with high cheekbones, delicate eyebrows that she can arch separately and a long slender swan neck. She kind of looks like Audrey Hepburn in *Breakfast at Tiffany's* with a black poodle on her head. She immediately seats herself right next to Sonny like that is her rightful place in the universe. Sonny looks at her and smiles.

Julie picks up an empty chair and plunks it down between me and Vince.

"So why are you not talking to me these days, Vince?" she asks as soon as her butt hits the seat.

After a few rounds of one word answers, she finally gets Vince talking about art classes, comic books and animation. Then Vince mentions my Super 8 and Julie decides I need to join the conversation. I try to focus on her chatter about film studies and screenwriting, but all I can think about is the way Meredith and Sonny are leaning toward each other flirting like crazy. Meredith's tiny hands keep fluttering over to Sonny's arm or his knee. I can feel their playful little dance like a white hot supernova radiating at the left side of my face.

Next thing I know, Julie is nudging me, asking if I want to see Vince's sketchbook. No, I don't really care, but I force myself to play along because I need a distraction from the Sonny and Meredith love connection. Vince lumbers off to get his sketchbook. After giving me an affectionate squeeze on my arm, Julie stands up and walks over to Alex while Jeff starts talking about some prank he pulled off in English class last year and Meredith giggles along.

It is so hard not to look over at Sonny. So hard.

Out of desperation, I focus on Chester, who is entirely focused on Jeff. He is drinking in every word Jeff says, following every movement of Jeff's hands. This feeling, sort of familiar and sort of alien, creeps up on me. I have seen this behavior before. Wait, no, I've done this before! Other things I've noticed about Chester click in and a wild idea hits me. Hard.

A surprised sound pops out of my mouth. Luckily, Jeff is into telling his story and assumes I'm reacting to whatever he just said. He lifts his beer can at me and says, "I know, can you believe it?" But I am not reacting to anything he's said. No.

I think Chester has a crush on Jeff.

I mean a real crush, like the crush I used to have on Jeff. It's not just the look of worship on his face right now, it's also the way he's been stealing looks at Jeff out of the corner of his eye. Or the way he stutters when he tries to say something to Jeff, even just simple things like yes or no.

My mouth is hanging open while my brain keeps replaying this one thought over and over. Chester has a crush on Jeff. Chester has a crush on Jeff. CHESTER has a crush on JEFF!

"Earth to Erika, you still with us?"

Everyone is looking at me, waiting for some response but I'm frozen.

The can of PBR I've nearly finished isn't improving my social skills, but I'm not drunk on beer. I'm drunk on weird. So it's really annoying when Sonny pulls the beer can out of my hand and gives me a bottle of Coke saying, "I think you better switch brands."

It is ten kinds of humiliating when Meredith chirps in with, "I remember my first time drinking beer."

I swallow a mouthful of Coke and glare acid at Sonny, but he settles back in his chair without noticing. Meredith points one of her bony shoulders toward me and settles her hand on Sonny's thigh.

"Who exactly invited you here?" I hear myself ask in a loud voice.

"I'm sorry, who are you? Do you own this roof?" she snaps back.

I can feel the syrupy fizz I just swallowed fighting its way back up my throat. I want so much to jump up and slap that girl over and over. Or to beat Sonny around the head and neck with this pop bottle.

"Mellow out, little cousin, or we're leaving." Julie's hand gently covers my clenched fist, her bracelets jingling. "Hey, Erika, come and look at this," she says, all nice and normal. Her thumb rubs over my wrist. "Better get a look before Vince changes his mind and hides it away."

Jeff shrugs one shoulder at me slightly and rolls his eyes.

I allow Julie to pull me out of my chair and over toward Vince. He thrusts out his open sketchbook toward us; it's open to a pencil drawing of Wayne wearing one of the Imperial uniforms from *Star Wars* with Darth Vader standing behind him. It's actually a great drawing. My face smiles at Vince because that's what I'm supposed to do. He flips to a picture of Chester as C-3PO. Somehow he's managed to capture the Chesterness of Chester's face in metal edges and angles. Next, there's a picture of Nick in Obi-Wan Kenobi's robes between Jeff and Sonny in outfits that looked like Luke and Han. My stomach flutters dangerously, but the smile stays fixed on my face.

"Come on, quit stalling. Show her," Julie places her free hand on Vince's shoulder.

He flips another page and now I'm staring at my own face. My hair is styled in two buns like Princess Leia's, but otherwise it looks exactly like me from the neck up. From the neck down it's a sketch of a Playboy centerfold body—big boobs, a tight waist and bubble hips—dressed in a very skimpy version of Leia's white dress. This ridiculous version of me-but-not-me is standing next to an old-fashioned Hollywood movie camera. *Wait.* I lean closer, carefully examining the movie camera. I've seen that exact version of a movie camera before. It's in the sketch Sheriff McCombs found in Cassie's scrapbook and accused me of drawing.

Vince. If Vince drew that picture, then that must mean…

My pop bottle hits the roof in an explosion that sounds like a gunshot. I snatch the sketchbook out of his hands and start flipping through the pages.

"Hey!" Vince protests and reaches to grab it back, but Julie stops him, laughing.

"See? I told you she would love it. You're an amazing artist, Vince."

What I'm looking for is inside the front cover. It's the exact same sketch of Cassie with wings that I discovered in the janitor's bathroom during the last week of school. This version is in pencil instead of fluorescent crayons, but there's no mistaking the style. The secret bathroom artist is Vince?

After closing the book and handing it back, all I want to do is escape. Without a word, I scramble over the wall, climb down the ladder to the lower roof and stumble through the door to the balcony without looking back.

Julie calls after me, "Erika? Wait, Erika," but I don't even slow down.

Once I'm down in the main lobby, I realize I'm trapped with nowhere to go. My house is looming empty in the darkness. Candy Man is still out there, possibly lurking around my neighborhood. My heart is screaming for me to get away, away, away. My head is screaming where, where, where? I end up pressed in a corner stall in the main lobby bathrooms with the lights out, tears dripping down my face.

The door to the lobby opens and closes, but I keep my body pressed to the wall and stay silent.

The familiar smell of cigarette smoke washes over me. Alex.

"So yeah," Alex's voice is all mellow and calm. "What exactly sent you over the edge? Getting treated like a drunk? Or Vince drawing you like a hooker in earmuffs?"

"Everything," I answer.

"Riiiiiight." I hear the slithery sound of fabric rubbing against brick. What is she doing? "No one can say you aren't having a rough summer, kiddo. Here's the thing—" She stops to take a deep drag from her cigarette. "If you want those girls gone, they go." Her exhale comes out in whoosh. "But do you really want to be that girl?"

"I'll just go."

"No, you won't. I let you get away with that one time. Take it from me, running away gets to be a habit."

I feel trapped and claustrophobic. The smell of cigarette smoke is suddenly overpowering, pressing down on me.

"But—"

"No ifs, ands or buts, Erika. You stand up, square your shoulders and come back up to deal with the girls. Or I tell them to go away. You choose."

"Why are you doing this?"

"I told you why. Now choose."

Silence. Alex lights another cigarette. I'm going to puke! Apparently her third option is smoking me to death.

"Alex?"

"Not going anywhere." Maybe that's supposed to sound reassuring, but it sounds more like a threat.

"The sheriff found a drawing of Cassie in her bedroom. He really wanted to know who drew it, but I didn't know. Just now, seeing that sketchbook, I realized Vince drew it. He drew another picture of Cassie on a bathroom wall at school, too. That's weird, isn't it?"

"Why don't we go back up and talk to Vince about it?"

"What? You mean just tell him I saw it?"

"Yeah! Just look him in the eye and ask a question or two. Radical concept, huh?" Alex's voice is oozing with sarcasm. "Oh, wait! Unless you think Vince is a deranged lunatic and he's got Cassie buried in his basement. In which case we should probably call the sheriff. Should we call the sheriff, Erika? Tell him to bring a shovel?"

"Maybe you could ask Vince about it for me?"

"I'm going to pretend I didn't hear that."

In the blackness, with my eyes closed and the smell of smoke threatening to asphyxiate me, it's amazingly easy to convince myself to do it. I scrub my face with my t-shirt until it's pretty dry then snap open the latch on the stall and feel my way toward the glow of Alex's lit cigarette.

A sink whooshes on and the glow sizzles out.

"Good girl," Alex says as the door opens onto the dim orange-ish light of the lobby.

I'm shaking a little as I follow Alex up the ladder, but when I step over and everybody looks at us, I manage to stay vertical. "Sorry I freaked out. My best friend is missing and...I'm in a really, really bad mood."

Julie is leaning forward looking sad and worried. "We're sorry, Erika."

She's the only one who was really trying to be nice to me before I lost it. So I focus on her, my shoulder turned squarely away from the lovebirds and say, "Forget it, okay? You were being great, Julie. Every time I meet you, you've gone out of your way to be nice to me. I'm sorry I'm such a freak."

There's a moment of silence.

"About that artwork?" Alex says.

Damn her!

"Um, Vince?"

He looks up at me like a dog waiting to be kicked. I feel bad for him and mad at him all at the same time.

"Look, your sketches are great."

He snorts. It's obvious he doesn't believe me.

"Thing is...do you mind if I ask you a question?"

No one says anything, but they are all watching.

"Did you ever draw a picture like that of Cassie? Not a *Star Wars* picture, but just a drawing of her in Hollywood?"

"Yeah, I did! Did she show it to you?" He sounds amazed.

"Um....well....thing is...."

Alex comes to my rescue. "The sheriff has it, V. He asked Erika to tell him who drew it."

"How did he get it?" Vince blinks, looking between Alex and me. "When was this?"

"He found it in her room," I say, thinking about the other stuff that was there.

"Oh," Vince manages to pack that one syllable with a ton of hurt. "She said she would keep it forever. She said it would be her lucky charm. That's the only reason I gave it to her." He looks up at me, "Do you think the sheriff will give it back?"

"Not a good idea," Alex tells him and nudges me.

"Um, Vince? Did you also draw Cassie as an angel in the janitor's bathroom?"

He looks down into his beer and shrugs.

"Hey! How do you know about that?" Chester looks like he's going to leap out of his chair any second. There's no hint of a stutter in his speech. "Why would someone like you be in Kenny's bathroom?"

"What do you mean someone like me?"

Before Chester can explain, Sonny says, "He means someone who doesn't get beaten to a bloody pulp on a regular basis."

I can't help myself. I look over at Sonny. We all do. What I see is a fire in his eyes that is focused on me. What did I do to deserve this anger?

"What Chester means, Erika, is there are some kids at school who can't use the regular bathrooms without getting tortured. Kenny left that bathroom open for them. Not for pretty girls who want to waste a little time or skip a class."

"I'm not—

"Cool it, Sonny," Alex breaks in. "This is our Erika you're barking at. Don't get so high and mighty on your damned fool crusade that you forget about the innocents. The world is not all about the villains and their victims."

Sonny nods, looks down and scrubs his hands through his hair. Meredith strokes his neck. This is the second time Alex has mentioned Sonny having a "damned fool crusade" and I'm dying to ask what she means, but first I focus my attention back on Chester, who has a crush on Jeff and has to use Kenny's bathroom to escape torture. He's still leaning forward looking at me with an intense expression that is nothing like the anger I saw in Sonny face. Every bad thing I've been thinking and feeling about Chester disappears.

"I was in there during exam week," I tell him in a soft voice. "It was a bad week."

Chester nods. "The pig calls? Yeah, I guess that was pretty bad for someone like you." The tone of his voice says he's giving me a compliment."

Everyone settles into their chairs without any additional arguments. Jeff launches into another story about a prank, this time on his Physics teacher.

Meredith stays quiet. Sonny stays quiet. I keep my eyes away from them until I can't stand it and steal a peek…only to realize they're both gone.

When I swivel around, looking for them, Jeff aims a wicked smile at me and says, "The loving hearts club snuck off to get a little closer in private."

"Jeff! Did you tell Sonny what I told you to tell him?" Julie asks.

Jeff's smile grows overly innocent, "Why whatever do you mean, Jules?"

"Jeff! My little cousin has been around. That girl has been around and over and through. I told you to make sure he knew." Julie's voice is not amused.

"He's a big boy. I'm not his priest or his mother."

"Yeah, but I didn't think he was the slut seeking missile you are." Speaking of missiles, that one is a direct hit. Jeff looks so hurt, I almost feel sorrier for him than for me. Julie crosses her arms over her chest. "Men! You are all useless. Hope he knows to use two maybe three rubbers if he decides to get it on with her," Julie says, dead serious.

It's the worst possible moment to laugh, but Alex starts snickering. Then Vince laughs. Chester giggles like a little girl and that gets me laughing despite the pain in my gut. Eventually, Jeff and Julie catch the laughing bug, too.

"If you really wanted to scare him," Alex chokes out, "maybe you should have told him she's a virgin who screams if you touch her panties."

Eventually, the laughter wears off and everyone resumes talking. I join in and pretend I'm not dying inside. No one says anything when I switch back to beer. After everyone stretches out and starts snoring, my eyes stay stubbornly open glaring at the night sky.

I hate Sonny. I hate him and I hope he dies of some rare disease that makes a guy's muscles turn to mush.

***

On Monday morning, I find Nick sitting all alone in the dark theater, staring up at nothing. I'm still feeling raw and prickly about the whole Sonny and Meredith thing, so I tiptoe around to avoid talking to him. Minutes click by and I start to feel nervous, wondering if he's feeling sick or something. But we've been quiet for so long, I'm not sure how to break the silence. Instead, I walk down the left-hand aisle to get a look at him from the front.

Nick's crying! There are fat tears running down the lines on his face and dripping off his chin. I look around wildly for help, but the projection room is dark. The doors are all closed.

"First picture ever played here was *Shopworn Angel* with Gary Cooper," Nick's voice seems to be drifting over to me from a thousand miles away.

"Are you okay, Nick. I mean, are you sick?"

"Ah, noooo..." His voice trails off into this heavy quiet as his eyes follow the stage curtains up to the scaffolding, the stage lights and finally settle on the dirty chandelier. "Never you mind me. Just feeling all sorry and sore today."

That makes two of us. I put down my broom and walk over to sit in a chair that is one away from his. We just sit still and say nothing for a few minutes. Nick's eyes are roving over the ceiling. I pretend to do the same, but I'm also looking him over for any signs of illness. There's a piece of paper crumpled in his left hand and a torn envelope in his right. I can see the words "Final Notice" stamped in red on both items.

"The organist played *The Star Spangled Banner*. The mayor gave a speech. And there were not one but two separate vaudeville acts." Nick smiles at me. "There were some singers who chattered a bit in between the songs and a juggler who told jokes. All that was before the movie even started. It was a really big event when this place opened. The line for tickets went all the way down the block past Sherman's Department Store. Did you know that?"

I shake my head, uncertain if he really wants my answer.

"I paid some kid a whole nickel to wait in that line for my tickets."

More silence. Finally, he turns to look straight at me and says, "You're a good girl, Erika. You work hard. Don't think I don't notice. But you can't work a miracle."

His words have me squirming all the way down to my toes. Is he going to tell me not to come any more?

"I love it here. I'll work harder," I say.

"You work any harder, you're going to scrub through the floor." Nick chuckles at his own joke.

Just look him in the eye and ask the question.

I look squarely at Nick and ask, "Are you saying I can't help you any more?"

"What? What gives you this crazy idea? As long as I own this theater…ahhhhh, well…." His voice trails off again. A terrible suspicion comes over me.

"Nick? You were talking about trying to sell the theater before. You haven't sold it yet, have you?"

"Nobody seems to want it." His words are so sad they made my whole body ache. "Everybody wants to build brand new shoebox theaters with little screens for little movies. No one wants a big cinema palace like this anymore, with the leaky roof and the cranky air conditioning and all the bulbs to change and the full stage setup for live performers that never come these days. No one wants this sort of place except crazy old men like me. And I can't keep it up. Look at this place."

He looks around, waving his arm to include the flaking ceiling, the tarnished brass and the burnt out bulbs.

"Oh, it was so beautiful once, but now look at it. I'm losing the battle. I don't want to watch this place crumble and stand by helpless. But I can't afford….ah, never mind."

Nick shakes his head. "There's a man calling me from Cleveland. Wants to come down and look at the place a week from this Saturday. Says he's got some big ideas. Says he owns three old theaters and he's turned 'em all around to make big profits. Says he can turn around the Bixby, too."

"How?"

Nick shrugs, "If I knew that, maybe we wouldn't be in this mess." He looks up and around again, the trails of tears still on his face. "I doubt his other places ever looked this bad, though. He'll probably take one look around at this poor old shopworn girl and he'll run all the way back to Cleveland."

Nick plants both of his hands on the armrests, heaves himself out of his seat with a long groan and starts to shuffle away. But he stops suddenly and looks back at me with one finger pointed upward.

"That reminds me. I have something to show you. Something I found just for you."

I hear Ben Kenobi saying, *That reminds me. I have something for you...your father's lightsaber.*

"For me? What is it?"

"Stop by my office before the first show," he says and winks at me before continuing his slow shuffle up the aisle.

***

It's impossible to focus on cleaning the theater because I can't stop staring at all the cracks, peeling paint, exposed wires, burnt out bulbs, chipped concrete, worn velvet, and carpet stains. I guess I've gotten so used to the Bixby that I stopped noticing her flaws a long time ago. After my conversation with Nick, I can't seem to find a spot that doesn't have some kind of blemish. If the Bixby is a shopworn angel, she sure isn't aging gracefully.

Something needs to be done, and fast.

Sonny is in the concession supply room taking inventory. When I knock on the open door, he eyes me with suspicion then looks back down to make a mark on his clipboard.

"What do you want, Erika?"

"Listen, Nick is really sad about how the Bixby looks." I say, trying to keep my voice low, an imitation of Alex's voice last night.

"This theater looks like hell because it *is* actually falling to hell. It's practically disintegrating around our heads." He's trying to act like he doesn't care, but I can see flickers of sadness behind the blast of his words.

"Let's fix it up a little bit."

"When? When do we have extra time on our hands to paint and spackle and re-wire?" He throws a box of napkins against the far wall with much more force than necessary.

"Maybe we could come in next Wednesday—"

"That's my only day off! And one day isn't enough to whip this place into shape."

"I'm not saying we could fix everything, but we could make it look better. Maybe we could get volunteers to help."

"Who?" Sonny asks. "Who's going to volunteer?"

"I can get some guys from the VA to lend a hand." Alex's voice startles me. I turn around to find her standing in the doorway, leaning against the frame. "And I'm sure you and Jeff could get some volunteers. Especially if I host a keg party to make the work a little easier." She winks at me and I turn back to Sonny, buzzing with triumph. Alex is on my side!

Sonny, on the other hand, is clearly struggling. "I promised Heidi we'd do something next Wednesday," he says, but I can tell by the tone of his voice that his resistance is softening,

"She can come, too! Maybe she wants to help out," I say.

Sonny looks like he wants to stuff the inventory checklist down my throat, but Alex puts one hand over his left arm.

"Nick has somebody coming down from Cleveland. Someone talking about investing," she tells him in a low, stern voice. "With the ticket sales from this movie, we have a little extra cash to buy some paint and a few other supplies. I might be able to sweet talk Maggie over at the hardware store into some discount prices. Erika's idea isn't bad. In fact, it's pretty good and you know it."

Sonny shakes her hand off his arm. "Fine! Whatever!" He starts pushing around boxes with a vengeance. Alex makes a two-handed pushing motion towards me, so I back out the door and hurry up the stairs toward Nick's office. When I pause near the top step, I can hear Alex and Sonny still arguing in very low voices but I can't make out the words. Leaning way out over the handrail, I'm ready to sneak back down to eavesdrop when Jeff suddenly pops out of the men's bathroom.

"Er-EEka!" he yells at the top of his lungs, announcing my presence to anyone within the county line, "Morning sunshine!" I give him a weak smile and keep moving.

Nick's on the phone, but he hangs up when I walk into his office. Huge smile firmly back in place, he points a stubby pencil toward a cluttered table where a large poster is draped over everything.

"Tell me what you see there," he whispers, full of excitement.

The poster is yellowing and fragile, obviously very old. It's for a movie I've never heard of called *Metropolis*. There's a metal man-robot with glowing eyes that looks faintly familiar.

"It looks kind of like C-3PO!" I say.

"Ah ha! Good girl! Our Mr. Lucas has definitely studied his old movies. And look here, look here…" He stands up and peels back the edge of the poster to show an old *Buck Rogers* poster. "You ever seen one of these?"

When I shake my head, Nick launches into a lesson on film history, mainly emphasizing what he calls "Mr. Lucas's influences." He shows me more old movie posters and tells me stories about the movies that dazzled and amazed him when he was young. When he tells me about an actor they called "a man with a thousand faces" who portrayed such terrible monsters that his movies caused ladies to faint in the theater, he stands up to re-enact a famous scene from *Phantom of the Opera*.

No one has ever talked to me about these things before. I am so completely under Nick's spell, that I'm shocked when Alex walks in and I realize the first showing must have ended. The clock on Nick's desk tells me we've been talking about old movies for over two hours!

I jump up. "Oh wow, I better get back to work."

Alex grabs my arm and says, "Just a second, Erika." Then she proceeds to tell Nick about "Erika's plan" to fix up the theater with a special volunteer crew willing to work for beer and pizza.

Nick claps his hands. "You are a good luck charm, my Gypsy Girl! We'll not abandon ship and give up the fight just yet, will we?"

"No, Nick." I promise. "We won't ever give up."

They're not going to get me without a fight.

Tuesday July 26, 1977

Dear Cassie,

As I write this, I'm blasting side four of the *Star Wars* soundtrack on our stereo in hopes that music written to tell a story about saving the entire galaxy from evil will fill me with the courage and power to save my theater.

Today I found a letter addressed to Nick from Agent Brown of the Internal Revenue Service when I emptied the trash in his office. I'd seen Nick holding the letter yesterday. He was horribly upset and we talked about the trouble he's having keeping the theater from falling apart. What he didn't tell me is that he owes years of back taxes to the federal government. Years!

Now the I.R.S. is trying to shut down the Bixby and I feel so sick about it.

What am I going to do without this theater? What will Nick do? It will kill him if the government chains up the front door and auctions off his theater. He poured his whole life into the Bixby.

All along there have been plenty of hints and clues that Nick is in serious financial trouble. But I was sure everything was getting better, especially with all the ticket sales *Star Wars* has been bringing in. Alex even told me there was a little extra cash on hand to help us fix up the theater for an investor who is coming down from Cleveland next week.

When I found the letter, I walked straight up to the projection booth to confront her.

"Did you know about this?" I asked, holding out the stained and crumpled notice Nick had thrown away.

Instead of answering me, she grabbed the paper and wadded it up. "That is private information, Erika."

I was beyond freaked out!

"That letter says they're going to seize the theater if he doesn't pay his past due taxes in full." I was practically screaming at her.

She told me to calm down. She told me Nick is on a repayment plan, but the I.R.S. is wrapped in red tape and one office never knows what the other office is doing. She told me Nick has made all his scheduled tax repayments on time and the government will not seize the theater.

Suddenly, my brilliant little idea to enlist a few volunteers to clean up the theater seems stupid and insignificant. What is a little paint and polish going to do to stop the U.S. Government? I asked Alex that question, and she laughed. She actually laughed!

"If we get this investment money, maybe we'll be able to repay the government ahead of schedule," she said. Then she told me she already had ten veterans from the VA Center willing to come and help us fix up the theater. "The only problem now is making sure we have enough beer and pizza on hand."

I told her I didn't want to fix up the theater if it was going to be chained up and auctioned off to some stranger.

She shook her head. "That's not going to happen, Erika. Trust me."

I want to believe her, Cassie. I really, really do. But she never looked me in the eye one time while I was in her booth. She was doing this and that with the film reels, getting ready for the next showing, and her eyes were everywhere except pointed toward me. And then she made me promise not to breathe a word about this "tax situation" to anyone.

So I am worried sick, but I can't share this with anyone. Except you.

Erika

| TWENTY-FIVE |

A VICIOUS SUMMER STORM RIPS THROUGH THE COUNTY TUESDAY night. I'm home alone carefully folding up my latest letter to Cassie with the stereo near maximum volume when the electricity goes out, plunging the house into an inky darkness punctuated by bursts of lightening. I freeze, completely disoriented. With the music on, I wasn't aware that a storm was brewing, but now I can hear rain pounding on the roof. Gusts of wind are making the house creak and groan as if every board is in pain. The pear tree is slapping and scratching at the windows. My flashlight is carefully hidden away in the Bixby dressing room but I know Anita keeps some candles under the kitchen sink. I'm inching my way toward the kitchen when the phone rings. I abandon my quest for light and stumble toward the sound.

"Erika, this is your mother. Has the storm hit there yet?"

"Yes, ma'am," I say, trying to keep the terror out of my voice. "The lights just went out."

"It's a nasty one. They've spotted three different tornadoes around Central Ohio. There's no way I'm driving home in this."

My stomach drops. "You're not coming home tonight?"

She barks orders about how to stay safe, but I can't concentrate on her words with the thundering darkness looming all around until I hear a word that penetrates my panic.

"What did you just say?"

"I said the shotgun is loaded. Get it out of the closet and keep it close to you in case we have any unwanted visitors. Understand?"

"Yes, ma'am."

"Just keep your wits about you and you'll be fine," she tells me before she hangs up.

The cold, heavy weight of my mother's shotgun doesn't fill me with anything like reassurance at first, but then an image of Leia blasting a rifle at Stormtroopers pops into my head. I cradle the gun in my arms and take long, slow breaths, concentrating on the living Force energy flowing through me. I picture a blue light growing inside my chest, pulsing out to my arms, my legs, my head.

It works! A calm stillness seems to settle over me and I realize that there is absolutely no way I'm going to huddle in our basement clutching a shotgun all night. I'd rather be torn to shreds by a tornado than buried alive under this house. So I gather the candles, matches, a transistor radio and my bedspread before climbing up to the attic to make a warm little nest. There's only one way up to the attic, the trap door outside our bedrooms, so no one is going to sneak up on me here. Despite the wind, rain and thunder pounding all around, I fall into a deep and dreamless sleep as soon as I shut my eyes.

***

When I wake up, light is streaming through the round attic windows. The air is boiling and my nightshirt is soaked with sweat, but I've made it safely through the night. Beneath my little makeshift cocoon, the phone starts ringing. There's no way I'm going to rush to answer it. It's probably Anita and I'm in no hurry to talk to her anyway. The fifth or sixth ring is suddenly cut off followed by the jingle and bang of someone jerking up the receiver and then slamming it back down.

All my senses jump to hyperdrive alert. Someone is in the house! All the hairs on my body stretch out, waiting. I press the back of my hand against my mouth and teeth and wait. My heart is slamming all out of whack in my chest. Finally, I can't stand the stillness any longer. I roll over on my belly and inch my way over to the trap door that leads back down to the hallway. There's a place where the wood is warped enough to give a good look at most of the hallway below when I press my cheekbone against the floor.

I can't see anyone so I wiggle and squirm around to get as full a view as possible. Suddenly, the door beneath me drops down. My left hand is clutching the folded ladder so the top half of my body pops out of the ceiling, but I don't fall all the way down to the floor below. Instead, I'm hanging upside down screaming like crazy and so is someone else.

Anita! It's just my stupid mother!

The phone started ringing again.

"Erika Shana Williams, you just scared ten years off my life. What are you doing?"

What I'm doing is trying to climb my hands back up the ladder, so I can get out of this ridiculous position and she certainly isn't helping. The phone keeps on ringing away while I grunt and struggle to get upright.

"Answer me!" she yells at the same time I yell, "Answer the phone!"

I stop struggling to glare at her and my mouth firmly shut. The phone is on the tenth ring by now. Anita stomps over, snatches it up and snarls, "What do you want!"

This is the same woman who used to smack my bottom if I didn't answer the phone "like a little lady" with, "Hello, this is the Williams residence."

"Oh, Sheriff! I'm so sorry. Hello."

New alarm bells go off in my head.

"No, no, just a little accident. I tripped and dropped the phone." Pause. "No, I'm not the least bit hurt. How can I help you?"

My face is probably turning purple from hanging upside down, but I can't make myself move a muscle. "Now?" She turns around and narrows her eyes into slits aimed at my face. "What's going on? Has she been into anything I should know about?" I try to look innocent, but it's kind of hard with all the blood that's pooling in my head. Anita crosses her free arm over her chest and spends the next few minutes saying "Oh" and "I see" and finally, "All right, give us a half hour."

After she hangs up, she turns, settles her hands on her hips and shakes her head at me.

"What are you doing up in the attic at—" She stops to look at a tiny gold wristwatch that I've never seen her wear before "eight thirty in the morning!"

I decide the truth is the easiest way to go. "Just sleeping."

"In the attic!?!? That's the worst possible place to be in a tornado. Why aren't you in the basement?"

I finally push myself all the way back up and lower my bare feet to climb down the access ladder. "I'd rather die in a tornado than huddle in the basement all night."

Anita lets out a colossal sigh, but lets the subject drop. "That was Sheriff McCombs on the phone. We've got to go down to his office."

"Why?" My heart is doing butterfly gymnastics in my chest.

"Just get dressed."

She turns around, dismissing me, but I'm not ready to go. "Who did you think you were slamming the phone on?"

She looks back at me with an expression like she just swallowed a sour pickle. "I said get dressed. And get washed up, too. You smell like a filthy locker room full of moth balls."

Oh. There must be trouble in paradise with Richard.

I keep my thoughts to myself and get ready as quickly as possible; trying not to think about the last time I spoke to the sheriff.

When we arrive at the station, a mousy looking woman in a tight pantsuit leads us into a tiny little room with a big mirror and no windows. She tells us the Sheriff will be with us in a few minutes before handing each of us a typed page with our statements about the break in at our house. "Please read them over carefully to make sure everything is accurate, then sign and date the bottom," she says before walking out.

Anita sets her paper on the table then takes mine and places it on top of hers. "This is a load of crap," she tells me, then leans in close to my ear. "We're in an interrogation room," she whispers, sending a chill down my spine. "Be careful."

When Sheriff McCombs arrives, he sits across from us and flashes a smile that makes my skin crawl.

"Rodney West has confessed to breaking and entering into your house," he tells us, "and he freely admits to damaging your property. He claims he was looking for some money Cassie took from him. Do you know anything about that, Erika?"

"No, sir."

The sheriff nods. "This guy is a piece of work. Once he started talking, he wouldn't shut up. He admitted to some things I never even guessed. The money he claims Cassie owes him had to do with selling acid stamps and marijuana cigarettes at rock concerts. Says he's been getting people to ingest these acid stamps when they didn't even know what it was. Says he likes getting people all wacked out as a joke. Can you believe that?"

Ears ringing, I shake my head. If Rodney told him all that, he probably told him about the money I gave to Cassie.

Suddenly, the sheriff's face gets deadly serious. Here it comes.

"Here's the part that's not making a lick of sense to me. This kid freely admits to just about everything except he swears, and I mean he's really vehement, swearing up and down that he did not slash up Cassie's costumes."

"Her costumes?" Anita sits forward. "You mean her dance costumes were....slashed?"

Sheriff looks at me. "You didn't tell your mother about that?"

"No, sir."

The sheriff sits back and looks over the two of us carefully. "Walt Abbott tells me you and Cassie used to pop in and out of each other's bedroom windows all the time. Said he's seen you scuttling about in his yard more than once this summer. You been up to Cassie's room since she's been gone?"

"Oh come on!" Anita snaps, slapping one hand on the table. "Erika worshipped that girl. Why would she ever...oh, come on! Are you serious?"

"Don't know that the why of this thing is very important. Could be a young girl could get jealous over a fella the other girl dated...or how many shiny costumes and hours of attention her mom gives the other girl."

Anita snorts and shakes her head. I'm seriously considering throwing up.

"On the other hand, don't know that I was saying Erika did anything to those costumes. But if you were in there before the break in, I need to know what you saw. Answer the question."

"No sir, I wasn't in there. Not since Cassie left. Only the day I was there with you. I swear I—"

"Enough Erika." Anita sits forward and starts firing questions at him without waiting for any response. "Do you have any witness, other than your good buddy Chief Walter Abbott? Did anyone else see Erika go into the Abbott house any time this summer? Do I need to get my daughter a lawyer? Are you going to read us our rights?"

"Relax, Anita. I'm just saying—"

"No, I'm just saying," she practically spits the words at him, "I know what this is. Your buddy Walt Abbott points a finger at my child and now you're on her case? Well what if I point the finger at the Costas girl? You want to talk about jealous, there's your jealous. You want to talk about spoiled and vindictive, there's your girl. Last year during the pageant, I caught the little bitch messing with Cassie's tap costume."

"Well, I don't think—"

Anita pops out of her chair, too angry and worked up to sit still. "Oh, I know what you think. Little Tammy's got a set of parents that belong to the country club and the Rotary and all that garbage. And that makes a big difference doesn't it?"

"Now, Anita, calm down."

Oh man, that's the wrong thing to say to my mother when she's in one of her crazy furies. Even though she's on my side, I'm getting very nervous. She looks like her head might start spinning and pea soup will spew out of her mouth. "Don't you patronize me! And don't think I've forgotten our 'little talk' back when I moved to this godforsaken village. Remember that? Remember telling me this town is not like New York and you do not allow a single woman with a big pregnant belly to parade herself around with no wedding ring on her finger."

The sheriff is turning purple.

"Watch yourself. I'm just following up on something Walt told me."

"Really? Well maybe you should take a closer look at Walt. Cassie was the queen of that castle in more ways than one."

That gets the sheriff to his feet. "Walt worshipped that little girl," he yells. "What are you saying? What are you trying to say?"

At this point, Anita yanks open the door, hooks my upper arm and jerks me to my feet too.

"Yeah, Walt worshipped his pretty daughter all right. Whenever he wasn't thrashing her with his belt, he kept his eyes on her every move like she was his own personal property. He was always watching Cassie...and not like a daddy is supposed to watch his little girl!"

"That's outrageous!" Sheriff roars as Anita marches me out of the building with her chin held high.

When Penny opens her front door, she takes one look at us and says, "What happened?"

"Sheriff McCombs," Anita tells her, then stands still for Penny's hug. "Do you have anything to drink in this house?"

Penny nods and ushers us into her kitchen. "How do you feel about a Bloody Mary?" she asks.

"Ecstatic!" Anita drops into one of Penny's kitchen chairs.

While she's gathering the ingredients, Penny gives me a good long look. "Erika, are you losing weight?"

My mouth forms an automatic "no" but Anita jumps in with, "Of course she is. She's been disappearing all summer. She's losing it everywhere except those boobs!"

Why is it impossible for my mother to say anything even half nice about me without saying something disgusting, too?

Penny's husband, Ted, shuffles in wearing a bathrobe and stops when he sees what his wife is doing. "We're drinking before noon today?"

"They've been to see Sheriff McCombs," Penny says, splashing pickle juice into her cocktail shaker.

"Oh," Ted answers as if that explains everything and grabs a beer out of the fridge. "You want me to put you in touch with our attorney?"

Two hours later, the adults are still drinking cocktails while I sip iced tea.

Penny asks about Richard and Anita grumbles something about "a little tiff."

"Uh oh!" Penny chirps, "What's going on?

Anita directs a disgusted look toward me. "He was all hot and heavy to take us both to the Ohio State Fair next month." Her tone makes it sound like he offered to throw up on our living room sofa.

"Well what's wrong with that?" Ted asks.

"Maybe we should stay out of it," Penny says, tilting her head toward me.

"No come on," Ted insists, waving around his fourth beer. "What's so wrong with a guy offering to take his girlfriend and her daughter to the fair?"

Anita pulls her spine up perfectly straight and fixes Ted with her most condescending look. "First Wayne. Now Richard. No one ever offered to include my little girl on dates when she was a little meatball rolling around at my feet. I just want to know why they're all so hot and heavy to have her along now that she's sprouted these huge buzooms!" She cups her hands out in front of her own nearly flat chest to illustrate the point. Everyone, all three adults and even, I swear, Penny's deaf old schnauzer turn to stare at my boobs.

I think everything, including my eardrums, are blushing.

***

Julie walks into the Bixby on Saturday afternoon with a huge smile on her face. "Who's in the mood for a barn buster tonight?" she asks.

"Where is it?" Sonny asks while Jeff punches one fist in the air and says, "Dy-no-mite!"

"What's a barn buster?" I ask Chester quietly as Julie sketches something on a napkin for Sonny.

"It's an all night party," he tells me. "A bunch of friends pitch in money for kegs, they build a bonfire and everybody drinks and smokes from sun down to sun up in some old rickety barn." He looks toward Vince. "Can you get your dad's jeep?"

Vince looks irritated and shakes his head. "I told you what happened, man."

"He's still pissed?" Chester sounds amazed. "You hit one deer. I thought he just took your keys away for a month?"

"I hit another one," Vince mumbles and turns his back on us. "And swerved into a tree."

"Whoa! Bad luck, man."

When Julie hears that Vince and Chester aren't coming, she asks if I want to squeeze into her car with Jeff, Sonny and Meredith. I'd rather have my guts removed with a spoon.

"I have some chores I have to do for my mother tonight," I tell her.

"Oh, darn," she says.

"Yeah, darn," I echo back trying to make my voice sound sincere.

Sunday July 31, 1977

Dear Cassie,

A new nightmare!

Walking home from the Bixby last night, I was about a block from my house when an uneasy feeling suddenly crept over me. Despite the heat, my skin turned ice cold. I ducked down under the branches of a pine tree and scanned the neighborhood. At first everything seemed nice and normal and I was starting to think it was an attack of paranoia. Then I saw Candy Man's VW Bug in the parking lot next to the Pit Stop, right where he could watch the front door of my house.

My stomach slithered down to my shoes.

The obvious solution was to sneak back the way I came and hide at the Bixby. I gripped my set of keys and started back, but then I remembered something that stopped me in my tracks. My letters to you, those terrible Polaroid pictures and even that film cassette of Tammy—I'd left them all in a box on my desk. What if Candy Man was planning to break into my room again?

How could I be so stupid?

I circled around the block and made it all the way to the peony bushes that border your back yard when I spotted another car. The neighbor's porch light lit up a little bit of the front fender. It was a sky blue Maverick and it was parked in the grass behind my house with all the lights off and the engine running. I couldn't see who was inside, but I could see the lit end of a cigarette through the driver's side window. I crouched down and waited, hoping it might be Anita's boyfriend or someone else she knows, even as my stomach twisted and churned. I watched whoever it was smoke one, two, three cigarettes, tossing each glowing butt out of the driver's side window toward the alley. My feet and neck were starting to ache and twitch from all the tension.

I know what you're thinking, because I thought of it, too. It could have been someone looking at your house, not at mine. But even if that was true, I didn't want whoever it was to see me go back into my house and I had no way to get in without being seen.

Time slowed down to a trickle. Even with all my aching, twitching agony, my eyelids were drooping. I tried to sit and curl up, but the grass was getting damp and itchy. Digging around in the pockets of my windbreaker looking for a stick of gum, I heard the heavy rattle of my Bixby keys. It was time to give up and hide away in my safe and comfortable dressing room.

Keeping to the darkest shadows, I hustled my butt back to the theater, but not walking on the sidewalks or streets made the trip take twice as long as it usually does.

Guess what was parked right square in front of the side entrance to the Bixby when I got there.

That same stupid blue Maverick!

There was no way for me to sneak in. The driver, whoever it was, was sitting in that car still smoking up a storm with all the windows cracked just an inch. At that point, I almost sat down and howled with frustration. Or walked over to the sheriff's station to ask for help. Then I remembered a terrible scene between Sheriff McCombs and Anita that happened a few days ago. And there I was wandering around in the middle of the night, way after curfew. The sheriff would never understand.

Maybe I should have walked to Penny's. But I just walked back home. Once again, creeping through the shadows and avoiding the yards with outside dogs. Still, even with all the caution, the Hanson's hound dog just about scared the skin right off my body. In the end, I was in the process of climbing in my bedroom window when I saw that same blue Maverick cruise down my street.

Now there's no way that it was a coincidence, right?

One look at the pile of broken junk in my closet reminded me that Candy Man was out there, too. So I wedged our kitchen broom above my bedroom window to stop it from sliding up and turned on every light in the house. I reclaimed Anita's shotgun from the closet, pulled the green hallway phone with the long cord into my bedroom, shut the door and moved my dresser in front of it.

There is no way I can possibly tell you how scared I was, Cassie. And yet, I was so tired I kept flickering in and out of sleep the rest of the night until the noise of Anita tripping over the phone cord and cussing loudly ripped me out of this endless dream of running in mud.

In the shower, with water running over my head, I tried to piece it all together, but my brain keeps chasing itself in nonsense circles.

Candy Man's VW Bug was parked at the Pit Stop. Who owns the other car? I don't ever remember seeing it before.

I'm seriously thinking of getting out an old sheet and writing, "What do you want from me?" on it then hanging the thing on our front porch, but I know Anita would tear it down immediately.

Erika

BIXBY
STAR WARS

AUGUST 1977

"I think of my body as a side effect of my mind."

-Carrie Fisher

"I think the Force is in you. Force yourself."

-Harrison Ford

"I've learned that the [Star Wars] movies will never finally end. It just goes on and on and on....I accepted that a long time ago."

-Mark Hamill

| TWENTY-SIX |

ON MONDAY MORNING, ANITA WAKES ME UP BEFORE EIGHT o'clock waving another list of chores and dollar values in my face.

"If you know what's best for you, you'll have that list completed before you go hang out with your friends at the Bixby," she says. As she's leaving my bedroom, she stops and turns around, "Oh, and I expect you to be home by eight o'clock tonight. We have a guest coming."

What I say is, "Yes, ma'am."

What I'm thinking is, *Walking home before the sun sets sounds like a brilliant idea to me, guest or no guest.*

She doesn't make an announcement like that when Penny comes over, so I'm not really surprised when I come home to find a guy I've never seen before sitting on my front porch. This must be Richard. What surprises me, shocks me actually, is how young he looks. This guy has got to be at least ten years younger than my mom!

As I approach, he's lounging on the steps eating a gigantic slice of watermelon. Even though he's wearing paint-spattered coveralls and his sandy brown hair is sprinkled with sawdust, I can see that he's absolutely gorgeous. Movie star gorgeous. My feet stop while I stare at him in amazement. This guy is nothing like my mother's usual boyfriends.

He looks up, face all sticky from the melon, and says, "Hey, are you Erika? I'm Richard. Come over here and get some of this melon."

He's so friendly and casual and beautiful that I can't help smiling back at him. Without any hesitation, I sit down on the other side of the porch steps and accept an even bigger slice of melon than the one he's eating.

When Anita steps out on the porch ten minutes later, we're in the middle of a contest to see who can spit watermelon seeds the farthest. I tense up, waiting for an explosion, but all she does is laugh and shake her head.

"Glad you could tear yourself away from the theater to join us, Erika," she says and settles herself on the front porch swing. Richard immediately jumps up and joins her.

"You work in a theater?" he asks. "Far out!"

Before I can respond, Anita says, "My daughter has given up just about every day of her summer to volunteer at the Bixby theater downtown." I am absolutely shocked to hear the pride in her voice.

"The Bixby?" Richard looks at me with something close to awe. "That place is amazing!"

"You know the Bixby?" I ask.

"Oh wow, are you kidding?"

"Richard," Anita says, placing a hand on his arm. "Erika doesn't know anything about you. Tell her how you know about our theater."

For the next half hour, Richard tells me how he grew up in his father's paint and wallpaper store reading the books on historic architecture his father kept on hand. Apparently his father was obsessed with authenticity in older homes and businesses. Now Richard is equally enthusiastic about preserving historic landmarks.

"Did you know the Bixby was the first theater in this part of the state to be equipped with sound?" he asks.

Well, of course I know that because Nick told me all about it. I find myself telling Richard about the opening night as Nick described it, but then my voice stumbles when I mention the maintenance problems Nick is having.

"We're organizing a volunteer day on Wednesday to fix up the place a bit, but I'm not sure anything we can do in one day will help that much."

Richard gets this excited look in his eyes, points a finger at me then swoops into the house. Anita shrugs one shoulder and sips her drink. "He gets like this sometimes," she tells me.

Through the open front door, I hear Richard on the phone calling some friends to help with the "Bixby Restoration Project." Between calls, he manages to talk Anita into lending her talents to the project.

"I hope Nick appreciates the whirlwind that is about to descend on that theater," Anita tells me.

***

On Tuesday, Jeff announces that a bunch of his football buddies are coming to help us fix up the theater. Vince and Chester are bringing a group of guys they know from the AV Club. Alex says that the group of Vietnam veterans who will be volunteering has grown to twenty men.

When Nick hears that, he looks uncomfortable. "Doesn't seem right to ask those boys to work for free after all they've been through," he grumbles.

"It makes them feel good to help out someone else, Popples," Alex tells him in voice I could barely hear. "It lifts them up."

When we arrive at the theater early Wednesday morning, there are so many volunteers milling around that no one seems to know what to do or who to ask. It's a mess. Richard knows what should happen, but he's not exactly a born leader. Instead of taking charge, he bounces around shaking hands and pointing out all the wonderful architectural details.

An ear-splitting whistle brings the room to silent attention. My mother is standing on the stairs with both hands in the air.

"Everyone with formal technical skills get on this side of the room," she yells, pointing her left hand left. "Everyone else on this side of the room." She points her right hand right.

Before I know it, she has everybody assigned to a team and every team assigned to a task.

As an unskilled worker, I'm assigned to paint the lobby walls with a small group of volunteers, which includes Julie. We're just getting started when Sonny walks in late, holding the door open for Heidi to follow.

Heidi immediately points to the paint can in my hand. "Can I help Erika paint? I'm really good at painting."

"Have at it," Sonny says and walks into the theater.

We paint the walls in the lobby a creamy white that makes the old paint look dirty yellow while Mrs. P watches us from a stool and points at places she wants to be sure we don't miss. Heidi really is good at painting and a hard worker, but she can't get on a ladder, not even a step stool, because her balance isn't good.

"Sorry I'm so jiggely-wiggely," she tells me.

"I think you're perfect," I assure her.

Around noon, Meredith shows up in a cute tube top and cut off jeans with her massive hair tucked under a bandana. She looks so clean and fresh and cute. I want to smash her. Luckily, Anita intercepts her as soon as she walks in. Out of the corner of my eye, I watch a brief heated exchange before Meredith walks over to join us with my mother hot on her heels.

"This little princess has decided to join us for a little painting," Anita announces in a falsetto. "I'll go get her highness a little brush," she warbles before mincing away.

"Who is that bitch?" Meredith asks the group as soon as Anita is out of range.

"That bitch is my mother," I tell her proudly with something like love swelling in my chest.

"Wow! No wonder you're such a freak," Meredith says with absolute sincerity.

"Merri!" Julie exclaims in horror, but all I can do is laugh.

"I recommend you make sure you're painting like fury before she gets back," I say, nodding toward a clean roller.

The group settles back into a comfortable working silence as Mrs. P rocks and hums and occasionally snaps her fingers at us from her stool. Heidi is painting directly below the spot where I'm perched on a ladder. When I glance down, she's looking up at me with a smile on her face.

"I have your invitation to my birthday party in my purse, Erika," she whispers.

Up until this second, I had totally forgotten about Heidi's birthday. With all the stuff that has happened between accepting her invitation and now, I'm instantly dreading the party. But I smile and say, "Great" with as much spirit as I can muster.

We all paint on in silence for a while until Meredith asks, "Hey, Erika, do you have a boyfriend?"

Heidi giggles and I shrug.

"Meredith." Julie's tone is a warning. Heidi looks at her in alarm, but Meredith keeps right on painting without acknowledging her cousin. "Did you know Vince is in love, I mean capital L-O-V-E love with you?"

"Vince?" Heidi looks confused. "Erika is too pretty for Vince."

Bless her sweet, sweet heart.

"Meredith!" Julie's voice is getting harsher, "Drop it."

I don't know what's going on, but I'm sick and tired of secrets.

"No, don't drop it," I say, my voice sounding worn thin to my own ears. "What do you want to say Meredith? Just say it."

"Oh well…it's just that Vince got a few beers in him Tuesday night after you left and announced to everyone that he was in love with you and he would kill anyone who tried to hurt you. Then he got all weepy and said you didn't like him, but you sure spent plenty of time staring at Sonny."

I plant my paintbrush on one hip and glare at her. When I open my mouth to say that I can't stand Sonny, I feel the weight of Heidi's eyes watching me, waiting. "Vince was talking nonsense."

We stare each other down for a minute until she shrugs and turns back to her painting. "Wouldn't matter to me if you were panting over him. Sonny is just a little summer fun. I'm not going to be dating a high school senior from the middle of Nowheresville next year."

I keep my lips zipped and focus on rolling the paint on the wall.

Julie starts babbling that it's too bad I'm not interested because Vince is such a sweetheart. Am I sure I'm not interested? Not even a tiny bit? Because Vince will worship me and never cheat on me or treat me bad because he is really SUCH a sweetheart.

I'm getting pretty irritated with Julie, but it's Meredith who finally comes to my rescue.

"If he's that damn amazing, why don't you date him yourself?" She asks, throwing her roller down on the metal paint pan.

"He's not in love with me," Julie says, very seriously.

"Oh come on! Listen to yourself. Vince is a spaz."

"Shhhhh...He may hear us."

"No, let's get one thing straight. You've never dated any nice boys, have you? No! You dated Jeff until he made out with that missing beauty queen at your own graduation party. Who are you to tell Erika she should date this nice, ugly boy? And why are you back here hanging out with Jeff again?"

"Drop it," Julie says between clenched teeth.

"Yes, by all means, let's drop it." Meredith storms away to the bathroom.

"She stomps and fights a lot," Heidi whispers to me in a voice that probably carried into the theater. I giggle. Mrs. P clicks her tongue and shakes her head.

Meredith doesn't come back to join our group again. She gets recruited by some of the veterans to help them do something with the wiring.

The rest of the day goes pretty smoothly. We all paint, polish, scrub, haul, wire and repair as much as possible until after the sun sets. As promised, Nick shows up with plenty of beer and pizza. Then he walks around ooohing and aaahing over everything that we've done. Anita doesn't even bat an eyelash when Alex hands me a cup of frothy beer. I sip some, but it doesn't taste like anything I want to drink after all that work. So I open two Cokes, one for me and one for Heidi, and listen to her excited chatter about her birthday. That girl has more energy than the sun.

Saturday August 6, 1977

Dear Cassie,

Disaster! After all that work, it's a complete and total disaster.

This is how it went down. Harold P. Commisford arrived in a brand new Cadillac that was so shiny in the afternoon sun you needed safety goggles to look at it directly. The man who stepped out looked oddly similar to Nick – on the short side with a bald head, giant ears and a wide grin that connected his floppy earlobes. But everything about Mr. Commisford screamed money. From his white leather shoes, to his tailored linen suit, fedora hat and silk tie with monogram HPC pin. He was carrying a golden walking stick and there were diamonds on his fingers and cufflinks. This old man glittered like a disco ball.

While we all stood inside staring, this guy stood on the sidewalk, looked up at the marquee and stretched out his arms in a thrusting motion that seemed to say, "Look at that! I've found Heaven." For a second I wondered if he was a preacher who wanted to turn this theater into a church. Alex says that's one of the sad but common fates of historic theaters that can't make money.

Eventually he got tired of worshipping the marquee, but he didn't walk in right away. First he turned around in a slow circle and pointed to various buildings around the square. Then he took a little notepad out of his breast pocket and made notes with a thin gold pen.

"Is it me or is this guy a hoot?" Sonny asked no one in particular. Jeff, Vince, and I all kept silent. Alex snorted. Mrs. P crossed herself. Maybe all that shiny metal made her think he was a man in uniform.

Outside, our visitor tucked his notepad and pen back in his pocket, patted his heart two or three times then headed for the door. Vince and I scrambled back into the theater, but stayed just inside the doors with our faces pressed to the cracks. Everyone else acted busy except Mrs. P. She just kept staring.

Once inside, Mr. Commisford pumped Nick's hand with so much enthusiasm I was afraid for Nick's shoulder. Then he opened his arms and looked around smiling this huge smile and shaking his head. Finally he said, "Look at this place. Just look at it! It's a real old-time movie palace! Who knew this jewel was sitting here in this poor, blue collar community? Unbelievable!"

Nick looked upset. I heard Vince suck in air between his teeth and looked over. "Not good," he whispered. "Nick is proud of this town. Been on every civic committee."

Basically, the whole tour was this guy giving the same performance. Every time he walked into a new area, he would hold out his arms like Jesus on his way to Heaven. The theater, the stage, the projection room....I thought the guy might actually kneel down and weep when he stood in the balcony. For his part, Nick made it a point to list out every fault he could think of. On one hand, you could say Nick was being scrupulous with his honesty. Personally, I think Nick was annoyed by this guy and hoping to scare him away, but the long laundry list of overdue maintenance, damages and looming expenses had the opposite effect. The more problems Nick listed, the more happy and excited Mr. Commisford acted.

At the end, when Nick had finally run out of bad things to say about the Bixby, Mr. Commisford turned to him and said, "You've got a lot of problems, sure, but there's so much potential here. I think we should talk business."

Nick kept his feet firmly planted and eyed the other man with suspicion. "Like I told you on the phone, I won't even think about twinning this place. That's would be an abomination."

"I agree, I agree. Wouldn't work here anyway with the theatrical stage. No twinning."

I must have been looking as lost as I felt, because Vince whispered," Twinning is cutting the theater into two theaters." I looked at him like he was crazy. He chopped his arm up and down "They build a wall right down the middle."

I heard Nick say, "What I just can't seem to understand is how this place is going to start making so much money."

By this point, I was getting a little impatient and irritated with Nick. This guy was a Fruit Loop, but he was a rich Fruit Loop and he'd been nothing but nice and positive. After hearing all about the Bixby's warts and problems, he still wanted to talk business. Nick was being so unfriendly!

"Oh, there's lots of money to be made here. Let's go into your office and have a chat shall we?"

After they disappeared into Nick's office, Vince and I joined Jeff, Sonny, Alex, and Mrs. P in the lobby. The popcorn machine was just starting to churn out the kernels. We all whispered half-formed thoughts at once while the popping intensified.

"What do you think?"

"Is the roof really gonna cost that much to fix?"

"Nick is not happy."

"Maybe he's a con artist."

"Shiny man."

That last one was Mrs. P's contribution. We kept talking for a few minutes, but what happened next stunned us into silence.

There was a crash as Nick's office door flew open and hit the wall. We all heard Nick's voice roar, "Out!"

There was a few seconds that felt like silence even though I could hear murmurs of the other guy talking fast. Then Nick bellowing, "Ooooouuuuuuut! Get out of my theater. Get out right this minute."

Mr. Commisford appeared at the top of the stairs, smiled down at all of our upturned faces and shrugged dramatically with his whole body. In no particular hurry, he started to descend with one hand on the carved banister. Nick, nearly purple in the face, appeared at the top of the stairs where the other man had just stood and glared at his back like the force of his eyes could shove the offending creature out the door.

At the bottom of the stairs, Mr. Commisford looked at us and said, "I did try to make him understand, children."

"I said get out. Don't you talk to my workers!"

His smile took on a melancholy tint, "This place won't last till Christmas, I'm afraid. Such a shame."

Then he walked out the front door with Nick yelling, "And don't you come back to my theater."

When the door clicked shut, there was only the sound of the popcorn.

Eventually, Nick settled down enough to talk to Alex and she was able to get the whole story out of him. It turns out Harold P. Commisford turns old theaters into adult movie theaters. What he calls "art movies" but are really dirty movies. And he also wanted to bring in live exotic dancers, turn the balcony into a bar and feature stage plays with naked characters and burlesque shows. A total "adult entertainment experience."

Harold P. Commisford shall heretofore and forever be known as Dirty Harry by the Bixby crew.

After we all got done laughing and giggling about Dirty Harry, Alex told everyone Harry was right about one thing. The theater can't last much longer, even with all this extra business from *Star Wars*. She didn't look at me or mention the tax issue. Instead, she told us that the air conditioning is ready to go. She said the blizzard we had in January seriously damaged most of the windows in the second and third floor dressing rooms, the fire system is not up to code and a whole bunch of other stuff I can't remember right now.

Plus, and this was the worst blow, Alex told us she will be leaving soon. She and another nurse from Vietnam are going to start an organic farm near San Francisco. They already signed the papers on the property six months ago. Alex has been putting off her own dreams to help Nick. He can't afford to hire a union projectionist and most of them won't work for him anyway because he's been using non-union people. No matter what, she's leaving in September.

What a disaster!

And yet I'm glad Nick isn't going to let Dirty Harry turn the Bixby into a wretched hive of scum and villainy.

Erika

| TWENTY-SEVEN |

WHEN I GET HOME FROM THE THEATER, ANITA AND RICHARD are sitting on the porch listening to the Cincinnati Reds game on the radio and playing cards. Right away they ask me about the big business man so I tell them the story. At first they're amused, but then they start saying things like Nick is a fool. He has no business sense and the world is changing.

"He's running that place like a charity," Anita says.

"Yeah, maybe you're right. Maybe we shouldn't have done that work for him," Richard says.

Oh that makes me so mad! "You would rather he runs it like a disco whorehouse?"

"Watch your mouth!" Anita snaps in her mother monster voice.

I'm choking on my anger all the way to bed. When I try to climb out on the roof to cool down, the sound of Anita and Richard talking and laughing makes me want to throw up. Worse, with the lovebirds camped out on our porch, it's impossible to escape this house. All I can do to relieve the tension is plug the headphones into our stereo, crank up the *Star Wars* soundtrack and practice screaming into my pillow.

The next day, Chester is bouncing around the theater asking the same questions about Dirty Harry over and over. He's driving me bonkers. I corner Vince outside the supply area and ask him to get Chester to shut up or go away. I give him my saddest eyes and put my hand on his arm.

"No one can get Chester to stop talking, not even Chester," Vince says.

"Is there any chance you can make him go away?" I beg him. "Please."

Vince stands there wobbling back and forth until a sneaky look comes into his eyes. "Make a deal with you. I'll get Chester to go away. You agree to let us make a movie with your camera."

"Yes, I mean... Wait! Just one film cassette? They're only four minutes long."

"Okay, one film cassette. Do we have a deal?" he asks, backing away from me slowly.

"Where the Super 8 goes, I go."

"Deal!" Vince says, then hurries away while dread and anxiety wash over me. In order to get rid of Chester for now, I've signed up to go somewhere with the two of them and shoot a short film. Dumb move!

Just four minutes, just four minutes of film, just four minutes.... that's the chant I keep in my head the rest of the day.

We end up in Chester's garage on Jefferson Avenue, three blocks from my house. Turns out my presence fits right into their plan. Otherwise, Chester's twin sister was going to have to play the "beautiful space ghost" and...oh my! She looks like Chester in a skirt, poor thing.

They try to explain the story, something about an ancient Roman ghost story adapted to take place in the future, in space, then they show me comic strips Vince calls storyboards. They've already created silvery Roman costumes out of painted sheets and tin foil. I change into my costume in the tool shed

In order to get the timing right, Chester makes us do three practice runs with a stopwatch and no film in the camera. Then the actual filming starts. First with me behind the camera while Vince and Chester act like two space explorers arriving on a new planet. Then Vince takes over the camera for shots of Chester trying to sleep on a silver inflatable pool float with boxes flying all around. The boxes are actually being tossed around by Chester's sister and me from outside the shot. Then there's a tight shot of Chester looking up from sleep to see me in my space-age toga standing above his head. He follows me to the garden—a small strip of white pebbles with silver whirly gigs—where I point at him, then point down at the dirt and stomp my foot. The last shot is Chester pulling a plastic model skull out of the dirt then turning around to find I'm gone.

Despite everything, I'm having fun.

So, after we finish the film, I sit and listen to Vince and Chester chatter about other ghost stories that could be filmed.

"Like the abandoned railroad bridge past the cemetery." Vince tells me. "a girl committed suicide there in the 20's, now people see her walking the track.

"I'm not climbing up there!" I tell him. "Are you crazy?"

"I would do it," Chester says.

"It's got to be a girl," I remind him.

"With a dress and long hair, who could tell from so far away?" Chester shrugs.

"Yeah, Chester is a good actor."

"I've been doing plays since I was five years old. I was the lead in *Peter Pan* last year. I'll show you."

Chester jumps up and runs inside, leaving me alone with Vince. I really want to back out of this project. It worked earlier when I wanted some peace and quiet, so I take a deep breath, lean toward Vince with my begging eyes and put my hand on his arm. "Vince, the thing is—"

Vince leans in and kisses me. On the lips! A quick smacking kiss like you give your mom. I'm so shocked and horrified, I freeze up with my mouth open. Then he grabs me and presses his open mouth to my open mouth. His lips are two warm slugs smashed up against my teeth. I try to turn my head away and lean back, but he presses in harder, squirming his mouth around and making this mum, mum, mum sound. I gag and shove his chest hard with both hands to get him off me. He falls right off the bench we're sitting on and I jump up.

"Erika, please."

I grab my camera and get out of there as fast as I can. I'm halfway home before I realize I'm still wearing the silly costume. My clothes are in Chester's shed. I should go back, but I can't do it even though I feel ridiculous and exposed in this costume. It's a painted sheet cut into a simple dress with another sheet draped over one shoulder and aluminum foil flowers at the hem. There's more foil flowers clipped in my hair and baby powder whitening every inch of exposed skin. It feels like I'm wearing a neon sign that says, *Look here!* So I duck into the back alleyways to get home.

The sky blue Maverick is idling with all the lights off in the alleyway about half a block from my house. I duck behind the spruce tree near the corner. My whole mouth, already burning from that gross kiss, suddenly tastes of metal. I watch as a cigarette drops out of the window, holding my breath. Time stretches out. Ten, maybe twenty minutes go by before the car starts rolling forward. It rolls super slow past my house, then it rounds the curve toward the next street and disappears.

I pick up the hem of that toga dress and run like crazy for home.

Anita and Richard are on the back porch drinking some kind of fruity frozen drinks and playing Chinese checkers. They both stop and stare as I hurry toward them.

"This has GOT to be a good story," Richard says, wiggling his eyebrows.

"Do I need to start you on birth control pills, or is it too late?" Anita asks then they both giggle like little girls. I walk inside without bothering to answer.

***

The next morning I find Richard in our kitchen drinking a cup of coffee and standing in front of our open refrigerator. My mother is nowhere in sight.

"Hey Erika, did you know somebody stole all the food out of your fridge?" ha asks me, deadly serious. "The thief only left behind three bottles of Tab, some orange juice and a tub of margarine."

"That's normal," I mumble and shuffle past him to grab a box of Cap'n Crunch.

"I was going to make breakfast," he tells me with such sad, puppy dog eyes that I can't keep up the hostility.

"I wouldn't do that if I were you," I tell him. "She hates the sight or smell of food in the morning. All she wants is coffee and orange juice."

"Oh, I know about her crazy eating habits! All messed up if you ask me...which she keeps reminding me she didn't." He flashes a sheepish grin and closes the refrigerator door. "I meant I was going to make a decent breakfast for the two of us."

"You don't have to do that," I tell him, scooping a handful of cereal out of the box.

"Eat? I consider it a pretty vital function."

"No, I mean you don't have to make stuff for me or be all nice to me. In fact, it's probably not a good idea." The memory of Anita's words to Penny echoes in my memory. *They're all so hot and heavy to have her along now that she's sprouted these huge buzooms.* I have to fight the urge to cross my arms over my chest.

"Okaaaaaaaay," he leans against the counter and takes a hearty gulp from his cup. "Should I throw Tab bottles at you? Will that convince you to help me find some food?"

I hold out the box of cereal and shake it. He eyes the Cap'n suspiciously and makes no move to take any. "That stuff is toxic, man."

I shrug and take another handful. "Now you sound like her," I tell him, setting the open box on the counter.

As I'm leaving for the Bixby ten minutes later, Richard is sitting at the kitchen table eating green beans straight from the can. "I'm buying some damned groceries for this house!" he tells me as I'm walking out the door.

"Have at it," I yell back over my shoulder. "And may the Force be with you.

***

The most incredible, heavenly scent invades my bedroom the next morning, drawing me out of bed and down the stairs toward our kitchen.

"Ah ha!" Richard yells as soon as I walk through the doorway. He waves a baking sheet in front of me, blasting my senses with that delicious aroma. "No one can resist the lure of my homemade granola. Step into my parlor and prepare to be amazed."

As soon as I sit down at the kitchen table, Richard slides a bowl under my nose. It's a mound of ripe berries with a layer of crunchy nuts and grains sprinkled on top. Richard stands over me with his arms crossed. "Come on, Mikey. Let's see how you like it."

The first bite is so amazing, I have to close my eyes. Damn, why did he have to do this? Now I'm going to miss him when he leaves.

"What's the matter, Erika?" he asks, sitting across from me. "You really don't like it?"

"It's the most fantastical thing I've ever tasted," I tell him, unable to keep the sadness out of my voice.

"You say that like it's a bad thing."

My mother's relationships never last longer than a few months. She finds a summer romance after every recital and ends it before her fall dance classes start. When I open my eyes, Richard is watching me with such concern. I can't tell him it's August so he'll be out of the picture in less than a month. Instead, I make my lips smile.

"I don't want you to get cocky."

He laughs like that's the funniest joke he's heard in a long time. "Too late!" He stands up and heads back toward the oven. "You want me to pack up some of this to take with you to the theater today?"

"Theater's closed today." My stomach drops. "I have to go to a birthday party."

"Good grief, Erika! You make it sound like you're going to a funeral. What will it take to make you cheer up?"

That's a good question. "I wish I knew," I tell him and focus every bit of my attention on the most delicious breakfast I've ever eaten.

Wednesday August 10, 1977

Dear Cassie,

Today was Heidi's birthday.

Richard drove me to Heidi's party. You know, I really do like Richard better than any of Anita's other boyfriends and I don't think he cares about the size of my boobs. Not only did he drive me to the party, he stopped at Woolworth's, helped me pick out the best gift and he even paid before I could dig out my own money. His eyes never once drifted anywhere near my chest.

There was a map drawn on the back of Heidi's invitation, but we still managed to take a few wrong turns and got a little lost. Richard didn't lose his sense of humor. We were twisting and turning down this crazy rollercoaster of a country road and he started imitating hillbilly banjo music and yelling, "Hee haw!" Between the road tickling my stomach and Richard's comedy routine, I couldn't stop laughing.

Then the road ended. We went over a hill and it just ended...with a thick stone wall. Richard stomped on the brakes so hard the car skidded sideways and kicked up gravel. Our front fender ended up inches from the wall. I almost peed my pants, but Richard stayed totally calm, cool and collected. Eyes forward, he whistled long and low.

"Would you look at that." He said it like we were out for a leisurely drive and just came across something interesting. Even though my heart was practically sitting on my tongue, I looked out to see what he was whistling at.

Beyond the garden wall that almost killed us, there was a sea of flowers in every color of the rainbow. No grass. Only flowers, flowers and more flowers in a wild kaleidoscope of blooms. I could see a white farm house in the distance, but it was a small island among the flowers. The effect was crazy beautiful. Like the magical planet I've been creating in my head.

My car door opened and there was Sonny, wearing cut off jeans, a Bud Man t-shirt full of holes and one of his heaviest frowns. "Everyone okay?"

"Sorry about the skid out, man," Richard said. "We're looking for the Johannson Farm."

I opened my mouth to tell him this must be it, but Sonny's lips moved faster. "You found it. Let me guess, there was no warning sign? About a half mile back?"

Richard shrugged, "We were goofing around. Might have missed it."

"No, it keeps falling down." Sonny shot me a grim look. "I asked Jeff to make sure the sign was very easy to see this morning."

"No big thing." Richard fished Heidi's birthday present off the floor and tucked it under my left arm. "Nice flowers. Your folks own a flower shop or something?"

Sonny cracked one of his rare smiles. "No shop. We like to call this the Heidi Sue Botanical Gardens. Heidi's my sister. The birthday girl. Flowers are her super power."

Heidi?

After Richard drove away, I stood in a daze looking around at all the amazing flowers – a birdbath filled with pansies, candy-colored snapdragons mingling with frilly bushes of white daisies, fat pink peonies surrounded by silvery lavender plants, a row of sunflowers standing tall and proud as soldiers against a fragment of rusted iron fence, plum and purple irises with fat bumblebees hovering.

"This is all Heidi's work?"

I walked away from Sonny, my eyes drinking in the colors – hollyhocks, geraniums, daylilies and a single bird of paradise while Sonny explained.

"Heidi has a rare gift with flowers. Anything will bloom for her. From spring thaw past first frost, she's out here for hours. Planting, weeding, trimming...she even talks and sings to the flowers. And there's the flower power girl herself."

Heidi was bouncing up and down on the front porch.

"Erika! You came!"

"Heidi, I am in love with your flower garden!" I told her.

Heidi giggled. "Come and join the party. Everyone wants to meet you!"

Everyone? I froze as Heidi bounced away, leaving a trail of giggles behind her. Sonny noticed I wasn't moving. "What's wrong?"

"Who is everyone? Sonny hooked my elbow and leaned toward me. "Yeah…about that. There's something I have to tell you."

I was starting to panic. Really panic. "What?!?!"

"My mom's maiden name is West." Silence stretched out.

"You know," Sonny said, "as in Rodney West. As in Candy Man. He's my second cousin."

I looked at him in horror. "You mean Candy Man is here? Now?"

"No, he doesn't come around here much. There's a messy family thing… not quite a feud. It's hard to explain. I thought you should know…in case anyone mentions anything. I don't want you to feel weird."

"I always feel weird."

Sonny cupped his hand behind my neck, his thumb resting on the sensitive place behind my ear. My insides turned buttery.

"Relax, you won't feel weird here," he said. "Next to this family, you'd have to be a real freak show not to feel downright normal." A wicked grin crept over his face. "And if you don't have fun today, I will personally kiss Deputy Wayne Todd full on the lips."

When we walked around the house to the back yard, a tiny woman with long copper braids and paint-splattered overalls practically tackled me with a hug.

"Welcome to the family," Sonny said, walking away.

"This is Mom!" Heidi said.

She held me out at arm's length for a long look while I tried not to squirm. "Call me Bev." She pointed at an older version of Sonny with crinkly eyes and blonde hair going very white. "That's John. We don't do any of that Mister and Missus nonsense around here."

"We are very happy you came, Honey," she whispered then quickly turned to Heidi. "Heidibug, make sure she meets everybody, okay?"

Everybody was quite a group. Heidi grabbed my arm and dragged me around to introduce me to two grandmas, one grandpa, three great-aunts, the neighbor guy and his very fat beagle before we finally landed on Cousin Jeff sitting in a lawn chair with a beer in his hand.

"Er-REEK-a!" he yelled.

Next I met Jeff's dad, mom, and a tiny woman with fiery red hair everyone called Auntie Boo. She immediately grabbed my arm and whispered in my ear that she's from the West side of the family and has no use for most of "that worthless bunch." From there, I lost track of the people I met. There were at least twenty more people – cousins, second cousins, friends, and friends of friends. I was exhausted by the time Sonny set up a chair for me next to Jeff. Heidi was still bouncing around, the belle of the ball.

Grandpa started doing sleight of hand tricks and Jeff's mom said, "Oh here we go," a little too loud and poured a tiny bottle of booze into her lemonade.

Bev crouched between Auntie Boo and Jeff and whispered, "How many drinks has your mother downed?"

Jeff shrugged. "Lost count."

"Lovely," Bev sighed while grandpa pulled a quarter out of my ear.

Everyone was talking and laughing, shouting over everyone else. Someone, a cousin I think, tried to walk on his hands and knocked over a folding table full of food. The beagle ate five cupcakes before anyone could stop him. Grandpa moved up to card tricks. One of the great aunts offered to read my palm and told me I needed to follow my heart "across the sea."

When Heidi opened her gifts, she cried at each and every one. She opened mine and yelled, "Mom! Erika got me a Bedazzler. I've always wanted one."

"Watch out Marie Osmond! Heidi is going to be bedazzling," Sonny said in a teasing tone from where he was stretched out on the grass. While Heidi tore into the next package, I caught him shifting a sideways look in my direction.

"Good job," Jeff whispered. "She really has been wanting one forever."

"Doesn't every girl?" I whispered back.

Most of the way through the gifts, Jeff's mom wobbled over to fall into a rope hammock that was strung between two maple trees.

"At least she didn't fall asleep on the table this year," Jeff muttered.

Not long after that, Heidi announced, "I'm hot! Let's swim now."

I wasn't wearing a swimsuit. I have not asked Anita to buy swimwear for me since the summer before sixth grade when she pinched my emerging right nipple in the ladies dressing room and said, "Is this a pudgy fat roll or are you developing boobs this early?"

Bev found a black one piece suit and said, "This may not fit exactly but you can wear one of Sonny's t-shirts over it." She gave me a tattered t-shirt and ushered me into the bathroom. I put on the bathing suit. It fit ok. I mean, as well as any bathing suit ever feels like it fits. Then I put on my own t-shirt and walked out. Bev was tying Heidi into a life vest.

"I'm not so good at swimming, but I like to float," she said.

I followed her down the grassy slope toward a sparkling, lazy creek that runs behind their house. At one point, she got a little wobbly on her feet, so I hooked my arm through hers and tried to ignore the way my butt felt very exposed to the world. I was glad to have water to jump into when we got there.

All the parents except Jeff's mom joined us. There were lots of black tubes for floating and a rope swing tied to a sturdy tree branch. I floated near Heidi and didn't get involved in most of the splashing or rope swinging, but I thought it was so cool that all the parents took turns swinging out over the water. Jeff's dad did an awesome Tarzan call.

Everything was perfect. The sky started to mellow into peach and pink clouds. I was leaning my hair back into the water when I felt a wet hand gently shove my right leg causing my tube to rotate around. Rolling my head to one side I found myself almost nose-to-nose with Sonny treading water. He hooked my tube with one arm.

"So, are you having fun? Or do I need to pucker up with Wayne?"

"I don't know if I want to let you off the hook" I whispered back, forcing myself to look at him without pulling my head away. "It would be so much fun to see you kiss Wayne."

"I'd rather kiss a Jawa."

"What is the problem between you and Deputy Wayne Todd?" I asked.

Most of the humor melted out of Sonny's eyes. "Never mind. You already have enough reasons to think I'm a bad guy."

"I don't think you're a bad guy." Our eyes locked. His shoulder was touching my arm and I wanted so badly to let my hand wander over the skin beneath the water's surface.

Sonny made a low growling sound in his throat and disappeared under the water. Then he emerged behind me, circled my neck with his wet hands and put his mouth close to my ear. "You are so exasperating."

With the sun disappearing quickly, I was shivering and covered in goose bumps when we got back to the picnic tables. Sonny shoved a sweatshirt at me and said, "Put this on."

After the deserts, Sonny stood up and said, "Are you ready to go, Erika?"

The ride home in Sonny's truck was quiet, but not tense at all. My body felt like it was wrapped in a warm glow. "Tell me about you and Wayne Todd."

"It's complicated," Sonny muttered.

"Please."

"Not tonight, Nancy Drew. Ask me some other time, okay?"

We didn't say anything else until he turned on my street and stopped in front of the house. My eyes automatically scanned the area for the blue maverick. That gave me a new idea.

"Do you know anyone who drives a light blue Maverick?"

"No, why?" Sonny replied.

"There's been one around the neighborhood cruising by my house and the theater kind of slow and stuff."

I could feel his eyes on my profile. "I don't know any blue mavericks," he said slowly.

Sonny put the truck in park and looked at me. "We're going to start taking you home," Sonny said. "Jeff or me or Vince. No more walking home alone."

I opened my mouth to argue, but Sonny made a slashing motion and leaned out his window to wave toward the porch. No one was standing there, but I noticed a curtain twitch. Anita?

"See you tomorrow, Little Buddy," Sonny said cheerfully.

I wanted to stay, but I knew it was time to get out of the truck.

"Welcome to the family," Sonny said, leaning out his open window as he pulled away. I stood there in front of my house, wearing his sweatshirt and watched the taillights disappear down the street.

Welcome to the family. He said that twice. Twice. It has to mean something, don't you think?

Erika

| TWENTY-EIGHT |

On Thursday morning, I float to the theater in a bubble of happiness that bursts the second I walk through the side entrance. Julie and Meredith are standing in the lobby, giggling away with Sonny and Jeff. Meredith's hands keep touching and rubbing and scratching some place on Sonny's body like he's her little pet. It's disgusting.

No one notices me, so I duck and hurry into the theater to start cleaning and immediately run into a worse problem. Vince is already in there pushing the Bissell around. The memory of that horrible kiss comes back to me as I back slowly out of the theater.

There's only one place to go. Cleaning the bathrooms may be the most disgusting job at the Bixby, but it will keep me away from everyone for a good chunk of time.

Over two hours later, Chester finds me in the men's bathroom polishing the hand dryers. He shoves a brown paper sack under my nose.

"My mom washed and folded your clothes," he tells me. "There's also five dollars in there to pay you for the film cassette we used. Can I have it?"

I close my eyes. "Oh, Chester. Um, I'm sorry, I just, I—"

"You still have the movie we shot, right? You didn't smash it up or throw it away, did you?"

"Why would I do that?"

"Vince told me what happened."

"Oh, wow." I feel like I'm going to dissolve into the bathroom floor.

"I told him it was a stupid thing to do." Chester lifts my arm and tucks the bag under it. "How mad are you?"

"I'm not mad, I'm mortified. I don't like Vince at all that way!"

"I know; you're in love with Sonny."

I jerk away from him reflexively with every intention of denying it, but, when I look at Chester, I see a boy who has a crush on Jeff and can't use the school bathrooms without being tortured. "Is it that obvious?"

"Sonny has no clue, if that's what you mean. He can be pretty stupid about girls." Chester jerks his thumb toward the lobby. "Look at that rude ho bag he's letting hang all over him. Probably thinks he can save her from herself or some stupid idea like that. Sonny can't resist pathetic cases. Don't worry, it won't last."

His words remind me of Alex teasing Sonny about his "damn fool crusade." Suddenly, I realize Chester may have something I want much more than money.

"Chester, I have your movie. I'll give it to you and you can keep your five dollars. I just have one condition."

Chester gives me a very suspicious look. "What condition?"

"Do you know what Alex means when she talks about Sonny's crusade and villains and victims."

"Oh sure, I was one of the victims."

"Of Sonny?"

Chester gives me a dirty look. "You can't possibly be that dumb can you?"

"Tell me everything and I'll give you your movie. I might even agree to shoot more movies if you keep Vince far away from me."

He presses a finger over his lips and backs up to peek out the bathroom door into the lobby. Then he motions me to the back wall of the bathroom and tells me about the beatings and the torture he endured during his freshman year.

"I was going to kill myself. I really was," he tells me with dry eyes and no trace of emotion in his voice.

"What happened?"

"Sonny caught two guys beating the crap out of me behind the gym, and he stopped them. I mean, he was better than Batman,

Erika. You should have seen it. He tore those guys up! He's got moves like Bruce Lee. Better than Bruce Lee."

"I know he gets into a lot of fights—"

"No, he hurts people who hurt other people. Big difference. You know that linebacker he beat up last year?" I nod. "He caught that guy holding down a girl trying to make her do stuff, Erika. You know; sex stuff. Everybody talks about how he put that guy in the hospital. Nobody talks about that girl. She went to the hospital, too. They pressed charges on Sonny, but they didn't do anything about what happened to that girl."

"Who was she?"

"Doesn't matter. What matters is that Sonny is like a real life Jedi. Kinda cool, huh?"

"Damn it, Chester. I was hoping you would tell me something terrible about him so I could get over this stupid…thing."

We grin at each other like a couple of idiots.

***

On Sunday night, we're back up on the roof, but there's a real strain. I'm busy not looking at Vince, sitting far away from Vince and trying to act like Vince isn't making my skin crawl. For the first time ever, I'm happy to see Meredith and Julie arrive but Sonny looks like he swallowed sour milk.

"Don't worry, we're not here to stay," Julie says and pushes her cousin toward Sonny. He stands up and crosses his arms, waiting.

"Sorry I threw up in your truck." Meredith's tone says she is not really sorry at all.

"Is that all you're sorry about?" Sonny asks.

"Yeah, it is." She pulls some money out of her pocket and tosses it at him. He keeps his arms crossed so the bills land at his feet. "Oh, wait, I'm also sorry you are such a pathetic hillbilly," she adds, then storms away.

"I tried to warn you," Julie says sadly, and follows her cousin.

Chester catches my eye and winks. I frown at him and shake my head, but he keeps making kissy faces, wiggling his eyebrows and winking at me for the rest of the night. Either I'm going to kill him or I'm starting to like him.

Tuesday August 16, 1977

Dear Cassie,

Guess what? I'm shrinking without even trying! Today, while cleaning the front glass cases in the lobby and reaching all the way to the top corners, my pants almost fell off!

There was this huge breathy sigh behind me. It's a sigh I've learned to recognize very well. Mrs. P was shaking her head and pointing at me. "Why you no have pants that fit?"

"They used to fit fine," I told her, then tried to hold my left arm over the waistband and clean with my right. Problem is, that's really awkward. So I kept forgetting, then having to pull up on my pants.

Another huge sigh. So I said, "I'm really sorry. I'll get a pin or something."

"No," she said with a dramatic slashing motion and a stern shake of her head that startled me. "No pin. You work hard. You live in this rich country. You get new pants."

"I promise, I will get new pants soon." In my head, I was trying to guess how cheap I could find the required black pants.

"No, now," she said, walking up to me. There was a nudge in my back. I turned around with an excuse ready on the tip of my tongue, then I saw that Mrs. P was nudging me with a roll of bills.

"You go to departmental store and buy pants that fit. Maybe you find cheap and buy nice shirt or something."

If Anita were waving money at me, I'd snatch it up, but Mrs. P must be handing me Nick's money. How could I take Nick's money knowing what I know?

"I'll ask my mother for the money to pay you back as soon as—"

"No!" she said again like a bullet shot. "You do good work here and you need pants to keep working. Nikolas pays you nothing, while he pays that boy who never works so hard."

"Three boys," I correct her without thinking.

"We only pay Vincent," she tells me. "Sonny, he is working community hours and Jeffery, he cashes his paycheck and puts it back in the concession till when he thinks I won't notice. I always notice." She pushed the roll of money into my hand and walked away. I was too stunned to put up any sort of fight.

I walked to Sherman's Department Store with that wad of money in my pocket. I didn't even bother to count it until I walked into the store and realized I needed to figure out how much I had in order to know which pants to buy. So I stood there in the middle of the empty sales floor and carefully unfolded the roll of bills Mrs. P had pressed into my hand..... and nearly sat down right there in the middle of the blue, black and white pattern on the floor. Mrs. P had given me fifty dollars!

There was no way I could keep all of it. I grabbed the cheapest pair of black pants I could find and took them to the dressing room. Even though I picked up a size smaller than the loose pair I was wearing, there still seemed to be too much room. I even checked the tag to be sure I'd picked up a size 10. I almost bought them, but then I went out and grabbed the size 8. The sales woman, blue haired and bored, followed me with her eyes and made no comment.

Still, I was so excited I told her, "I need a smaller size" in amazement. She didn't even bother to nod. Back in the fitting room, I nearly jumped up and down when the pants slid over my hips and zipped up easily.

Now, I'm sure you can't possibly imagine. I know you've never been chubby in your entire life. My only experience in dressing rooms for the past three or four years has involved wiggling and squeezing into last year's sizes and trying to pretend everything was fine. Until Anita would twist me around roughly and pinch her nails into my flabby skin before announcing, "Better get a larger size," in a voice that could peel paint.

I've never ever had to go for a smaller size...and definitely not two smaller sizes. Back on the sales floor, I looked over the jeans for a few minutes before finally taking back a pair of Levis. Now, I'm not going to pretend I looked like Kelly Garrett in those jeans. But I didn't look terrible. And Mrs. P had told me to buy pants and maybe something else.

"I'll pay her back," I told my reflection in the mirror. When my reflection glared back at me accusingly, I moved on to pleading with myself, "It would be an insult not to accept her gift."

I might have stood there arguing with my reflection all day, but then I heard a horribly familiar voice yelling, "Mother, I'm telling you this isn't the same size they gave me last time!"

It was Big Red. A banging door and crash of hangers announced her entry into the dressing room.

A softer fluttery voice said, "Now dear, there's no reason to get yourself into a mood. A few pounds is nothing serious."

"Mother, are you deaf? I have not gained anything. That idiot woman gave me the wrong size." Wow. If I used that tone of voice with Anita just one time, I'd be dead and buried before I could open my mouth to apologize.

"Your face looks a little fuller, but it looks good," Mrs. Costas fluttered on. I held my breath. The other dressing room door banged open again.

"Boys like a girl with a little something to hold onto," Mrs. Costas' voice was still mild.

"MOTHER! SHUT! UP!" Every word was a separate scream. Then the door banged shut again.

"Now Tamra Lynn Costas, don't let yourself get so worked up."

Part of me wanted to enjoy the fact that Big Red was getting bigger, but the way she was yelling at her mom was making me queasy. Without changing out of the jeans, I grabbed the black pants and scrambled out of the dressing rooms as quickly as I could.

The lady behind the counter didn't even raise an eyebrow when I told her I wanted to pay for two items and wear the jeans out of the store. As she handed over the receipt, another round of yelling erupted from the fitting rooms and she whispered "That child is getting as nasty as her daddy."

Back at the theater, I did a twirl on the sidewalk in my new jeans to show them to Mrs. P before changing into the black pants in the bathroom. Again, she made me twirl and walked back and forth a couple of times like a fashion model. Then she clapped and laughed, "Much better. Is much better. What else?"

At that point, I tried to say, "This is all I needed," and hand her back the rest of the money, but she wouldn't take it. Instead, she gave me another sudden slash of her hand.

"Go back again soon and get something nice for top. Something not for work. Something like the other girls wear. Maybe tomorrow."

I tried one more time to protest, but she just shook her finger at me and said, "Say, 'Thank you Mrs. P.'"

"Thank you, Mrs. P," I echoed. Her eyes looked warm, so I added, "I didn't even realize I'd lost that much weight."

"Know what I think?" she said, and walked up to pat my cheek, "I think there are many things about you that you don't see." And then she walked away to the booth muttering something in Greek.

Taking my cue from Jeff, I slipped the money back into the concessions cash drawer before the eight-thirty showing.

Erika, Size 8

| TWENTY-NINE |

WHEN I STEP OUT OF THE SHOWER WEDNESDAY MORNING, Anita is sitting on the bathroom counter. She's staring into space with her knees tucked up under her chin like a little girl. I wrap a towel around my body and wait for her to say something.

"I loved that man. I really did."

"Richard?" I ask, fighting to sound indifferent.

"No, Elvis. I can't believe he's really dead. The King of Rock and Roll is dead."

She seems to be waiting for me to say something. All sorts of meaningless words dance through my head. In the end, all I say is, "I didn't know."

Anita nods like I've said something profound. "Well, you wouldn't know anything about it. The whole thing—" She clears her throat. "I don't like to remember much about that time."

There are hundreds of questions buzzing in my brain, but I keep quiet.

After a minute or two, she goes on. "Elvis Presley was a bright shining point of light when everything else was dark and ugly." There's something in her voice that makes me think of a rusty unused door opening after a hundred years. "You used to ask me about your grandparents, but you finally gave up. Do you remember?"

I nod. Do I remember? Is she kidding? How could I forget? She threatened and punished that curiosity right out of me. Forbidden subject. When Anita dictates that a subject is forbidden, she makes darn sure I'm too afraid to ever mention it.

"What did I tell you about them?" she asks.

Part of me isn't willing to trust this Anita. Still, I can't stay silent. "They were not nice?"

Anita snorts before nodding. "What else?"

"They don't want anything to do with either of us because I'm a bastard so there's no use trying to contact them."

"Did I ever tell you your grandfather is a preacher man?" The tone of her voice is so hard and so bitter I take a step back.

"You said they were very religious and that's why you don't have any use for churches."

"That's right." Anita nods once, staring past me into nothing. I'm about to try prodding her into saying more when she seems to wake up and gives herself a little shake. "That's right," she repeats and looks me over with clear eyes. "I'll let you get dressed," she says, hopping off the counter in one quick movement and walking away.

The disappointment and confusion is so intense that my mouth tastes like burnt ashes. I grab my new jeans and give them a rough shake. An envelope falls to the floor. The words *I always notice!* are printed in big block letters on the front. Inside, I find the money that I slipped into the cash register last night. I don't know whether to laugh or cry.

After getting dressed, I spend a few minutes in my bedroom debating my next move. When I realize what I have to do, I feel sick but also weirdly exhilarated. Closing my eyes, I breathe deeply and focus on the pulse of pure living energy coursing through my body.

Yes, the energy seems to whisper. *You have to do what you feel is right, of course.*

I track down my mother in the kitchen. She's sitting at the kitchen table, staring out the back window toward Cassie's house. The coffee pot is empty and cold.

"Hey, Mom? Do you want to have a cup of coffee with me at the Landmark Diner?" I wave Mrs. P's money at her. "My treat?"

Anita focuses on me, her eyebrows shooting up when she notices the jeans, but she doesn't comment. Instead she nods, grabs her purse, jiggles her keys in the air and sweeps out of the house, leaving me to follow her or be left behind. Neither of us says a word for the entire eight minute drive to the diner. I watch the seconds tick away on her dashboard clock. When the car stops, we look at each other.

"Let's do this," she says and I can't help feeling she has some idea there's a bomb I'm about to drop on her.

Doreen greets us like we are her oldest and dearest friends when we walk in the door. Her hair is still piled high, but it's been dyed an alarming shade of yellow. The diner is empty except for two old men playing checkers at the lunch counter. "Sit wherever you fancy, girls," Doreen says, waving her hand to take in the whole room and gives me a sly wink.

I give her a weak smile and rush to the corner booth that is farthest away from any door or window. Anita follows much more slowly and takes her time sitting across from me. My whole body is buzzing as Doreen hustles over with the coffee pot. We both turn up our cups and sit silently as she pours.

"What else can I get for you?" she asks.

I give her the best smile I can paste on my face. "Just the coffee for now. We have something important to discuss."

Anita steeples her fingers together. Her eyes never leave my face. After Doreen hustles away, she crosses her arms on the table. "We do?"

I take in a huge gulp of air and nod. Carefully, one by one, I place the nine remaining Polaroid pictures of Cassie's injuries from last summer on the table in front of her. She studies each one, picking it up, nodding, then turning it face down. After what feels like a million years, she takes a sip of her coffee, eyeballing me over the rim.

"Why did you take the pictures?"

"She asked me to. She made me promise to do something with them if her father ever—" My throat closes up, refusing to say the words. "She made me promise to use them to make him pay for it. All of it. She was always talking about it, about how we could make him pay for hurting her."

"Oh my poor, foolish girl." Anita reaches across the table and grabs my hand. "You couldn't save her. You couldn't stop him.

And I really don't see how you can use these pictures now to make him pay for what he did to her."

This is not what I want to hear. I yank my hand away from hers. "Mother, you don't understand."

"I understand much more then you think I do."

"No, you don't. If you did—"

"Cassie Abbott is not the only runaway you know," she says.

"What?"

"The other runaway you know is me. Your own mother. I ran away from home at sixteen."

Kapow! Wham! Slap! I did not see that one coming. I'm speechless.

"The things I'm going to tell you now are private, Erika. You are never, ever to repeat a word of this. Got it?"

I nod, unable to do more than listen to her in amazement.

"I know you think I've been a terrible mother. Believe it or not, I wouldn't really disagree with you. Every hurt feeling and harsh thing I've done, I'll bet you could write out quite a list. Am I right?"

I shake my head even though I've already written this list, more then once.

"Of course I'm right," she answers herself. "You know what? There isn't a single thing on that list of yours to compare with the garbage I endured from my own mother." She stops and drills one index finger into the gray Formica tabletop while her eyes drill into mine. "You may not believe me, Kiddo, but it's the absolute truth."

We sit in silence once again, staring at each other. I'm trying not to squirm. After an eternity, she finally sits back and lowers her eyes.

"I never intended to tell you this, but you need a dose of reality here. Maybe what happened, why I took off, will help you. Let's start with the iron. My mother used to iron everything, even the bed sheets. There was always some point in the day when she had that big old electric iron in her hand. If she found a stain on my clothes or I was annoying her—" Anita makes a violent jerking motion with her right arm. "She'd whip that electric cord out of the wall and beat the hell out of me with it. One second she'd be ironing and the next second she'd be screaming like a banshee and trying to kill me. No warning at all. Have you ever noticed we don't have an iron in our house? To this day, the smell of a hot iron will make me vomit."

"I'm sorry," I say. The words are stupid, inadequate. "No one should have to live like that."

"No," Anita agrees. "And it wasn't just me, my father got hit, too. Not that I'm excusing him."

My wires feel crossed. Anita watches the confusion making me squirm and laughs. Not just a short bark, but a full belly laugh that seems entirely inappropriate to me. Then she takes another drink of coffee.

"That's right. The preacher was a mellow little man with his face always pressed in a book. It was my mother who did all the beating and the screaming and the intimidating. He ignored what was going on in his own house. You know, he actually used to lock himself in the church office to hide from her. The whole time he was leaving us alone to deal with her. So no, I'm not excusing him. In some ways he's worse than her."

"Us?

"I had a younger brother, Eddie. He was just a year younger than me, so we were like bread and butter. We were the Two Musketeers until Eddie ended up in the churchyard next to Grandma Ione when I was thirteen."

My breath is frozen in my chest. For all of a split second I have an uncle....and then he's dead.

"After we buried Eddie, Mother got a hundred times worse. Even the solid stupid old church ladies started to notice. Not that they ever did anything about it. They'd just give me peppermints and tell me there was a greater reward in Heaven. Back then I was oh so grateful for their little bits of kindness. Stupid cows."

She snorts loudly and we fall silent again for a bit.

"One more example, then we move on out of this trip down memory lane. I told you I loved Elvis. Well, good old Mother and Father were strictly united on that subject. Rock and roll was sinful, savage black music. TV was sin. We didn't have one in the house. Anything remotely sexy was a filthy sin. Of course Daddy just said these things in a mild tone and gave me a book. Mother went flaming nuts. Oh, and dancing was evil, too. All forms of dancing. I wasn't allowed to take dance lessons. Dancing was part of the Devil's curse on mankind."

My face must look as horrified as I feel, because Anita points at me and starts laughing again.

"I'm not even joking, kid! Devil's curse!"

"But how did you learn dance?"

"Where there's a will, there's always a way." Anita smiles, looking away toward the diner windows. "A pretty little southern belle named Miss Renita lived in my neighborhood. She had a Dance Education degree from some tiny little women's college in Georgia and a set of twin boys she couldn't handle. I helped her with the brats and she gave me private dance lessons."

She slaps the table and points at me. "In fact, Miss Renita is part of this next thing I need to tell you. Elvis was going to appear on the *Ed Sullivan Show.* No TV at our place, so Miss Renita let me watch it with her and the boys. Not only did we watch it, we actually got up and danced to it. Right there in Miss Renita's living room we were trying to swivel our hips like Elvis the Pelvis and laughing...oh did we laugh!"

Anita drifts off again, lost in the memory. Even though it sounds happy, there's a haunted look in her eyes. "As luck would have it, two things happened."

"One," Anita holds up one finger, "Renita's nosy neighbor was a member of Dad's congregation and he saw us dancing. Then the idiot stopped by the church to unburden himself of this shameful knowledge, that the preacher's own daughter was contorting herself to the devil's music."

Something icy and black forms in my stomach.

"Two," Anita wiggles two fingers in the air between us. "I was cursed with an itch you're not supposed to scratch. A feminine itch, if you follow."

Oh yes, I follow. The thing in my stomach grows fangs and bubbles acid.

"So my mother hears about the dancing and comes after me like fire and brimstone... only to find me scratching somewhere a good Christian girl should never ever touch. That time my punishment involved hot water, a wire scrub brush and Clorox bleach. I'll let your imagination fill in the rest of that picture."

The picture is gruesome.

Anita shrugs her shoulders, picks up her coffee, and drains the cup.

"Believe it or not, I still loved Elvis," she continues. "To me, he was all that was pure and good, but not too pure or too good. Even that nasty hag couldn't beat, boil, or scrub the black music devil out of me. As soon as I could, I got out of there. I hitched a ride with an older boy who told me he'd take me all the way to New York City. He dumped me at a truck stop in Pennsylvania, but I made it to New York eventually. Thanks to a little secret help from Miss Renita."

Silence settles between us.

"Did you give Cassie any money to get away from here?"

"Aren't you a smarty pants?" Anita says, but there's no hostility in it.

"Has she called you since she left?"

"Now you're sounding like Walt, Erika. Or the sheriff."

"Mom? Has she? Has she called you or written or anything?"

"No," she says with her right hand over her heart. "I swear I have not heard from her. Has she called you?

"No. Do you think she's okay?"

Anita puts down her empty coffee cup and settles both of her hands over my hands. "Listen, running is ugly. It's not romantic. It's not fun. But sometimes it just needs to happen. There's a lot of horrible people out there. I fought my way through some terrible situations. Cassie has plenty of courage and she knows how to play the cards she's been dealt. If I could do it, she can do it, too. Do you hear me?" I nod and Anita looks into my eyes for a few seconds longer than necessary before pulling her hands back. She picks up the stack of photographs and gives them back to me.

"It's up to you to decide if you want to wage this war with Chief Abbott. I really don't think you can win. I don't think you are tied in any way to that promise Cassie forced on you. If you decide to take him on, I will back you as best I can, but I want you to think long and hard on this before you do anything foolish, do you hear me?"

I nod, entirely incapable of forming words.

"I'm going over to Penny's. Do you want to join me?"

When I shake my head, she smiles and taps the rim of my untouched coffee cup. "Why don't you order a soda or something else you actually like?"

After she leaves, Doreen sets a glass of Coke in front of me and pats my shoulder. I look up. That hair is really atrocious, but her smile is still so sweet.

"I meant to bring you some flowers after you rescued me," I tell her.

"Maybe you should get your momma some flowers." She pats my shoulder again and retreats back to the lunch counter, leaving me to wonder exactly how much of our conversation she overheard.

Thursday August 18, 1977

Dear Cassie,

Yesterday I learned that Elvis is dead, Anita is a runaway and I come from a family of monsters. Today I let myself sit and watch *Star Wars* again from beginning to end.

I noticed something new, something I'd never noticed before.

There's this point when Luke Skywalker asks Ben Kenobi what happened to his father. Then there's this weird look, for a brief second, on Ben's face before he says, "He was killed by a young Jedi named Darth Vader—"

Ben's look is just a flicker really, but once I saw it I couldn't stop thinking about it.

He's not telling the truth.

The next two showings I went back in to watch that part. On the third trip, Sonny followed me.

"What are you looking for?" he asked.

"Watch Ben's face." I whispered back. "Watch it carefully…there!"

I looked at Sonny's profile hovering over me in the darkness.

"It's something….yeah."

"He's lying," I said

"Or it's just a bad shot."

"It's Alec Guinness," I replied. "He won an academy award. It's not a bad shot."

Right now I can't stop thinking about that look, that moment. What is Darth Vader? Who is he? I'm not being stupid and trivial like Chester and Vince when they get into their crazy discussions. I mean, in the movie he's pure evil. All black metal and nasty. But, according to Ben Kenobi, he was a Jedi once.

My mother was a tortured little girl once. You told me your father used to sing silly songs and acted like you hung the moon before you turned 12. Even Candy Man and Sheriff McCombs must have been somebody's little boys once upon a time.

How does it happen? How do people become monsters? And is anyone really and truly a monster to the core? I used to think Anita was. Now I'm not so sure.

Good night, Cassie. Sleep tight…wherever you are.

I hope you don't have to fight too hard to find your way through the bad people and the garbage.

Erika

| THIRTY |

EARLY FRIDAY AFTERNOON, CHESTER COMES RUNNING INTO the Bixby lobby yelling, "Fight! Fight! Big fight!"

I grab him. "Are you okay, Chester? Did someone hurt you?"

He shakes his head, frantic and out of breath. "Not me. It's Chief Abbott. He's trying to kill Candy Man!"

Sonny and Jeff rush outside. Chester latches onto my arm and drags me out the door after them. Mrs. P is standing outside her booth with the fire extinguisher in her hands looking baffled. I can hear Walt screaming his head off even before we get out under the marquee to see the full scene.

What we find is pure insanity! Chief Abbott is yanking on the collar of Candy Man's shirt, throwing wild punches that aren't really landing because the blond fireman I saw arguing with Wayne, Bryan, is struggling to keep himself between Candy Man and the Chief's wildly thrashing fists. Another fireman with a thick black mustache is standing behind Chief trying to get a grip on his arms, but then Chief butts him with the back of his head. Mustache guy clamps one hand over his nose, but keeps fighting to get a good grip on Chief with his free hand. Blood quickly covers his hand and chin.

The sight of that blood, ugly crimson in the afternoon sun, seems to activate both Sonny and Jeff. Both rush forward, but Sonny pushes Jeff back. "Don't be stupid, Cuz. This isn't football. Go get some help."

I inch closer, even though I'm terrified. Mrs. P shoves out her left arm to block my way then steps in front of me with her fire extinguisher held forward like a weapon.

Sonny grabs the back of Candy Man's shirt and manages to help him slip out of it, leaving the Chief holding a useless piece of fabric. Feet planted wide, knees bent, hands hovering next to his head, Sonny puts himself between Candy Man and the Chief with a look of fierce determination. "Enough!"

Instead of running away like a sensible person, Candy Man hops up and down behind Sonny. "I told you I never touched your damn daughter. What is wrong with you?"

Even though there are two people between Chief and the object of his fury, he won't slow down one bit. If anything, he jerks harder and throws more wild punches to get at Candy Man. The blond fireman is able to get two fistfuls of his shirt and drive him back at least five feet.

Chief straightens up, takes a breath and seems to back down a little bit so his men relax slightly. That is their mistake. Without a sound Chief lunges away, circles around Sonny in two steps and grabs a fistful of Candy Man's hair then cracks Sonny in the side of the head, right next to his left eye. Sonny staggers, but gets a firm grip on Chief's wrist, managing to take some of the power out of his pounding on Candy Man.

I have never heard a real fight before. On TV a fight is all nice clean popping sounds. In real life it's all skin slapping skin, ugly grunting and breathing. Heavy, hollow, panting breathing. Those breaths. I know that sound.

As the three guys close in around Chief and try to stop him, Candy Man screams like a girl and the sickening sound of pounding and panting goes on and on.

I remember climbing up the metal rungs of the TV antennae tower to Cassie's bedroom window. I'm upset. Tears blur my vision. Anita found an empty donut box in my room and told me she was going to send me to a fat camp for little piggy girls who won't quit eating. I hear the sound of that heavy, hollow, panting breathing before my head is high enough to peek over the window sill. It takes a few seconds to blink away my tears, but then I see very clearly. I see exactly what he is doing to her and I scream. Cassie hears me. He doesn't hear me. He's too intent on hurting her. She looks over, our eyes meet and her mouth shapes one word. "Run."

"Stop it! You're going to kill him!" Sonny's words shake me out of my most horrible memory and suddenly I know how to stop this.

My hand touches my back pocket. After my talk with Anita, I have kept the Polaroid pictures with me at all times, wrapped in paper napkins from the diner. Slowly, I take one step back, then another, then another. Neither Chester nor Mrs. P notices, they are too focused on this terrible thing happening in front of them. I take out the pictures and pick the two that are the most graphic, the most hideous. Shoving the rest back into my pocket, I circle around Mrs. P and run toward the fight with a picture in each hand facing forward. I need to make sure Chief can see what I have and so can the two firemen trying to stop the fight.

A direct hit and only a direct hit will start a chain reaction.

Chief pulls up his left elbow, set to deliver it to Sonny's face.

"Chief!" I scream, "No! Stop it! Stop it right now! Look at me! Look at me!"

Chief stops. Everyone stops.

"Look at these pictures! Look! Look what you did to your little girl. I saw you! I saw you in her bedroom. I saw what you did to her!"

Chief looks at me with his weird, dead eyes and says nothing. Candy Man manages to break loose and scramble away. The blond fireman snatches one of the photos out of my hand and looks it over closely then looks up, flips it around for the other fireman to see.

"She ran away from that." My voice is breaking under the strain. "She ran away from you. She ran away to stop being tortured by you!"

Both firemen turn to look at their Chief.

"She's lying," he says.

"Why would she lie?" Sonny asks calmly, his eyes focusing on first one then the other man. He helps Candy Man stand up and they both back away. "What possible reason would Erika have for lying?"

Brian is the first one to throw a punch, a nice clean blow right below Chief's ribcage, then follows it with two more to his face. Black mustache pushes him back, then delivers his own uppercut to Chief's jaw, grabs his shoulders and plants a knee in his gut. It is a quick and brutal fight. The two men take turns pounding their Chief into submission. When the sheriff and his men finally arrive, Chief Walter Abbott is lying on the sidewalk in a fetal position while the two men stand over him with their arms crossed. Sheriff McCombs takes one look at the scene and orders his deputies to handcuff the two firemen.

I start to protest, but Sonny quickly clamps a hand over my mouth and captures me in a bear hug. "Let it play out," he whispers in my ear. "No more battles for you today." I stop struggling and let him half pull, half carry me into the Bixby, one Polaroid still clutched in my hand.

Sonny insists on taking me home immediately. I try to argue, but the fact that I can't stop crying is not working in my favor. When we pull up in front of the house, Anita and Richard are playing Yahtzee on the front porch. Sonny helps me out of the truck and supports me as I slowly shuffle up the front walk. Anita takes one look at us, jumps up and rushes forward to grab both my arms.

"What is it?" she asks.

"I've done something really stupid, Mom," I manage to say before crumpling into a fresh round of tears. She wraps me in a hug, something she hasn't done in years.

Quickly, Sonny gives her the barest explanation of what happened. "It wasn't stupid. In fact, I might even say it was brilliant," he tells her then gives me a firm rub on my back before leaving.

"It was stupid," I say into her soggy shoulder.

"Time will tell," she says. "It was certainly brave." She steps back and pats both my arms. "Who knew my little girl was such a brave little soldier?"

"I'd rather be a Jedi," I tell her.

Richard tries to convince me to join them for a game of Yahtzee but, as much as I like Richard, the noisy rattle and roll of the dice is shredding my nerve endings. All I want to do is curl up in a ball and sleep. Unfortunately, as soon as I flop into bed, my mind starts screaming and it's impossible to stay still. After starting a load of laundry, washing a few dishes and pushing the broom through my mother's dance studio, I emerge back on the porch feeling desperate.

"I need chores," I tell my mother.

"Are you kidding?" Richard asks. "Can't you ever relax, Cinderella?"

Anita shoots him a dirty look, then turns to give me her full attention. "Actually, I have a very special job for you. I was just thinking about this yesterday." She points a finger at me. "I think this will be right up your alley, my little artsy camera girl."

She leads me inside to the reception desk and points to a messy pile of flyers, junk mail, notebooks and catalogs stacked on the chair. "Suzie chose most of the group recital costumes last year, but I wasn't thrilled with the result."

"I didn't notice a big difference."

"Exactly! I was looking for a breath of fresh air; new ideas. Instead, Suzie gave me more of the same looks I've been doing for years. You know—" Her fingers flutter through my hair playfully. "I've been meaning to watch the movies you took of this recital. It's not just the dancing, I need to know which costumes look good, which ones move well, and which ones look...awkward. You know what I'm trying to say?"

"You want to know which costumes love the camera."

"Bingo! And you had the opportunity to look at my dancers through the lens." She taps a fingernail on my forehead. "Try to remember which acts really stood out in your mind. I know you won't remember everything, but go through these catalogs and mark what you think will work best. Think about colors and patterns and movement."

As soon as she rejoins Richard outside, I pounce on this new project. Scooping up the stack in my arms I waddle into the kitchen leaving a trail of junk mail and flyers behind me. The possibilities feel electrifying. I rush back to the reception desk, grab a pad of paper and black marker then absently start picking up the items I dropped on the first trip.

The postcard is just inside the kitchen door.

My head is filled with visions of sequins and satin, so it takes a moment to register what I am seeing. There, on our kitchen floor, is a picture postcard showing one perfect palm tree, with the sun setting over a white sandy beach in the background. Once the image registers in my brain, I sit right down on the kitchen floor and stare at it. Hands shaking, I reach out to touch it to make sure it's real.

Yes, it's really there.

I close my eyes, hold my breath and flip it over. Heart pounding in my ears, I whisper a prayer to every living thing that this postcard is what I think it is. That it means what I think it means. Slowly, I open my eyes to see the back. It is blank! It is our signal. Cassie has made it to Hollywood and she is safe.

Pressing the card to my chest, I rock back and forth as tears of joy flow and happy little squeaks escape my throat. Cassie made it. She is safe.

I brush my fingers over the card, hoping to find some tingle of her living energy there. The only thing the card reveals to me is the postmark. It was mailed at the end of July, over two weeks ago. It has been hidden in a stack of junk mail for over two weeks.

Perhaps I should walk outside and show it to Anita, but I can't do it. This is a precious secret I need to hold in my heart for now. Earlier today I started a rebellion against Chief Walter Abbott. Finding this postcard now, today, I feel as though the Force is telling me I did the right thing.

Saturday August 20, 1977

Dear Cassie,

I am so glad you made it! As I write this, my heart is filled with so much hope that my chest hurts. Or maybe that's fear. It's hard to tell the difference any more. I'm afraid to write it all down; afraid the hope will dissolve away like a mirage or explode into something more dangerous than I ever imagined.

Yesterday I started a rebellion against your father. It was an act of desperation. Today I discovered my act of desperation might have been the direct hit we needed to start a chain reaction that will finally destroy that man!

Anita woke me up this morning by tearing the sheet off my bed and yelling "Time to rise and face your followers, little Jedi."

We have been getting along better, but this was not a good moment.

I snatched the sheet back and growled, "Leave me alone!"

She yanked back on the sheet and said, "I'm not exactly thrilled about it either, but we have visitors. Get your butt downstairs."

Terrible memories flooded my sleepy brain. I sat straight up. "Who is it?"

"Don't freak out." That's all Anita would say.

Deputy Wayne Todd, who is no longer a deputy, and Assistant Fire Chief Brian Anderson, who has been suspended without pay, were waiting for me on the front porch. Brian was suspended because he beat the crap out of Walt yesterday. He beat the crap out of Walt because I showed him two of the most gruesome Polaroids we took.

There was a tense moment where I stood there and didn't know what to expect. Wayne gave Brian's shoulder a light shove and said, "Go on, tell her." And I knew, instantly, even before Brian stuttered through his story, I knew he was the witness who saw you on the state road hitchhiking the night you left town.

"I was sick of it. I should have done something, but I was so sick of it. The chief was always having us chase down his crazy daughter and drag her home. I knew something was not right, I mean I didn't know exactly, but I knew something—" The guy sucked in a breath and just stood there looking at me, waiting for me to say something.

"Thing is, if you came forward, if you went on record about seeing her that night, then the Chief would have known you left his daughter out there and didn't bring her home, right?"

I understood. I really did. If I didn't have this postcard in my pocket, maybe I would not have been able to forgive him. With the postcard, I felt so powerful.

Wayne stepped forward and quickly explained that several firefighters and concerned citizens convinced the City Council to hold a special meeting about Chief Abbott. There's all sorts of proof he's been misusing city resources in lots of ways, but most especially he's been using his firefighters to keep you as his prisoner. Those pictures of your injuries? Wayne said those pictures will be the nails in his coffin.

I had one question. "What about the sheriff?"

Wayne explained that Sheriff McCombs is an elected county official and nobody but the State Highway Patrol or the Feds can do anything to him. But the City Council appoints the fire chief and they can fire him.

"There's not enough evidence to put together a case for corruption against McCombs," Wayne explained, "but he's not an idiot. He'll cut ties with Abbott once all this comes out, to keep his image clean."

In the end, I gave them all eight remaining pictures to help their case. Wayne doesn't think I'll have to speak to the City Council, but I told him I would do it if they needed me.

Anita keeps reminding me that a wounded, cornered animal is ten times more dangerous than the average predator. She doesn't know about your postcard yet.

Erika

| THIRTY-ONE |

Anita drops me off in front of the Bixby a little before ten o'clock on Sunday. She and Richard have decided it is too dangerous to let me wander around town on my own. This is annoying, but also comforting. She reminds me that Richard will pick me up at eight-thirty and zooms away.

Standing in front of the marquee with her exhaust fumes still burning my nostrils, I notice the glass windows and displays all look smudged, gritty and gross. Sonny prohibited me from cleaning outside and today is not the day to break his rule, but this is ridiculous!

The deep, penetrating blare of a warning siren goes off next door and the fire station doors roll up. Hypersensitive to anything next door, I watch as the ambulance zooms out. My blood freezes when it immediately stops behind me. Medics jump out, pop open the back doors and yank out the metal gurney.

The front doors of the Bixby explode open and Sonny rushes out with a look of pure terror in his eyes. All I can do is stare, my own terror swelling. He shoves at the air toward me, signaling me to stay back as the men rush inside.

Then the world is totally silent. Sonny and I are alone.

"Who?" I finally force myself to ask.

"Nick." I watch his throat muscles convulsing until I have to look away.

We stand out there for an eternity. No length of time has ever felt so heavy. A few people walk out of other buildings and stare.

I make it my job to glare hard at each and every one of them, willing them to go back inside. A couple of deputies rush out of the sheriff's station and jog toward the theater.

As they approach, I hear something I will probably hear in my heart for the rest of my life. A pale wavering ghost of Nick's usual voice moans, "Oh it hurts. It hurts. Oh my God it hurts."

Alex's voice chants, "I know, I know it does Popples. I know. Hold on. I know. Hold on."

I feel sick as they load him into the ambulance; I can't watch as Alex jumps in and the doors slam shut.

After the ambulance speeds away, I stand silent waiting for Sonny to say something, anything, to make this less awful. But Sonny is quiet, too. When I look over, he is still watching the empty place where the ambulance disappeared from view. I take his arm and lead him inside, much the way he led me home yesterday.

Inside we find four firemen milling around the lobby, mixing with the two deputies. Mrs. P is sitting on the bench in the lobby, so I drop down next to her. With all the uniforms, I'm surprised to find her strangely calm, humming a slow sad tune. As soon as I sit, she places a hand on my head and pets my hair like a stray dog, still humming. Vince and Chester wobble around like drunks, looking confused. Sonny makes a beeline for the theater.

One fireman, I don't know his name, approaches Mrs. P and kneels in front of her. She stops humming to listen, but continues caressing my hair. I hear, "heart attack" and I hear "compound fracture" and I hear "critical condition." He keeps stopping to ask if she understands. She nods. He looks doubtful, but keeps talking.

A deputy starts asking some basic questions in a quiet, careful voice. It's not his fault that he's not Wayne, but he needs to shut up.

Sonny bursts out of the theater waving a piece of paper. "What is this? What the hell is this?" he yells, waving the paper at one of the firemen. The guy takes the paper, looks it over carefully, then whistles to bring his three fellow firemen to come look. There is a murmur of conversation. One of them looks over at me, then quickly looks away.

"There is nothing wrong with our sprinklers!" Sonny screams at the men. "There is nothing wrong with our alarms. All of our fire exits are clear. We just tested everything this month. It all works perfectly! Perfectly!"

I stand up and wobble over to the cluster of firefighters, holding out my hand. After a brief hesitation, they hand over a Notice of Fire Code Violation signed by Chief Walter Abbott and dated today. The notice says we have twenty-four hours to correct the violation or...the rest of the text blurs.

"He's doing this because of me," I tell them.

"Stay here," one of them says and signals the deputy, "We're going to check to see if this is a valid violation."

"You know it's not," Sonny screams at them, but Chester and the deputy convince him to let the men do their work.

"While we're waiting, can someone tell me exactly what happened?" The Deputy looks around with pencil to notebook.

Chester steps forward. He explains that he and Vince were cleaning around the theater seats when he heard a smacking sound on the stage. "I turned around, man, but I couldn't understand the lump on the stage."

"The lump?" My voice is so shrill I barely recognize it.

Chester sighs and mumbles a quick "Sorry" in my direction before continuing with his story. "Alex, that's Nick's niece, she's our projectionist, she ran out of the booth screaming and ran straight for the balcony railing. I thought she was going to jump over it! Then she turned around and ran out toward the lobby."

The deputy looks at Sonny with some degree of nervousness. "You were in the lobby?"

Sonny gives the guy his most vicious look. I put one hand on Sonny's arm. "Please, Sonny? What happened? I have to know."

Sonny focuses on me. "I heard screaming from the balcony and thought Alex was hurt, so I was halfway up the stairs when she came flying down screaming, 'Get help. Go next door. It's Popples. Go!'"

Both Sonny and Chester start talking over each other, saying they were frozen for way too long, not knowing what was happening. Unable to move. Unable to help. The whole time Nick was laying on the stage seriously hurt and maybe even dying. Both are fairly sure Nick's condition is partly their fault for not moving faster.

At this point, the deputy is very decent. He tells them that he's sure they acted as quickly as could be expected, that time in an emergency plays tricks on the mind.

I can't listen to any more of this. Nick was upset by Chief. He was probably trying to fix whatever Chief Abbott told him was a violation. And Chief was only here looking for me. He was messing with Nick to mess with me. I'm sure of it. This is all my fault.

The door to the back lot opens and Jeff walks in with a big careless grin on his face saying, "Hey, hey, hey what's happenin?"

It takes him a few seconds of looking around, blinking in the dim light before he picks up on the bad energy. "Okay, seriously," he says in a less enthusiastic voice. "What's happening?"

Sonny explains while I walk back to Mrs. P.

"Do we close?" I ask.

She shakes her head immediately. "No. We have a business to run." Jeff tries to tell her we can put up a sign and close for one day, but she will not listen to a word of it. She slashes the air and says, "No, no, no. We keep movies running for Nikolas. He wants movies running."

So that is what we do. Moving slowly, in a fog, Vince, Chester and I wash, polish and prepare everything. Sonny and Jeff practice running the projector. Alex has taught both of them how to do it, but they've never worked a feature film without supervision before today. Mrs. P walks around humming and patting us all in turn and calling us "good children." The deputy who is not Wayne stands at the front lobby doors heading off any curious people who peek in to ask why the ambulance was here earlier.

After an hour, the firemen reconvene in the lobby and give Mrs. P a clean inspection certificate. They have not been able find a single problem that qualifies as a fire code violation. None of them look at me or Sonny as they file out of the theater.

The day grinds by. The movies are shown as scheduled.

When I collapse into Richard's car at eight-thirty, he says, "Must have been a great day. You look miserable."

I'm too numb to cry or explain.

I feel as though thousands of voices suddenly cried out in terror and all of those voices were mine.

***

When I wake up the next morning, I can't remember why I have this horrible aching feeling in my chest. I make it all the way to the bathroom before I catch my reflection, my raw bruised eyes looking back at me like a stranger, and remember that Nick is in the hospital.

I shuffle back to my room and curl up into a useless ball.

When the hall phone starts ringing, I glare at it as though it's an alien creature until the thing shuts up. I count ten rings before it falls silent the second time. The ringing starts up a third time and I can feel the noise in my chest. I try smashing my pillow to both ears, but the sound penetrates relentlessly. Tears pour out both eyes and pool at my temples before soaking into the pillow. Ten rings later, the noise stops yet again.

Why not answer? I don't know. I guess I'm afraid to pick up the phone and hear more bad news about Nick.

About fifteen minutes later, there's pounding on the front door. I look out my window and see Sonny's truck. No, no, no. That can only mean bad news. So I sit still, hugging my knees. He pounds a few more times and yells my name. I watch from the hall window as he walks around the house, trying to look in. When he finally stops pounding and turns away, something inside me rips open. If I let him leave, I'll be alone with time stretched out forever.

I run downstairs, fumbling with three new locks Richard installed, before running carelessly out the front door and straight into Sonny's chest. His arms come around me, probably just a blind reaction to this messy person plowing straight into him. My arms are pinned awkwardly between us and I keep my head ducked, pressing my forehead against his chest, drinking in the smell and feel of him. Intensely aware that I'm only wearing a short nightshirt and panties, no bra. At the same time, I'm also miserable for thinking these thoughts right now.

I wait to be pushed away. Instead, he pats my back.

"Is he—?" I can't make myself say it.

"He's still in intensive care," Sonny's voice is gentle, just inches from my ear.

"Will he be okay?" I look up, begging him with my eyes to say yes.

I could swear he's fighting with himself, trying to tell me the lie I want to hear, but in the end he says, "They don't know. No one knows."

***

At the theater, Alex lines us all up and walks back and forth like a general addressing her troops. Dry eyed, she lists out in precise detail the situation with Nick. It was not a severe heart attack, but it wasn't mild either. He broke his arm in the fall, and the blood thinners for the heart attack are causing his arm to swell up. They need to operate on the arm, but they can't do that until his heart is stable. There's some problems with his insurance. There's also problems with a bank loan Nick took out to do some emergency repair work after January's blizzard. Even though Nick has been making all the payments on his back taxes on time, he's missed a few payments on his loan and now the bank manager is spooked, thinks the theater is going under and needs to be sold off in pieces to salvage some money. Worst of all, during our clean up day, one of Alex's veteran buddies pulled her aside to talk. Apparently, Nick has patched and re-patched the drain pan on the air conditioning when it should have been replaced a long time ago. Water has been leaking out, finding cracks, running into ducts, rusting wires, weakening plaster and generally causing problems on top of problems. Alex's friend warned her there was no way to measure the full extent of the damage without "ripping the place apart."

"In short," Alex stops and looks at us, "this is a calamity on all fronts."

"What about Dirty Harry?" Jeff asks. We all glare at him.

"If she hands this place over to a sex merchant with naked dancers and dirty movies, you might as well stop treating Nick cause he will drop dead the second he finds out," Sonny grinds the words out. I silently cheer for him, but Alex fixes him with her own glare.

"What other options are there?" she asks him. Then she opens her arms and says, "I'm open for suggestions. Anyone? Don't be afraid to speak up."

Silence. Then Sonny runs a hand through his hair. "Maybe we could do some kind of fundraiser?"

Vince nods, "Everyone loves this theater. They always say so. We could get an ad in the paper."

"Ads in the paper cost money. We're already behind on our bill to the paper." Alex waves her hands in the air, full of frustration. "And this is a business, not a charity!"

"I don't understand," I say, wincing at the sound of my own voice. "I mean, we've been getting all these extra people for *Star Wars*. You said it yourself; you said this has been the best summer for this movie theater since TV became popular."

"Erika, honey," Alex's voice is painfully sad, "one good rain storm does not make up for years of drought."

"But we're still selling lots of tickets. Lots of people keep coming back."

"It's not enough," Alex starts scrubbing at the back of her neck. "We would have to triple the ticket price and fill every seat in this theater a few times to get the bank off my back."

"Listen," Jeff says, "I know this guy who says a theater that shows a porno movie can charge triple the price and people line up around the block. Wait!" He holds up a hand toward Sonny, who looks ready to bust his jaw. "I'm not talking about selling out to Dirty Harry. I'm talking about a few 'special' showings. Nick would never have to know."

"This is not a horrible idea," Alex says. "I know someone. I could get one or two raunchy movies here pretty fast, but how do we attract an audience without causing the church ladies to picket the theater?"

"Flyers," Vince says. "I could draw something kind of…you know, naughty. But not too bad. We could take them to all the nightclubs and the new disco garden at the Sheraton."

"Well, it's a start." Alex looks over at Mrs. P. "Grammy, can you keep this a secret?"

"Ay have many secrets," Mrs. P mutters. She doesn't sound too happy though.

My mind is whirling. I'm dizzy with the idea that's growing inside me.

"That's a start for this week, but there's something else we could do. Something even better. Something that will make a lot of money!" I'm so excited, I'm practically bouncing up and down like Heidi.

"Good grief, tell us before you wet your pants!" Alex cracks the first shadow of a smile since Nick was taken away.

"Nick will love this idea. It won't need to be a secret. We could have a *Star Wars* festival!" I look around practically bubbling with excitement. Only Vince looks the slightest bit happy with this suggestion.

"We could have a whole weekend of not just showing the movie. We could show some older stuff that influenced this movie, like *Metropolis* and some of the old *Buck Rogers* stuff. We could have games. Face painting. Make t-shirts to sell. Vince could draw people like they are *Star Wars* characters for, I don't know, maybe ten bucks each? Penny told me three different girls have asked for Princess Leia hairdos at her beauty salon. She'll come and do weird hairstyles here to help out. We could sell special food and drinks with names from the movie. Like Jawa Juice or Wookiee Cookies! I mean there's nothing out there for people who love this movie to buy. The department store had one cheap t-shirt with an iron-on picture from *Star Wars*, and it sold out in one day!"

Silence.

"We can't pull that together for next weekend," Alex says. Everyone nods.

"No, of course not. We do Jeff's dirty movies this week. We could do the *Star Wars* festival the next weekend. That's Labor Day weekend!"

"Do we have to say Jeff's dirty movies?" Jeff asks, but he's laughing.

"We need the cash now. Plus, it's going to cost extra to pull this off and—"

"We could sell advance passes to the festival," Sonny breaks in, surprising me. "Hand out flyers at the pools, little league games, flood the high school during the first days of school. Print the cost as eight dollars for an all-day pass but offer the passes for a dollar less if they buy in advance."

"Look," I jump back in, desperate to convince Alex, "I know this isn't a charity, but we can still get lots of help and supplies very cheap or free if we tell people it's helping out Nick and this theater and it's also advertising for their business. There's no shame in it if we do it right."

Alex stares at me while Mrs. P pats my shoulder making shushing noises. Alex looks over at Sonny, "You're on board with this? I'm going to be back and forth with Nick at the hospital. I need you to be in charge here. What do you think?"

"I think it's a damn brilliant idea. I like it a truckload more than I like dealing porn."

"High school starts in what? A week and a half?" Alex watches us all nod. "And Jeff starts college after Labor Day?" More nodding. "Okay, I can't give you much money, but I can definitely get my hands on some of those old movies. Erika, give me a list of ideas. But listen. If this thing hasn't started to shape up by this Sunday, we give it up. Understood?"

We all agree, but my mind is already racing ahead. So many things to do. So many possibilities.

Maybe it's crazy, but I just have this feeling. If I can pull this off, if I can make this *Star Wars* film festival a success, I know Nick will be okay. I just know it. Deep in my bones.

***

Sonny and I take over Nick's office and huddle over his black notebook to come up with our strategy; or our game plan as Sonny calls it. When Sonny puts his mind to a project, he does not fool around! After telling me to call Anita and let her know he'll drive me home before eleven o'clock, we get down to business. Armed with a map of the city and the Yellow Pages, we create a color-coded priority list, diagrams, and strategy notes. Hours later I stand up to stretch my aching back and watch Sonny scribble some final notes. There's a pencil tucked behind each of his ears, his fingers are stained in rainbow colors from the markers we've been using and there's a deep line of concentration right down the middle of his forehead.

He looks up suddenly and says, "What?"

I can't tell him I was just realizing how much I love him, so I say, "I think it's time for you to take me home?"

When Sonny drops me off, I find Anita and Richard sitting in lawn chairs in the back yard. They're sipping cocktails and watching the Super 8 movies I've been making this summer.

My life flashes before my eyes. I never did get around to telling her how many cassettes I've used up and here she is watching that scene where Jeff and Sonny talk about cheating. My knees turn to water. When the film ends, the screen goes dark then pure white and I hold my breath.

Anita looks over at me. "You shot all of these?"

"Yes, I'm sorry. I'll make up for it."

She shakes her head and Richard winks at me. "Your mom asked me to get the movies developed last week 'cause I get a discount rate from the camera shop next to my store. I grabbed the box marked *used* and took them all in. We were just expecting Anita's dance stuff, but...wow! That episode with the thief, was that for real?" I nod. "Far out! And that one we just watched? You really managed to get those two guys. Are they brothers?"

"Cousins. Their dads are identical twins though."

"Wild!" Richard smiles at me.

Anita laughs and shakes her head. "I can't tell you how relieved I am to finally understand the toga. I thought for sure you were going to some kinky parties or something."

"Mother!" My face must be glowing in the dark. She just laughs harder. Richard starts laughing, then I start laughing too, but the relief does something weird to me and my laughter quickly turns to tears.

"What on earth is wrong with you now?" Anita asks.

I sit on the grass and tell them about Nick's heart attack, the Bixby's money issues, and the plans to charge extra for dirty movies next Saturday.

"Oh, I can help you get plenty of business for the naughty stuff," Richard manages to choke out after swallowing his drink the wrong way. "Get me some of those flyers."

"See, now that's a smart business idea," Anita waggles her finger at me.

Encouraged, I explain my big plan for a *Star Wars* film festival weekend.

Anita gets quiet. I'm sure she's going to tell me it's a stupid idea, so I rush to fill in the details, but she waves an impatient hand toward me. "Shush, let me think." We all sit there while Anita taps her fingernails together and looks up at the sky. "You'll need programs. If the studio sponsors the programs, I could put a full page ad in there for upcoming fall classes...something about reaching for the stars with dance."

"You'll help? Really?"

"You think I'm going to miss out on this advertising opportunity?" Anita turns to Richard. "What have you got?

Richard flashes the most ridiculous smile. "Three words, ladies. Photo murals of space!"

"That's four words, Richard," Anita cuts in, but he doesn't make any sign of hearing her.

"Imagine a room where one whole wall looks out over the Milky Way. Everybody has sunset beaches and happy tree forests. Yours truly read that article in *Time Magazine* back in May about this movie being the blockbuster of the year and I thought ahead. I found the guy who can supply the space murals. I'll create three of four space walls." Richard points at me. "You can turn them into games." Then he points at Anita. "And you can give me a half page ad in your programs."

"Deal," Anita and I chorus in unison.

We all sit back looking up at the night sky. Several minutes pass where no one says anything. I should go inside, but there's one more question burning in my brain.

"Do you guys really think my movies are...not bad?"

"Far out!" Richard says again.

"I think I might consider letting you take a film study course at the college next year," Anita tells me. "Once you can drive and I don't have to taxi your butt back and forth."

"Thanks, Mom." The words feel totally inadequate.

"You're welcome, Kid."

Thursday, August 25, 1977

Dear Cassie,

Remember when I told you that everything could explode into something dangerous? Well it happened. Your father wrote up a phony fire violation for the Bixby and Nick ended up having a heart attack and falling from the catwalk above the stage. Everyone—Anita, Richard, Alex and even Wayne Todd—they all keep telling me that these things may be related, but neither Chief nor I caused this terrible accident. Their words just deflect off my surface.

The good news is that the City Council held their emergency session last night and voted unanimously to fire Chief Walter Abbott. Wayne stopped by the house to give the Polaroids back to me. Apparently, there was no need for the pictures or for anyone to testify. Chief put the nails in his own coffin.

"That man has totally lost his mind," Wayne told us. "It would be funny if it weren't so damn sad."

"You don't feel sorry for him, do you?" Anita asked. Her voice was crackling with the same anger that was sizzling in my own throat.

Wayne shook his head, but the expression on his face was full something that looked suspiciously like pity to me. "He walked into that meeting smelling like a dirty barroom floor and started yelling crazy stuff. He was rambling like a maniac. He actually pointed at one councilman and said he knew the guy paid bribes to Sheriff McCombs to get his son off an arson charge. Then he pointed to another councilman and said that guy tried to sleep with Cassie. Then he started crying and screaming they were all a bunch of dirty cowards. It was hard to watch."

I wish I could have watched it, Cassie. After what he did to you and to Nick, I would have loved to watch that monster dissolving in his own ugliness. But I can't waste time thinking about him now.

There's another nightmare that I have to fight. As it turns out, in addition to the back taxes, Nick owes a chunk of money to the bank. Also, there's an issue with water damage from the air conditioning unit.

And now, thanks to your father, there will be medical bills on top of everything else. The bank manager wants to close the Bixby! But Sonny and I have created an amazing plan to host a *Star Wars* festival that could get us out of this hole. Our plan has to work. It just has to.

Yesterday, we walked into every business on the Downtown Business Association list looking for sponsorship and participation. The response was amazing! The Dairy Dream is going to mix up a special "Galaxy" ice cream for the festival. Kane's Sporting Goods is going to come make *Star Wars* themed t-shirts and jerseys on the spot. Doreen at the Landmark Diner told me she was already working on a new space-themed kids menu and would love to hand out samples and coupons at our event. The bookstore is going to bring a rack of science fiction books and movie magazines to sell. The owner of the karate studio on Main Street is going to give Kendo demonstrations, that's a Japanese form of sword fighting that he swears can make a true Jedi out of anyone. Chester is going to paint faces. Vince is going to draw caricatures. Sonny's mother is going to bake crazy cookies. Penny is going to do crazy hairstyles. Richard is going to make crazy space murals. My mother is going to create a commemorative program with an ad for her dance studio on the back cover and sell more ads to local businesses. All of that after just two days of work!

According to Sonny, we've already sold over a hundred festival passes. Plus, everyone who is selling anything at the festival is going to donate their profits to the theater. We even found an accountant who is donating his services to make sure everything is legitimate.

See what I mean? There's too much to do. I can't let myself sit around and wallow in misery. As Leia says, "We have no time for our sorrows, Commander."

Erika

| THIRTY-TWO |

The first words I hear Friday morning are, "You've got to calm down and tell me where you are, Honey. California is a huge state."

I crack open my bedroom door to listen to Anita on the phone.

"You don't have to know what to do, Honey. I can get you a plane ticket, a bus ticket, whatever. I can get you home."

My stomach lurches, but my feet walk steadily toward the sound of my mother's voice.

"Calm down, Honey. Breathe. Stay with me. I can get you home."

Anita is sitting at the kitchen table, both hands gripping the telephone receiver. Her whole body is positioned as if she's going to jump right through the wires. Richard is standing behind her, hands on hips. His eyes meet mine over Anita's head.

"Cassie?" I force the question between numb lips as he asks, "Who is Suzie Q?"

"Shhhhh!" Anita hisses at us.

My legs turn to Jell-o and I end up with my butt on the kitchen floor. Richard hurries over to help me stand up. I grip his arm. "It's Suzie on the phone? Not Cassie? You're sure?"

Enlightenment creeps over Richard's face. "It's not your friend Cassie," he whispers. "It's definitely someone called Suzie."

I close my eyes with a shudder. Suzie. It's just Suzie on the phone. Not Cassie.

Anita shushes us again, so Richard pulls me out to the back porch. He relays the bits and pieces he's heard, but didn't understand. I understand perfectly. Suzie's greasy boyfriend dumped her and now she wants Anita to rescue her. I explain the situation to Richard, then tell him I'm going to head over to the newspaper office to see if they will run an article about our festival.

"I should drive you," Richard says, his eyes shifting between me and the door to the kitchen.

"No, you stay with Mom," I tell him and hurry back upstairs to get ready before he can argue. Twenty minutes later, Anita is barking orders into the phone. From the tone of her voice, it's obvious she's no longer talking to Suzie. Richard is pacing around the kitchen stirring something in a big mixing bowl. They're both so distracted it's easy to slip out the front door.

It's been almost a week since I've pedaled to the theater on my bike. The rhythm of my feet pumping as the air ruffles through my hair and the pavement whizzes by under my tires feels amazing. When I get near the newspaper office, I'm not ready to stop riding so I circle around the square at least ten times. With each pass I feel more and more powerful, more and more hopeful. A memory pops into my head of Cassie running up the hill on our last night together and rolling down with a wild sort of glee. For just a second I can feel her next to me, running away from the demons. A sensation that is entirely unfamiliar settles over me. I think this is what they call peace.

After parking my bike by the front door, I head into the newspaper office with a new sense of calm.

***

As soon as we finish cleaning the theater for the Saturday matinee, Sonny hands his truck keys to Chester and tells him to drive me home. His face is grim.

"What is wrong with you?" I ask.

"You don't need to be around here when the perverts start showing up," Sonny grumbles.

"Not everybody who watches a dirty movie is a pervert, Sonny," Chester tells him, but I recognize the closed look on Sonny's face and know there's no use arguing.

When we pull up in front of my house, it's obvious no one is home. They are probably off somewhere rescuing Suzie and I'm not looking forward to sitting home alone all day. Suddenly, I remember our space ghost movie.

"Hey, Chester, you want to come get your movie?"

"Oh yeah!" Chester says, his face splitting into the first smile I've seen from him since Nick's fall.

The only problem is that all of the brightly-colored plastic film cases look alike. His original cassette was clearly labeled *Chester*, but all of the developed films have blank labels. We sit on the porch opening canisters and holding the film up to the light trying to find the right one while I tell him about coming home to find Anita and Richard watching my movies.

"I thought she was going to rip off my face for wasting all that film, but she was really cool about it," I tell him, reaching for another canister. "She even said I could take a film class at the college."

"You know there's a film study class at the high school, right?" Chester asks. "Hey, I think this might be our film!"

Before I can answer a flash of blue catches my attention. The sky blue Maverick is back. It's parked in the alley behind my house. "Chester," I whisper between clenched teeth. "Do you know that car?"

Taking my cue, Chester stretches the film above his head and pretends to examine it while looking at the Maverick out of the corner of his eye. "No. Why."

"That damn car has been haunting me for weeks."

"Do you know a girl with big hair who likes to twirl it around one finger?" I stare at him. "Cause that's what I'm seeing," he tells me, carefully winding up his reel.

Yeah, I know someone exactly like that—Tammy freaking "Big Red" Costas. I drop my film, jump off the porch and run up to the driver's side door yelling, "What do you want?"

"Erika!" Tammy gasps. "You almost scared me to death!" She opens her door and climbs out. I step back and hold up my arm to let her know she should stay away from me.

"What possible reason do you have for following me around?" I ask. "What is wrong with you?"

"I just want to talk to you," she says in a low voice.

"You could have talked to me before school was out, but you oinked at me instead. You told lies that got everyone oinking at me. Oh, and remember when you pushed me down the stairs at the recital? Now you want to talk?"

"Look, I don't know what that tramp…what Cassie told you about me, but you've got it all wrong."

"Cassie never told me any damn thing about you, Tammy. What do you think she told me?"

Tammy is looking at me very, very carefully now. It feels like she's searching for some tiny piece of something on my face. Finally, she whispers, "You know."

This is getting so old. "Look, Tammy, you want to talk to me, then speak plain English and drop this whole 'you-know-something-don't-you' paranoia act."

Her eyes twitch around before they land on something behind me. I turn my head and see Chester walking toward us. I wave my hand to tell him to stay back and turn to face Tammy again. "What do you want?"

Tammy leans forward and whispers, "If my dad finds out about the film, he will kill me. Really kill me. Dead. With a ball bat. And if he finds out about all the drugs—" She stops cold. "You really don't know any of this do you?"

I shake my head. Tammy turns to get back in her car. She's about to drive away without explaining anything. There is no way I'm going to accept that. I take a few steps forward and kick the car door shut as she tries to open it.

"Hey!" she practically squeals into my face. We're inches apart, so close I can smell the nicotine on her breath.

"Does any of this have to do with Candy Man?"

We're practically nose to nose so I brace myself for some impact. Instead, Tammy melts. She collapses into the side of the car and slides down until her butt hits the ground. The whole time her eyes stay locked with mine.

"You do know," she says quietly.

"No, I really don't know anything. Talk! Talk now or I will march myself over to your house and make stuff up to tell your dad. I'll tell everyone about your drug problem and your missing movie."

"Shut up!"

"Talk!" I practically spit the word in her face. "Now!"

There's a long stretch where we glare at each other. She drops her eyes first. "Candy Man sells...party supplies for really wild parties."

This is old news. "Drugs. Yeah. Everyone knows that."

"Well, the cops started messing with him last summer. All of a sudden they cared way too much about party drugs. Two different times one of the sheriff's men pulled him over, grabbed his whole stash and took off. So he started giving Cassie and me some stuff to take places."

"You and Cassie were selling Candy Man's drugs?"

Next thing I know, my butt is on the pavement next to hers.

"It wasn't that serious or anything," Tammy's voice is suddenly defensive. "It was just us taking some of his stuff to parties. We were his sales girls. We'd get all dressed up...like they do at Studio 54."

"We're in Nowhere, Ohio. There's no Studio 54 here!"

"Guys would get high and slip us extra money. I made more money doing this than I did for an entire summer last year." There's a sort of zombie look on her face.

"But now Candy Man wants to hurt you?"

"No, he just wants to destroy that stupid home movie we shot at Slim Jim's party. His car is in some of the shots. He wants to be sure Chief doesn't see it. I have to be sure my daddy doesn't find out. You have no idea what he will do to me!"

"Movie? What movie? What are you talking about?"

"We dropped some acid. We were a little wild. Cassie had this movie camera, one of those home movie cameras like the one you used to film our dance recital. It was all her idea. She wanted to make a movie."

"Cassie had my Super 8 camera?"

"No, this was an older one. It was kind of beat up and it had some tape wrapped around the handle with letters and numbers…I think. I was pretty messed up."

"Tammy, what kind of a movie did you make?"

Tammy gets very interested in staring at her own feet.

"Tammy? What kind of movie?"

She whispers something so low that I have to lean in very close and only catch the last four words. "…with our clothes off."

"You took your clothes off with someone filming you?"

"Shhhh!!!" She looks around us with wild eyes.

Chester is standing near my porch. He can't hear us, but I lower my voice to a whisper and ask, "Tammy, when did this happen? Was it the night Cassie ran away?"

She nods and keeps on nodding while tears stream down her face. "That was the worst one."

"How many times did you freaks get naked with a camera?"

Tammy glares at me through her tears. "It was always Cassie's idea."

"I don't care!" I tell her and it is true, but I do want to understand one more thing. "Is this the real reason why Candy Man tore apart my room?"

"Yeah. Cassie told us she'd destroy the film, but then she started saying maybe we should give her money. We got in a fight, then she stormed out. I was so messed up! When I got home, there was a note from Cassie taped to my bedroom window. It said she was taking off, but she would send 'the thing you want to find' with 'a little bird.' I was so sure she meant she had given the movie to you. So did Rodney."

"So you and Candy Man, you've both been following me around to get this film?"

"Right," she nods once more. Then we sit there staring at each other.

There's one used but undeveloped film cassette hidden in my backpack. It's the stupid film I shot of Tammy after I found out she was the cause of all that oinking. I've been meaning to destroy it. In fact, it's even labeled *Defective – Do Not Develop*. Now I know why I have not been able to smash it.

"I may know where it is." The words escape before I have time to think about their effect.

Tammy's eyes narrow. "You said you didn't know anything!"

I push myself to my feet and put some space between the two of us. "I didn't, but now that I've heard your story I have an idea where it might be."

"Where?"

"If I find it, I'll call you."

Tammy jumps up, ready to fight but I'm not the least bit afraid of her.

"You and Candy Man need to leave me alone. I swear to you, if I see either of you two lurking around here again, I will find that film and I will personally deliver it to Daddy Costas, you hear me?"

"Erika, is everything okay?" Chester is standing behind me. I see Tammy focus on the reel of film in his hand.

"That's not it," I tell her. "That's a developed film. The film you want is still on the original cassette."

"You made a movie?" Chester asks Tammy. "You like making movies, too?"

"Oh yeah, Chester! Tammy loves to make movies." I can't keep the glee out of my voice as Tammy turns a gruesome shade of purple. "Why don't you tell Chester all about your special movie, Tammy?"

Instead of answering, she turns and gets into her car. Chester and I stand together as she tears away.

"There is something wrong with that girl," Chester tells me.

"You have no idea how right you are."

Tuesday, August 30, 1977

Dear Cassie,

Suzie is back, but she is now a skeleton covered in mosquito bites and lice. Yes, that's right. Lice! She has to use special shampoo, sleep on special sheets and use a special comb. And she is living in our house. My skin is crawling. Our sweet Suzie Q, who used to smell of strawberry shampoo and peppermints, now reeks of chemicals and body odor.

She called Anita four days ago, begging for help. Her loser boyfriend lost his job, lost his car and every bit of money they had. Then he took off and left her in a sleazy motel with a month's unpaid bill. Suzie called Anita from the motel office, hysterical. Anita thinks the jerk took Suzie along for the little bit of money she had saved and dumped her the second her cash ran out.

You know what she's most upset about? He didn't marry her! That's the worst part in her mind. That he didn't marry her. Isn't that sad?

You know what is even more pathetic? Anita paid Suzie's motel bill, arranged a prepaid cab to pick her up and purchased her plane ticket home. Now all Suzie does is sit in our spare bedroom with the lights off and the shades down and stares at nothing. When she speaks, she calls me "You" instead of Erika or Sweetpea or Honey Bun. She sleeps at least twelve hours a day. I haven't seen her cry one single tear, but she looks and smells worse than your dad.

I don't know what to say to her, so I avoid her. Anita keeps telling me to give her time. Right now, I feel like Suzie died, but we forgot to bury her.

Cassie, I hope you are doing better out there than Suzie. I really do.

Erika

| THIRTY-THREE |

It's the first day of school. Anita shuffles past me in the hallway as I'm standing in front of the hall mirror frowning at my reflection.

She stops. "You got a ride to school or are you hoofing it?"

"Sonny from work is giving me a ride."

"Jeff's cousin?" she asks. I nod. "Sonny is the darker guy sitting behind Jeff's movie star act in your movie, right?"

I'm startled by her phrasing, the way it mimics what I used to think about Jeff and Sonny. "He's not as good looking, but Sonny is a really decent guy."

"Kenny Rogers says never fall in love with a dreamer. Your mother says, never fall in love with a pretty boy."

"We're just friends," I roll my eyes at her.

"Right, that's why you're giving yourself the evil eye in the mirror. Wear your turquoise blouse. And remind me to get you some decent shirts. It's time you stop wearing those shapeless things."

When I climb into the truck, Sonny pushes an open box of Little Debbie cakes at me and mumbles, "Don't talk. I hate mornings."

We pull into the school parking lot to find Chester and Vince surrounded by six or seven people I sort of vaguely recognize, but don't really know. Everyone looks half asleep except Chester, who's jumping around talking so fast his lips are a blur. Everyone in the group takes a stack of flyers about the festival.

"It's show time, folks," Sonny announces, "let's make some money even if we need to ignore a few classes." Then he smiles a wicked smile and walks away.

I notice one of the girls in the group staring after him with dreamy eyes. Then she looks at me. "Aren't you the one who ratted out Slim Jim's party last year."

"No she was not!" Vince jumps in. "That was a lie Tammy Costas told and most people were stupid enough to believe it."

"Aw man, Jenny," Chester says, still bouncing around, "You don't want to get on Sonny's bad side! Mess with Erika and that's where you'll be."

"Tammy Costas lies about pretty much everything," another girl with sleepy eyes mumbles and the girl named Jenny bites her lower lip.

The whole thing bothers me much less than I would have thought possible because I've made up my mind to do something crazy. Something brave. Something that's making me so nervous my heartbeat is thundering in my ears. I mumble, "See ya," and walk toward the main office to find Principal Nelson.

On the way, I practice what I'm going to say and try to forget the last time I spoke to Nazi Nelson, the day of that awful scene at Cassie's locker.

Nelson is standing in front of the main office looking around with a big, dopey grin on his face. "Hello, Miss Williams," he says like he is just thrilled to see me again. "Saw your picture in the Sunday paper. I'm very sorry to hear about the trouble at the Bixby, but I think this festival is an excellent idea. Excellent. Very creative."

The words I've rehearsed flutter right out of my head. I stutter meaningless words of thanks until he says, "Ready for a new year?"

"Can I make an announcement?" I blurt out, then feel my skin burn bright red.

"During morning announcements?" he asks.

"Yeah, sometimes you let the cheerleaders announce their car washes and stuff. I thought maybe—" I open my new three-ring notebook and pull out the announcement I've been working on for two days.

"Forgive me, but you take me by surprise." He pulls out a pair of half glasses to read the paper I'm holding out. "You don't seem like the type of student who would ever make a special request to speak to the whole school." He takes the paper, slowly reading and muttering the words. Then he looks up at me and takes off the glasses. I'm in agony.

"This isn't a school-sponsored event," he says. My stomach drops down to join my heart in my shoes. "Now, don't look so morose. I'm going to let you read the announcement, but you have to include a statement that this is not a school-sponsored event. Got it?"

I nod. He keeps waiting, so I add, "Yes, sir. Thank you."

He smiles again. "Good, I wanted to make sure you still had your voice. I'll tell you a secret if you promise not to repeat it to the whole school?"

"Yes, sir."

"For our first date, Mrs. Nelson and I went to the Bixby. Don't remember what movie was playing because I was so nervous. Prettiest girl I ever dated." He winks at me and I smile back. "We always go back, every year, on the anniversary of our first date. I love that old theater. Those shoebox theaters they build by the malls are terrible. How's Nick doing?"

Just like that, my heart and my stomach are back where they should be. I give Nelson, who is not really a Nazi at all, the latest update on Nick.

During the morning announcements, I clutch my notebook paper in both hands. Finally, when Nelson says he's going to end with a special announcement from Erika Williams, I step up to that big metal microphone and almost pass out on the spot. But then I picture Nick standing there with an old movie poster he wants to show me. I can see his ear-to-ear grin and hear him saying, "There's my Gypsy Girl!" I press the button on the microphone and read the full announcement, from beginning to end, without stuttering or stumbling one time. Nelson gives me a thumbs up and I walk out of the office on a cloud.

By lunch, I've passed out all my flyers. When I walk out to the courtyard to eat, I find Sonny sitting on the brick wall near the Chemistry lab glaring into a paper bag. Jenny is sitting next to him while a few other people from the morning sit on the grass. He pats the empty space on his right side.

"Would you look at this?" he pushes the open bag toward me. Inside I see an apple, a hard-boiled egg, two oversized lumpy cookies, a bag of chopped up veggies, and some kind of tiny sandwich.

"Is your sandwich supposed to be that tiny?"

"Exactly. One of my mother's new creations, no doubt."

"Well, she did give you two gigantic cookies."

"Actually, one of those is for you." He pulls out the miniature sandwich and drops it into his lap. Then he fishes out a cookie and presents it to me with a flat hand. "This is your Wookiee Cookie. Make sure you like it before she bakes a million of 'em."

Jenny pretends not to pay attention, but I can feel her prickling on the other side.

The cookie is pure heaven. It's full of butterscotch and chocolate chips with caramel piped on to look like Chewbacca's hair. One bite and I almost fall backwards. "That woman is a genius."

Sonny shakes the baby sandwich at me. "What about this tragedy?"

"What's actually on it?" someone asks.

"Does it matter?" Sonny asks the sky.

I snatch it out of his hand, open the bag and take a wee tiny bite. The bread is some kind of rye with sunflower seeds baked in and there's something thick, creamy and sharp cheesy inside with layers of bright green leaves, shredded radish and very thin sweet pickles.

"Uh, excuse me? It's not exactly a sharing sandwich."

I pull out my standard bologna, cheese and mayo on Wonder Bread and drop it in his lap. "Eat that you ingrate."

Sonny picks it up and smiles. "We have not had bologna or Kraft cheese slices in my house for two years. Ever since my mother got on her natural foods kick." He opens the bag and takes a wolf bite. With the food still in his mouth, he starts singing, "Hello bologna my old friend."

Everyone laughs and the jokes flow for a few minutes.

The sleepy eyed girl from this morning suddenly plops down on my other side and says, "I'm so bummed out. They messed up my schedule so I have to drop Mr. Davidson's film class."

After talking to the girl, I find out her name is Carolyn and the film studies class is during my study hall period. I hurry over to see my guidance counselor. The teacher has to sign an add card for me to get into the class. So I head out to track him down. It turns out Mr. Davidson used to work at the Bixby fifteen years ago. He leans over my add card and whispers, "I have a waiting list for the class, but no one knows who is on it or who is first in line. I'll just say it was you. Keep it our little secret."

After signing my card, he buys four tickets to the festival.

I find Tammy waiting at my locker after my last class.

"Have you found it?" she asks as soon as she sees me.

"Not yet," I tell her. "Maybe you and Candy Man should buy tickets to the film festival this weekend. I think I'll have it by then."

She looks ready to jump down my throat, but then Sonny shows up with a fresh stack of flyers in his hand. "Costas? What are you doing here?" he asks. It's obvious he remembers Slim Jim's story about Tammy's campaign to make the last days of my freshman year miserable.

"Oh, Tammy was just telling me how much she wants to buy a ticket to our festival, weren't you, Tammy?" She shoots me an evil look and stomps away.

"Is she getting a little chubby?" Sonny asks. I want to grab his face and kiss every inch.

SEPTEMBER 1977

"*Star Wars* is probably the most influential film of my generation. It's the personification of good and evil and the way it opened up the world to space adventure, the way westerns had to our parents' generations, left an indelible imprint. So, in a way, everything that any of us does is somehow directly or indirectly affected by the experience of seeing those first three films."

-J. J. Abrams

Friday, September 2, 1977

Dear Cassie,

Tammy Costas just poked her big red head through my bedroom window and asked me to help her break into your house. Can you believe that? Either that girl belongs in a mental ward or…well, I guess this dirty movie you two made must be ridiculous. Thing is, I have a used cassette of film I could give her. The Force has a powerful effect on the weak-minded. Tammy is definitely weak-minded. If I play it right, she'll be convinced she's found the dirty movie she's looking for and she'll never get the thing developed. But there's a small, cold, mean little part of me that wants her to squirm a little while longer.

So I told her to climb back down my pear tree and go home. Instead, she hooked one leg through my window and sat there squinting toward your house.

"Candy Man said Chief Abbott left town this morning. No one's staying at the house. It's the perfect time to search for that camera or the film, but Sheriff McCombs will send Rodney to prison if he goes within a hundred feet of that house or this place."

Thank you, Sheriff McCombs!

I could feel Tammy's eyes on me. "Look, if anyone could figure out where she stashed it, you could."

"Good night, Tammy."

I counted one hundred thirty seven potatoes before she finally left. I heard her say, "If my dad murders me, it's going to be on your head."

As if it's my fault she got high and took her clothes off on camera!

After she left, I switched off my light and crawled into bed, but sleep was a million miles away. (Didn't I write something like that in my first letter to you?)

It isn't just Tammy and her incredible nerve that has me back out of bed. I'm so scrambled and fried over the festival. This was my big idea.

What if it's a huge disaster? What if people start asking for their money back because the festival is boring? What if...wait.

Do I hear screaming or is that some kind of night bird? Anita's not here. Maybe Suzie turned on the television or...I'd better go check this out.

Erika

| THIRTY-FOUR |

I POKE MY HEAD OUT OF MY WINDOW. IT'S DEFINITELY SCREAMING I'm hearing and it's coming from the direction of Cassie's house. I climb out the window and let my feet carry me toward the noise. The Abbott house is totally dark, but the screaming is getting louder. After climbing down the pear tree, I walk toward the alley. Suzie is standing in our back yard wearing only her nightgown, both hands over her ears. Tears are pouring down her face and her mouth is opening and closing, but her screams are totally silent. Then I hear something that turns my blood to ice.

"You stink like sin! You whore! You stink like sin." It's Walt's voice. He didn't leave town. He's in there beating the holy crap out of someone. I can just barely make out his shadowy form through the open kitchen door, one arm swinging wildly, lashing out at someone. Someone with a mess of big hair.

Tammy! He's beating up Tammy!

I look at Suzie, but I can see she's clearly useless. So I run for our kitchen with every intention of calling the operator for help when another shadowy form sprints toward me through the side yard.

"Erika! What the hell is going on?"

Sonny! I reach out and grab two fistfuls of his shirt.

"It's Tammy!" I scream. "Chief is killing Tammy!"

A fresh round of screaming erupts. Sonny doesn't hesitate. He takes off straight for Cassie's house yelling, "Stay back," over his shoulder.

After watching that horrible fight in front of the fire station, I have no doubt that Walt Abbott can and will kill both of them. No doubt. Once inside, I don't even look at the telephone. Instead, I grab Anita's shotgun and follow Sonny's path.

Hokey religion is no match for a good blaster at your side.

As long as I live, I will never forget the scene in that kitchen when I step through the back door and slap on the light. There's broken glass everywhere. Chief is standing in the middle of the room with his belt held high and Tammy's hair clutched in the other hand. Tammy is scratching at his arm with both hands, twisting and screaming like a wild animal. Sonny is holding a kitchen chair, legs pointed toward Walt like a lion tamer.

I cock that shotgun just like Anita taught me and take aim at Walt's chest.

"Hold it! Stop it! Stop it right now," I yell like an officer on an episode of *S.W.A.T.* Both men freeze and stare at the gun, but Tammy's still struggling. "Let her go, Chief. Let her go right now!"

Even a crazy ex-Marine knows better than to argue with a loaded shotgun. He releases Tammy's hair and she scrambles away.

"You gonna shoot me, girl?" Chief asks in a voice that sounds, I don't know, almost hopeful.

My heart is booming. The floor under my feet doesn't feel solid. The walls are pulsing in a weird way. It would be so easy to pull this trigger, so easy.

"If she does shoot, I'd say it might be justifiable." Sheriff McCombs walks through the open doorway with one hand on his own gun belt. "Three different neighbors called Dispatch to report you were in here trying to kill some girl and there's not one person in this county who doesn't think you're a dangerous maniac who's lost his damn mind."

Is the sheriff telling me I can shoot Walt and get away with it? The room starts spinning and I have to bite down hard on my bottom lip to stay upright. My entire universe has narrowed down to the place where my finger is curled around the trigger.

"If you're going to shoot, get it over with," Walt growls at me. He snaps his belt between both hands and takes a step forward.

"Walt, leave the girl alone," Sheriff McCombs bellows. "She pulls that trigger, it'll be self-defense."

Something is terribly wrong here. The sheriff is standing behind my right shoulder with his own gun still in the holster when he could have easily put a stop to this nightmare by now, yet he's acting like I'm in mortal danger. I glance over at Sonny. Our eyes meet and an electric volt of understanding burns though me even before he shakes his head ever so slightly.

No. I refuse to act like some weak-minded Stormtrooper.

I lower Anita's shotgun and back up. "This is all a misunderstanding, Sheriff."

"A misunderstanding?"

"Yeah" Sonny drops his chair and yanks Tammy to her feet. "This is just a terrible misunderstanding. We thought Chief Abbott was out of town, so, when we heard something over here, the three of us thought we should come investigate. Right, Chief?"

"All right," Chief draws out both words and starts wrapping his belt tightly around his right hand. "We'll say it was a misunderstanding." His eyes never leave my face.

"Sorry about the misunderstanding, Chief." My voice sounds like it belongs to a stranger.

Sonny pushes Tammy toward the door, latching onto my arm and pulling me behind him. Sheriff McCombs and Walter Abbott watch us leave without looking at each other.

When we get to my back yard, Tammy yanks her arm away from Sonny and crosses both arms over her stomach. The moonlight clearly shows her bottom lip is swelling up and there's a few cuts on her face and arms. Suzie walks over and silently put her hands on Tammy's shoulders.

"That's it then?" Tammy asks us. "He gets to do that to me and we're all going to pretend it didn't happen?"

"Yep," Sonny's voice is almost cheerful. "We're going to pretend you didn't break into the Abbott house. We're going to pretend I didn't trespass and threaten the homeowner. We're definitely going to pretend Erika didn't point a deadly weapon at Chief Abbott in his own kitchen. That's exactly what we are going to do. Oh, and we're going to thank our lucky stars while we're at it."

"And my mom's shotgun," I add softly.

Sonny rolls his eyes at me. "I'm taking Tammy home," he tells me, and steers her toward the front of my house. His truck is parked on the wrong side of the street with the driver side door hanging open. Tammy pulls away and marches to her own car, the infamous blue Maverick. We watch her burn rubber down my street.

"You're welcome," I yell at her taillights.

"Get some rest, Annie Oakley," Sonny whispers. "This never happened." His lips briefly touch my temple, then he walks away.

"Hey, Sonny?" He turns around with one hand on his door and one foot in the truck. "Why were you here tonight?"

"I was never here," he says with a half smile. I open my mouth to protest. "But if I had been here, I might have been driving by to make sure everything was peaceful when I saw the blue Maverick parked near your house. I might have stopped to check it out when I caught sight of you running around in your nightshirt."

"If any of that would have happened, I would have said thank you," I tell him. "I might have even told you you're my hero."

Sonny gets into his truck and looks out at me with a very Jeff-like megawatt smile. "You don't need a hero, Erika."

Monday, September 5, 1977

Dear Cassie,

I shot lots of film, trying to capture the spirit of our film festival, but I never seem to get the perfect moments on camera; the moments you want to save, hold next to your heart and replay forever.

The first perfect moment happened Saturday morning. When I woke up, I found a black tank top hanging on my bedroom door. *The Force is strong with this one* was printed on the front and *Bixby Theater, 1977* was printed on the back. I tried to thank Anita, but she shook her head. "Thank Richard. It was his idea. But I am happy to see you in something feminine for a change."

When I walked through the Bixby's side door, I was bristling with my lists, totally distracted. Jeff started wolf whistling while Mrs. P clapped.

"That shirt is hilarious," Alex said leaning on the counter.

Later, there was this older guy, like college age. Not bad looking. I mean, nothing amazing, but very tan and athletic with thick brown hair. He was following me around asking stuff about the theater until Sonny said, "She's too young for you, man."

"Somebody sounds a little jealous," Penny said and winked at me.

Sonny didn't argue the point, he just turned and walked away. That means something, don't you think?

Inspired by my tank top, most people working or volunteering for the event had their own shirts made.

Heidi's mom bought her one that said *A little short for a Stormtrooper?* which Heidi thought was the most wonderful thing ever.

Anita's said *I don't like you either.* (She let me pick the line since she doesn't really remember much of the movie.)

Photographers from five different newspapers showed up all three days. According to Alex, those news stories are going to be more effective than any advertising we could purchase.

The Japanese sword stuff was kind of boring to me, but every male age two to ninety-two loved it. The face painting started to look more like a KISS concert than anything alien, but the customers seemed happy. Vince was practically swamped with people wanting his character portraits. He told me his arm was about to fall off and he even had orders from people who didn't want to wait in line during the event. The Wookiee Cookies and Galaxy ice cream were a huge hit.

A few people didn't understand that we were going to be showing bits and pieces of older movies mixed in between the *Star Wars* screenings, so we got a few complaints, but most people told us we should have more events like this one.

The best, most perfect moment happened today. I was shooting film of two kids having a sword fight with wood sticks when Sonny put his hands on my shoulders and gently turned me toward the front entrance doors.

One of the paramedics from the fire station was pushing in a wheelchair where Nick sat smiling from ear to ear. He looked at everything. Talked to everyone. Shook hands with every volunteer and clapped when he saw the *Metropolis* poster featured in the inside case.

When he saw me, he pointed and said, "That way. There's my girl."

By this time, tears were pouring down my face.

"Did I tell you yet, you're my lucky charm?" he asked me. "Now why are you crying?"

"Happy," I whispered.

"Well what do you do when you get sad? Dance a jig?"

Everyone laughed and so did I. Thing is, he's much more frail-looking and blurred around the edges, but he's still Nick. Still alive. Still smiling. He posed for some pictures with all of us, but then he started to wilt so they took him home.

I asked Sonny and Alex not to tell me how much money we made. I just asked them to tell me if we made "enough."

When everyone had gone and we'd cleaned up most of the mess, Alex said to me, "We aren't free and clear and rich, but we have enough to pay the bills and keep going for a while."

What more is there to ask for?

Cassie, I think this needs to be my last letter to you. Not because I'm angry or giving up hope of ever seeing you again. I just think it's time to live my life instead of writing it all down for someone who may never read it. It's time for me to say goodbye.

My hope for you is that you finally outrun all your demons. I hope you have more than enough of whatever you need to keep going through the garbage. And I hope the Force will be with you…always.

Erika

| ACKNOWLEDGMENTS |

THIS BOOK, NOT TO MENTION MANY OF MY HAPPIEST FANGIRL memories, would not exist without the amazing talents and vision of George Lucas. His movies swept me into a galaxy far, far away from my mundane existence and helped me to survive childhood without losing my creative spirit. There are so many of us who owe you so much...please forgive us if we don't always express our appreciation in the most socially-acceptable ways.

This book is my fan letter to every member of the original trilogy's cast and crew, but most especially to Carrie Fisher. I promise I will never be tempted to join the "small, but merry band of stalkers" that she jokes about. That said, I do hope she realizes what an empowering role model she's been to an entire generation of girls who couldn't or wouldn't fit the perfect little princess mold.

The Bixby is a fictional theater loosely based on the Midland Theater in my hometown of Newark, Ohio. The kind and patient staff of the Midland allowed me to ramble around the entire theater, ask some crazy questions and take a ludicrous amount of pictures. The notebook where I recorded their names is missing, but I really do appreciate all of their assistance. If you live anywhere near Licking County, please consider visiting and supporting this incredible community resource.

My early research into the financial struggles of historic theaters during the 1970's led me to discover an incredible book that I highly recommend – *Cinema Treasures* by Ross Melnick and Andreas Fuchs. Anyone interested in discovering the elegant cinematic experience of a more civilized age should check out the book and also visit the online community at CinemaTreasures.org. I owe a huge debt of gratitude to AlAlvarez, TheaterBuff1 and Wes Stillwagon for sharing their thoughts, memories and photographs of 1977 theater life in response to my posting there.

This is not just a book about *Star Wars* or historic movie theaters. At its heart, it's a story about finding your tribe. And so I must thank my own tribe of fierce and beautiful misfits.

Trish Yeager—who started our friendship by forcing this weird fangirl to stop watching *Twin Peaks* in my dorm room long enough to venture out on a Friday night—was quick to step in as my Book Coach when the going got rough in the final draft. Trish introduced me to Teresa Franklin-Kern, who somehow manages to be both wonderfully creative and a rock-steady emotional presence in times of happiness and trouble. Trish also introduced me to Tony "Boomerang" Stillings who has brought more love, joy and laughter to my life than I would have ever thought possible. Tony and Teresa, in turn, brought Thomas Ganley and Chris "Shummy" Shumway to the party. Thanks for being the best tribe of friends a girl could hope to find! I love you one and all. I also want to thank Anne Yeager, whose quick fingers helped me achieve a respectable ranking in a national *Star Wars* trivia contest, and the entire Yeager clan for always welcoming me into their homes and to their holiday buffets.

My mother, Sue Weiland, never stops telling me I'm good enough, I'm smart enough, and gosh darn it doesn't matter if other people like me. It is terrifying to think about everything she has given up to ensure that I had a safe and happy childhood. All she has asked me to do for her in return is to stay out of jail, get a college degree and finish this book. Here it is, Momma. Three out of three. Finally! Also, I need to thank her friends, Ann and Tim Rehbeck, who burned through plenty of paper and ink to deliver early drafts of this novel to her.

My grandmother, Wilma Slay, came from the twin schools of hard knocks and tough love. She was neither the soft nor cuddly sort of grandmother. We fought like mortal enemies stuck under the same roof for years, but I am eternally grateful to her. Because she nurtured a deep love of books and of storytelling in our family. Because she taught me that it is never too late to follow your artistic dreams. And because she took me to see *The Empire Strikes Back* when my mother said she could not possibly sit through another *Star Wars* movie.

My aunts, Linda Green and Sally Dailey, as well as my uncle, Jim Dailey, always encourage me to believe in the beauty of my dreams (and they never grumble when I show up on the doorstep to "crash" their vacations). My uncle, James Green, once looked at me on a lazy summer afternoon and asked, "Trisha, when are you going to write your book?" I regret not being able to hand him this book before he left us, but I will always be grateful for the unconditional love and support he gave to me during my most awkward teenaged years.

It was Holly Hardin who flat out forced me to join the Society of Children's Book Writers and Illustrators and to attend their Los Angeles writing conferences back when this story was just a distant glimmer in the darkest, unexplored corners of my imagination. There's a good chance I'd still be dreaming of writing a novel "someday" if I had never gone to that first conference.

My SCBWI critique group—Suzanne Morrone, Emily Jiang, Rebecca Fallow and Alexis Whaley—helped me struggle through the first draft of this book and refused to let me give up.

My AWC critique group—Jane Haessler, Gaby Anderson, Sweta Bhaumik, Josh Bugosh, Emily Carpenter, Ellie Decker, Suzi Ehtesham-Zadeh, JD Jordon, Tom Leidy, Chris Negron, Luis Nunez, Thom Shelton, George Weinstein, Fred Whitson, and others—helped me stumble through the final draft.

Thanks to the incredibly talented and determined folks at Deeds Publishing—Bob, Jan and Mark Babcock. They not only believed in this project, they made my vision a reality. I will always be eternally grateful for their partnership, experience, wisdom and perseverance!

Diane Cannataro's faith in my storytelling skills was so strong that she pre-purchased this novel back in 2008 before I'd even finished the first draft.

Lastly, I cannot possibly express the depth of my gratitude and love for my fiancé, Michael. I don't think he truly understood what he was getting himself into when he met a single writer at a literary festival and invited her to explore the starlight. Thank you for sticking with me and supporting me through this journey. You are my scoundrel, my rogue leader and my Jedi hero all in one.

| AUTHOR'S BIO |

Trisha Slay lives in Dahlonega, Georgia where she divides her time between making sure this country has plenty of opportunities to pause for refreshment every day and working on her next novel, tentatively entitled *Sometimes We Strike Back.* She has a weakness for ghost stories, unsolved mysteries, wildflowers and homeless pets. She would love for you to visit her at www.trishaslay.com or to share tips for living a stronger, healthier, more creative lifestyle at www.creativitydiet.com.

CPSIA information can be obtained at www.ICGtesting.com
Printed in the USA
LVOW081712200513

334280LV00006BF/11/P